BLOOD IN THE VALLEY

The Vigilati Series

Book Two

J.K. HOGAN

Cover Image by Roser Portella Florit

J.K. Hogan

http://jkhogan.com/
http://twitter.com/JK_Hogan
http://www.facebook.com/OfficialJKHogan
http://www.goodreads.com/jkhogan
http://www.amazon.com/author/jkhogan
http://officialjkhogan.tumblr.com

"These heroines roll with the punches, get back up, acknowledge their weaknesses, kick some major butt , and love their men."

~Mama Kitty Reviews

"[The female characters] are beautiful, intelligent, and can kick-butt and take names. They are right there on the front line protecting those that they love! This is an excellent read you will not want to put down!"

~Faerie Tale Books

Praise for Fire on the Island

"Fire on the Island is a paranormal tale that mixes together a good brew of essential elements—love, death, mystery, intrigue, magic and demons, to name a few—that brings the reader into a modern day world with the age old battle of good vs. evil. The reader will love J.K. Hogan's pairing of romance with the paranormal as she weaves a tale that pulls us into this mysterious and magical world."

~ Ricki R.

"This is an action-packed paranormal romance book with a very lovable cast."

~Lizzy's Dark Fiction

"I love to read a good paranormal romance. One that will sweep me into it and take me on a magical adventure. Fire on the Island does exactly that and I loved the journey. This book is rich in detail and world building. It has a unique take on witches and demons and I was captured by this story."

~The Book Tart

Praise for Blood in the Valley

"I was a big fan of Fire on the Island, book I in the Vigilati Series, and Blood in the Valley was even better. Raven was a perfectly imperfect heroine and one I loved from the first chapter. And Drew gave me the happy sighs. A slightly geeky Cajun determined to get his girl? Yes, please. But my favorite thing about this series is that is really is a girl's fight. The heroines are on the front line in the good vs. evil war, and while the heroes do support and fight beside them, the battle is won or lost based on the heroine's intelligence, strength and courage. There's no sitting around, waiting for the white knight to save the damsel in distress. These damsels save themselves, along with everyone else, thank you very much."

~Romance Reader at Heart, Novel Thoughts and Book Talk

"I found myself resenting every interruption while I was reading because I wanted to see what was going to happen next, with the romantic developments, the archeological dig, and the paranormal aspects. Hogan struck a wonderful balance between the different elements that satisfied both my romance reader and my paranormal/fantasy reader."

~The Book Pushers

"It's an exciting paranormal romance with passion, heart, and humor. The characters are complicated and relatable and my emotions were all bound up for their journey. I couldn't put this book down!"

~The Book Tart

"Unique, with lots of action, a strong heroine, and a sexy hero, Fire On the Island is a recommended read. I will be picking up book 2 when it comes out in May. Hogan has created a world that I want to revisit frequently and I have high hopes for this series!"

~Romance Reader at Heart, Novel Thoughts and Book Talk

"In a nutshell, I can't wait to read this again. And again. The simple beauty of Hogan's writing transported me from my apartment into the beautiful wilds of the Scottish islands, sitting on the back porch with Isla and Jeremiah. Absolutely stunning. "

~The Canon

Dedication

For Rowan, my heart.

In Memoriam

For Ray, who lent me the voice for my crazy character.
Rest in peace, old friend.

ACKNOWLEDGEMENTS

Thanks to Nancy Thompson, the best editor a girl could have!

Special thanks to Larissa Ione for taking the time to give advice to a reader who hoped to be a writer someday.

CHAPTER ONE
Las Vegas

Ray Sabatier never intended to start a family. He saw no need to pass the kind of upbringing he'd had onto some poor, innocent kid. His father was a drunk and, more often than not, had left Ray in the care of his psychotic bitch of a wife while he went on binges of drinking and whoring.

If Ray ever expressed his displeasure over their situation, all he got was a backhand in the teeth for his trouble. He knew that, had he stayed with them, he would have died—either by his father's hand or his own.

So he worked odd jobs, scrimped and saved until he had enough to purchase his first motorcycle, a broke-ass 1980's Honda cruiser. Not a minute later, he left their slum apartment in Mid-City and took to the road. Joining up with some friends, older guys—twenty to his sixteen—he lit out of New Orleans like his ass was on fire.

Life on the road was hard. Harder than he'd thought. There was never enough money, but there was an endless supply of drugs, sex, and booze. Soon, Ray began following in his father's unfortunate footsteps. He took to grifting to get the money needed for his next buzz.

He started off slow, picking pockets, stealing socials, and the like. Eventually, he evolved to more intricate, longer running cons and actually did quite well for himself. He could have retired a young man, if it hadn't been for his vices.

By age twenty-three, Ray had joined up with a biker gang based out of Vegas. Needing a place to dump his shit between rides, he purchased a tiny apartment above a Chinese restaurant. The restaurant owner accepted cash, no ID, no background check, no questions. For that, he could handle the odors...and the yelling.

Inevitably, he grew tired of riding with the gang. Because of his father, Ray had a problem with authority, and the leader of the gang was just like any other asshole who got off on ordering people around.

When he'd finally had enough, Ray went to the leader—a man who called himself Bone Picker—and politely suggested that they part ways. Oh, they let him out all right. With three broken ribs, a collapsed lung, and a couple of bruised kidneys.

There in that one-room apartment, Ray put down as many roots as a man like him ever did. He settled in there, riding his bike up and down the Vegas Strip, scamming tourists for their money, walking the thin line between sobriety and death. For once in his life, Ray was happy. Almost.

Yeah, Ray Sabatier had never intended to have any children. But on one cold, dreary November night, that decision was taken out of his hands forever.

Having just polished off several glasses of Jack, Ray was nodding off on the couch, lulled by the sound of driving rain. A brisk knock sounded on his door, causing his entire body to tense.

Who the hell would come to his door? He didn't owe anyone any money. And he didn't want to let himself think of who he was afraid it could be.

Ever since he'd left home all those years ago, he'd never stopped waiting for the knock. The knock that would signify that his father had found him and was ready, willing, and able to put the final nail in his coffin. Or fist, as the case may be.

Ray hadn't seen his father since the day he left, and he'd heard the bastard drank himself to death in a back alley off Bourbon Street. But that didn't stop the waiting and the clench in his gut anytime he had an unexpected visitor.

Heaving himself up off the couch, he paused to button his jeans but didn't bother to throw a shirt on.

Ray flung the door open, causing the woman standing on his busted welcome mat to jump. She glared at him when he looked her up and down, his signature leer firmly in place. His shrewd eyes missed nothing. From her serviceable flats and her drab grey suit, to her mousy brown hair and mud-colored eyes, which were narrowed on him behind horn-rimmed glasses, her entire getup screamed government. He'd seen the type enough to know. They'd been all over him at juvie, and the couple of times his pop had beat him up bad enough to warrant the whole white coat routine. The public defenders, the social workers, he figured they dressed in such a way as an attempt to be unobtrusive, to blend in, to put people at ease. It had the opposite effect on him. Just made him feel twitchy and a little nauseated.

Instantly on alert, Ray eyed her suspiciously. "Yeah?" he said, raising his chin slightly and scowling at her.

Opening a file, she looked at him, then down at the file, then back at him. Definitely government. "Raymonde Sabatier?" she asked.

"Who's askin'?"

Holding out a thin hand for him to shake, the woman looked rather like the cat that ate the canary. Ray's eyes darted around the hallway, looking for a means of escape in case shit got critical.

"I'm Barbara McCoy from Nevada DCFS. We were recently contacted by the Louisiana CPS office. They've been looking for you for four years, Mr. Sabatier. You're a hard man to find."

"DC who?"

"Department of Child and Family Services. We have your daughter."

"My what?" Blinking, Ray looked at her like she had just grown a second head. Then he burst out laughing. Doubling over, he gripped his aching sides as he gasped for breath between bouts.

"Did old Two Scalps put you up to this?" he asked breathlessly. Two Scalps was a Native American pimp that occupied the next unit over, affectionately known around the neighborhood as Two Scalps, due to his two-toned hair color. He and Ray often traded practical jokes.

Miss Barbara McCoy from DCFS sniffed and pegged him with an icy glare. She spoke carefully, as if she were addressing a slow child. "I can assure you, Mr. Sabatier, that I don't know anyone called 'Two Scalps.' This is not a joke. You have a daughter. She's four years old. The mother died from internal hemorrhage shortly after giving birth in New Orleans, but not before she named you on the child's birth certificate."

"What's to stop her from putting any old name she can think of on there?"

"Lucky for you, you're still in CODIS from your little stint in juvie. CPS ran a paternity test when they were searching for the child's closest relative. You're certainly welcome to run your own, but I wouldn't expect a different result."

She paused for a moment while Ray absorbed that information, watched him coolly as he ran a shaking hand through his jet black hair. "You're just going to hand a child over to me?" he asked, his voice none too steady.

"You're her only relative of record, so you have legal parental rights to her. You don't have a record, other than the juvenile offense." She eyed him as if she knew the only reason he didn't have a record was because he hadn't yet been caught. "You're really our only option, and now that we've found you, we are obligated to turn her over to you. Of course, if you can't, or won't, take her then you can sign over your rights to the state. But you would have to come down to the courthouse and do some paperwork," she said, pursing her lips and raising a brow at him.

Ray narrowed his eyes. "How *did* you find me, anyway?"

Miss McCoy just chuckled and shook her head. "We have our ways, Mr. Sabatier. I'm going to go get the girl now. Please wait here."

Her meaning was clear. *Don't ghost out again, you bum.*

He knew he should bail. Grab a duffel and beat it down the fire escape. But pure, morbid curiosity had him rooted to the spot as he watched Miss McCoy climb back up the stairs with a tiny child in tow.

Cocking his head, Ray studied the little girl who was trying desperately to hide behind the social worker's skirt. There was no gentleness in the touch when Miss McCoy pulled the child out to face him. Her dark sable hair was chopped off bluntly at her chin and was tangled about her face. She had amber-colored eyes and dusky skin; how much of which was heritage and how much was dirt, he couldn't say.

"What's her name?" he asked.

She turned sad eyes down to the girl. "She was never given one. She's listed in the system as Baby Girl Trevigne, although I think the foster parents have been calling her Mary."

He curled his lip at the injustice of that and let out a sound something akin to a growl, causing Mary to cower away again.

He winced at the reaction. "Winning father of the year already," he muttered.

Ray was frozen in place as Miss McCoy shoved a handful of papers at him, briefly explaining that they were to prove that the girl had been delivered safely into his hands and that the state would be relieved of any and all legal responsibility…blah, blah, blah. He was sure he must be gaping at her like a fish as he initialed by the x's.

He was still stuck on the fact that they were giving him a child. *Him.* Raymonde Julien Sabatier, formerly a motorcycle gang member who now hustles on the Vegas strip. They were just going to leave her here like Daniel in the lions' den. What was the world coming to? Ray honestly felt sorry for the kid.

Miss McCoy cleared her throat, shaking him out of his thoughts, and he realized she was holding out his ID to return it to him. He felt a dizziness that was akin to panic as he took it from her. She made a grand show of checking her watch and backed a few steps away from the little girl. Reaching into her purse, she pulled out a card and handed it to him. "I have to get going now. Feel free to call me if you have any questions, Mr. Sabatier. Number's on the card. I'll be dropping by a couple of times the first month to make sure she's being taken care of. Other than that, she's all yours."

Ray gaped at her as she set a pint-sized suitcase on the ground beside Mary, turned on her heel, and left. He looked down at the child. She stared back with wide, frightened eyes. She was trembling, and her knuckles where white where she clung to her teddy bear.

Sighing, he stepped to the side and gestured toward the doorway. "Well, go on then." Never taking her eyes off of him, she skirted around him and ran inside like a skittish colt. Stunned, Ray stared down the empty stairway for several moments, as if he expected the social worker to come back and say it had all been a mistake.

When no such thing happened, he cursed under his breath and headed back through the door. "Holy shit! What am I gonna do?"

ꕥ

When Ray returned to his shabby living room, he saw the girl curled up on the couch. She watched him with wide-eyed fear, but he saw a sparkle of curiosity there as well.

Sitting on the coffee table across from her, he regarded the child silently. Her eyes were dark amber with flecks of gold in them and rimmed around the edges with darker brown. She had eyes that haunted his memory. His father's eyes.

He studied the girl's sharply angular face, her pert nose and high, slashing brows. The edges of her eyes were turned up slightly, and she looked decidedly feline.

He'd been so shell-shocked, he'd forgotten to ask the social worker what the mother's name had been. While it was obvious that Miss McCoy didn't have a very high opinion of him, he imagined she probably assumed he knew who he'd been sleeping with. Ray racked his memory for what, or who, he'd been doing four years ago.

Something about the girl's face caused a memory to tug at the back of his mind. The name *Lisette* floated through the haze, along with a memory of the toffee-skinned, brown-eyed Creole girl he'd spent the weekend with during one of his few returns to New Orleans. Trevigne could have easily been her last name, but he probably never knew what it was.

Timeline fits, he thought, and the kid is a dead ringer for Lisette. He closed his eyes briefly, and he'd have given his right arm for just one more glass of whiskey. But he figured it was a little early to go on a bender in front of his daughter.

His daughter. He started to curse again but caught himself, remembering she was still in front of him. When he opened his eyes, she cocked her head sideways like a gloomy little bird.

> *Then this ebony bird beguiling my sad fancy into smiling,*
> *By the grave and stern decorum of the countenance it wore.*

The lines popped into his head unbidden, but they seemed strangely fitting. His stepmother had liked to read Poe to him at night—The Crazy Bitch's idea of a bedtime story—and some of it had stuck with him.

"Well, you need a name," he said to the silent girl who continued to stare at him with those hundred-year-old eyes. She reminded him of how he'd always imagined the raven looked, so regal and proud yet melancholy and lost at the same time. He saw the same in the little girl. This girl who was supposed to be his daughter. "Raven sounds like as good a name as any. What do you think?"

Still, she said nothing, but the corner of her mouth tilted up ever so slightly, and she gave him the faintest hint of a nod.

"Raven it is, then. We'll see about making it legal tomorrow." He stood up, went to a small linen closet, and pulled out blankets and an extra pillow for her. Making a palette for her on the couch, he tucked her in as much as she would let him. He watched her for a few minutes as her eyes began to droop, exhaustion overwhelming the fear, allowing sleep to come.

Once he was sure she slept, he trudged into his bedroom and flopped down on the mattress. Flinging an arm across his eyes, he let out a soft groan. "What the hell am I going to do with a kid? I'm the last person who should be taking care of a child."

That may have been the truth, he thought, but he was all she had. So he would just have to try to do right by her, and he would have to start by swallowing down the mind-numbing fear.

These thoughts were weighing on his heart as he drifted off to sleep. He was joined in his dreams by a familiar image of a tiny, dark-haired woman with milky white eyes. He'd been dreaming of her since he was a child. When she opened her mouth to speak, it was to say the same phrase she always said, only this time there was more.

Ne t'effraie pas, mon petit. Don't be afraid. Never doubt that she is yours, for she is destined for greatness.

CHAPTER TWO
New Orleans

Raven had skills. Here, she was in her element, she thought as she looked up at the back of the charming six-story apartment building. This was what was behind the facade that faced the street. Water-stained brick and rusty fire escapes. Perfect.

She was dressed, head-to-toe, in black—tight Lycra pants and a form-fitting, scoop-neck top—to avoid being seen. Her mass of long, sable hair was tamed into a tight French braid. She couldn't risk getting anything snagged on the way up.

The years spent with her father had been quite educational. She learned the art of the con, how to spin an unravelable backstory, and how to pick the perfect mark.

But every plan has its flaw, so he also taught her how to be invisible. How to get in quick, get what she needed, get out, and never be seen. It was that particular skill set that had led her to start her business in private security.

Her partners created and installed the most intricate and impenetrable security systems available to the private citizen. Her job? To crack them. She made her living breaking and entering, legally. She was hired by independent clients to attempt to breach their security systems.

She was the best. If she couldn't do it, no one could. If she succeeded, and she usually did, they sold the client on a state-of-the-art system. It was cake.

Raven narrowed her eyes at the sixth-floor terrace. She would use her special talents to gain access to that apartment, but not for work. This one was personal and just as illegal.

Yeah, she had skills all right. But more than those she had from a childhood of grifting with Ray. Her other abilities were much more dangerous.

She'd known all her life that she had power. Never having been able to define it, she supposed others would probably call it magick...call her a witch. But she'd never been much for labels, and certainly not one for practicing any type of religion, however Pagan in nature.

It wasn't as if she honed these skills as one would any learned talent. It was just a little extra energy humming under her skin, just a little extra perception, just...extra. To her, it was as natural as breathing—just like, to the rest of the world, it was as unnatural as if she'd sprouted gills to breathe with.

Raven's knowledge of her family lineage began and ended with her father. Ray had never told her who her mother was. She wasn't sure he knew. And Ray's own parents were long dead. That left Raven without a clue as to how or why she'd been born this way.

Desperately seeking those answers that could explain her existence, Raven began researching using the only clue she had—the symbol branded over her collarbone on the left side.

That was yet another thing in her life that needed explaining. The symbol had simply appeared on her skin when she was eight, and no amount of rubbing, scraping, or screaming had gotten rid of it.

The mark was about two inches in diameter, with three nesting circles, and three slashes across them that formed the points of an invisible triangle. Inside the smallest circle was a glyph of a spider.

She'd been researching that symbol and others like it ever since she struck out on her own—she was fifteen when the law had finally caught up with Ray and took him away for the first time. She'd come close in Rome, finding a book with that symbol on the cover, but someone had come in before she could grab it. One thing Ray had made sure to teach her was never to leave a trail. She wanted to get in and out with the book, without being seen. If it meant she'd have to take a five-finger discount, so be it.

When she came back the next day, the book had been sold. It only took a little coaxing using one of her 'special talents' to get the shopkeeper to give her the purchaser's information. She tracked it here, to New Orleans, and the apartment of one Dr. Andrew Deveraux.

Funny that the search would bring her back here, to the city where she'd been unceremoniously brought into the world.

Casing the area had been easy. Dr. Deveraux led a fairly predictable life, coming and going at around the same times every day. He taught a class at Tulane and wasn't due back for a couple of hours.

Opening her pack, she dug out a climbing rope attached to a grappling hook. Old-fashioned, yes, but the classics were such for a reason. She took a step forward and froze. She raised her face and sniffed the wind as her hackles rose.

Turning only her eyes, she scanned the other side of the street. Someone was watching her. Had been for weeks. So far, they'd yet to make a move. Shrugging a thin shoulder, she turned back to the apartment building. She had nothing to hide. Between her lifestyle growing up with Ray and her special abilities, she'd already spent too many years with too much to hide.

One of those extra talents Raven had as long as she could remember was being able to manipulate energy and space. She could see it as a tangible thing, a solid mass that she could push and pull against, using nothing but her mind. It was this ability that was going to help her into Dr. Deveraux's apartment.

Deciding it was time to make her move, Raven swung the hook over her head and tossed it toward the terrace. Using her energy, she pushed at the air currents around the hook, keeping its path true.

The hook flew over the terrace railing and caught between the wrought iron pickets. Perfect. The fading light of dusk concealed her as she scaled the wall with nothing but the rope. When she reached the top, she swung over the railing and landed on her feet without making a sound.

Studying the sliding glass door, Raven took out her lock picking kit and chose the instruments she needed. She slid her tools in and easily engaged the lock with a deft flick of her wrist.

Using caution born of instinct and experience, she pulled on the door and slipped inside, closing it behind her. She waited a moment to allow her eyes to adjust to the near darkness. With the drapes drawn and the sun going down, the apartment was nothing but shadows.

She knew the layout, had studied the blueprints of the building. But the decor of the room was the wildcard. She skirted the perimeter of the living room with her back against the wall, keeping low to the ground.

Raven hitched up her small tactical pack higher on her shoulders and scanned the living area. The furniture was spartan, and the room was neat as a pin. She would have to be careful, because she had a feeling Dr. Deveraux would notice even the slightest thing out of place—not that it would matter, of course, as she'd be long gone by the time he came home.

Making her way along the wall, she edged over to a large oak bookcase. She pulled a penlight out of her bag and scanned its contents. Dickens, Tolstoy, Brontë, Dostoyevsky, to name a few. Raven guessed he kept all of his intellectual books out where guests could see, and probably had another bookcase somewhere else with all his sci-fi thrillers and murder mysteries.

She checked every spine of every book, even though she knew the book she was looking for wouldn't be in such an obvious place. But Raven wasn't one to cut corners. She tiptoed through the first door she found—bathroom.

She moved on, edging across the front door to the other side of the living room. Careful not to move anything, she opened all the cabinets in the massive entertainment center facing the couch. Nada. Raven took only a moment to drool over the incredible stone fireplace before she rounded a corner into a narrow hallway.

When she entered the next room, she realized it was a study. She would have to take more time there. Lots of places to hide a book. She flicked the light on her watch, saw that she had over an hour and a half before her drop dead, get out, deadline.

She tackled the enormous cherry wood desk first. The man didn't have much furniture, but what he did have was all insanely huge. A girl had to wonder if he was compensating for something.

Sixteen drawers and two cabinets later, she still had nothing. A quick search through the four file cabinet drawers that weren't even locked told her that Dr. Deveraux kept nothing of value in the study.

Slinking back out into the hallway, Raven checked the remaining doors. The next two were closets, but the final door at the end of the hall led to the bedroom. This room was outfitted with much more personality than the rest of the space. Clearly Deveraux was quite confident he'd be spending a lot of time there.

The walls were a rich maroon color, the furniture was mahogany. The size of the four poster bed lived up to the rest of the apartment. It was dressed in warm brown to match the floor-length drapes.

Raven took only a moment to admire the room before scanning for hiding places. Where would the man keep his important documents? His valuable possessions? She moved toward a large bureau across from the bed.

Carefully rifling through it, she opened one of the lower cabinet doors to reveal a small black safe. *Jackpot,* she thought. She shrugged out of her pack and pulled out a doctor's stethoscope.

Another cliché, but Raven was a back-to-basics kind-of-girl. She placed the ear tips in her ears and pressed the chest piece against the cool metal, two inches to the left of the combination dial. Slowing her breathing to prevent noise interference, Raven turned the dial gradually, listening for the tumblers to engage.

Click. Twenty-three right. Slowly, she spun the dial back to the left. The closer she got, the softer the clicks would be. She held her breath for the space of a moment. Click. Sixty left.

Her foot was falling asleep from the crouch, and a single drop of sweat slid down from her temple, but she held completely still. The last number would be the hardest, she strained to hear.

Raven concentrated hard, her focus narrowed so that all she heard were the tumblers and her own heartbeat. Probably why she didn't notice the front door swing open or the soft footsteps padding through the living room and down the hall.

She heard nothing until a strong hand with a grip of steel clamped down on her shoulder, at the same time a deep voice boomed out right beside her.

"What the *fuck*?" Deveraux shouted as he pulled her back.

Years of grifting with Ray had taught her how to get out of many sticky situations. The key was not to think, not to hesitate. Just react. And so she did.

Raven leapt to her feet and spun around to face him in one fluid motion, striking out as she did so. When her right fist connected with his solid jaw, pain shot down her arm even as she sent a wave of energy into the punch to increase the impact.

The big man spun, fell sprawled out on his back, and shook his head. Since she clearly hadn't knocked him unconscious—which was a shock in itself with the amount of energy she had shot him with—Raven wasted no time.

She sprinted down the narrow hallway, shoved open the sliding door, and leapt over the terrace railing, snagging her rope on the way over. Using her power, she manipulated the space around her to cushion her fall so that she was able to hit the ground running.

Raven didn't stop until she turned into a dark alley, where she pressed her back against an aging brick building and took a moment to catch her breath. Here, concealed by shadow, she could watch and see what Deveraux would do.

It was only seconds before the tall, well-built, blonde man walked out onto the terrace, holding his jaw and scanning the street below. He glanced toward her alley and narrowed his eyes, almost as if he knew she was waiting there.

Raven tensed, and watched some more. He scrubbed a hand over his spiky blonde hair, shook his head, and went back inside. Breathing a sigh of relief for the reprieve, Raven took off at a dead run to where she had parked her motorcycle, two blocks down.

Close. Too close. But she had to figure out a way to get that book.

CHAPTER THREE
Blowing Rock

Dr. Andrew Deveraux was soul-weary, bone-deep tired. He had come to the little town of Blowing Rock, North Carolina expecting the best. As an anthropologist and professor at Tulane University, he was often asked along on archaeological digs as a consulting scientist. He helped identify artifacts and research the anthropological history of the area.

Typically, he loved going out to the dig sites. It was the *Indiana Jones* type of field work that every scientist wished for. This time, however, it had been one headache after another. A recent rock slide had unearthed some remains, and the research team had been called in to identify what may be a Catawba Indian burial ground.

While many of the local residents wanted answers, wanted to find out more about the history of their area, there was a group of conservationists opposed to the dig. At first, the research team got tangled in a massive web of red tape, trying to get the permits for the dig site.

Eventually, they got the dig authorized, but they were still dealing with protesters on location. They had picketers, chanters, and even a few who threw food and empty bottles at them. Drew hadn't signed on for that kind of shit, but once he started a job, he finished it.

He'd had a rough day of trying to examine artifacts in the field while dodging rotten food flying past his head. Drew needed some time to relax. Instead of stopping at his hotel in town, he kept on driving farther up the mountain.

The road was a surprising thrill, his late model Camaro hugging the curves on the switchbacks as the altitude increased. Finally, the road leveled a bit, and he saw a neon sign up ahead.

Cliffdweller's Inn & Tavern. Since a double whiskey sounded real good right about then, Drew swung the sleek, black sports car into the gravel parking lot. Unfolding his long legs, he stepped out into the cool night air, stretched, cracked his back.

Drew leaned against his car as he tilted his head back to study the building. It was stone, seemingly built into the bald mountain face behind it. He guessed it had probably been there since well before he was born.

The porch was wood and was listing in a way that made Drew wonder about building codes and fire hazards. But light poured from the windows, and music, mingled with voices, floated out to him. Seemed as good a place as any to stop for a drink, so he carefully negotiated the rickety porch and went inside.

The interior of the tavern was immaculate, unlike the outside. Hardwood floors sparkled, the dark, cherry bar shone from regular polishing. A fire roared in the hearth and, along with the stone walls and exposed rafters, made the room seem more like a cozy den than a dive bar.

When Drew stepped over the threshold, wiped his feet, and hung his coat on the rack, the animated conversation paused as the other patrons eyed him for a moment. He wasn't sure why, but he tipped the brim of his leather cowboy hat and walked across the room to the bar.

Talk resumed, and Drew guessed he must've passed muster. He took a seat on one of the cracked vinyl barstools and nodded at the bartender. As the man approached, Drew couldn't help but stare. The guy was huge, bald, and covered in tattoos. At least on the parts that were showing. Dude could have been a stunt double in a Jason Statham movie. Safe to say that Drew would probably piss himself if he ran into this joker in a dark alley.

But the man simply gave him a bright smile that almost looked ridiculous in contrast to his don't-fuck-with-me exterior. "Don't mind them, they're just not used to out-of-towners makin' it this far up the mountain."

"How do they know I'm from out of town?" Drew asked.

Baldie just laughed and winked at him. "What can I get for ya?"

"Bushmills, neat. And make it a double."

"Tough day?"

"Something like that."

The bartender poured him a generous amount of the staunch Irish whiskey and slid the glass over to him. Drew gave him a grateful smile. "Thanks, uh..."

"Micah Cliffton," the guy supplied while extending a hand for Drew to shake. "Welcome to Cliffdweller's. Let me know if you'll be needing a room," he said, nodding toward the glass of amber liquid.

"Drew Deveraux," he replied and tried not to wince as Micah's handshake crunched his knuckles. "Nice to meet you."

Drew dug his keys and a credit card out of his pocket and handed them to Micah. "Start a tab. Not sure how much I plan to drink. Just put the room on the card if I need to crash."

The bartender nodded, put the keys and card in the cash register drawer, and set the Bushmills bottle beside Drew's glass. He handed Drew a key attached to a carabiner. "Room 213. I'll run it if you use it."

Drew nodded his thanks and watched as Micah moved down the bar to wipe up a spill. He swirled his whiskey in his glass, breathed in the spicy scent, and drank deep, relishing the burn as he exhaled.

Hit the spot. His shoulders relaxed as he closed his eyes and hunched over the bar. He hadn't truly realized how stressed-out he'd been until the tension finally started to ease. He sighed as he took another sip of sweet liquid calm.

His phone screeched at him from inside his pants pocket, breaking the spell and causing him to jump. He fumbled trying to pull it out, flip it open.

"What!" he barked into the handset.

"Damn, brother. What the hell?" His best friend, Jeremiah's, voice washed over him, soothing like the whiskey. The one person who wouldn't stress him out.

"Sorry, man. Had a shit day, and the phone scared my balls into my throat."

Rich laughter rolled out of the speaker. "Got it. We were just calling to check up on you."

Drew heard a muffled female voice in the background. He smiled and shook his head. He couldn't believe that confirmed bachelor, Jeremiah Rousseau, was half of a 'we' now. Of course, anyone who met his wife, Isla, would see exactly how that happened. She was enchanting. Actually, if he were being honest, Drew thought with a smirk, he should say 'bewitching'.

"Shit, man. This dig has been hell. Permit issues, protestors, food throwing, you name it."

"Where y'at again?"

"North Carolina. Little one horse town up in the mountains." Drew winced and looked around, hoping he hadn't offended anyone. No one seemed to have overheard.

"Sure that's hell on you, Mr. Big City," Jere teased.

"Hey now, I'm from the bayou, hear? Just 'cause I live in the city now...," he broke off, chuckling at the good-natured teasing. The only time his Cajun came out was when he was talking to Jeremiah, or anyone else who still lived in New Orleans. Well, that and when he was turned on or riled up.

"Listen, Drew, I did have another reason for calling. You in a place you can talk about...you know?"

Drew glanced at the burly bartender a few feet away. "Nah, man. I'm at a bar. Let me go outside."

"Day was really that bad, huh?"

Drew rarely drank, and when he did, it was usually when he was stressed. "You have no idea. I can't wait until we wrap this dig. Hold on a sec." He put the phone down long enough to shrug into his coat, picked it back up, and stepped out into the chill. Hell, September in motherfucking Appalachia was worse than February in New Orleans.

Shivering, he rested his back against the stone exterior of the tavern and tugged his hat down lower. "All right, I'm out. What've ya got?"

"Marduk got a lead on a *Praeda* up in Baton Rouge, so Isla and I went to track her. Turns out she's gone missin'. Cops think she's dead."

Drew cursed sharply and wished like hell he'd brought the Bushmills out with him. Jeremiah was a parapsychologist and a paranormal investigator. His research on an ancient and previously unknown race of witches called the *Bruixi* had led him to Scotland last year. It was there he'd met and fell in love with Isla.

She just happened to be one of those witches, and they had learned that she was also from a revered lineage called the *Vigilati,* who were bred to guard the gateways between the human world and the spirit world and prevent invasion by demons called *auchrim.*

Together, they were determined to find out more about Isla's heritage and the dangers they were facing. Because he was an expert on antiquated languages, Drew had been recruited to translate a book that Jere had picked up in Rome. It was written in a form of Old Latin even Drew was having trouble with.

They had learned a lot, including the fact that Isla was what the *Bruixi* grimoire, as they had taken to calling it, referred to as a *Praeda.* Supposedly, that meant she had been sired by one of the head demons, called the *Lochrim.* Later, Isla's own mother had confirmed it.

Because of the blood they shared, Isla was able to kill the demon and free the souls he had been feeding on. As far as they knew, she had been the first ever able to kill a *Lochrim.* Isla and Jeremiah had made it their mission to track down other *Vigilati* and *Praedos,* to make sure they knew what they were up against. If Jeremiah had never come along, Isla could have been taken by Alastore, her *Lochrim* father, and never known what she was.

"Where did Marduk come up with this lead, anyway?"

"You know wolf-boy, he only tells us what he thinks we need to know. Which is usually less than nothing."

Marduk was a *feradux*, an ancient race of shapeshifters that existed to protect and guide the *Vigilati.* When a *feradux* commits a crime, he is called into active service of his *Vigile.* Only a blood sacrifice to save her would free him.

Marduk had made his sacrifice by saving Isla's life and nearly got himself killed in the process. But he chose to stick with the couple and help them in their mission. Drew guessed that he had, too.

"So, you're back to square one, then?"

"Pretty much, man. You come up with anything more in the translations?"

"Tell you the truth, the University has kept me pretty booked up the last few weeks, so I haven't been able to work on them much. I've got it with me though—in a locked case, of course—so hopefully I'll have some down time when I'm not at the dig."

"All right man, keep us updated."

"Sure thing, you, too. Take care."

Drew closed his outdated POS flip phone, leaned his head back and breathed deep the crisp mountain air. If it weren't for all those idiot protestors, he might actually like it here. He wished they could see that the research team wasn't trying to destroy anything. On the contrary, they only wanted to catalog, to preserve. Some people could never see past their own narrow ideas.

Drew glanced up when he heard the rumbling of an engine. Too loud and raw to be a car, so he wasn't surprised when a black motorcycle roared into the parking lot. It looked like some sort of hybrid between a cruiser and a sport bike.

The rider skidded to a stop not ten feet from where Drew stood, concealed in shadow with his hat brim low. Not wanting to attract attention, but too curious to let the opportunity pass, he edged a bit closer to look at the bike.

Ducati Monster. *Nice*. The rider swung a leg over and stood behind the bike. Small. That was his first impression. Definitely female. The second-skin leather pants and fitted motocross jacket left nothing to the imagination. The black full-face helmet, fingerless riding gloves, and the calf-high shit kickers, covered in buckles and straps, just added to the picture.

He hadn't even seen her face yet, but Drew felt his body stand up and take notice, even through the whiskey haze. She stood in the pool of light that came from the parking lot lamp, and he could see that she was petite and slender but with just enough curve.

When she reached up to pull the helmet off, the short jacket rode up to reveal a strip of dusky skin over a stomach that was nearly as ripped as his own, and showed off not just one, but—dear God—two belly button piercings. One on top and one on bottom.

The helmet came off, and an incredible cloud of dark, straight hair cascaded down from it and whipped in the wind. As she walked, quick and purposeful, from the bike to the sad little porch, she flicked a glance his way.

The wind had snaked her hair around to cover her face, so all he saw were her eyes. Almond shaped and exotic, the tilt at the corners played up by one of those tricks women did with eyeliner designed to make a man beg. Those eyes were the color of the fine whiskey that waited for him back at the bar, and there was a smile in them.

She disappeared inside the bar, and Drew swore he actually heard his cock whimper. "That's a negative, Ghost Rider. We're not here to pick up chicks, we're just here to get our buzz, get some sleep, and get back to that godforsaken dig," he mumbled in the direction of his belt buckle. Clearly, some parts of him were not happy with that plan.

When Drew reentered the tavern, Mystery Woman was nowhere to be found, so he determined it was safe to go back to his bottle. He climbed back up on his stool and nodded at Micah. Cue Ball just smiled at him while chatting up another customer.

Two more glasses of Bushmills later, Drew was pleasantly buzzed, and the room was spinning only a little. Pouring himself a little more, he pushed the bottle back toward Micah. "You can close me out."

"How 'bout that room?"

"Yeah, I'll take it. Go ahead and ring me up."

The bartender turned to swipe Drew's credit card, and didn't seem to notice when the small, leather-clad woman skirted the side of the bar and poured herself a drink. Sidling up to Micah, she hip-bumped him and leaned her head on his shoulder. "Hey, big guy," she said in a husky voice that Drew thought would sound amazing crying out his name.

He was barely able to suppress the groan that wanted to escape. *Down boy!* Damn, he was acting like a horny teenager.

Micah kissed the top of her head without stopping what he was doing. "Hey, Rave. You don't have to work tonight?"

"Had a day job for once. Looks like I'm going to be around tonight. You want me to take over for a little while? You never take breaks."

"Nah, I'm good. Why don't you go get some rest. You don't get enough."

Drew couldn't hear the rest of the conversation over the buzzing in his head and the heartbeat in his ears. Whether that was from the alcohol, the arousal, or both, he couldn't say. He still couldn't see her face, just that long fall of sable hair that nearly reached her finely formed ass. God, he wanted to see her face!

His attention was drawn back to the conversation as Micah laughed at something the woman had said. She tossed her hair back and flicked a glance toward him, and he finally saw her.

The sight caused his blood to run cold. He would never forget that face. The slanted, whiskey-colored eyes with their dark slashing brows, the sharp cheekbones that suggested some Native American descent somewhere down the line. The straight nose, plump, sinful lips, and stubborn jaw.

It was the one he'd seen right before the closest he'd ever come to being knocked the fuck out. Having shed the leather jacket, she wore a black top that bared one shoulder. If he didn't instantly recognize her face, he would have known her by the brand on her collarbone, also bared by the neckline of that shirt.

The woman who had broken into his house, punched him into next week, and fucking *disappeared,* had just walked into this little tavern in the same shithole Appalachian town that he happened to be in. What were the odds?

Drew managed to play it cool, pretty sure she wouldn't recognize him in his dirty dig clothes and with his hat pulled down low over his eyes, and he was damn proud of himself for not reaching over the bar and strangling her. But he was going to get some answers. Oh yes.

She grabbed a key off the rack behind the bar. Tag said 237. Drew filed that knowledge away for future use as he watched her take a glass and sashay toward the stairs, throwing a 'goodnight' over her shoulder at Micah.

He waited a few seconds before speaking up. "Your girlfriend?"

Micah laughed again, a deep, booming sound. "Hell, no. She ain't my type. I prefer my women not to be able to kick my ass six ways to Sunday. If I went that way." Drew couldn't help but laugh when the man winked at him.

"Who is she?" Drew was trying for innocence but clearly missed the mark. Micah's expression went blank, and he shook his head. "No one you need to worry about. Trust me, man, that ain't the tree you wanna go barkin' up."

Drew narrowed his eyes and searched Micah's face. He gave away nothing. There was clearly a history there and he'd find out eventually, but Drew had bigger fish to fry at the moment. "Duly noted. Well, I think I'm going to head up. Thanks."

The big man nodded and gave Drew directions to his room. He didn't have to know that room 213 wasn't where Drew was going.

CHAPTER FOUR

Swaying only a little, Drew made his way to the old staircase at the end of the bar and began to climb. He stumbled on the third step. Damn thing could use a repair, he thought. He kicked the offending step and winced when the blow reverberated up his leg.

He made it to the second floor without breaking his neck, and decided he should stop by his room to put down his bags. When he reached the door, he looked down in confusion at his empty hands. "The fuck?" he murmured. Where was his stuff?

Oh yeah. Dig, driving, drinks. Crashing at the tavern. Got it. Shaking his head, he moved down the hall, stopping at the door to room 237. He looked left, then right, before he put his ear to the door. He heard no sound coming from inside the room.

Great. Either she was asleep or she wasn't in there. This situation would require a bit of stealth on his part. Drew grinned while taking another credit card out of his wallet. Biker Chick wasn't the only one with a few tricks.

Drew slid the credit card into the crack between door and frame, and gently wiggled the handle. He nearly shouted when he heard the telltale click. Carefully, quietly, he eased the door open and stepped into the darkness of the room.

ജര

Raven had come up to her room and crashed hard. She generally worked and traveled by night, but today's client had requested a daytime system test. Since she couldn't turn off the nocturnal just like that, Raven had been up for over twenty-four hours.

She was already half asleep by the time she made it through the door. She'd stripped to the skin and thrown on an oversized Saints jersey that nearly reached her knees. Normally, she slept in the nude, but she didn't plan on getting up anytime soon and she didn't want to flash housekeeping if they thought the room was empty.

In her line of work, she traveled from place to place, going wherever the next client needed her. She'd just finished up a big job in Blowing Rock, a vacation home—and love nest—for a US Senator. He'd recommended her to some other top-shelf clients in the area, raving about the expertise and discretion of her company.

Since Raven was going to be in town for the next couple of weeks, she rented a weekly room at Cliffdweller's and helped Micah at the bar whenever she had free time. She didn't need the money, but she hated down time. She always needed to be moving, doing, so she pitched in where she was needed.

It had been just after midnight when she'd collapsed facedown on the surprisingly comfortable bed, dead to the world. It was close to three a. m. when she heard the first noise outside her door.

At first, it was a light thump followed by a muffled curse. Her eyes flew open, but she wrote it off as some drunk from the bar trying to find his room. She'd almost gone back to sleep when she heard a faint scraping sound, followed by the distinct turning of the handle.

Raven was instantly on alert but not overly worried, as no one else but Micah had a key to her room. Her whole body tensed as she heard the door pop open.

Her back was to it, so she couldn't see. Not her typical sleeping position—she never put her back to the door—but she'd crashed so quickly. She kept still, not wanting to let on that she was awake and lose the element of surprise.

She sent a low frequency energy wave rippling through the air. It would send back visual information as it bounced off the intruder, a lot like sonar. Not enough detail to discern identity, but enough to let her know what she was up against.

Extremely tall. Six-five, maybe six-six. Long, rangy build. Not a body builder type, but plenty of muscle to work with.

She watched the shimmering outline the energy wave sent to her neocortex. He didn't seem in too big of a hurry, and her internal warning system was not yet sensing a threat—other than the fact the guy had just broken into her room.

Raven perceived no immediate mortal danger so she decided to play dumb, let the guy think he'd caught her. Who the hell was it, anyway? Had The Watcher finally decided to show himself? Maybe he'd finally tell her what the fuck he wanted.

Footsteps echoed on the hardwood floor as the stranger walked over to the small writing desk. He grabbed hold of the spindly ladder-back chair that went with it, dragged it back to the door, and, presumably, sat down in it.

Hell, she hoped this guy didn't think he was being stealth. He did surprise her by suddenly flicking on the overhead lights. Her eyes had always adjusted quickly to changes in light, and tonight was no exception.

She sprang upright in the bed, clutched a hand to her chest, and blinked as if she'd been jolted awake. Playing the startled damsel in distress should buy her a little time to figure out what was up.

When she glanced toward the door, Raven saw that the tall guy had wedged the back of the chair up under the door knob and was sitting back with legs stretched out and arms crossed over his chest. The dirty leather cowboy hat was pulled down over his eyes and obscured most of his face.

She barely suppressed a snort when she realized he actually thought he had her trapped in there. Guy had no idea who he was dealing with. Putting just the right amount of shake in her voice, she spoke to him.

"Wh-who are you? What do you want?"

The man leaned forward to rest his elbows on his thighs, lowered his head, and pulled the hat off. After he raked a hand through messy ash-blonde hair, he looked at her and sneered. "Gotcha."

Raven gave him a hard stare. He was dressed differently, in a khaki work shirt and camo cargo pants, stuffed into steel-toe boots. All of it, including his skin, was covered in a fine layer of dirt.

The face was different. Harder, more world-weary than a year ago. But she recognized him. The good Dr. Deveraux had finally found her, and she never even knew he'd been looking. Touché. Well played, Doctor.

Raven dropped the act, seeing no point in it since he clearly knew who she was. With a toss of the covers, she threw her legs over the side of the bed and spun around to face him. She knew the jersey barely covered her lady bits, and she got a small sense of satisfaction watching his eyes zero in on the hem for just a moment before flicking back to her face.

So blue, she thought. Those eyes. A rich, sky blue. And that was enough of that. She could moon over hot guys when they weren't holding her hostage, however ineffectively.

She tilted her head and let a small smile play over her full lips, giving him what Ray had always called her curious bird look. "You got me. Now what are you going to do with me?"

As she watched his eyes dart around the room, it occurred to her that he hadn't thought this through any further than getting in the room. She decided to play along. For now. If she could get him talking, she might be able to get more information about what was in that book.

"Contrary to how it may look, Cliffdweller's isn't that kind of inn." That surprised a laugh out of him that had her fighting the urge to smile back.

Leaning back in the chair again, he crossed his legs, like he was settling in. "Why don't we start with your name."

With no reason to lie, she shrugged a deceptively delicate looking shoulder. "Raven."

"Raven...," he prompted, and urged her to continue with a wave of his hand.

"Just Raven. For now."

"Okay, Just Raven, why don't we start with why you're not the least bit scared of me, even though I broke into your room."

She flashed him a smile designed to distract, to seduce. "Come on, Doc, you're about as stealth as a bull in a china shop. I think the whole inn knew what you were up to."

One corner of his mouth tipped up in a half smile. "That bad, huh?" he said.

Raven noticed his voice slurred a little when he spoke. She narrowed her eyes at him. Bloody hell, was he drunk?

"Besides, I thought you were The Watcher. Finally ready to make a move," Raven said.

His brows drew together as he tried to process that one. "Uh, The Watcher?"

"I'm being followed. Have been since before that night at your place. I'm not sure what he wants, and I'm not inclined to care until he makes a move."

CHAPTER FIVE

Drew sighed and plunged his hands into his hair. Questioning this woman was like pulling out his own goddamn teeth. "Damn, okay. Let's try another easy one. Where are you from?" he asked.

She gave him another inscrutable look and looked down at her hands. "Everywhere. Nowhere."

Drew shook his head. This girl should go into intelligence, because she gave away nothing. "All right. Let's get right to the point, shall we? Why, the hell, did you break into my apartment last year?"

"I guess I thought a big shot professor who was born with a silver spoon in his mouth would have fancier stuff. I guess I was wrong. By the way, how come you look like you've been living under a bridge?"

Drew scrubbed both hands over his face and frowned at her. "I was out in the field, helping with an archaeological dig. I'm not just a professor, I'm a scientist. Anyway, I call bullshit. You weren't there to rob me. I know what the hell you were after."

Raven stood and stretched her arms over her head, causing the hem of the jersey to creep even higher. She sneered at him when his eyes stayed locked on her face, although a muscle in his jaw twitched with the effort. "If you've got it all figured out, what do you need me for?"

"I want to know why. Why you were after it, and how you found out about it."

"It?"

"The book."

Her brows rose at that, and Drew reveled in the fact that he had finally been able to rattle her. The look was gone as quickly as it had come, and her face was once again a mask of indifference.

"Mmkay, well, I have to work in a few hours, so I'm gonna grab a shower. Make yourself at home." On that note, she turned her back on him and tugged the jersey over her head.

Drew nearly swallowed his tongue when he realized she wore nothing underneath. She was covered from her slender neck down to her shapely legs in bronze, toffee-colored skin. That was no tan job, she came by that genetically.

She swept her dark mass of hair over one shoulder as she rifled through her drawers. Drew's brain shorted out when he caught sight of her tattoo. It was a stylized drawing of a raven with its head resting at the base of her neck, wings spread out across her shoulder blades.

Halfway down her back, another raven curled around the bigger one's body, wings also spread, tail feathers resting at the small of her back.

Drew had never been a fan of tattoos on women, but that one on that woman was the most unbearably erotic thing he had ever seen. He cleared his throat twice before he was able to find his voice again. "Raven," he said softly. She stopped in her path to the bathroom but didn't turn. "I know what you are and why you want the book. I can help you get the answers you're looking for, but you're going to have to talk to me."

She paused for another second before she left to take her shower. Drew decided to take her up on her offer to make himself at home. He stretched out on the bed and lay down on top of the covers. He closed his eyes and tried to get rid of the image of the most finely made body he'd ever seen out of his head.

"Not why we're here, man," he told himself. Hell, what had he gotten himself into?

ജ്ജ

Raven stood with her arms braced against the dingy shower wall tile, with her head bent under the spray. She took deep breaths from down in her diaphragm to slow her racing heart.

Answers. That's what he'd offered her. Even after she had broken into his apartment to take them from him. *I can help you get the answers you're looking for, but you're going to have to talk to me*, he'd said.

She bit her lip and closed her eyes to the burning she felt behind her lids. She hadn't realized just how much she wanted—no, needed—those answers until they were offered to her.

Sighing, she smacked her hand against the tile. But a man like Drew Deveraux wasn't the type to give something for nothing. He'd want answers from her, too. She wasn't sure what the questions were, but she'd bet her life that they were coming.

Question was, could she give enough to get what she needed from him while she protected the rest? There really wasn't any choice. She had to know. Had to find out where she came from.

The water began to run cold, so she cut it off and stepped out. She toweled off quickly and put her jersey back on. No need to give the guy a coronary, she thought with a sneer.

She went back into the bedroom, expecting round two of twenty questions. What she didn't expect was to see the handsome Dr. Deveraux passed out on her bed. Curious and more than a little intrigued, she rounded the bed and sat down on the other side.

He was on his side, facing her, with one arm coiled under the pillow. In sleep, the worry lines eased, and he looked so much younger. Again, she wondered what had happened to him in a year's time that had roughened his facade.

Unable to stop herself, she sifted her fingers through the sandy hair, noting that where it had always been impeccably groomed, he had neglected it so that it was now curling at the ends. It pissed her off that she found that so adorable, but she continued her exploration, allowing her hand to slide down over his prickly jaw. She swiped her thumb across his lips, softened in slumber, as well.

He heaved a weary sigh and snuggled further into the pillow but didn't wake. He had classic all-American boy looks. Square jaw, straight nose except for a small deviation on the bridge that suggested it had once been broken.

Raven felt her heart trip a little as she watched him breathe. That was enough to cause her to back away, get off the bed, get dressed. *Not cool, Raven. Not even a little,* she told herself. Looking back at the sleeping man on her bed, whose feet hung off the end, somehow she knew he was very, very dangerous. If not to her life, then to her heart.

CHAPTER SIX

Drew woke to the sound of someone jackhammering inside his skull. No, wait, that was just his cell phone vibrating against his head. He blinked at the rather blinding light streaming in through the windows of...Where the hell was he?

Somehow, he managed to flip the phone open and bark into it. "Somebody better be dead or dying. Seriously."

"Uh...hey, uh, Professor D?"

He couldn't suppress a groan at the sound of his student intern's voice on the other end. "What is it, Hammer?" he asked with practiced patience. The kid's real name was Martin LeRoux, but he'd earned the nickname Hammer after some drunken karaoke incident freshman year. Drew didn't want, or need, to know any more than that.

"We found some remains. I thought you might want to take a look at them before we start excavating."

"Human?"

"Yeah, it looks that way. Hey, where are you, anyway? I knocked on the door of your room before I left this morning."

Drew glanced around the room and tried to get his bearings. Right, the whiskey, the inn, the woman. Raven...

"I decided to check in to an inn farther up the mountain. It has more character. Plus, I can be sure the activists won't find me. I'm gonna come by and check out of the hotel today.

"All right then, see you at the site?"

"Be there in twenty."

Drew shut the phone, rolled onto his back and threw an arm over his face. He was going to get up. Right after the room stopped spinning. Whatever had possessed him to drink so much? He'd had bad days at work before but damn.

Raven must have taken off after her shower, he thought. He remembered she said she had to work. Yeah, she was probably a hundred miles from here by now.

Gathering the mental fortitude to sit up, he swung his long legs over the side of the bed, resting a moment when the room pitched wildly. He glanced with longing at the bathroom door and thought he might kill for a hot shower.

With a shrug, he got up carefully and headed for it. Shit, he'd already taken her bed. He guessed one shower wasn't going to make it any worse.

When he emerged from the bathroom, Drew felt decidedly more human. He looked down at his dusty clothes that lay crumpled on the floor. With a sigh, he picked them up, and put them on.

He was definitely going to stop by the hotel, grab some clean clothes and the rest of his stuff, and check out. Hammer could hold his horses for a few more minutes.

Drew quickly scrawled his room number, his cell number, and the address of the dig site on a complimentary pad of paper. Just in case. He didn't hold out hope that she'd use them, or that she'd even come back, but it was worth a shot.

ജ്വ

With the sun beating down on the dig site, it was an unseasonably warm day in Black Valley, the lowland between Barron's Bald and Whistler Mountain. Drew had foregone the leather hat for a red bandana he'd tied over his head to keep sweat out of his eyes.

Wet blonde hair stood on end when he pulled the thing off to mop his face. His head ached from the blinding sun, and his calves burned from crouching over sector C19 of the grid.

C19 was where the skull had been found. In fact, the team had unearthed the first full skeleton. It stretched from C19 to C21, with phalanges and various other loose bones scattered across B20.

The dig site had been divided into a grid formed by posts and string. The team would have to carefully photograph and record the contents of each two foot square sector as they appeared, before beginning to excavate.

Drew was doing his best to gain what information he could from the still partially buried skeleton. From the shape and width of the pelvis, he could tell the specimen was female. Measurements he'd taken of the femur and tibia—the long bones in the leg—put her at barely four foot eleven.

His observations of the sternal ends of the clavicle, or collarbone, and the fourth rib led him to estimate her age from twenty-two to twenty-four years old when she'd died. He could tell all that even before the skeleton was fully extracted.

However, determining ethnicity, cultural subset, and actual age of the remains would require removing the bones, carefully cleaning them, and running a multitude of tests. Luckily, that was what the team was for.

Drew was just there to tell them what they were looking at and what should be done with it. He cocked his head as he studied the skull. Something was off about it, but he couldn't place it. Not yet.

He stood to let the team do their work, and to stretch out his screaming muscles. A commotion rose up from the cluster of picketers at the edge of the roped-off area and he turned to check it out.

Someone was pushing their way through the crowd amidst a litany of protests, including several shouts of 'scab' that caused Drew to roll his eyes. Fucking union maid over there, he thought.

He lost interest in the latest chants, turned his back on them and ducked under the pop-up tent that served as the team's base. Hammer poked his head in and nodded at Drew.

"Mornin' Professor. What'd you make of Daisy?"

"Daisy?" he asked, raising a brow at the redheaded grad student.

Hammer ducked his head and twin spots of pink appeared over his cheek bones, mottling his pale skin. Drew sure hoped the kid had put on sunscreen.

"S'what the team's calling her."

"Ah. Female, obviously. Height around 4'11", no older than twenty-four. Ethnicity as yet undetermined."

"But she's got to be Catawba, right? This area, the layout of the site. Gotta be."

"Hammer, what do I always tell you?"

"Assume nothing, miss nothing. Yes, sir."

"That's right. Assumptions lead to carelessness. We'll be able to answer many of our questions once more of the skeleton is excavated. It will be a couple of hours yet. Go ahead and take lunch, yeah?"

The young man nodded and turned to leave but stopped and looked back. "Oh, we have a new intern coming in to take Jessy's place. A visiting student from the University of Edinburgh."

Drew stared hard at Hammer for a few seconds, then inclined his head. "Good to know. Oh, and Hammer?"

"Sir?"

"Put on some goddamn sunscreen."

"Yes, Sir."

ᔕᗢᗡ

Drew pushed aside the sun shade that shrouded the tent, planning on going back to oversee the excavators, but he was waylaid by the head of the archaeological team. Dr. Oswalt Larkin was in his mid-fifties and looked entirely too much like Burt Reynolds for his own good, complete with the precisely manicured 'stache.

Dr. Larkin, or "Oz" to his friends, was the head of the Archaeology Department at Appalachian State University, the local college. He had assembled a highly skilled team of fellow scientists and grad students from both ASU and the University of North Carolina at Asheville. Along with Drew's interns from Tulane, there were around forty people in and out of the site on any given day.

"Dev, you get a chance to take a look at our Daisy?"

Drew rolled his eyes at the nickname Oz had given him when he'd been Oz's TA for a few years at Brown. "Hey, Oz. Yeah, I got a look at her. She's a beaut. Made a few rough determinations based on what I could see, it's all in the report."

"I read it." He crossed his arms and gave Drew a bland stare.

"But that's not the information you want."

Oz shook his head and took a step forward, crowding Drew's space with his enormous ex-marine presence. "Any ideas as to who she was? What she is? I need to know what I'm dealing with here."

Drew barely resisted the urge to step back. Instead, he crossed his own arms over his chest and regarded the other man. While Dr. Larkin was shorter, he easily outweighed Drew by close to a hundred pounds of solid muscle.

"You know I won't speculate. Too easy to make a mistake."

Oz cursed a blue streak, but his tense posture eased up. He clapped Drew on the back, and Drew was sure something popped out of joint. "I know, I'm just up to my ears in protestors and government types, all wanting to know what the hell we've found."

He kept talking as he exited the tent, beckoning Drew to follow. "The sooner I know whether or not Farmer Bob over there stumbled onto a Native American burial ground, or a modern relocated cemetery, the better."

"I feel for ya, man, I really do. But if you want to speed up the process, you're better off lightin' a fire under your team's collective ass, rather than mine."

Larkin barked out a laugh that startled a couple of the young interns and winked at Drew. "You're probably right. I'd better go do that. Check with me later."

Drew nodded at Oz. "I'll go see if there's anything I can do to help," he said with a wave over his shoulder.

As he passed by sector A4, Drew decided to check on the group of students excavating some earthenware shards. Whether those where Catawba artifacts, or just pieces of modern day urns and flower pots commonly found in cemeteries, remained to be seen.

He noticed a slender young woman with flaming-red hair tucked through the hole in a baseball cap who leaned over a corner of A4. She viciously stabbed at the dirt around a shard with a rock breaker. If she kept on like that, she'd bust the pottery into a million pieces.

He crouched down and grabbed her delicate wrist to stay her hand. "Stop! You're being too rough."

Light green eyes lined in some kind of kohl lifted to connect with his bright blue gaze, and they both froze. Her eyes widened in shock, and she snatched her hand away as recognition sparked. He started to speak, but she stopped him with a sharp intake of breath, cutting her eyes to the left where Larkin stood with a group of grad students.

Drew cleared his throat and gave her his hand to pull her up. "Miss, ah..."

"Murphy. Brynna Murphy. Visiting student from U of E," she said, shaking his hand.

"Dr. Deveraux. Drew. Miss Murphy, can I have a word with you inside the tent, please?"

"Of course." She lowered her head and followed him.

Drew escorted Brynna into the empty tent and rounded on her. "Brynna. What the hell are you doing here?" Brynna was a friend and former employee of Isla's. Drew had met her the summer before when he'd traveled to Scotland to help Jeremiah with the research on the Bruixi. He didn't know if she had any ties in the States, but he sure as hell knew she wasn't a student.

The diminutive Irish woman shrugged and glared at him. Amazing how she recovered from her shock so quickly, he thought.

"Exactly what you heard. Visiting student from U of E to help with the excavation," she said in her lilting Irish brogue.

"Bullshit. You're not a student, you're not an archaeologist, and what you were doing out there—beating a piece of pottery to death with a rock breaker—was most *certainly* not excavating."

Brynna snorted and rolled her eyes, which only served to further infuriate him, but she didn't deny it. "Well, for the record, I did go to the University of Edinburgh. Awhile back, anyway." Looking put upon, she heaved a sigh. She narrowed her eyes at him and Drew got the feeling she was sizing him up, deciding whether or not to trust him.

"I'm here to find another witch. One like Isla. I've tracked her to this area, and the dig is my cover. If you don't want anyone else finding out about the *Vigilati*, I'd suggest you give me a crash course in archaeology."

With that, she turned on her heel and started to march out of the tent. "Now wait just a fucking minute!" Drew commanded, grabbing her arm to stop her. A white-hot shock blasted up his arm and into his body, knocking him back a few steps.

He looked on in astonishment as her eyes narrowed and the pupils contracted into a thin black line. Not her eyes. Cat eyes. A low growl radiated up from her chest.

"Don't test me, Deveraux," she snarled, punctuating each syllable with a flash of a fierce set of fangs. "I am *feradux*.

And you are coming dangerously close to threatening my charge."

Drew tried hard to keep from trembling, he really did. But she was terrifying. He held up his hands, palms out, and approached her slowly. "Whoa. Whoa, easy there, tiger," he said, then winced at his own choice of words.

No, a tiger she was not. Not with eyes that green. Some kind of wildcat, probably. Cougar would fit in with the landscape here in Appalachia.

She seemed amused by his phraseology and her lips twisted into a wry smile, but he could still see those killer canines poking out from under her upper lip.

"Chill. Out. Brynna. We don't have to be at cross purposes here. I want to protect the *Vigilati,* just like you do. I'm just doing it by helping with the research Jeremiah and Isla are working on."

She nodded, and her features went back to normal. "I haven't made contact with my *vigile* yet. She doesn't know about me. I'm not sure she knows about herself. I most recently tracked her here, but now she's off the grid again. I've been keeping an eye on her for a while now, and she's a slippery one. You'd think she was born suspicious."

Understanding dawned as he put the pieces together. Followed the *vigile* to Blowing Rock, hard to keep track of her...The Watcher. "Raven," he breathed.

Brynna narrowed her eyes and took a step towards him. "What do you know about her?"

"Nothing, except she was the one who broke into my apartment last year to steal the grimoire from my safe. She knows she's a witch, but not much more than that. Doing her best to find out though," he answered, absently fingering his jaw as if it still held a bruise from that punch a year ago.

Drew's brow knit together in confusion when a memory teased at the back of his mind. "Wait, she said The Watcher had been following her even before she broke into my place. So it can't be you. There must be someone else after her."

Pinching the bridge of her nose, Brynna raised a hand to stop him from speaking further. "Stole the—what watcher? Drew, what are you—" she broke off when she heard a noise outside the tent. She lowered her voice to a whisper. "We need to talk, but it's not safe here. Where are you staying?"

"Cliffdweller's Inn & Tavern, about six miles north on Blowing Rock Highway. Meet me there at eight?"

She gave him a quick nod and turned to leave again. "Wait! I just have to ask...," Drew started. She raised a brow at him and he took that to mean he could continue.

"How did you go half-cat like that? I mean, when Marduk—"

"Marduk is nowhere near as old or powerful as I am. He's just a pup compared to me." After that little revelation, she left the tent without looking back.

Drew raked a shaking hand through his irritating curls, and wondered just how well Isla knew her little Irish friend.

As Drew emerged from the tent, he caught a glimpse of light reflecting off of something on one of the mountain overlooks. The overlooks were small parking areas on the road that snaked around Whistler Mountain, where cars could pull off and enjoy the view of the valley below.

He shaded his eyes from the sun with his hand and he looked up at where he'd seen the light. A figure in black sat astride a vicious motorcycle and stared out over the valley. The sunlight had caught the chrome on the handlebars.

The full-face helmet was intact, but the sable hair streaming out the back of it told him it was Raven. His body knew it even before his brain did, as his blood began to sizzle in his veins. So she hadn't left town after all, he thought.

That told him everything he needed to know right there. She was dying to hear what he knew, but was too proud to ask. Well, that was just too damn bad, because he wasn't going to give an inch. If she wanted information, she'd have to come and get it.

He raised a hand in greeting to the dark silhouette that was Raven. The helmet flashed as she dipped her head in an answering nod, kick-started the Ducati, and sped off.

CHAPTER SEVEN

Drew finally dragged his tired, aching body into the tavern after another trying day. The protestors had escalated, hollering threats of bodily harm and harassing interns as they came in and out of the dig site.

It was becoming harder and harder to pinpoint the reason for their animosity. He wasn't sure they even knew anymore. He and Oz had talked about hiring a security company to keep everyone safe and guard the site at night. Somehow, Oz Larkin maneuvered it so that Drew had agreed to be the one to look into it. He'd put in a call to a highly recommended company called Stiles & Nash Security.

He was waiting on a return call to confirm, but the receptionist thought they had a consultant in the Boone area that could meet with him. Drew thought it may be overkill, but if it made everyone feel safe, maybe they'd be able to excavate the site quicker.

Cliffdweller's was busy for a Thursday night, he noted as he headed for the bar. They were somewhat close to a university, but to Drew, the crowd looked more biker than student.

He sat on one of the barstools and nodded at Micah, who immediately waved and came over. The burly, bald guy's smile was just too bright for Drew's frame of mind, though he politely smiled back.

"Hey man, how're things goin' at the boneyard?"

Drew winced and rubbed the back of his neck. "How'd you know about that?"

"Honey, welcome to Small Town America. Everyone knows about that," Micah answered sympathetically and winked at Drew.

"It was pretty rough, actually. We're making a lot of progress with the dig, but the protesters make it difficult. I've even had to look into hiring private security. Ever heard of Stiles & Nash?"

Micah nodded, scratched the stubble on his jaw. "Matter of fact, they did my security at the inn. They don't normally work on small-time operations like mine, but I know a guy who knows a guy."

"I'm hoping between Tulane, ASU, and UNCA, we can come up with enough cash to afford them."

An inscrutable look passed over Micah's face for a moment. Then it was gone. "Ain't so much about money with those guys. Not always. Trystan Stiles and Ryder Nash are good people."

Micah gave a quick decisive nod, as if that was that.

And Drew supposed it was. "You know them, then?"

"Oh, we go way back. Used to ride with a gang based out of Vegas back in the day. The three of us were little shits, all balls and no follow through. Our buddy Ray got out a couple of years before we did, and he helped us get back on our feet.

"Eventually, the boys started their security company, and I saved up enough money to buy the place I was bussing tables at."

Drew smiled at the pride he heard in the other man's voice. It was a lot, coming from a bad start and making something of yourself. Lord knew, he had experienced that in his own life.

"What happened to Ray?" he asked innocently enough.

The nostalgic smile disappeared from Micah's face and he looked down at where his hand rested on the polished bar. He shrugged. "He didn't hold it together as well as we did. I haven't seen him in years, but last I heard, he was doing two-to-five in High Desert. Prison," he clarified when he caught Drew's questioning look.

"Shame," Drew said. What else was there to say? They settled into comfortable silence while Drew continued to wait on Brynna.

She was late, and he was disconcerted to say it irked him. He was severely disturbed by any kind of chaos, even tardiness. With the exception of his little bender yesterday, Drew was always impeccably groomed and meticulously punctual.

He guessed it stemmed from the way he grew up, in a little hovel on the bayou, south of New Orleans. He spent the first eight years of his life either getting beat on by his old man or watching his mama get it.

Finally, dear ol' Dad hauled off and broke Drew's collarbone, which resulted in a hospital trip, complete with a CPS visit. Stanton Deveraux did not pass go, he lit out of town like the devil was on his heels, and Drew never saw him again.

They'd struggled, Drew and his mama, with only her puny income from cleaning houses to live on. But Yvonne DuBois Deveraux was nothing if not a fighter. She kept on cleaning, kept on saving, and she somehow found the time to invest in her hobby. Writing.

She was eventually able to turn that into a career, an income, and they lived comfortably on that for a few years. They were happy, for a hot minute anyway. Drew was never quite able to shake the effect his childhood had on him, and it manifested itself in his slightly obsessive-compulsive tendencies.

But they managed, and they loved. Until his mother had met Bostonian publishing mogul Everett Wheaton. They had a whirlwind courtship, and an even quicker engagement. They were married, and just like that, Drew was whisked off to a boarding school in Maine to prepare him for an Ivy League lifestyle.

It only took him a year to get kicked out. Then they sent him to military school, where he overstayed his welcome even faster. After that, he'd begged his mother to let him come home. Home to New Orleans, not to her. He moved in with the Rousseaus, and Esme Rousseau became his mom in all the ways that counted. Just like Jeremiah and Matthieu had been brothers of his heart.

He never spoke to his own mother again. Just like that, the first and last family relationship he ever had was subjugated by a prevaricating asshole in Gucci. And that, as they say, was that.

Sure, he had people he loved. Friends like Jeremiah and Isla, Esme and Matty, whenever the kid bothered to be around. Hell, even the wolf was beginning to grow on him.

But those kinds of codependent, symbiotic relationships that came from deep connection—parent and child, blood siblings, lovers—those, he had long since given up on. If you didn't allow people to get that close, those relationships couldn't destroy you.

Like his father destroyed his mother. Like his mother destroyed him.

Drew shook his head, trying to clear it of the melancholy thoughts. He turned toward the door when he heard it open, and waved to Brynna. Looking back at Micah, he slid his credit card across the bar to him. "My friend's here. Will you send a Sam Adams in the bottle to that corner booth? And an Irish car bomb for the lady."

"Sure thing. Run a tab?"

"Why not? It's not like I have far to go."

ꙮ

Drew greeted Brynna and escorted her to the corner booth. The table sat caddy-corner to the bar, and Brynna sat where she could see the entire room, while Drew had to turn to see the bar. He wondered if all *feradux* were so cautious, or if it was just Brynna's nature.

Marduk had never seemed so uptight. Then again, he'd had Jeremiah to help him keep Isla safe. That thought brought Drew back to the most pressing matter. Why the hell Brynna was here.

He opened his mouth to start grilling her when the waiter brought their drinks over. Brynna raised an eyebrow at Drew as the young man placed the Irish car bomb in front of her. A tall, frothing glass of Guinness with a shot of Jamison's floating in it. It was Brynna's favorite drink. It reminded her of growing up in Dublin.

"Good memory, Professor," she said, and laughed when he pretended to shine a medal on his chest. "You know, I never could figure how you and Jeremiah became friends. But you're both total goofballs."

"Well, I try," he said and took a sip of his beer. "As much as I'd love to catch up, I've had a long day, and I really need some answers."

Brynna pegged him with a hard stare. "You may be Jeremiah's friend, but I don't really know you at all. Therefore, I don't trust you."

Drew inclined his head to her. "Fair enough. How about this. You ask, I answer. I ask, you answer. Sound fair?"

She jerked her head in a quick nod that made Drew grin. "I'll even be a gentleman and let you go first. Ask away."

Her brows knit as she thought about it. Smart girl. Don't show your hand too quick.

"Okay. What do you know about the *Vigilati*?"

He didn't break eye contact with her when he answered. "I know everything that Jeremiah and Isla know. What they've decided to share with you is their business. I'm helping them in their research, trying to find more of the *Vigilati* to help them learn their powers, and educate them about the dangers they face."

Drew let her digest that answer for a moment before he posed his own question. "How long have you known Raven was your *vigile*?"

"Since just after Jeremiah and Isla left for New Orleans. I got the call, and I tracked her to San Francisco. She lives like a nomad, as her job requires her to travel constantly. She's very good at staying under the radar, so tracking her is a full time job. I wasn't even sure she was still here, but she is."

"Yes." He shrugged when she narrowed her eyes at him. "I saw her, earlier today."

"Well, trust me, if you saw her, it was because she wanted you to. Finding her if she didn't want to be found would be an impossible task for a human like you."

"Human like...never mind, not sure I even want to know. Your turn."

She didn't pause to think this time. "What is the grimoire?"

"A grimoire is a book of magick."

Brynna glared at him. "No shit. I know what *a* grimoire is. I want to know what *the* grimoire is. The one you've been talking about. You're hedging."

Laughing, he held up his hands in surrender. "Not hedging, just being an ass. A couple of years ago, Jeremiah was traveling in Rome where he came across a book with a *Bruixi signa* on the cover. Of course, he didn't know what it was at the time, only that he'd seen it before."

"What's that got t'do with you?"

Drew pinched the bridge of his nose, begging for patience. "I'm getting there. You know from the dig that I'm an anthropologist. I'm also a specialist in antiquated languages. The book was written in a form of Old Latin even I have never seen before. We've been able to surmise that the *Bruixi* race originated in Latium—an ancient region in Italy that predates the Roman Empire."

"What does it say?"

"I've only been able to translate bits and pieces so far, although we've learned a lot from that. I'm on the verge of a breakthrough though, as I've just about got the full alphabet deciphered."

"I had no idea anything like that existed."

"We didn't either. My turn. What did you do?"

She narrowed her eyes at him. "I'm sorry?"

"What. Did. You. Do. I've learned enough about the *feradux* to know what kind of thing has to happen to get them sent out on 'active duty'."

"No," she held up a hand to stop him from arguing. "That information is off the table. Try another question."

Drew decided not to push her. For now. "Why haven't you made contact with Raven?"

On safer ground now, Brynna flicked a glance over to the door behind the bar then returned to Drew. "I will soon. She's a runner. So skittish, I was afraid, once she knew what I was, she'd go off the grid and never come back."

"Yeah, I could see that."

"All of this watching and tracking, and I still have no idea how much she knows. Or how little. Makes it a little hard to start the conversation. 'Hi, I'm Brynna, your shapeshifting animal spirit guide. Nice to meet ya.'"

"Good point," Drew said, laughing.

"So how do you know Raven?"

"She broke into my apartment last year. I found her trying to crack my safe."

Brynna choked on the whiskey she'd been rolling around in her mouth and leaned forward, eyes wide. "Are you serious? What was in it?"

"Just the grimoire. Nothing else."

"How could she possibly know you had that? You said Jeremiah was the one who originally bought the thing."

"I have no idea how she found out about it, but she certainly made an impression when she came looking for it," he said as he fingered his jaw. "I'm pretty sure it was just coincidence we ran into each other here. So why now?"

Brynna blinked at him, confused. "Why now what?"

"Why would you need to make contact now? You've been sitting on this for nearly a year, and now you've decided to unleash your inner *Catwoman* on her. Why?" His intent gaze never wavered. He may not be an investigator like Jeremiah, but he wasn't an idiot. Brynna was worried about something and, God help him, he wanted to know if Raven was in danger. He didn't really want to examine that instinct too closely right now.

Brynna sighed and cast a worried glance around the room. "I don't know. It's just a feeling I have."

From the limited experience he'd had with these magickal beings, Drew had learned not to ignore their 'feelings'.

"There's something about this place," she whispered and waved her hand toward the bar.

She'd lost him with that. "What, the tavern?"

She thought that through for a moment, raising her eyes to the ceiling. "No. No, not the tavern specifically. It actually feels pretty safe here. It's this town, or somewhere near it. It has this...static, a hum under my skin. Kind of like how it felt in Scotland only...more."

"Do you think there could be a *locus* here?"

Nodding, Brynna took a long draw on her whiskey-flavored Guinness. "Possibly. Only a *vigile* would know for sure, but I'm wondering if that was why Raven was drawn here. I know something's brewing. I wouldn't have been called so soon otherwise."

"But how are you—"

Brynna raised a hand to cut him off and her eyes turned feline again. "There are some things you aren't meant to know, Andrew."

Drew resisted the urge to flinch and look away from her unwavering stare. He let out an awkward laugh and held up his hands in surrender. Again. No one ever called him Andrew but his mother and Isla.

"Okay, message received. Relax." He gave her a lopsided grin. "I'm a scientist; I can't help the curiosity."

Her eyes cleared and she sat back against the booth. "Sorry. That happens sometimes."

Drew wanted to draw the conversation back to the topic at hand, so he reached into his briefcase and pulled out his iPad. He began to feel a tingling sensation at the back of his neck. It became hot almost to the point of pain.

Sitting up straight, he whirled around to face the bar, searching the back of the tavern for the person who was surely staring holes into his head. But there was no one. He continued to search, feeling sure, if he looked hard enough, he'd see.

He jumped when Brynna touched his arm. He turned back and gave her a sheepish grin. Opening the browser, he pulled up a custom Google map he'd created. "The three of us have started compiling the coordinates of all the locuses we've found so far."

Drew watched Brynna as she scanned the map, committing it to memory. Suddenly, she looked across the bar to the doorway in the back, as if she'd sensed something, just like he had.

After a few moments, Brynna turned her attention back to Drew and his map. He had a feeling they'd be adding the little town of Blowing Rock to that map very soon.

As he headed up to his room an hour later, Drew's phone jangled in his pocket. He paused in the stairwell to drop his duffel bag and fish the phone out with his one free hand. He flipped it open with his chin to answer it.

"Deveraux," he barked.

"Dr. Deveraux? This is Trystan Stiles with Stiles & Nash Security. Is this a bad time?"

"Huh? Oh, no, sorry. Long day."

"No worries, we all have those from time to time. So, Randy briefed me on your situation there at your dig site, and I think we may be able to help you."

"Randy?"

"Our receptionist slash office manager slash den mother," the man answered with a smile in his voice. "She said she talked to you earlier."

"Yes, sorry. Didn't catch her name." Drew stopped on the landing in between floors, set down his heavy briefcase, and sat down with a sigh. "I'll be honest with you, I'm just a consulting scientist on this dig. I kind of got roped into taking care of this security stuff."

Rich laughter rolled across the phone line and somehow calmed Drew's frayed nerves. "Isn't that always the way? We normally only do, uh, system analysis and interface design for private citizens and businesses. Occasionally, we'll do private security—usually as a favor to someone."

"To what do I owe the pleasure, then?"

"Someone put in a good word for you."

"Oh really? Who?"

"Well, I can't mention any names, but let's just say I got a call from a big, bald, scary sonofabitch. Could have been anybody really."

Drew made a mental note to thank Micah for his generosity later. "Great, where do we start?"

"As luck would have it, we have an associate on a job in your area. She is what we call an efficacy analyst, but she knows enough about the private security branch to meet with you and assess your needs."

"That would be great! How do I get in touch with her."

"She'll find you."

"But—"

"Listen, great talking with you. We'll be in touch after your meeting."

"Wait—"

"Have a good night!"

The phone beeped as the call ended, but Drew just stared dumbly at it. She'd find him? The fuck? These security people were a couple cards shy of a full deck.

"Whatever," he mumbled, scrubbing a hand over his face, "'m goin' to bed." Exhaustion slurred his words and thickened his accent.

Drew hauled himself to his feet and trudged up the remainder of the stairs to find his room. All he wanted was to face plant onto the bed.

CHAPTER EIGHT

Raven came in the side door of Cliffdweller's that led through the kitchen and out to the bar. She caught sight of Drew in the corner booth with a stunning redhead. The slender woman had a riot of flaming curls around a cherubic face.

It was her eyes that were most striking. Clear goldish-green, with long dark lashes rimmed in black with what had to be the best eyeliner job Raven had ever seen. The woman gave Drew a bright smile and laughed at something he'd said.

A white-hot ball of jealousy curled in Raven's gut as she hovered in the doorway, watching them. What the hell, she thought, embarrassed with herself. She'd only met the guy twice, and fifty percent of those encounters had ended in her punching him.

No, she had no claim on the handsome and polished Dr. Deveraux. Despite the way his voice made her toes curl, and his smile made her want to climb into his lap and kiss it from his lips... Wait, what? Where had all that come from?

She shook her head, trying to break the spell. She had to get a grip. If you let people get to you, it gave them the power to hurt you. Love, especially, came at too high a price. Higher than she was willing to pay.

People may mean well sometimes, but, in the end, they disappointed. They hurt. They left. She could still remember her father's words when the first boy she'd ever 'loved' had broken her poor little twelve-year-old heart.

"Listen to me, little blackbird. If you forget everything else I've taught you, remember this. You can't trust anyone, Raven. Not even me. Trust leads to carelessness. It gives other people power over you that you can't afford."

She admitted it was a bit cynical, but it was also very, very true. Raven loved her father dearly, with his laughing eyes and salt and pepper hair that always fell into his eyes. She loved him through his cyclical battles with addiction, loved him through his eventual failure each time.

She loved him still, and, God, she missed him. But Ray had been right. Even he, himself, disappointed. Hurt. Eventually, left.

She shook her memories off and turned her attention back to Drew and the Mystery Woman. Raven wondered who she was and what she wanted. Not that it was any of her business, but she knew Drew wasn't from here, so why would he be pursuing a romantic interest right now, during his dig with all its politics?

The sound of his voice drifted out across the room as he told some sort of animated story to the woman. Raven couldn't hear the words, but she allowed the sinful sound to wash over her.

His voice was deep, almost gravelly, and when he let his guard down, she could hear the Cajun, loud and clear.

When he was aware of himself and those around him, like he was now, he spoke in those cultured, educated tones. He could have passed for a French expat, living in the U. S. , who'd lost most of his accent, but it was still there. Just a little around the edges.

Raven tried so hard not to be affected by it, but it was fucking hot. Besides, being turned on by the man didn't equal trusting him. She identified with him on some level, though. To the casual observer, he might seem like a trust-fund baby, always had money and never knew what it was like to do without. To struggle.

But Raven saw shadows in those sky-blue eyes, ones she'd often seen reflected back at her in the mirror. It was the look of someone who'd pulled themselves up from nothing, had clawed and fought their way to where they were, and who wasn't going to let anyone take it away. She knew what that was all about. When she looked in his eyes, they practically screamed *been there, not going back.*

In that and the fact that he had the precious book—the key to her history and answer to all her questions—he intrigued her.

Raven continued to watch the couple without fear of being seen. Despite the fact that she had some seriously stealthy skills by trade, her powers also gave the ability to create the illusion that she wasn't there.

She tried to hear what they were saying by edging farther through the door. She wasn't proud of it, but she was curious by nature. Her Kryptonite, Ray had always called it.

Suddenly, Drew sat up straight in his seat and turned his head to stare right in her direction. Surprise lanced through Raven, because no one, *no one,* had ever been able to see her when she went ghost.

She could tell by the way his eyes darted around the room that he hadn't seen her, but he sure as hell had sensed her. Raven would definitely have to examine that closer later on, but for now, she shrank back into the shadows.

The redhead touched his arm to regain his attention, and he pulled out a small tablet computer to show her something. She listened to him for a moment, then she, too, looked over directly to where Raven was.

The woman smiled and winked in her direction, then mimed zipping her lips before turning her attention back to Drew.

Raven couldn't quite contain her gasp, so she clapped a hand over her mouth and backed up into the hallway. That woman had known she was there. Maybe she'd seen Raven...maybe she was psychic. Raven didn't know, but she didn't like being so vulnerable.

She always counted on the ability to blend into her surroundings, and it terrified her that the woman may have found a chink in her armor.

As she made good her escape, Raven's phone began to play a throbbing Black Eyed Peas beat. She smiled as she answered the call. "Hey, Trys."

"Hello, love, how are you?"

Trystan's voice had always been the calm in her storm, and she closed her eyes for a moment to let the chaos that roiled inside her smooth and still.

"I'm good. I wrapped up the Senator Blaisdale job today, and I am positive his detail will be calling you to set up a new system immediately."

"That bad, huh?"

"Let's just say that a young MacAulay Culkin could have done better."

Deep laughter boomed out from the phone, allowing the little ball of warmth to grow inside her. Trys, Ryder, and Micah where the only connections to the past with her father that she had, and she knew they all tried to fill his shoes whenever they could.

"With that done, I'm good to go on the Markham Estates job whenever you give me the go ahead."

"Actually, I'm going to squeeze in one more on you. Not our usual deal, but this one's a personal favor and requires some special attention."

Raven had a nagging sensation that she wasn't going to like where this conversation would lead her, though she was helpless but to follow. "Oh? Government or Richie Rich private?"

"Well, neither. You know the archaeological dig going on over in Black Valley?"

And that was the sound of the other shoe dropping, alarm bells, and a big *Danger, Will Robinson,* all rolled into one. "What about it?" she asked, suspicious.

"They've been having some trouble over there with protestors."

"And?" She drew the word out for emphasis.

"The protestors have escalated quite a bit, throwing things, harassing the interns and scientists as they try to come in to work. Dr. Larkin, the head guy on the dig thinks it's only a matter of time until it intensifies into something more violent and destructive."

"And you think we can help how?"

"Just take a few precautions like having a live security detail during the day while folks are there. Rig some cameras and motion lights. If they're so concerned with their artifacts, it may be worth talking about erecting a fence around the site that can be locked."

"So what's all this got to do with me?" she asked, though she could guess what her old friend was about to say.

"Since you're in the area, I thought you could meet with their guy and discuss what they think they need versus what we're willing to provide. It would keep us from being down a man in the office here."

"Sure thing, Trys. You know I can never say no to you anyway," she said, grinning. "Who's their guy and where do I find him?"

"Name's Deveraux. He's staying over at Micah's. And since you tend to crash there when you're in the area, he should be easy for you to find."

"Trys, I don't think—"

"Really appreciate this, love. Call me after you speak with him, and we'll talk about setting it all up."

"No, listen—"

"Doll, I gotta run. Meeting Ryder for a consult in ten! Call me later. Bye!"

Raven gaped at her phone as the line went dead. Wow. Trystan certainly had unrivaled powers of manipulation. His silver tongue could probably convince a Viking warlord to do what he wanted, she thought.

As far as she knew, Trys had no idea she and Drew had ever met, but something about the whole situation had set off her suspicion radar.

"Well," she said quietly to herself, "I guess I need to go find my client." Perhaps she would keep up the tradition of how they kept meeting, just for old times' sake, she thought with a devilish smile.

CHAPTER NINE

As he stood in front of room 213's bright red door, Drew realized this would be the first time he'd actually gone into the room since booking it the night before. His mind drifted to the night spent in Raven's room, wishing he had been slightly less unconscious for it.

He'd go inside, drop off his briefcase and computer, then head back to the car for his duffel. He looked forward to a long, scalding shower and the blissful oblivion of sleep. God only knew when he would end up having to meet with this security consultant.

Drew stuck the old-fashioned key in the lock and he pushed the door open. Nothing but the light from the hallway illuminated the room. As his eyes adjusted to the darkness, he shut and locked the door behind him.

Drew flicked the light switch that turned on a couple of lamps in the small living room. He had to hand it to Micah, the rooms at Cliffdweller's were quite nice considering the low rates he was charging.

The room Drew had been given was actually a small suite with a living room, a large bathroom and walk-in closet, and a bedroom. There were balconies attached to both the living room and the bedroom.

With a weary sigh, he put his laptop bag, and the small locked case that held the grimoire, on the antique claw-foot writing desk. He glanced at the closet, sighed and promised himself that he would unpack tomorrow after getting back from the site.

Eying the bedroom door, and the good twenty feet of real estate he'd have to cross to get to it, he chose to flop down on the plush chocolate-colored leather couch. He let out a groan and his eyes rolled back in his head, because the feeling of finally getting off his aching feet was nearly orgasmic.

Drew propped his feet up on the solid oak coffee table and checked out the cozy little living area. On either side of him were recliners that matched the couch. In front of him was a large stone fireplace with a remote-controlled gas log fire.

Mounted on the wall above the heavy mantle was a thirty-two-inch flat screen plasma TV. Nice. Drew picked up the multi-functional remote and opted to turn on the fire rather than the television. He drifted off to sleep in the haze of exhaustion and much needed comfort.

He wasn't sure how long he'd been out when he sat up, instantly and inexplicably awake. He glanced around the room to see what could have woken him, but all he saw were the quiet shadows flickering from the firelight.

Just about to give up and surrender to oblivion again, he heard the slightest noise from the direction of the bedroom. It was so incredibly faint, he was sure he'd imagined it—except for the fact that his entire body went on alert, all synapses firing. The hair on the back of his neck rose, and instinct told him that he was most definitely not alone.

Drew silently cursed the lack of some kind of weapon as he crept into the darkened bedroom. On the right side of the door was a half wall that jutted out into the room, and he would have to walk around it to see who or what was in there, thereby leaving himself out in the open and vulnerable.

Drew swallowed and rounded the corner as cautiously as possible. He braced himself as he switched on the lamp on the bureau. He was proud of himself for not jumping a mile high and screaming like a little girl. He really was. Outwardly, he simply froze. Every muscle in his body going rock solid still. Inside, he was still trying to extricate his balls from his throat with as much grace as he could muster.

There was most definitely someone in the room, and that someone was dressed to kill. Raven lay curled up on his bed, and, instead of her riding leathers, she wore a vintage Queen t-shirt that was several sizes too small, revealing several inches of toffee colored skin where her belly button rings twinkled at him.

She also sported denim cut-off shorts. And they were...Cut. Off. Miles and miles of leg—from the fraying denim to her bare feet with the toenails polished to a shiny black—tempted him beyond reason.

He saw that she had plaited several braids on her temples that followed her hairline, which gave her almost a Mohawk look. The ends of the braids fell to her waist, each was tipped with a black feather. On anyone else, it would have looked silly, but on Raven...it was the hottest thing he'd ever seen.

Only the right side of her face was illuminated, leaving the rest in shadow. He could see the shell of her ear, pierced all the way up to the delicate little spike at the top. He had no idea when the hell he started finding body piercings so sexy. Maybe it was just the essence of Raven, bad-ass chick wrapped in mystery...Apparently, that was his type now.

He followed the line of her profile, from the square jaw and full lips, to the straight nose and high cheekbones. Her brows were dark slashes over smoky amber eyes and her inky lashes dusted the soft skin over her cheeks.

It was almost as if she were asleep; he'd begun to think she was until she shifted, bringing one black fingernail to her lips to nibble on. Her eyes fluttered open and pierced into him, full of sensual promise.

He knew it was a trap. She wanted something. He knew this even as his body flared to life, lust surged through him, and everything in him reached out to her. He bit down on the inside of his cheek to jolt him out of his stupor.

She was still after the book. He knew it, even if is body didn't. He couldn't let her play him. He needed to gain the upper hand, because it seemed as though he'd been one step behind since they'd first met.

ꕥ

Pretending to check the lock on the sliding-glass door to the balcony, Drew sighed. "We've got to stop meeting this way," he muttered. "You know, you can just knock. Funny thing, that. Usually gets people to answer the door."

She chuckled, a dark husky sound that caused his cock to sit up and pay attention. "But Professor, this is our special little dance."

"So it is...Raven, I meant what I said before. I'll be glad to give you the answers you're looking for. You only have to ask. Until then, feel free to make yourself at home. I've got work to do."

Turning on his heel, he left the room and hoped he didn't imagine the surprised gasp his words pulled from her. He really just wanted to get some more sleep before heading back to the dig at oh-eight-hundred, but he also wanted to see how their 'special little dance' played out.

Drew sat down at the writing desk and decided to catch up on a couple of emails to give Raven time to formulate her next move. He pulled his laptop out of its case and booted it up, making sure that the locked case was within his view on the desk.

The case was solid metal with a five-number combination lock. The only bad thing about it was there was a key that could override the combination. He always kept the key on his person; right now it was in his pants pocket.

When he opened his email program, he sorted through and deleted some junk, answered an email from the dean about the progress of the dig. He wrote a quick one to Jeremiah, now that he felt he had enough evidence that Raven was, indeed, a *vigile*.

Jere,

Think I've found another vigile *here in Blowing Rock. She's looking for answers, but I'm not sure how much she knows. She's a runner so I don't want to scare her off. Could use some advice. Or better yet, you and the missus could come for a visit. Let me know,*

D

Drew lost track of time until his ears picked up a slight shuffling sound as Raven entered the living room and padded over to where he was working.

"Hey." She stood next to him and poked him in the shoulder with a finger. The childlike action made his lips twitch with the need to smile.

Humoring her, he dropped his hands from the keyboard and scooted his chair back from the desk just a bit. "Yeah? Did you need something?" Drew could tell his nonchalant attitude was confusing her. Based on the way her full lips turned down in a pout and her brows drew together, he thought it probably pissed her off a little, too.

His cell phone beeped to signal an incoming text. He turned from her to check it, and he saw that it was a quick answer to his email from Jeremiah. *OMW,* it said. Good. Jeremiah would know how he should handle...this. Looking back at Raven, Drew bit back the urge to smile.

She looked a little uncertain as to what to do now that she was no longer so artfully posed for seduction. She huffed in frustration, and Drew's hands itched to pull her into his lap.

Turned out he didn't have to fight that urge because she straddled him. He closed his eyes briefly as he searched for control. He found his body had none as his arousal swelled to meet her. Those bottomless eyes of hers held him transfixed as a small smile played at her mouth.

She bit her plump lower lip and swiveled her hips a little to put just the slightest pressure on his erection. His head fell back against the chair and his hips involuntarily bucked against her. The expression that flickered across her face was that of a hunter who had her prey in her sights.

His brain struggled to process this as all the blood drained to the lower half of his body. When her mouth closed over his, he gave up the fight. The instant their lips touched, a shock of electricity rippled through him. It sizzled under his skin and raised the hair on his arms. Her sharp gasp told him she'd felt it too.

He fell into the kiss, opening for her. Her tongue plunged into the depths of his mouth, each stroke causing his pulse to jump.

Unable to stop himself, he wrapped his arms around her to keep her right where she was. His hands followed the path of her spine and over the rough fabric of her shorts to grasp her softly rounded backside.

He used his grip to jerk her more firmly against him and swallowed her surprised moan. They wrestled for control of the kiss, each with their own motive in mind, until she began to rock against him. Her elegant fingers plunged into his hair. She tugged sharply on his curls, angling his head to deepen the kiss.

He nearly went off like a rocket, going wild beneath her. He rolled his hips to push back against her, broke the kiss to burn a trail of nips and bites down her jaw and throat. He pulled a strangled moan from her as he sucked up a mark on the sensitive skin behind her ear.

The long fall of sable hair fell across his arms where he held her, its silky decadence causing him to shudder. Her hand left his hair to slide down his chest where his shirt lay already unbuttoned. Every molecule of his being focused on the path of that hand as it grazed the quivering muscles of his belly, and lower.

He saw stars shoot behind his closed lids as her hand closed around him in a firm grip, stroking him through his pants. She kept up a driving rhythm that mirrored what her tongue was doing in his mouth. She broke off to graze his pulse point with her teeth as she gave him a squeeze.

A tingling at the base of his spine set off alarm bells, warning him that he was close. He bit his lip hard enough to draw blood. The pain focused him enough to keep from embarrassing himself, but also enough to realize her other hand had left his hair and he could no longer feel it on him.

He felt a slight tickle at his hipbone that caused the blood in his veins to turn to ice. His hand snapped out to catch her wrist as it pulled away from his pants pocket. A tiny key dangled from her grip.

Her eyes went wide as his face hardened, and he glared at her. She'd made him forget. She'd made him want her enough to ignore his instincts and let his guard down. Stupid, but it wouldn't happen again.

Nudging her off his lap, he stood with his hands fisted and jaw clenched. "Get out," he said in a voice devoid of all emotion. He would give away nothing. Not anymore.

CHAPTER TEN

Raven did herself a favor and didn't argue with him. She knew she'd fucked up when she saw that look in his eyes. The cold, dead scowl looked at home on his patrician features, as if he too often wore that expression, and she suddenly wished she could put that easy smile and boyish charm back in place.

She'd blown her shot; now he'd never let her near that book. Strangely, Raven found herself just as upset that he'd probably never let her near him again. Time to leave, she thought. He refused to look at her as she stole one last glance before slipping out the door.

Once on the other side, she flattened herself against the wall, pulse pounding, unable to catch her breath. What had she done? She'd set out to get access to the book and she'd damn near fucked the man in his desk chair. It was only at the last minute she'd remembered her initial goal and made her grab for the key. She'd been distracted. Distracted by just how good it felt to be held by someone, by the power she felt at having caused such a reaction in him.

Distraction made for a sloppy grab. He never would have caught her otherwise. For some reason, she was glad he had. It was ridiculous, of course, last thing a good grifter needed was to go soft on a mark.

But somehow, she couldn't help but be sad that he was disappointed in her. Raven had lived her life not caring what anyone thought. It was all about survival back then, just as it was now. So why was she suddenly so worried about Drew and the possibility that she'd hurt him?

When she thought of the empty, glacial tone of his voice when he'd told her to get out, she shuttered. That man had a mouth built for smiles and sex, not scowls and angry words. Raven sensed that there had been too many of those in his life.

Raven was faced with emotions that she couldn't remember ever having felt before, even after all the cons she'd run with Ray—regret. Remorse. Maybe even a little shame. The feelings curdled in her gut like sour milk as she slunk down the hall and back to her own room.

She squared her shoulders and steeled herself against the unpleasant emotions, just like Ray had taught her back in the day. She'd find a way to make it right with Drew and get a look at that book. As bad as she felt about manipulating him, she still had a goal that needed to be met.

She may be an accomplished professional now, backed by a legitimate company, but you can't take the grifter out of the girl, as the saying went. Tomorrow, she had a job to do, making sure good people were safe. She had to focus on that first, then she would figure out how to get back in Dr. Deveraux's good graces.

CHAPTER ELEVEN

A makeshift lab had been set up under one of the tents at the dig, and Drew was busy looking at a bone fragment from the skeleton they'd found under a high-powered microscope. The skull had been fractured post-mortem, and they believed the shard was one of the pieces that had broken off.

Since the researchers were still digging out the skeleton, Drew had chiseled out the fragment to have a look. Pulling away from the microscope, he frowned. He increased the magnification and refocused, looking through the lens.

There were some unusual striations on the bone that he'd never seen before, and without the rest of the skeleton, he couldn't get the full picture of what they meant. Something else was bothering him about the fragment as well. He had nothing specific to back it up yet, but he had a hunch that this fragment was not so ancient.

Of course, he'd need to send off samples for various tests, and the university would probably want to have the bone radiocarbon dated. While the people buried here could very well be Catawba, Drew had a feeling that this bone hadn't come from one of them. He knew that the powers that be at the universities would need more than his speculation, so he would have to wait to do the tests once the skeleton was extracted.

Drew heard the familiar cacophony of angry shouts and obscenities that signaled someone's arrival at the site. He ignored the disruption and continued to study the bone. He looked up from the scope and turned as Oz entered the tent. The movement caused a curl to flop forward into his eyes, and he shoved it back in frustration.

"'Sup, Boss?"

"Hey Dev, you're meeting's here."

"My meeting? What meeting?"

"Stiles & Nash Security? She said she's here to see you. Brought some muscle with her, too. Maybe they can quiet down that crowd."

Annoyed that he had to drop everything for this *consultant* who didn't know how to use a fucking phone, Drew shut off the microscope and yanked the plastic cover down over it. Oz eyed him carefully, a silent question in his eyes.

Drew shrugged and gave him a half-smile. "Yeah. Must have forgotten that was this morning. I'll take care of it."

"I appreciate you handling this for me, Dev."

"No problem, Oz." Drew wiped his hands on a rag from the lab table and put on his aviator sunglasses. May as well get this over with, he thought.

Drew stepped out of the tent and cast his eyes skyward, frowning at the angry gray clouds that were gathering. If the rain came, they would have to call it an early day and cover the excavation area with tarps to protect it.

He spotted the huge black Escalade first. A bit extravagant for a security company, in his opinion. Then he saw her. She wore a black fitted leather blazer with a high, popped collar. Her long, long legs were hugged by black pencil slacks that ended just above the black snakeskin pumps.

Her hair was scraped back into a tight French braid, the tail of which brushed her finely formed ass. This time, the black feathers were at her ears, instead of in her hair, but the effect was the same. Raven.

Even as his anger at the events of the night before surged through him, his entire body screamed out for her, so loud it was nearly deafening inside his head. Raven.

She was flanked on either side by muscle-bound meatheads that he could only describe as goons. The pair were dressed alike, from their camo pants and combat boots, to their black t-shirts—and if they didn't say *Security* on the back, Drew would eat his own hat.

That was where the similarities between Thing One and Thing Two ended. Guido on the left was clean-cut, with a military brush cut and cold, dead eyes. Guido on the right was covered in more ink and metal than Drew had ever seen on one body. The guy's long brown hair was pulled back in a low ponytail, and his eyes were hidden behind silver wraparound Oakleys.

Drew eyed the trio suspiciously as he approached. "What is this?" He directed his question to Raven, as she was clearly the top dog in charge. She stepped forward, impossibly steady in those towering heels, and held out a hand to him.

"Raven Sabatier, Stiles & Nash Security," she said, obviously pretending never to have met him before. There was a challenge in her eyes as she waited for him to take her hand. He shook it briefly then dropped it like it burned him.

"Miss Sabatier," he said with a nod. "I'm Dr. Deveraux. I'm a consultant on the dig, and I'll be handling the security setup." Her lips quirked into a smile, and he wondered if she'd noticed that he failed to give her a first name.

"Nice to meet you, Doctor. Why don't you tell me a bit about your needs—"

Drew jumped as a big hand clapped him on the back. He wondered if Oz would ever stop sneaking up on him like that. "Hey Dev, introduce me."

Drew felt an unwelcome surge of possessiveness when he saw the older man eyeing Raven with interest.

She raised a brow at him. "Dev?"

Drew rolled his eyes and shook his head. "Old college nickname. Ms. Sabatier, this is Dr. Oswalt Larkin. He's running the dig. Dr. Larkin, Raven Sabatier."

Oz leaned forward to take her offered hand, but, instead of shaking it, he raised it to his lips and brushed a kiss over her skin. Drew gritted his teeth and felt his hands curl into fists but was eased some when he saw Raven's body tense. At least the advances were unwelcome. For now, anyway.

"Oz, if you'll excuse us, I'm going to show Raven and her...associates around the site."

"Sounds good, Dev. Let me know what you all figure out. Raven, pleasure to meet you," he said with a lascivious wink.

Raven's only acknowledgment was a nod. When they were alone, Drew pulled Raven aside. "What are you doing here?" he hissed, glancing back at the Bobbsey twins.

She rounded on him, eyes piercing. "I'm doing exactly what I told you. I'm part owner of Stiles & Nash. I was in the area on a job when the boys called and told me about the security problems at the site. I had no idea I'd be dealing with you until they sprung it on me."

Her calm, collected attitude rankled so he poked at her. "And I'm just supposed to believe you? I think we both know that you always have an ulterior motive."

A look strangely close to regret crossed her face before her features became, once again, carefully blank. "You're right. You have no reason to trust me, of course. I'll call Trystan and see if he can send out another consultant. May take a couple of days, but he'll get it done."

She pulled out an iPhone and began tapping on the screen. Drew ran a hand through his unruly curls and marveled at how she made him feel like a petulant child. Which was ridiculous, because *she* had been the one trying to play *him.*

Nevertheless, he sighed and placed a hand on her arm to stop her from calling. "No, that won't be necessary. I'm sure you take your profession very seriously. If you're willing to help us, I'd appreciate it."

He guided her around the cordoned off perimeter of the dig site, explained the gridding system and what was set up inside each tent. She was silent while he talked, sharp eyes darting around the valley as she looked for unseen threats.

"Why, exactly, are they protesting the dig, Dr. Deveraux?"

He laughed, chagrined, and the action felt rusty, as if he hadn't done it in far too long.

"You really can call me Drew. I was just being an ass before."

"Drew," she said, testing it out. Rolling it around on her tongue. He wanted to kiss it off her lips, while, at the same time, he wanted to hear her gasping it while those black nails clawed his back.

He shook his head when he realized he'd been staring at her mouth. She chewed her lower lip and gave him an expectant look, and he finally remembered she'd asked him a question.

"Oh, uh, well, it varies. There seem to be two camps among the angry mob. There are the conservationists who don't want us tearing up their nature. Then there are the spiritualists, the ones who believe we shouldn't disturb the 'final resting place' of whoever is buried here."

Raven nodded, eyes narrowed at the picketers. "They may have a point."

"You agree with them?"

"I'm not saying I do. Not saying I don't. But I firmly believe that there are some things in this world that we are just not meant to mess with. I can't comment as to what those things are. However, threatening people, possibly hurting them, is not a way to get your point across."

"I just want to stop this before anyone does get hurt," he answered, turning worried eyes to search her face.

"Has anyone gotten violent?"

He held out his hand and waved it back and forth in a noncommittal gesture. "Not exactly, but things are escalating. My interns are getting harassed as they come into work in the morning, yelled at, shoved a little. They throw things sometimes, but so far no attempts at real bodily harm."

She said nothing, but Drew knew she was taking it all in as her eyes continued to search the perimeter.

Raven studied the layout of the site, the grid, the four pop-up tents, the orange snow fencing that marked the perimeter. It would be so easy for someone, anyone, to get in.

To destroy equipment, tamper with the findings, even hurt someone.

An area out in the open like this would be hard to secure, but they had the cover of the valley working for them. She tipped her face up to one of the ridges above and noted a rocky ledge that jutted out over the site.

She pointed at it and she turned back to Drew. "Can we get up there? It would really help to get an overhead view."

"Sure. I think there's a trail," he said, then grinned broadly at her, flicking his eyes downward. "You're gonna want to change your shoes."

ഇൽ

Once they made the ledge, Raven was still for a long time as she looked out over the valley below. Drew thought she looked ridiculously adorable in her black widow business attire, stuffed into borrowed hiking boots.

Unable to stand the suspense, Drew broke the silence. "So what would you recommend for us?"

She didn't look at him. She continued to stare down at the site, envisioning her plan as she laid it out to him. "Four motion sensor security lights, one mounted at each corner. Eight solar powered security cameras with live feed and battery backup—four visible and four hidden. Here, here, here, and there." She pointed out the proposed locations of the hidden cameras.

"Why have some visible and some hidden?"

"The visible cameras will distract an intruder. They'll be worried about avoiding those and won't know they're being recorded by others."

Drew nodded, "Makes sense."

"I think two live guards during the day while there are people here, and a night guard as well. You don't really have any way of protecting the contents of the tents. Also, you need to implement a reverse curfew. Basically no one is allowed here after dark, and no one is allowed to be here by themselves, at anytime."

"You can make all this happen?"

"Absolutely. It's what we do. If this turns out not to be enough, we can talk about burying a line that will trigger an alarm and a distress call."

"Great, set it up," Drew said.

Raven stepped away to make a few calls, just as Drew heard the distant rumble of thunder. Soon they would have to shut down for the day.

"The boys have got everything lined up for you, and we'll have a team out to install everything tomorrow."

"Thanks. So, how did you hook up with Stiles & Nash?"

She gave him a wary look, as if weighing the pros and cons of trusting him. "Trys and Ryder were friends of my father's. I grew up with them always around, along with Micah. Almost like three older brothers. A few years back, they told me they wanted to start their own security company and could use my 'special skills'. So I bought in. I'm more of a silent partner, though. I like to be out in the field."

Drew's mind flashed back to the conversation he'd had with Micah on this same subject, and a lightbulb went on. "Ray," he whispered.

Raven's eyes snapped to his face, and her head jerked back as if he'd struck her. "What did you say?" she hissed.

Knowing he was on dangerous ground, Drew cleared his throat. He wasn't going to lie. "I said, Ray."

"Where did you hear that name? You know *nothing* about my father!" She began to turn and walk away from him.

Enough was enough. Drew grabbed her by the shoulders and turned her back around. She tensed against him, muscles twitching in her arms. "Hey," he said calmly, and waited for her to look up at him.

The depth of anger he saw in her eyes startled him, but he wasn't going to give up. He had a feeling she'd had too much of that. "I didn't mean anything by it. Micah told me about him, but I didn't make the connection until just now, when you were talking. We don't have to talk about your father." *Yet.*

He felt her slowly relax, muscle by muscle, and led her over to a rickety old bench someone had erected. "Okay?" he asked.

"Okay. Sorry."

"No problem."

"No. I mean about last night. I'm sorry. I grew up having to con to get what I wanted. Needed. Sometimes I forget I don't have to do that anymore. I can just ask."

"Can you? Ask?"

She laughed. Deep, rich, and husky. The sound caused a shudder to ripple under his skin.

"Touché, Dr. Deveraux. Look, I don't trust you. I can't. The world I was raised in, trust can get you killed. But I really want to know—*need* to know—what is in that book. I need your help."

A lot of guys would use this opportunity to gloat, to rub it in, dangle her weakness in her face. But he didn't. He simply nodded.

"I can do that. You need to understand one thing though. We're dealing with some heavy shit here. This information has the power to hurt a lot of people I care about, so I have to be very careful about what I say. In order for me to help you, you're going to have to answer some questions, even some about your past. Can you do that?"

She toyed with the tail of her braid, and studied him from beneath her lashes. "I can only promise that I'll try. I can't promise I won't get defensive, though."

"And I can't promise I won't tell you to get the fuck over it." His smile softened the words, and she smiled back.

Against his will, his eyes were drawn to her mouth, and he couldn't help but remember last night—before shit had gone downhill. He leaned in close until his breath fanned her face. Her eyes fluttered closed and her lips parted, and he almost forgot—almost—what he was going to say.

"Raven?" he asked in a husky whisper.

"Yes."

"You kiss me again? You better mean it."

Her strangled gasp was drowned out by a loud clap of thunder, and the sky began to dump buckets of rain on their heads.

"Shit, gotta get down there to help batten down the hatches," he said, taking off his windbreaker and offering it to her.

She stared at it in her hands for a moment, as if she couldn't figure out what to do with it, or why he'd bothered to offer it. He'd bet the latter.

"Earth to Raven. Time to go!" Hand in hand, they took off running down the trail and headed back down to the valley.

Drew couldn't believe that she'd asked him. Now it was time to play ball. He just had to make sure he didn't scare her off again.

ꙮ

Jeremiah flopped onto his back on the bed and tried to slow his raging heartbeat. His chest heaved as his lungs burned for air, and his skin was slick with a sheen of perspiration. He was pretty sure his new wife had just killed him. Twice.

But as Isla leaned over him and smiled, soft skin sliding against his, silky curls tickling his chest, he decided that this must be what heaven was like. She kissed him softly, lingering to suck on his lower lip, and damned if his body didn't try and show some interest again.

He smacked her bare butt and rolled them so he was on top of her. "Damn, woman! You'll be the death of me."

Her laughter rang out, tinkling like faerie bells, warming him all over. "Oh, you *love* it," she answered in her thick Scottish brogue.

"Yes. Yes I do," he agreed. He kissed her pert little nose and was rewarded with a flash of the dimples. "Love you."

The afterglow was interrupted as the door to their bedroom burst open to reveal a tall, dark haired, lanky boy sporting icy eyes and a cocky grin. Jeremiah was thankful that he had covered them up, because the sight of them bare-ass naked would not have stopped Marduk from coming in. It would have just embarrassed them to no end.

Marduk flopped down at the foot of the bed and gave them a cheeky wink. "So, what are we doing this morning?" he asked. His wicked smile indicated he knew damn well what they'd been doing.

"Son of a bitch, wolf. Boundaries! What have I been telling you?"

As usual, the shapeshifting pain-in-the-ass *feradux* ignored him. "When are we leaving for North Carolina?"

Fuck. Jeremiah swore the little bastard had his shit bugged. He could practically hear Isla's wheels turning.

"North Carolina? Jeremiah?"

"Isla, I just found out about this last night. I was going to talk to you about it then, but you sort of distracted me," he said, giving her a wide grin and flashing his overlong canines. Unlike the kid, there was no wolf in him. Just a genetic accident, apparently. "I don't even know how the flea-bag found out about it."

"I went through your emails, that's how," Marduk said, without remorse, and ducked the pillow that was thrown at his head.

"Found out about what? Just tell me," Isla pleaded.

"Drew thinks he may have found another *vigile* where he's working in North Carolina. He's not sure how to handle it, so he asked for our help."

"Drew? Deveraux? Ask for help?"

"I know, right? Shows you how desperate he is."

"Well, what are we waiting for? Let's get on the road!"

"Actually, we're waitin' on *Rougaroux* here to get the hell off our bed so I can get my naked ass dressed."

After showering, Jeremiah stepped out into their bedroom and was toweling off when he heard his phone ring. He checked the display and saw that it was a restricted number. Only one person ever called him from a restricted number.

When he hit the speaker button, he didn't wait for the person to speak. "Matty?"

Silence.

"Matty, is that you? Say something."

More silence. But Jere could hear the faint sound of breathing on the other end. "Look, Matty, if you're in trouble, just say the word and I'm there...and I'd really like you to meet my wife."

Jeremiah's brother had gone off the grid a few months ago, and he hadn't been seen or heard from since. But Jere knew Matty had been checking up on him, and was sure his brother knew he'd been in Scotland, and that he'd gotten married.

He jolted when the line went dead, and resisted the urge to throw the phone across the room. Holy shit, his brother was infuriating. He sighed when he felt Isla slide behind him to rub his tense shoulders.

"Was it him?"

"I think so. I don't know. I just don't know what his damage is. I mean, anymore than usual."

Ever the voice of reason, Isla pressed a kiss to his temple and spelled it out for him. "He'll come around when he's ready, Jeremiah. I think he just wants you to know he's alive."

"I hope you're right," he answered and rubbed the ache over his heart from the hole Matthieu's absence had left in it.

CHAPTER TWELVE

Raven needed some air. She had been running from the overwhelming sense of panic she felt since the storm had started. Revving the Ducati, she felt the 1100cc twin cylinder engine purr beneath her as she sped up the mountain.

Heedless of the wet road, she leaned to the inside as she negotiated the switchbacks, hugging the curves with the sleek machine. She had to get away.

What had she agreed to? She had asked Drew for help. She *never* asked for help. To her, it was the equivalent of crawling over hot coals and begging. But she'd felt so bad for trying to con him. He'd been so angry, but that wasn't what got to her. He'd seemed almost...hurt.

So she'd swallowed her pride, climbed over her mountain of baggage, and asked him to help her find out about herself. And now she was feeling the cold, bony fingers of panic close over her throat.

Give nothing away. That's what Ray always said. God, she loved her father. Missed him. But she was beginning to realize how royally screwed up her world view was thanks to him. Besides, Ray knew nothing about Raven's mother or what happened to her, and he refused to talk about his own parents, so she really had no other options to explain her strange abilities.

The rain began pouring down on her and, while she may be reckless, she wasn't stupid. She guided the bike over to the side of the road, swung off, and rolled it into the cover of some trees.

Since she was dressed simply in cargo pants, t-shirt, boots, and a rain jacket, Raven decided to go for a little hike until the rain stopped. Maybe she would be able to catch hold of her tenuous control.

The Blue Ridge mountain range was one of her favorite places to visit. The forest was thick with tall pine, sourwood, and blackgum trees, padded with smaller flora like dogwood and rhododendron.

Natural game travel had worn a small path through the thick of it, and Raven dug in, pushing her body to the limit to try and shut off her mind. Her muscles burned as she tackled a sharp incline.

Her hackles rose when she realized she was being followed. Her watcher was silent, an excellent tracker. But Raven's power to command the space around her acted like an early warning system when another warm body was in the area.

Unconcerned, she kept hiking until she came to a small heath, a fertile clearing in the woods stuffed full of mountain laurel, azalea, wintergreen, and various berry bushes. It was beautiful, like an *arroyo* in the desert.

She was checking out the intricate web of a writing spider when a twig snapped behind her. Raven whipped around, then froze, pulse pounding in her ears. Standing in front of her was a huge-ass cat.

She searched her limited database of Discovery Channel shows and what she knew of the area, and decided it was probably a mountain lion, a cougar. The creature looked at her steadily with its clear, green eyes.

It took a tentative step forward, and Raven jumped back, cursing herself silently for the sudden movement. "Oh shit. Oh, *fuck,*" she whispered when the reality of her situation struck her. She was deep in the woods, high on a mountain.

No one knew where she was, and few knew how to contact her. She wasn't expected anywhere that she would be missed, and now, she was literally staring into the eyes of the beast.

Afraid to move again, Raven felt the edges of hysteria pulling at her consciousness as she began to sing in a shaky voice. "Soft kitty, warm kitty, little ball of fur." The stupid song from her favorite TV show popped into her head, and she was unable to stop it. The big cat sneezed, a noise that sounded suspiciously like a laugh.

She waited, and they stared at each other, until the creature stretched out its front legs and slowly slid to the soft, mossy ground. Not knowing much about animals, Raven couldn't be sure, but she didn't think this was typical behavior for a wild cat. She guessed it was good news that the thing wasn't growling or preparing to pounce.

Unsure of what to do, Raven did the first thing that jumped into her head. She mirrored the cat's actions. She took off her rain jacket and laid it on the ground, lowering herself to sit cross-legged on top of it.

"Okay, now what?" she asked quietly. The cougar groaned softly and slowly belly crawled toward her.

Everything inside of Raven was screaming to run, but she knew that was the worst thing she could do.

The cat's nose was inches from her toes, and she could feel herself trembling. Unable to stop herself, because she clearly had a death wish, she reached out to stroke the animal's silky head. It nuzzled her hand and purred. Actually purred.

Raven wasn't sure this day could get any weirder. Then it did. The cougar suddenly sat up, entire body alert, ears twitching. She was baffled by the animal's very human-like behaviors. While she'd spent most of her life fully enveloped in the idea that things were rarely as they seemed, Raven was a city girl. That she'd just basically had a silent communication with an apex predator was enough to give even her the willies.

The cougar turned back to her and after a few tense moments, it bounded into the woods without a backward glance.

"Okaaaay," she said to herself. Raven's heart was still stuttering in her chest as she dusted off her wet pants and shook out her jacket. She wiped the clammy sweat off her forehead with a shaking hand. "Time to get back to civilization before I run into another wild animal."

As she made her way back down the trail to her bike, Raven could still feel the cat's eyes on her. It was following closely, but completely silent and out of sight. As if it were escorting her safely back to the road.

Bizarre. The incident had scared her enough that she felt the uncommon urge to be around people. She pulled out her phone and dialed the inn.

"Cliffdweller's," Micah's deep voice answered.

"Hey big guy."

"Hey Rave, what's happenin'?"

"Oh, little of this, little of that. Can you put me through to room 213?"

"Sure thing, baby doll."

She heard a click then the line began to ring. There was a growl in the voice that answered. "Hello?"

"Drew. Were you sleeping?"

"Raven? No." The gritty, sleepy tone of his voice called him a liar, but Raven let it go.

"So about our deal..."

"Yeah?"

"Can we start tonight?"

"Ah, sure. You could meet me in the tavern. I just need to shower and get dressed."

Raven bit her lip because, damn, that was a mental picture. "'Kay, I'll be there in twenty." Raven's stomach fluttered as she hung up on him before she could change her mind. She couldn't be sure if it was an attack of nerves over sharing her personal business with a virtual stranger, or anticipation of seeing Drew again that caused her to be so jittery. Shutting down her thoughts for the ride, she stowed her phone, put on her helmet and kick-started the Ducati.

The bike was a streak of black and chrome as she raced down the curvy road, feeling like the devil was on her heels. Maybe he was. Raven knew she was about to find out what kind of skeletons were in her closet.

ᘓᘐ

Drew was waiting at the bar, nursing a beer, when Raven walked in. She looked adorable as she searched the room for him. Her dark hair was pulled back in a messy ponytail that showed off the braids at her temples.

She wore a simple, nearly sheer white v-neck tee, like the kind men used for undershirts. Her long legs were encased in ratty denim, a low slung pair of holey jeans. The denim was frayed at the bottoms, and it drew his attention to feet that sported black flip-flops and red nail polish. She had a ring on each of her pinky toes.

God, seeing those made him think of sucking on each of the delicate little digits, and the image made him instantly hard. He resisted the urge to adjust himself. Instead, he smiled at her when she waved and slid into the corner booth.

A throat clearing behind him drew his attention, and he turned to find Micah glaring at him. "Problem?"

The man's dark eyes flicked from Drew's face over to Raven and back again. A muscle twitched in his jaw, but Micah shook his head. "Nope. No problem."

"Good," Drew said, grabbing two beers and turning to meet Raven.

"Deveraux." Micah's voice was quiet and deadly calm.

"Yeah?"

"I like you," he said, then nodded in Raven's direction. "But if you hurt her, I'm gonna fuckin' crazy murder you. Dig?"

"Fair enough." He turned and stalked across the room.

Raven raised a brow as she watched him ease his bulky frame into the booth, and smiled. "Micah giving you trouble?"

"Oh, nothing I can't handle. Let's get started, shall we?"

"Okay. What's in the book?"

Drew couldn't help but laugh at her one track mind. "It's not that simple. The grimoire was written in a language that's not just dead, it's extinct. There's been no known written record of it ever having existed until now. Before, one could only draw conclusions based on references to it in other texts.

I've been working with friends to translate it for the better part of a year. It's slow going."

Raven's mouth dropped open and her brows shot toward her hairline. "So you don't know anything? What was all of this *'I can help you'* bullshit about then?"

Drew took her hand, rubbed his thumb over her knuckles in a soothing gesture. "Easy. I know a lot. But, like I said, what I know has the potential to hurt a lot of people I care about, so I have to play it close to the vest."

"Well, what do you need to know?" she asked impatiently.

"We can start with an easy one. What do you know about the symbol you have here?" He tapped a finger to his own collarbone. "The one similar to the book cover." Raven ran a hand over her hair, causing wisps of silk to escape the ponytail. Drew had to sit on his hands to keep from reaching out to touch them. "Nothing. Not really. It's what started my search that led me to Rome, to the book. It just appeared one day when I was—"

"Eight?"

Her eyes snapped to his and narrowed suspiciously.

He just grinned at her. "Told you, I know things. So you went to Rome. How did you find out about the book?"

"Easy. Google."

"You serious?"

"Hell, yes. You can find anything on the Internet, even a purveyor of ancient texts. The man wanted an exorbitant amount of money for it. In cash. I went to go find an ATM, and when I came back, the old fart had sold it."

"How did you find out what happened to it?"

She gave him a sly smile. "I did what I do best. Broke into the place, hacked the computer and found out who he'd sold it to. I tracked the asshole back to New Orleans and that led me to you."

"That asshole is my best friend, Jeremiah."

She shrugged, apparently unconcerned if she'd offended him. "What did he want with it anyway. What's it got to do with him?"

"Jere had an experience when he was a child, where he encountered a woman with a similar symbol. His wife also has one."

He watched her eyes widen and her face drain of color. He hadn't known someone with her skin tone could look that pale. "You thought you were the only one."

Raven simply nodded, unable to speak. Drew could practically see the wheels turning as she tried to adjust the world view she'd had all her life.

"What do *you* know about the symbol?" she asked in a shaky voice, turning the tables on him.

"The symbol is used in connection with an ancient race of witches called the *Bruixi* that predates the Roman Empire. A race so old that the world's leading expert in antiquated languages can't translate their literature."

He watched as understanding dawned. "You?" she asked.

"The very same. I love how you didn't bat an eye at the witch part. Explain."

"I've always known I had power. I always called it my special skills," she answered. "I never gave it a name, nothing so concrete as witches or magick, but I can do things that other people can't. Comes as easy as breathing. That's all I know about it, though."

"Jeremiah's experience when he was a kid led to his peculiar career choice."

"Which is?"

"He has a PhD in parapsychology, and he makes his living as a paranormal investigator."

"Shut up!"

"I'm serious. So, much like you, he had been searching for information on the symbol and that led him to Scotland, where he met his wife, Isla. Together, along with a few friends, they were able to learn more about the *Bruixi* than probably anyone left living."

Drew pulled out his iPad and brought up a picture of the leather bound book cover and pointed to the circular symbol in the middle. "This is a *signa.* It represents a highborn bloodline among those witches called the *Vigilati.* They were revered and often feared by the *Bruixi.* With me so far?"

She nodded absently, riveted by the story. "The *Vigilati* had been born to be guardians of this world. They guard the gateways between the spirit world and the human world, to keep the evil souls from crossing over."

Raven choked on a swallow of her beer. "Are you serious?"

"As a heart attack. The three circles represent the human world, the spirit world, and the barrier in between them. We think the slashes represent a set of standing stones, often present at these weak points in the barrier, called *locuses*."

"What about the image in the middle of mine, the spider? The one on the book doesn't have that."

"That's where it starts to get complicated, and honestly, I'm not the best person to explain that part to you."

"What are you saying? Who is, then?"

"My buddy Jeremiah's wife. No one knows more about this than Isla. Look, I know you don't trust anyone. Believe me,

I get that. But I'm a little out of my depth with this. They're coming here, be in town in a couple of days."

He held up a hand when she glared at him. "Wait. Before you freak, just hear me out. Isla will be able to give you more information about who and what you are than probably anyone else. It wouldn't be smart to pass up an opportunity like that."

Drew had a feeling that appealing to the reasonable side of her was the only thing that would have worked. And it did.

"Okay," Raven said.

"Okay?"

"I'll meet them. But *I* decide what I want to tell them."

"Of course," he answered with a grin. He suddenly realized that he'd smiled more in the last two days than he had in years.

Raucous laughter pulled their attention to the bar. Quite the crowd had grown while they were immersed in their discussion.

"We can't talk here anymore," Drew said, and Raven agreed.

"Why don't we go up to your room?"

He raised a brow at her because he *so* wasn't sure he wanted to go down that road again.

"What? Yours has a fireplace."

CHAPTER THIRTEEN

When they entered Drew's suite, Raven whirled around. "Let me see it. Let me hold the book."

After he'd shut and locked the door, he made his way over to the desk and began to dig through his briefcase. "So not gonna do that."

She actually had the nerve to look incredulous, like she hadn't tried to steal the book at least twice—that he knew of. Of course, he had more practical reasoning for keeping it to himself.

"It's not going to leave my hands until I've got it all translated. If something happens to it, the information left untranslated would be lost forever."

She closed her gaping jaw at least, but continued to glare at him. "And besides, Bonnie, your fingers are stickier than a tree frog's."

That surprised a laugh out of her, lighting her eyes and flashing straight, white teeth. He thought she was sexy before, but laughing, she was downright beautiful. He cleared his throat and tried to turn his attention back to his briefcase.

"I've got some print-outs of sections I've been able to translate so far that you can read if you want."

"Please."

Grabbing his briefcase and laptop, he gestured toward the huge couch. "Why don't you have a seat and I'll bring this stuff over."

She settled in the corner of the couch and pulled her legs up under her. Drew watched her for a moment, forgetting what he was supposed to be doing. She turned her head to smile at him, and he nearly passed-out from the need that surged through his body. *Down boy.* That was beginning to become his motto in life.

"Coming?" She nibbled her lip and cast her eyes down his body, as if she knew exactly what his problem was.

"Uh, yeah. You want the fire?"

"Oh, yeah."

He sat down next to her on the couch and set up his laptop on the coffee table. Picking up the remote, he flicked on the fire. From his briefcase, he pulled out a paper-clipped section of paper and handed it to her.

It was the section about the *feradux*. She had to find out about them eventually, and he didn't think she'd believe it coming from him. Hell, he wouldn't even believe it if he hadn't seen it with his own eyes.

He made sure not to give her anything on the *Praedos* yet. He'd let Isla handle that little nightmare. From the way Raven reacted to talk of her father already, he figured she wasn't going to take it well.

"You can start with those. I think you'll find them very informative," he said. She frowned at him, as if unsure how to take that. "I'm going to work on my translation program for a little bit. I've almost got it perfected."

She was already reading, totally engaged. Occasionally he would hear little gasps, whispered exclamations over what she was learning.

"Wait, *what*?" she hissed. "Shapeshifting witch slaves? Am I being punked?"

He laughed at her and...well, shit, there it was again. "No, you're not being punked, although I understand the feeling. Thing is, I've seen it."

"Seen it? What is *it*?"

"I've seen one, in the flesh. Isla's *feradux*, Marduk, can turn into a big gray wolf. In either form, he's a big pain in the ass."

She gaped at him and looked like she was ready to scream. He'd had some time to adjust to this craziness, so he decided to give her a minute.

"Yeah, okay. For argument's sake, I'm going to pretend I believe this and keep reading."

Drew just smiled, set down his laptop, and pulled out a spiral-bound notebook. Clearly, he wasn't going to be able to concentrate on the program, so he would work on his manual translations.

He was just getting into it when another outburst startled him so much he dropped the notebook.

"Blood sacrifice!" she screeched. "As in, real blood? I don't want anyone bleeding because of me."

He struggled for patience because he knew this was a lot to throw at her all at once. "It's not your choice. It's prophecy. It's their way of life, what they're bred for. Don't worry about it right now. You haven't even found your *feradux,* so there's no use worrying about the sacrifice."

After nearly an hour of staring at words that refused to make sense, Drew's eyelids began to droop. Lulled by the warmth of the fire, he cast a sleepy glance over at Raven, only to see that she was asleep, her head resting on the arm of the couch.

He should wake her, he really should. Nothing good would come of them sharing a room yet again. But at least she used the door that time. He'd call that progress. His limbs felt heavy, and he felt his body slowly relaxing, all of the tension from the day uncoiling.

Yeah, he should wake her. And he would. In a minute.

Before the minute was up, he was fast asleep.

Drew was wrapped in a cozy blanket of dry heat that filled the room, and he fought to stay under the spell. He felt more relaxed than he had in days. There was a warm, pleasant weight on his chest, so he lifted his heavy arm to wrap around it, and his hand plunged into a delicate nest of silk.

He let out a sleepy groan at the feel of it. He refused to open his eyes and let go of the hold he had on sleep. Besides, there was an incredible pressure massaging his dick. Before he could even question it, his hips were involuntarily bucking against it.

Drew forced his eyes open and looked down his body for the source of the sensations. He had shifted to lay lengthwise on the couch, with Raven draped half on top of him, between his body and the back of the sofa. Her head was pillowed on his chest, and his hand was buried in her now-loose hair.

She had a leg thrown across his hips, which explained the other pressure. She was, as he had been, sound asleep. She shifted in her sleep and her leg moved higher, massaging his length.

His head fell back against the arm of the couch, and he had to take several calming breaths to keep from losing it. He cupped her cheek with his hand and whispered to her. "Raven? Hey, Raven."

He watched as her thick, inky lashes fluttered to reveal those startling amber eyes. Had he noticed the flecks of gold near the center before? He watched as she slowly came awake, as awareness seeped into features.

He'd expected her to jerk away, to be horrified. Instead, those eyes clouded over with lust and grew heavy-lidded. Her gaze flicked to his mouth and her leg—that gorgeous, mile-long leg—began to undulate against him. He grabbed her leg with his free hand to still it.

Drew leveraged himself against the couch and flipped them so she was under him and he was half on top of her. Lowering his head, he brushed a kiss across her lips. When they broke apart, he reared back to look at her. "You sure about this?" he asked, his voice nothing more than a hoarse whisper.

She nodded and buried a hand in his blonde curls to pull him back down to her lips. She was aggressive, how he knew she'd be, nipping and biting, frantic beneath him. When her hand reached down to unbutton his jeans, he caught her wrist, bringing the hand up to kiss each one of her knuckles.

Drew's blue eyes were darkened with passion, and they captivated her. He looked at her as if she were something precious, even though he barely knew her. He brushed his full lips across her knuckles, and, unable to help herself, she dragged a finger across his lower lip. His pupils dilated until his eyes were almost completely black as he pulled her finger into his mouth, applied a bit of gentle suction.

Raven observed the action as if she were outside of herself, powerless to stop the flood of sensation that came over her. She'd been raised to never get close, to never trust anyone. Because of this, Raven had always used sex as a release and nothing more. A way to get off, not a way to be close with someone.

It was always frenzied, aggressive, bordering on abusive, but it was all she knew. She didn't know what to do with all of this...tenderness. She wanted him to lose that unflagging control. Needed him to.

He stopped every attempt she made to speed things up, continued kissing her at his leisure. His hands moved over her body in a thorough exploration. Each touch sent a wave of shudders through her. He finally allowed her to tug his t-shirt over his head, and her eyes feasted on the sight.

His skin was smooth, perfect. Not exactly tanned, but it had a certain sun-kissed glow to it. His broad shoulders and muscular chest that tapered down to a narrow waist made her think that he was probably a swimmer. God, the man was too hot for his own good.

He lifted off of her so she could yank her own t-shirt off. She laughed as his eyes popped when he saw she was wearing nothing underneath. His gaze traveled over her body, halting at her full breasts.

A shaking hand reached out to cup first one, then the other. His rough thumb dragged over a nipple, causing her to arch her back. When she tried to climb on top of him again, he wedged a knee between her thighs to hold her still.

A little shiver of anticipation danced up her spine at the aggressive act. Now they were getting somewhere.

Drew had other ideas. He kissed her with a lazy nonchalance, nipped her earlobe, scraped teeth down her neck. She felt his hand move to the fly of her jeans, and she allowed him to undo them. When she would have wiggled out of the offending garments, he held her fast. It was as if he wanted to unwrap her slowly, like an exotic candy or a much anticipated present.

That thought distracted her until she felt his hand slip inside her pants, underneath her black lace panties, to ghost a caress across her center. She arched up toward him, aching with the need for him to touch her. "Drew. Please."

Her husky plea seemed to set off something in him. His head surged forward and captured one of her nipples between his lips, and he sucked. The pleasure-pain sensation was almost too much, and Raven felt herself losing her grip on reality.

As if he sensed her need, he continued to stroke her. She cried out, bucked her hips and lifted up, seeking...something. When she started to clutch his back, to score him with her nails, he just continued his torture with a control she couldn't fathom.

Pleasure rocketed through her as her climax slammed into her. She arched her body up off the couch and into his hand. He worked her through it, and softened his touch as she came down.

When she could breathe again, she flicked sleepy, sated eyes up to his face. He was watching her with a steady look of awe. He brushed a hand through her tangled hair, and tipped her chin up toward him.

"That, was the most beautiful thing I've ever seen." And he meant it. As she searched his face, she saw no signs of deceit, anger, or manipulation. A sight she wasn't used to. No, she saw something she wasn't used to at all.

Not love. No, he was too practical for that. But genuine interest, caring. She knew, in that moment, that this would never be casual for him.

That familiar panic surged through her again. It gripped her heart and kicked her pulse into overdrive. The room began to close in on her, and she couldn't draw enough breath.

Drew felt her tense, saw her chest begin to heave and her eyes go wide, and he knew that the night was going to end differently than he'd expected when they'd begun.

"Raven? You okay?"

Instead of answering, she scrambled over him, nearly knocking him off the couch in her haste. She grabbed her shirt and pulled it on so carelessly that he heard a ripping sound. She looked so vulnerable as she hugged herself. Her eyes darted around the room as if she was looking for all the possible exits.

He reached a hand out to her. "Look, Raven—"

"No! I'm so sorry. Can't do this," she said and danced out of his reach. She said nothing else, just toed on her flip-flops and headed for the door like her ass was on fire.

Drew winced as the door slammed behind her. Flopping over on his back, he flung an arm over his eyes. "Damn. Skittish as a newborn filly." It seemed like he was destined to be in a constant state of blue balls around her.

He knew she had trust issues. He even understood where she was coming from. But enough was enough. He resolved not to make another move on her. He knew she wanted him. He was sure she knew he wanted her. But she would have to decide for herself if she could pursue a relationship.

Drew sighed, got up and wandered into the bathroom, hoping a cold shower would calm his hopping nerves.

CHAPTER FOURTEEN

Ray took a long, deep breath of the dry desert air. The first true fresh air he'd had in three years. Because it was his second strike, he'd gotten the max—five years—but good behavior had gotten him early parole.

He had done a lot of work on himself on the inside this time, getting clean, seeing a counselor. Hell, he even earned an associates degree in business. Go figure. He was determined to make it stick this time.

Of course, he'd already lost the most important thing in his life. His daughter. Raven had taken off when he was hauled in the first time. She'd been fifteen, young and jaded, tired of being disappointed every time he failed to sober up.

He'd always wondered where CPS got off, dumping an innocent four-year-old on a twenty-five-year-old alcoholic con artist. Yeah, he hadn't had a record, 'cept for that stint in Saint Bernard Parish Juvenile Detention Center, of course.

Maybe they truly were underfunded enough to dump a kid on any available parent, that they hadn't researched him enough. God, he loved her, but the poor kid hadn't stood a chance. Maybe if they'd told him about her ahead of time, given him a chance to get sober, find a legit job, he might have made a halfway decent father.

Well, if wishes were horses then beggars would ride, as the saying went. So he'd raised her the best he knew how. It was no small wonder she hadn't run away earlier. They'd kept in touch, and once she'd partnered up with Stiles and Nash and started the company, he was kept updated on her life.

But after the second time he was arrested, the calls slowed to almost nonexistent. She never visited him in prison. He didn't blame her. He didn't want the stink of his incarceration to taint her.

So, yeah, he was determined to make it stick this time.

He flagged down the car Trystan had sent for him. His friend had apologized for not being able to meet him in person, but he'd had a meeting downtown he couldn't get out of. Ray was just grateful he still had any friends at all.

The black Town Car escorted him all the way back to his apartment, the same one he'd been living in when Raven was brought to his doorstep. The boys had made sure his shit was taken care of while he'd been on the inside, so he knew everything would be just as he left it. Just like he knew his Harley would still be in the garage, well-oiled and gassed up.

He just had time for a quick shower before he was supposed to meet Ryder for lunch. Ryder had always been the most practical of their little group, so he'd promised Ray he would help him find a job, despite his record.

As much as he longed to fire up the Harley, the diner was only a few blocks away and gas cost money, so he opted to walk. Taking a shortcut down one of the alleys knocked off a bit of the trip, so that's exactly what he did.

By that time, the sun had dipped below the desert horizon, and it was almost completely dark. He was about halfway down the alley when he realized he was being followed. He forced himself not to run, not to turn and fight. He just kept walking.

There was a crash behind him that had him whipping around to scan the dark street. He saw nothing. With a frown, he spun back around only to freeze. Someone stood in the shadows in front of him.

A security lamp above them finally sputtered to life, shrouding them in a pool of flickering, fluorescent light. A woman stood alone in the alley. Small with long dark hair that brushed her elbows, with bangs that covered her forehead and swooped over one eye. From what Ray could see, she appeared to be in her early thirties, give or take. Her heels clicked on the pavement as she sauntered toward him.

"Hello, Raymonde," she said in a soft, lilting British accent. Great, he was going to get mugged in an alley by the fucking Queen of England.

He could do nothing but gape at her, allowing his confusion to show on his face. He didn't know her. He would have remembered that face, that body. Her eyes were tilted up like a cat's, her lips were full, the top one slightly larger, indicating just a hint of an overbite. It was damn sexy on her.

"Uh, I'm sorry. Do I know you?"

"Oh, Raymonde, I'm hurt you don't recognize me. Maybe this will help." She waved a hand over her face and her features began to change before his eyes. Her hair curled and browned to a deep sable, her skin darkened, and her eyes changed from dark to bright green.

Oh yeah, now he recognized her, although he was pretty sure he was tripping on something. Had he gone on a bender as soon as he got home that was now causing hallucinations? He looked back at the woman's fine-boned features that looked so much like Raven's.

"Lisette?"

"Yes, I suppose. That's one of the names I've used."

"I don't understand," Ray said, and he really, really didn't.

"Maybe this will help." Lisette waved her hand again, and once more began to change. Her hair shortened and turned to a drab brown, and her eyes changed to the color of muddy water. Gaunt cheeks were shrouded by wide horn-rimmed glasses.

Another face he would never forget. Now he was looking at Barbara McCoy, the social worker. He scrubbed a hand over his face, and when he opened his eyes, the woman's appearance had changed back to how it had begun. "What the fuck is going on?"

There were subtle changes now. The eyes had gone from dark to pale, with misty shadows swirling in them. Her dark curls whipped about her shoulders as if being blown by a ghostly wind.

This time, when she stepped forward, his body tensed to run. Her eyes were definitely freaking him out, and the whole face changing thing didn't help. "I was counting on you to serve your whole sentence, Raymonde. You are severely inconveniencing me."

"What? Why? How?" Oh wow, his powers of communication were unparalleled, but considering he had a modern day Medusa creeping up on him, he was going to give himself a break.

"Unfortunately, you have become the proverbial wrench in my carefully laid plans. I'm afraid I can't allow you to go free."

The fuck? He began to back away slowly. "Look, lady, I don't know what you want from me, but I certainly don't have any interest in your plans. So I'll just be on my way."

The woman's mouth tipped up in a half-smile, and light glinted off a small fang that poked out from under her lip. And that explained the overbite.

He turned to leave but was struck in the side of his head by something solid, metal. When he fell to the ground, blood gushed down his temple. A huge muscle-bound dude loomed over him, and he knew he was in trouble. Medusa hovered behind him with another goon and licked her lips, Ray imagined, over the sight of his blood.

"Goodnight, Raymonde."

Oh, shit. That was his last thought before his world went dark.

CHAPTER FIFTEEN

Raven lifted her glass to her lips with a shaky hand. After leaving Drew's room, she had gone on a long ride to clear her head. She wasn't even sure what she was so freaked out about. Men were perfectly capable of having casual sex.

Just because Drew wasn't like other guys she'd been with didn't mean that he was going to develop some kind of codependent attachment to her. Guys had no-strings sex all the time, without thinking a thing about it.

Deep inside, she knew that he just wasn't built that way. He would be the type of guy that showered affection on a woman, gave her everything she needed, protected her. If she wanted, she could have him wrapped around her little finger.

And would that be so bad? Would it be so terrible to be with someone who treated her like she meant something? Sure, it scared the shit out of her. Ray had raised her to believe that depending on someone, having them depend on you, made you weak.

What if he was wrong? The guy was in jail, for God's sake. He wasn't Socrates. What if being with someone, the right person, could make you stronger? She feared the loss of her independence, of her edge, but she had never been one to shy away from a challenge.

She had crossed the state line into Tennessee by the time she concluded that she wanted to see where this thing went with Drew. She was strong; she could handle any outcome.

It was late, but she spent a little more time roaming around Gatlinburg, then she headed back over the ridge toward Blowing Rock.

Now she was having a much-deserved highball glass of bourbon to calm her nerves. She just hoped Drew wasn't completely put off by her behavior. She also hoped that he would make another move on her so she could prove to him that she wouldn't put him off again.

She was just about to go see if he was still up when she felt someone watching her. Raven slowly turned her head and saw the redhead Drew had been with the other night, sitting at the other end of the bar.

Raven closed her eyes as a big wave of back-the-fuck-off-my-man washed over her. It was all she could do to keep from snarling at the other woman. The little ginger girl smiled, stood up, and made her way toward Raven. Oh, bitch wanted to play?

She slid onto the barstool next to Raven, still sporting that easy smile. God, she was stunning. Which kind of made Raven hate her even more. Something about her eyes, though. There was something so familiar about them, almost as if they'd met before.

"That's because we have." The woman spoke softly, her musical Irish accent like a balm to Raven's frayed nerves.

"Because we have what?"

"Met before. Hello, Raven, it's nice to finally speak to you."

"I don't understand. The only time I've ever seen you was when you came here to meet Dr—Dr. Deveraux. I certainly wouldn't say we've *met*."

Her laughter sparkled around them, had Raven fighting the urge to smile in spite of herself.

"I knew you were there! Bravo on the concealment spell, though. You're very powerful. But we've met since then."

Raven continued to stare at those captivating eyes that shone like jewels, accented by the dark kohl around them. They were so unique. Feline. *Shit*!

"The cougar," she said before she could stop herself, then clapped a hand over her mouth.

"Excellent. Clever girl."

"So you are a *feradux*?"

"You've been speaking with Drew, haven't you?"

"We had a brief conversation before we...fell asleep."

"I see," she said with a knowing smile. "We haven't been properly introduced. I'm Brynna Murphy." She held out a hand and Raven shook it.

"So why are you here? Why now?"

"I'm here to help you. I can teach you to focus your powers, do more with them, and how to protect yourself."

"Protect myself from what?"

"That's complicated. You have a lot to learn and very little time to do it."

Raven rolled her eyes and took another slug of bourbon. " Damn, I am *so* sick of hearing that."

"What?"

"It's complicated. Drew said the same thing when I asked him about my symbol. He's got some friends coming into town he thinks will be able to explain things to me though."

Brynna looked genuinely startled when she heard that. Her eyes went wide and she backed away from Raven. "Okay, uh, I have to go now. I'll find you again soon, but if you need me, just say my name and I'll come to you."

And then she was gone.

ഗ്ര

During the day, the tavern served food and coffee, drawing in both travelers and locals. The floor was quieter than usual for a Saturday lunch rush, the stormy weather keeping people inside.

Raven picked at a Caesar salad while she waited for Drew to come downstairs. They were supposed to have a meeting about the dig site security. And he was late.

He didn't strike her as the type that had a problem with punctuality, so she had to wonder if he was avoiding her. She couldn't say she blamed him.

Finally, he emerged from the stairwell, looking more rested than she'd seen him before. He was dressed simply in khaki slacks and a sky blue t-shirt that reflected his eyes perfectly. His floppy curls were still damp from his shower, and still begged for a cut.

He searched her out and smiled when he saw her. There was the dimple again, and her heart did its little stutter step that she'd come to associate with the man in front of her. He pulled up a chair and sat across from her at the table.

"Hey, sorry I'm late. Jeremiah called when I was about to leave. They'll be getting in tomorrow." He blew out a deep breath. "Hey," he said again.

"Hey. You look like you slept good."

"I did. Once I got to sleep."

She felt her cheeks heat, knowing she was the cause of his random insomnia. "I'm sorry."

"Don't be. Honestly. I don't want you to do anything you don't want to do."

Raven was at a loss for words. Because it wasn't that she didn't want to be with him, just the thought of relinquishing control scared her to death. She was a control freak, just as she knew he was. They were both alpha dogs, so she knew there would always be some struggle for control.

Clearing her throat, she blatantly changed the subject. "I've got a team out at the site, setting up the lights and camera system. The two day guards, Eric and Bex, you met yesterday."

"Right, the no-necks."

"That'd be them. They're good guys though. Dedicated to the job, and trustworthy."

"As long as they don't get in the way, I'm glad to have them."

"The night guard is a local, Alex Webber. We haven't used him before, but he comes highly recommended. And I meant what I said about no one going there alone, especially at night. The guards can't be everywhere at once."

"Got it. For the record, I agree with that. The site's too dangerous at night anyway."

"Good. Well, that's the update."

Drew stood and offered his hand as she did the same. "Thanks, Raven. I really appreciate this." He shifted on his feet as if he wasn't sure what to do next. It was clear that he wasn't going to make this easy for her.

When she saw her opportunity, Raven stepped closer and hooked her index finger in his belt loops. She gave him her best sexy eyes and slowly licked her lips. "Can I come over later?" she said, making her voice sound extra husky.

His eyelids lowered and his lips parted, but then he blinked and stepped back. "Sure, door's always open. But Raven?" He waited until she abandoned her act to look at him.

"Yes?"

"You don't have to con me into anything. The real you is good enough."

She was stunned into silence, shocked both because he could see through her ruse to get what she wanted, and also because he didn't care.

He took advantage of her shock by brushing a light kiss across her lips and running those long fingers through her hair. Then he turned and walked away.

Chapter Sixteen

It was close to midnight when Raven finally worked up the nerve to go to Drew's room. She wanted him. God, she wanted him, but she wasn't used to being so stripped bare in front of someone. Wasn't used to being without all of her carefully built defenses.

Eventually want, and need, outweighed her fears, and she found herself standing in front of room 213 again. She found out he meant what he'd said about the door always being open. It was unlocked, and when she pushed on it, it swung open on well-oiled hinges.

The suite was dark. Pitch, in fact. It was obvious that Drew had already gone to bed. And why wouldn't he? It wasn't like she'd called. She momentarily considered turning back, but she wasn't a coward.

Somehow it would be easier if he didn't hear her coming, so she kicked off her shoes and padded soundlessly into his bedroom. The drapes were open a couple of inches, leaving her a small sliver of light to go by.

She could just barely make out the outline of his body sprawled on the bed. In the dim glow of moonlight, and with her better than normal night vision, she could see that he was on top of the covers.

And wasn't it just surprising that the polite, buttoned-down professor slept bare-assed naked? Her mouth quirked up in a smile. It would make getting what she came for that much easier.

She stood in the shadows at the foot of his bed to give herself a moment just to look at him. His feet were long and slender, calves ropy and sculpted, thighs massive and powerful. His ridged abdomen flared out to a broad chest. His face was lax, peaceful, his mouth slightly open. He'd thrown both his arms up over his head where they crossed at the wrists. Perfect.

Closing her eyes, Raven pushed out a surge of power that burst through the air and coiled around his wrists like silken handcuffs. It would hold them there until she was ready to let him go.

A noise had Drew shifting in his sleep as he tried to determine the cause without coming out of his coma. The scent hit him first—dark and earthy, with just a hint of mint as it drifted up to him. He tried to reach for whatever was the source of the delicious fragrance, but his arms wouldn't move.

What the—? He blinked and tried to get his eyes to adjust, but could see nothing in the darkness. Forgetting why he'd woken up in the first place, he started to drift back under when a small but surprisingly solid weight landed on him.

"Raven?" he whispered.

A soft hand covered his mouth, and lips brushed his ear. "Shhh."

Teeth bit down on his ear and made him gasp. Drew was fairly certain he must be dreaming, because his brain was processing the feeling of a naked Raven straddling his hips.

Certain parts were already on board, all 'sex now, talk later' as she rocked against him. She leaned forward and the long silky strands of her hair brushed his chest. She licked a trail from his collarbone to his navel, his muscles quivering along her path. His lower half mourned the loss of her warmth, but he was intrigued with her direction.

He closed his eyes, gave himself over to pure sensation. She slid down his body and settled herself between his thighs. He could feel her warm breath across his overheated skin. When she put her mouth on him, he jumped. The sensory deprivation provided by the darkness was both thrilling and frustrating at the same time.

She teased him gentle tongue and teeth, and his hips rose off the mattress to meet her. She used a hand to steady him as she gave her full attention to the sensual assault. With his hands still bound, Drew's fingers flexed with the need to touch her, to guide her to just the right—"Oh, God," he groaned. Right there."

She hummed her satisfaction against his flushed skin, and he almost lost it.

"Raven, if you want this to go any further, you'd better slow down." She pulled off of him with a husky laugh.

She climbed back up and lowered her mouth to his, demanding entry. When she swept her tongue inside, something clicked against his teeth. Something had changed since they'd last kissed. Was that, dear God, a tongue stud?

Drew broke the kiss and blinked up at her. Her fine boned face was barely discernible in the scant moonlight. "There's something different about you," he said with a crooked grin. "Doesn't it hurt?"

"I've found that my rather supernatural DNA lends itself to quick healing. It can be useful at times." She trailed her index finger along his jaw, down his neck. Drew?"

"Yes?"

"Shut up." She straddled his hips again and lowered herself so that their bodies made a delicious connection. Her hips rose up and guided herself down on him. It was like nothing he'd ever felt before. It was perfection.

As he watched her through slitted lids, her skin glowed in the moonlight. She was exquisite, her slightly flared hips tapering into a tiny waist below full, high breasts. The slender column of her neck and her sensuous face were framed by the lush curtain of hair that fell to her waist.

Their moans mingled as she began to move. She lifted herself almost completely, then dropped back down until she was once again filled. Raven couldn't stop staring at him. That powerful body, strung tight with arousal was entirely at her mercy. So. Hot.

She sped up her rhythm and licked her lips at his reaction. He flung his head back, the tendons in his neck taut, and he strained against her invisible restraints. His entire torso bowed off the bed, pushing him deeper inside her.

His eyes were closed, a line of concentration forming between his brows, and his mouth was slack. His chest heaved in a pant that matched her own, and he dug his fingernails into his palms.

"Raven," he said between gasps, and damn if that didn't sound sexy in that gravelly sandpaper voice. His biceps bulged as he fought her power for his release. "Raven...let me..."

She was ready to feel his hands on her, but she had a sudden desperate need to see his eyes, to see the man who saw her. She stopped moving and barely kept up the momentum with a gentle swiveling of her hips. And she waited.

Finally, those long lashed lids fluttered open, and his eyes connected with hers. Darkened with passion, they were the color of midnight, dusky and unfathomable. She released the hold on his wrists so he could lower his arms.

She expected him to attack her, to fill his hands with her. But instead, he raised up off the bed and stroked a hand down her cheek with nearly unbearable tenderness. "Raven," he whispered again.

He smiled at her, and as she stared into those midnight eyes, sinking into them felt a little like falling.

Raven needed to move. To break the tension, she began to ride him hard, the heat in the room going tropical. Drew leaned forward and licked a line of sweat that rolled down between her breasts, and her stomach muscles fluttered in response. He pulled a nipple into his mouth, rolled it between his teeth.

She cried out as shockwaves rippled through her. They started as a coil of heat low in her belly and exploded outward, racking her body with shudders. She arched her back deep, braced her hands on his thighs. As the last of the aftershocks danced through her, she flung her head back and let her hair stream down over the skin of his thighs. The minute her satiny locks touched his skin, he lost all control. In a series of erratic, jerky thrusts, he found his own release.

Raven collapsed on him in a sweaty heap, a welcome weight draped over him. She buried her face in his neck, licked and sucked as he stroked a hand through her hair and down her back.

"God, just...damn."

"Mmmhmm," came her muffled reply.

Drew had almost drifted off to sleep while they lay in each other's arms, waiting for their breathing to slow, when she suddenly heard his voice.

"Hey, Raven?"

"Hmm?"

"Uh, how the hell did you tie me down?"

She raised her head slightly and looked into his dark blue eyes that glittered in the soft light. She felt a slow smile spread across her lips, and she bent down to kiss his nose.

"Magic."

CHAPTER SEVENTEEN

On Sunday, Raven tended bar. She helped Micah out when he needed her in exchange for room and board. It wasn't that she couldn't afford it, but money tended to corrupt things, so she traded when she could.

More braids along the sides of her head intensified the Mohawk look, and the spikes at the tops of her ears were two-inchers this time. She was dressed in her riding leathers, bondage boots, and a white wife-beater tank. She'd woken up feeling a little punk rock that morning.

Raven was wiping down tables when she heard the bells on the door jingle as someone came in. She watched out of the corner of her eye as a woman stepped inside and took a seat at the bar.

No more than a couple of inches taller than Raven, she was fit and muscular but still curvy in a very feminine way. Raven skirted around the end of the bar and approached her with polite disinterest.

"What can I get you?"

Bright jade eyes peeked out from under a thick black fringe of bangs, the rest of her hair a cascading mass of curls. Her face was adorable, Raven thought grudgingly, heart shaped and porcelain white with delicate features. The young woman gave her a friendly smile, dimples winking on both sides.

"What kind of scotch have ye got?"

She sounded similar to that Brynna girl, with a peculiar brogue. Not Irish, though. Scottish, maybe. What was this, a UK invasion? Raven just hoped this one didn't turn in to a grizzly bear or something. She shrugged a shoulder in response to her question. "Name your poison."

"All right, I'll have the Laphroaig sixteen year malt."

"Coming up," Raven answered. She took down the bottle and poured two fingers into a glass and slid it over. She treated the newcomer to a smile of her own. "You're not from around here, are you?"

She laughed then took a deep swig, savoring it on the exhale. "Got it in one," she said. "Scotland. Do you know anywhere around that's good for climbing or hiking?"

Raven spread her arms wide and grinned. "Just close your eyes and point. Everywhere's good."

Her eyes danced with laughter as she considered Raven's suggestion. "Do you have a favorite?"

"Actually, I'm not from around here either. I'm just passing through, really. Helping out a friend today." Wiping her hands with a rag, she extended one to the woman. "I'm Raven."

"Nice to meet you, Raven. I'm Isla." Isla shook the offered hand, and Raven steeled her face to hide her reaction.

She narrowed her eyes as she regarded the woman, suspicious that this could be the woman who'd come to speak to her about all of the witch business. Hadn't Drew said his friend's wife was named Isla? Maybe not. It was hard to remember, so much had happened since then. She felt her cheeks heat at the memory of just *what* had happened. Raven shook her head and tried to concentrate on what the other woman was saying.

"So where are you from, if not here?"

"Oh, here and there. I'm a bit of a gypsy. I was spawned in New Orleans, but I grew up in Vegas, mostly."

Isla choked daintily at her use of the word *spawned,* and Raven smiled again. There really was no better way to describe the way she came into the world.

"What brings you all the way across the pond to Dixie Land ?"

"Just visiting friends," came the deliberately vague reply, coupled with an impish wink.

Raven was usually uncomfortable around other women, and she found that they were usually put off by her, as well. Having been raised completely by men, she distrusted women as a rule.

Still, Isla had a certain charm—she might even call it magnetism—that drew Raven in like a moth to a flame. Before long, and despite wanting to hate the girl for being so fucking cute, she found herself relaxed, chatting comfortably with a total stranger.

Another strange occurrence was the peculiar charge she was getting from such close proximity to Isla. Her power shimmered and rippled under her skin, like standing in the middle of a lightning storm holding an umbrella.

Raven stared down at her arms where the fine hairs rose up and goosebumps broke out over her skin. "Curiouser and curiouser...," she murmured.

Isla looked up at her. "Hmm?"

"Nothing. You want another?" She nodded at Isla's empty glass.

The other woman shook her head. "I'd better not. I'm already getting warm as it is," she said, fanning herself as the whiskey burned its way into her gut. Isla pulled out an elastic band from her pocket and tied her mass of black curls up into a messy knot on the top of her head.

One of the inn's guests exited from the stairwell, nodded to them, and walked across the room to the front door. Isla waggled her eyebrows at Raven before swiveling her head to check out the guy's butt.

This gave Raven an unfettered view of the circular mark on the back of her neck. She sucked in a breath and stumbled backward, hand to her throat. She'd known, Drew had told her, that there were others. She'd even suspected that Isla was, indeed, his friend.

Still, the sight of that mark on another living, breathing human being, when she'd spent twenty-six years of her life believing that she was alone, rocked her to her core. She couldn't even find the breath to speak, just stood there, staring, as she felt the blood drain from her face.

Isla turned back to her, her face instantly a mask of concern. "Raven? Dearling, are you all right? Are you going to be sick?"

Raven shook her head fiercely as she tried to catch her breath, still unable to speak. To explain her strange behavior, she pulled aside the strap of her tank and bared her *signa* for

Isla to see. Those sparkling green eyes widened in surprise at first, then she flashed Raven a knowing look.

"You're Andrew's friend, aren't you?"

Raven nodded, at a loss for what to say.

"Don't worry," Isla continued, "we're going to get this all sorted out."

It was ridiculous, she knew, as she'd just met this woman, but her words calmed Raven, and the cold fingers of panic loosened their grip on her throat. She took a deep breath, visibly relaxed.

Isla's mouth quirked up in a half-smile, and she winked at Raven. "Do you feel it too?" She waved her hands around to illustrate her point. "It's almost...electric."

Before she could answer, the bells jangled again and a boy walked through the front door. A man, really, but he looked so... young. He was tall and lanky with a wiry yet muscular build. He was dark-skinned, darker than her. Greek, maybe, she thought. Italian? Whatever.

His straight black hair angled across his forehead in choppy layers but was shorter in the back. His features were sharp, his look very European, with the exception of his icy, pale blue eyes.

He had some very strange ink, too. Three dark rings around his neck and a complete sleeve up his left arm. Gorgeous imagery, intricate and detailed. Raven would love to get a closer look at the artwork.

The guy inclined his head to Isla, but when his eyes fell on Raven, he gave her a full and thorough once-over. After he dragged his gaze back up to her face, he grinned and winked at her. He turned his back on them, flopped down in one of the booths and faced the television.

Isla rolled her eyes dramatically. "Don't mind him, he's barely housebroken."

Raven snorted. "Bet he's more so than mine," she mumbled.

"Pardon?"

"Nevermind." She was saved from having to explain further by the door opening again, signaling the arrival of two very tall, very stacked men. One was lean and well muscled with a swimmer's build, while the other was a bit bulkier. They were both stunning, no doubt, but only one sent Raven's blood thundering through her veins. The man with Drew nearly matched him in height, but for Raven, Drew's presence filled the room until there was no space for anything else.

The stranger had a mop of sun-kissed brown hair and hazel eyes. He had an easy smile that crinkled the corners of his eyes as he looked over at Isla. Must be the husband, Raven thought. Her heart lurched a little at the soft look he gave his wife.

Raven had to blink back the unexpected moisture in her eyes and turn away from what was clearly a moment between two intensely connected people. The kind of moment she craved as much as she feared.

She feasted her eyes on Drew like a starving woman, and again felt the blush creep up to her cheeks from her memories of the last time they were together.

He was dressed simply, but to such perfection, it made her want to sink her teeth into him. His long, thick legs were covered in threadbare denim with raveled holes at the knees. He wore a plain white t-shirt, stretched tight across his broad chest. His square jaw and sharp cheekbones were as familiar to her now as her own, as she had licked and kissed every inch of them the night before.

The mist outside had dampened his dark blonde hair, causing it to curl more than usual. It was sexy, in an adorable, boyish way, and her fingers itched to tug on the locks. What a pick-up line that would be, she thought. *Can I pull your hair? Pretty please?*

Those expressive blue eyes mesmerized her, in part because of their beauty, but mostly because he was looking at her with an expression on his face that was akin to the one Jeremiah wore for Isla.

Her stomach fluttered, and she laid a hand over it as if to calm the feeling. Oh, get a grip, she thought. Just a fling. Seriously. Ignoring the little voice in her head that was saying *yeah, sure, keep telling yourself that,* she hoisted herself up onto the bar and swung her legs over the other side.

She hopped down and sauntered across the room toward him, swinging her hips flirtatiously, while Isla followed a safe distance behind. Raven stepped up to Drew and rubbed her body on him like a cat, snaking a hand around his neck to tug him down to her for a kiss.

He raised an eyebrow at her antics, probably thinking she was trying to con him again, when she was really just trying to distract herself. But he kissed her anyway. Oh, he kissed her like he meant it. As his tongue dove into her mouth, she literally purred and wrapped herself around him. She smiled into the kiss as she felt his body respond to her, but her thoughts scattered when his arousal rubbed against her.

Someone cleared their throat, and they jumped apart like guilty teenagers.

Jeremiah smirked at his friend. "So it's like that, is it?"

"Guess so." Drew ducked his head and blushed. Her man actually blushed!

Jeremiah glanced down at Isla, who was tucked against his side. "I guess we'll be needin' a room, 'cause I have a feelin' these two may disappear for a while."

Isla giggled, and Drew smacked his friend on the back of his head.

"Ow. What'd I say?" Jere asked with a wolfish grin.

Raven just smiled back at him, and gestured toward the bar. "Innkeeper's off today. I can sign you in." They followed her over to the bar, and she pulled out an old-fashioned appointment book. "We're old school here."

"You got a suite with two rooms? I'd rather my wife and I not have to share a room with Benji over there." He nodded at the dark young man who still sat in the back booth, completely engrossed in some crime drama on TV.

"What's his deal?" Raven asked.

"Not sure. I think he grew up somewhere without a lot of technology, so he's completely addicted to it now," Jeremiah said.

Raven flipped through the book to find what she was looking for. "I've got a two-room suite on the third floor. Has a Jacuzzi tub," she taunted, raising her eyebrows at Isla.

"We'll take it!" the couple said in unison.

Chapter Eighteen

Outside, the sky blackened and the storm raged. The hail pounding on the tavern's tin roof competed with the booming thunder that rattled the windows. The storm had been threatening since the initial soaking the other day, and it had finally decided to unleash its rage upon them.

The lights in the room flickered once, twice, then shut off entirely. Immediately, the backup generator Micah had invested in kicked in and fired up the emergency lights. It wasn't much light but enough to see their way around.

Raven carefully crossed the room to the front door. She locked it and flipped over the sign so it said 'closed'. She looked back to where Drew waited for her behind the bar and shrugged.

"Don't think anyone's coming out for a drink in this."

The hotel guests usually used one of the four private entrances in the inn part of the building for coming and going. Even Isla, Jeremiah, and Marduk were ensconced in their suite.

Drew assumed Micah wouldn't mind Raven locking the tavern up early, what with the perfect storm brewing outside.

Rejoining Drew behind the bar, she used muscle memory more than eyesight in the dim glow to pour them each a glass of the Bushmills he favored. Raven leaned back against the bar and faced him as she sipped.

"About last night...," he started, unsure of what he planned to say. He wanted to tell her he'd never experienced something so intense, so raw, and he wanted to get down on his knees and beg her to do it again.

He wanted to tell her that all she had to do was smile at him to set his pulse racing and palms sweating like a horny teenager. It was embarrassing, sure. But he fucking loved it.

She lowered her head, closed her eyes, and he swore she looked a little sick.

"Yeah," she said quietly, "sorry about that. I get kind of carried away sometimes. I know not everyone is into that kind of stuff. I should have asked. I can be a little...much."

He gaped at her, truly shocked that she was feeling ashamed about what she had done. What they had done. It had been the most unbelievable night he could ever remember having with a woman.

Gently he gripped her chin and tipped her face up to look at him. "Don't be ridiculous," he said sternly, hoping to get his point across. "For the record, you can feel free to get carried away all over me when*ever* you want, hear?"

A slow smile broke across her face until she was grinning broadly, and she looked more than a little relieved. What kind of people had this woman been with, to make her doubt herself?

"I meant what I said before, Raven. The real you is good enough. Don't ever feel like you need to be anything different than who you really are around me."

Again her eyes went wide, glittering gold in the low light, and she just stared at him for a long moment. Her gaze blazed a trail down from his face, with a brief pause to linger on his lips, all the way down to the growing bulge in his jeans.

He watched as she tentatively licked her lips, and her delicate white teeth sank into the plump lower one. She flicked her eyes back to his face and smiled. He felt the familiar jolt of lust surge through his body. It was amazing what she could do to him with just one look.

You are in so much trouble, buddy. Unable to resist any longer, he captured her mouth with his own and gave no quarter as his tongue swept inside. She leaned back, gripped his forearms, and he shuddered when her nails dug into his flesh.

He'd had to let her come to him, to prove that she really wanted him instead of running a con. He'd wanted her to take charge, to make sure she was ready for what was happening between them. And it had been worth it. Absolute bliss. But he was done holding back.

With a growl, he reached around and gripped her ass, lifted her up and set her on the bar. Her breath was coming in short gasps, wild eyes darted around the room as if she was sure someone would burst in on them any moment.

When he hesitated, she raised an eyebrow at him, then fisted a hand in his shirt and tugged him toward her. "Where were you going with this, Dr. Deveraux?" she asked.

He didn't take his eyes off of her as he began to unzip her soft leather pants. When he had them undone, he peeled them down, lifting her hips and pulling them all the way off.

His eyes nearly crossed when he realized that, dear God, she wore nothing underneath them.

She seemed to be content with letting him take control of the situation. She reclined back across the bar and propped herself up on her elbows. Tilting her head slightly, she watched him from under heavy lids fringed with inky lashes.

Drew turned to pull up a chair from the computer behind the bar and yanked his shirt over his head. Sitting in the chair, he positioned himself between her thighs.

He kept his eyes on hers as he teased her navel with his tongue, and then allowed himself to venture lower.

Her head fell back, dark hair streaming over the side of the bar, and she arched toward him. His hand joined his tormenting tongue to caress her, and he took delicious satisfaction in seeing her squirm. But the low, needy sounds she was making were causing his situation downstairs to become almost painful. With his other hand, he reached down, unfastened his own jeans, and freed himself. Her head flew up and she locked eyes with him again.

Raven's eyes rolled back in her head as the torturous but exquisite sensations washed over her. She had never seen anything sexier than Drew's golden curls between her thighs. She shifted her weight to one arm and reached out with the other, giving in to her earlier impulse. She buried her fingers in his hair, gripped tight, tugging him closer. His eyes flickered closed and he groaned, and the vibrations from it pushed her over the edge.

She collapsed back on the bar and her body bowed up tight. Drew stood and held her hips in a punishing grip as he pulled her forward and thrust into her. Their moans mingled as he leaned forward and kissed her while he surged against her repeatedly.

He took her hard and fast, with a heavy grip on the back of her neck with one hand and his other arm wrapped around her waist. Raven shivered when she felt the rasp of denim brush the inside of her thighs. It secretly thrilled her that his need for her was so desperate, that he didn't bother to fully undress.

His breath fanned over her ear, along with the delicious little groans he made as he pumped his hips. She was so caught up in him, she didn't even care that the edge of the bar was digging into her back.

But he did. He lowered her until her feet touched the floor and supported her with an arm when her knees began to buckle. He captured her mouth again, nipped at her lip with his teeth, plundered with his tongue. He broke it only long enough to peel her tank top off and toss it behind him.

He stared into her eyes for a moment and must have approved of what he saw there, because he spun her around and gently bent her over across the bar. He leaned over her back and brushed his fingers over her from behind. "Raven," he sighed against her ear, with a plea in his voice. "This okay?"

Though Raven struggled to even form the words to answer as the he continued his exquisite torture, she managed to bite out a reply. "Drew, please," was all she could manage. Apparently it was good enough, because he slid back inside.

She arched her back, reached behind her and took a handful of those curls she loved so much. She held on with everything she had. She guessed the hair pulling was a turn on for him, because he locked a strong arm around her chest and bucked against her.

When she was able to pry her eyes open for a moment, she caught sight of their reflection in a large mirror on the other side of the room. The sight of him working her across the bar was unbelievably erotic, but it was her own eyes reflected back at her that startled her.

Even in the dim, flickering light from the emergency lamps, her bright amber eyes glowed brilliantly, almost as if they were lit from within. "What the...," she whispered, but her voice trailed off when he made eye contact with her in the reflection of the mirror.

His mouth hung open, the tendons in his arms and neck stood out in stark relief as he shuddered against her. He lowered his head to the hollow of her shoulder and bit down on the sensitive skin there. He still watched her in the mirror as he pushed through the last of his release.

That sent her over the edge again as she crested wave after wave of sensation. When they finally came down, they leaned against the bar, panting. After several minutes, he stood and tugged her around for a kiss.

When she looked up at him, she saw such naked, visceral emotion written on his face. She knew he'd never had a connection like this with anyone, and neither had she, just as well as she knew this would be no casual fling for him.

She knew that should scare her—normally she would be speeding toward oblivion on her bike by now—but, with delicious aftershocks from their lovemaking rippling through her, the only thing she could think of was climbing into his arms and staying there for as long as she could.

CHAPTER NINETEEN

Raven had agreed to meet Drew at his suite in twenty. Just enough time for a quick shower and a change of clothes. When she emerged from the bathroom, completely naked, toweling her hair dry, she practically jumped out of her skin.

Brynna sat cross-legged in the middle of Raven's bed. "Fucking hell, you scared the ever-loving shit out of me!" That had been one of Ray's signature phrases, and it made her smile.

Shrugging, Brynna flopped onto her back on the soft mattress.

"Get dressed, *Vigile*, there is much t'be done."

"Whatever it is, it'll have to wait until later. I'm supposed to meet Drew to go over more of the book." They'd already had sexy time, Raven thought with a smile, so she dressed for comfort. She donned her favorite oversized Saints jersey and a pair of black *Ellen* boxer shorts.

Raven checked herself out in the mirror and looked at the gold number nine on her chest. Drew Brees. Interesting coincidence, she thought. She shared a private smile with her reflection because—with her flushed skin, bruised lips, and various marks along her neck—she looked well and truly fucked.

Brynna's face appeared over her shoulder in the mirror, riotous red curls like a halo around her head. Her bright green gaze was intense and inscrutable. "You're sleeping with him, then?"

Raven lifted her chin, meeting Brynna's eyes with a defiant stare of her own. "Not that it has jack and shit to do with you, but yes. So?"

Brynna's features softened as she cast a sympathetic look at Raven's reflection. "In the battle we will inevitably have to fight, loved ones can become collateral damage."

Hiding behind her comfortable mask of snark and indifference, Raven snorted and turned away from the mirror. "No one said anything about love, kitty cat. Just sex. Really. Good. Sex."

Brynna just shook her head and followed behind as Raven headed for the door. "I may as well come with you. Your Dr. Deveraux doesn't know half as much as he thinks he does."

"Suit yourself," Raven called over her shoulder.

Raven let herself in to Drew's room, anxious to learn more about the contents of the book, but she lost her train of thought when she caught sight of him. His hair was wet from his own shower, combed back away from the sharp planes of his face.

He wore nothing but a pair of low slung flannel pajama pants, low enough that his hipbones poked out over the waistband, and his finely sculpted oblique muscles were visible in all their glory. She stood in the doorway, just admiring him. He gave her a goofy grin when he caught her checking him out.

"Hey."

"Hey yourself."

He frowned when Brynna brushed past Raven and plopped down in one of the recliners. "Raven, what'd I tell you about picking up strays?" He laughed as Brynna flipped him off behind her head.

"Sorry, she followed me home. Can I keep her?"

"Only if she's housebroken."

"Hey, douchebags! I'm right here," Brynna yelled.

"How could we ever forget?" Drew said sarcastically. Making his way to his desk, he took the book out of the lockbox and set it on the coffee table, along with his laptop.

Three heads turned when they heard a knock on the door. "That'll be Jeremiah and Isla. Right on time." His head whipped around as Brynna shot up from her seat.

"What? They're *here,* now? Shit, why didn't you tell me?" Her eyes darted wildly as if looking for means to escape.

"Uh, because I haven't seen you since you came into town. I thought you'd be happy to see them, thought Isla was your best friend."

"I...I am. She is. I just—"

"They don't know you're here, do they? Do they even know you're a *feradux*?"

"Yes...No...I can't do this right now. I'm going to stay in the bedroom. Just cover for me!" she called over her shoulder as she disappeared around the corner.

"I'll do no such thing," Drew grumbled as he swung the door open and let in his friends. He gave Jere a quick back-slapping hug, then lifted Isla up and spun her around. She giggled when he dropped her back on her feet.

Raven stuffed down the flare of jealousy at seeing another woman in his arms and hid it behind a polite smile. "Hello again," she said, nodding at the pair and at Marduk who had come up behind them. "Anyone want a beer?"

"God, yes."

"Aye."

"Please," came the replies.

Raven wandered over to the mini-fridge and pulled out a sixer of Guinness Extra Stout. She slapped the bottles down on the coffee table in front of Drew's guests. "Help yourselves."

Drew relaxed into the recliner Brynna had vacated and watched Raven as Isla introduced her to Marduk. Her hair was still damp, hanging loose down her back, devoid of her usual braids. Her face was scrubbed of makeup, but she still had a healthy glow from their lovemaking.

Her body was dwarfed by the jersey she wore, the hem just brushing the bottoms of her tiny shorts. The rest was a smooth expanse of silky bronze skin. She looked more real to him than ever before, vulnerable but fierce. God, how she set his blood on fire.

Raven caught him watching, raised a brow and traced her lips with her tongue. Closing his eyes, he stifled a moan. Clearly not well enough as he earned a snort from Jeremiah, who was sprawled on the couch.

Finally, the others joined them. Drew smiled when, instead of finding her own seat, Raven sauntered over and sat across his lap with her legs hanging over the arm of his chair. He let out a barely audible hiss when the curve of her ass pressed against his erection.

Damn, it seemed he was doomed to be perpetually hard around her. Well, there were worse things. Isla joined Jeremiah on the couch, instantly melting against him. Rather than taking the other chair, Marduk sat on the floor in front of Isla who lazily sifted fingers through his hair.

It was a strange relationship between a *vigile* and her *feradux,* Drew thought. One that, apparently, Jeremiah had come to accept as part of their lives. There was a blinding flash of light, and, when his eyes adjusted, Drew saw the sleeping gray wolf had taken the boy's place.

Isla smiled indulgently down on her charge. "Traveling really takes a toll on him. He can stay human a lot longer than when we were bonded, but staying in one form for long periods of time still drains his energy. We'll wake him if we need him."

Jeremiah studied Raven quietly until she began to squirm, but she instantly froze at the sound of a groan from Drew.

"Raven, can you tell us a little about yourself? If we can get an idea of what you know about your abilities, we'll know where to start teaching you," Isla said.

Raven's body tensed until Drew began stroking the nape of her neck, and carding his fingers through her hair. She sighed deep and leaned into the caress. He had such a calming effect on her normally jumpy nerves. Since she'd met him, she'd been able to sit still longer than she ever had in her life. As his touch soothed her, she began to talk.

"I was an orphan," she said, unable to meet Isla's eyes. "At least, until I was four years old. My mother died in childbirth, but not before naming my father on my birth certificate. CPS searched for him for four years, trying to find a permanent home for me as I bounced from foster home to shelter to orphanage. Ray, my father, was born in New Orleans.

Most of his adolescence was spent getting the shit beat out of him by his father, or getting verbally abused by his stepmother. As soon as he could, he bought his motorcycle and joined up with a gang and headed out to Vegas. He got into some pretty hard shit, too much alcohol, too many cons, too many women. Exactly one too many women," she said with no malice.

"CPS finally caught up with him, dumped me in his lap, and that was all she wrote. He and I were inseparable, running cons together, grifting on the strip. It was great, for a while. But every time he failed to get sober, he'd go on a binge, do something stupid. The law eventually got him. He went to jail, I went AWOL."

"When did you first realize you had extra abilities?" Jeremiah asked.

Raven looked him in the eyes, saw no judgement there. "I can't remember not knowing. I've always known I had more—more power, more senses—than the average person. It was my normal."

"*Vigilati* are sometimes stronger with a particular element. I am very strong with fire, a trait that comes from my father." There was an almost imperceptible pause before the word *father*, and a shadow passed across Isla's lovely face. "Have you noticed any such propensity in yourself?"

Raven thought about that for a moment, tapping her chin with a black-nailed finger. "Possibly. Although I'm not sure if it would be considered an element, I have always been able to control space. I can manipulate the space around me to do all kinds of things—sense when someone is near me, move objects, add force to a blow." She gave Drew a sheepish grin. "That's how I was able to knock you out."

"Didn't knock me out," he grumbled, "much."

"It's obvious from your lack of response to Marduk's changing, that you know of the *feradux*," Isla said.

"Yes. I read some about it in Drew's book, and I've also met mine...in both forms."

In that moment, Marduk lifted his furry head and began a low growl, his hackles rising. He sniffed the air and growled louder.

"Is there someone else here?" Jeremiah looked at Drew, who looked at Raven.

"Yes." Five heads swiveled around to see Brynna standing behind Drew's chair. "I am."

Isla's mouth dropped open in shock as she rose to face her friend. Brynna eyed her nervously as Isla slowly enveloped her in a bone crushing embrace. Her eyes flashed dangerously right before she reared back and slapped Brynna across the face. Hard.

Brynna's head whipped back with the force of the blow, and she snapped her fangs at the other woman—they had elongated with the perceived attack. Before she could respond, Isla gathered her up into another tight hug, holding her until her fangs receded and her body was no longer coiled to strike. While Raven looked on in shock, Brynna leaned into the embrace.

When Isla finally stepped back, her green eyes sparkled with unshed tears. "How could you do that? Just disappear without a word?"

Brynna looked down at her toes and her red hair formed a curtain around her face. Absently, she touched her flaming cheek. "I don't know. I'm sorry. I was...called. I wasn't sure if I was even supposed to tell anyone."

"So, you are feradux then," Isla said, and the other woman nodded. "That, at least, you could have mentioned."

Isla turned her back to Brynna and returned to the safety of her husband's arms.

"I'm sorry," Brynna repeated dismally. "I hope you'll be able to forgive me.

Sinking down to take a spot at Raven's feet, much as Marduk had done, Brynna drew her knees up to her chest and rested her chin on them. Raven took pity on her little cougar, feeling a powerful kinship with her that was out of proportion with the amount of time they'd known each other.

Raven glared daggers at Isla as she stroked a hand over Brynna's silky hair. "Yes. She will," she said. There was a hint of warning in the tone that had Isla narrowing her eyes. Drew's arms tightened around Raven as if he thought she would attack.

Jeremiah cleared his throat and did the same with his wife. "Ladies, let's get back to the topic at hand, shall we? Raven, is there anything you want to ask us?"

Raven pulled the neck of her jersey to the side to reveal her *signa*. "Drew told me what the circles and the slashes mean. Do either of you know about the symbol in the middle? The spider?"

Isla shared a worried look with Jeremiah before making eye contact with Drew. He gave her a barely noticeable nod. Taking a deep breath, she looked back at Raven. "Drew must have told you about the *locuses* when he explained the symbol, yes?"

"Briefly," Raven replied.

"While the *Vigilati* are the guardians of the gateways on our side, there are spirits—demons, really—that guard them in the spirit world. But it's less about guarding, and more about breaking through."

"The demons are called *Lochrim,*" Jeremiah interjected. "They gain their power by draining the energy of those around them. If they gain enough power, they are able to manifest into the form of a human male. The goal is to lure humans into the *locus* and suck out their life force. They can't physically harm a human until the veil is thinned on the Pagan pinnacle days of Samhain and Beltane, but they can do so by other means."

"Other means?"

"They can possess a human, compel them to hurt themselves or others. They send out their minions, the *auchrim* to cause mayhem and chaos, then lead unsuspecting victims through the gateway."

"No one is safe from them, especially not us," Isla said. "It is the job of the *Vigilati* to contain them, keep the body count down, until the pinnacle day passes. It's what we were born for."

"Can't you just kill them?" Ever the practical one, Raven couldn't imagine—relatively, of course—why they wouldn't just destroy the threat.

Again, Isla and Jeremiah shared another cryptic look with Drew. "Until recently, it hasn't been possible. The *Vigilati* just didn't have the power to destroy these beings, but we've figured out a way. Within the *Vigilati,* there is a sect called the *Praedos,* who have the ability to kill the demons. They are marked with a glyph inside their *signa,* like mine...and yours."

"Great, so we kill them," Raven said with a shrug.

"It's not that simple. A *praeda* shares the blood of a *Lochrim,* and that one alone is the one she can kill. He will bear the same symbol on his forehead."

"Wait, *what*? Are you saying we're related to these demons?"

"Yes, that is exactly what I'm saying. We found out last year that the *praeda's* blood is poisonous to her *Lochrim*. That is how I killed my father, Alastore. The *Vigilati* line passes from grandmother to granddaughter, skipping a generation. My mother was seduced by Alastore, posing as her husband, the man I believed was my father."

"Well, that's impossible. My father is Raymonde Sabatier of New Orleans. My mother was the one I've never met."

Isla looked at her with pity in her eyes. "I'm sorry, Raven. He may not be your real father."

Drew felt her go utterly still and figured she was about to bolt, so he just held on tight and kept stroking her hair. To his surprise, she threw her head back and barked out a hearty laugh.

"Of *course* he's my father. We've had multiple paternity tests done, since Ray didn't even know about me until I was four. Besides, we have the same hair, the same smile. And I have his father's eyes. I've seen pictures."

Jeremiah's brows drew together in confusion. "That doesn't fit with anything we've learned. If he's your biological father, then we're back at square one. Raven, we need to talk to your father. He's the only one who can fill in the missing piece of your history."

This time, when Drew felt her tense in his arms, her entire body went completely rigid. Her face turned cold, then carefully blank. "Feel free. You can find him at High Desert State Prison. But you'll have to do it without me."

Before they could respond, Raven's phone rang. She checked the display and turned to Drew. "It's Nash. I've got to take this." She gave him a quick kiss and hurried outside to the hallway.

"Hey Ry, what's up?"

"Raven, have you heard from Ray?"

Her smile faded when she picked up on Ryder's ominous tone. "No, he knows better than to contact me from the inside."

"He's out. Got sprung yesterday. I was supposed to meet him for lunch and he never showed, never called. His phone goes straight to voicemail. I'm kinda worried about him, Rave. That's why I wanted to see if he called you."

An uneasy feeling curled in the pit of her stomach, but she ignored it. "Ry, it wouldn't be the first time he disappeared. You know how he is."

"No, Raven. He's always made sure I knew where he was. In case you needed him. There were times when he distanced himself from you for your own good. But Trys and I always knew where he was."

"Did you go to his place?"

"Yeah, that was the first thing I did. Talked to one of the neighbors, guy named Two-Scalps, and he pointed me in the direction Ray had taken to meet me at the cafe. Found a hooker who'd seen him cut down an alley. I checked it out..."

His pause got Raven's nerves jumping. "And?"

"And...there was blood. Not a lot. Not enough...But I'm convinced something's happened to him. I've got some guys on it here in Vegas, but the trail is cold."

Raven ran a shaking hand through her hair. Yeah, she had issues with her father, but he'd always been there. She'd always had the choice to see him or not, and the feeling that he may not be there anymore was like a cold fist gripping her heart.

"Okay, keep me posted, and I'll let you know if he contacts me."

"Check with Micah, too, will ya?"

"Sure thing. I've got some friends here that are helping me with something personal, so maybe they can help me with this, too."

"It's a plan. Keep your chin up, kid."

"Thanks, Ry. Bye."

When he saw Raven come back into the room, Drew knew instantly that something wasn't right. Her face was pale and drawn, and dark circles stood out under her eyes. She tucked a lock of her hair behind her ear with trembling fingers.

Without a word, he crossed to her and led her back to the chair to sit down. "What's happened?" he asked softly.

She sniffled delicately, and it broke his heart a little.

"My father is missing. I didn't know it, but he'd been released. He was supposed to meet his friend and my business partner, Ryder, for lunch and never showed. Ryder did some checking and found...blood where Ray was last seen."

Drew cast a worried glance to his friends. The timing was far too convenient. What were the odds that his friends would come into town to meet Raven, and put this all together on the very same day Ray is released from prison and disappears. No way could this be a coincidence, he thought, and said as much to the group. "We've got to find him." he said.

Jeremiah nodded grimly. "Yeah. The setup is too perfect. This stinks of *auchrim* manipulation. And even if it didn't, we need to talk to Ray about Raven's parentage. Until we do, we're at a dead end. I think it may be time to deploy Operation Cobra."

"You think?"

Isla looked up at her husband. "You sure, my love?"

"It's our best bet."

"Someone please fill me in," Raven said impatiently. "What the hell is Operation Cobra."

"*CliffsNotes* version. My brother," Jeremiah answered. "He worked as a special operative in a top secret group within the U.S. Army called G9X. Codename: Cobra. He's out now, as far as I know. Still does mercenary jobs for military or other organizations, but he also does PI work, in a sense. He's what the military calls a finder. He can locate just about anyone or anything, with little or no information to go on."

"The problem isn't just getting Matty to help," Drew chimed in. "It's getting a hold of him in the first place."

Jere nodded again. "He's MIA right now, but we always have a failsafe. An untraceable email address where I can send him a secure message. He made it very clear that it was *strictly* emergency only, like if something happened to Mom. But I've decided we're going to call this an emergency."

He pulled out his iPhone and brought up his email program. "All I have to do is send an email that says 'deploy Operation Cobra' and he'll find me. He'll call or just show up, but he'll find me."

"You'd do that for me? My father...he's not what you'd call an upstanding citizen."

"Yes, I would. You're one of us now. Kin to my wife, however distantly. And a friend of my best friend. That would be enough. But I have a feelin' your father's disappearance may be tied up in this battle we're fighting. I think we need your father to get through this."

Raven hoped like hell they didn't all come to regret it.

Chapter Twenty

Ray didn't move a muscle when he came to, his arms and legs bound to a ladder back chair. Just kept his head hanging down limply, eyes closed. How the hell had he gotten here? Right, he'd been snatched by the crazy bitch and her two goombahs. And from the way his skull ached, he must have gotten clobbered something fierce.

He cracked his eyelids the tiniest bit to assess his surroundings. It was dark, the room illuminated only by a couple of flickering fluorescent lights. He appeared to be in an abandoned warehouse, furnished with nothing but a few chairs and a tool cabinet.

Somebody's been watching too much Law & Order, he thought. Unable to help himself, he tensed when he heard the distinct sound of high heels approaching. The sound got nearer and nearer until it just stopped.

He could sense her in front of him, pure malice emanating from her in waves, nearly as tangible as the chair he sat in.

"I know you're awake, Raymonde," she said in a singsong voice. It made him hate the sound of his given name rolling off her tongue.

No longer seeing any point in the pretense, he raised his head and glared at her. "What could you possibly want with me? I. Have. Nothing."

She chuckled as she paced in front of him, and the sound made his skin crawl. "The answer to that is very simple. I'm surprised you haven't figured it out already."

His fingers ghosted over the bindings on his wrists. Could be a loose end somewhere. Got to keep her talking. "By all means, enlighten me."

"I want my daughter, Raymonde, and you are going to tell me where she is."

"The hell I am."

She stretched out a hand toward him and he got a close-up view of the vicious claw-like nails that extended out from her petite fingers. Instantly, a white-hot burst of pain sparked behind his eyes, and quickly spread until he thought his head would explode. He couldn't move, couldn't think. All he could do was squeeze his eyes shut and grit his teeth against the onslaught.

Ray had never felt such agony, not even when he'd been jumped out of the gang, not even when he'd had his mug smashed in by an inmate for refusing to be the guy's prison wife. It was like a fist squeezing his brain stem, while a thousand scarab beetles scrabbled around inside his head and tried to scratch their way out.

The woman dropped her hand and the pain receded. It left Ray feeling dizzy and disoriented, but still alive. Small favors, he thought. She pulled up a chair and spun it around to face him. Without a word, she straddled the seat, folded her arms over the back and rested her chin on them.

She cocked her head inquisitively and smiled that fanged smile. "Let's try again to have a civilized conversation, shall we?"

Ray sighed and shook his head, immediately regretting the motion. "Look, Lisette—"

"Lisette was just a name I used on a humid night in New Orleans. You may call me Azibel."

"Okaaaay, Azibel, why don't you tell me why you've brought me here."

She rose from the chair and paced in front of him again. The sound she made as she slapped a pair of black leather gloves across her palm made Ray want to scream. Or vomit. "My dear Raymonde, we are on the verge of a revolution. My people suffered a great loss last year. But now, we have hope of winning this war with those who would seek to destroy us. And, in turn, to destroy them."

Ray's mind spun in a million directions at once, while his fingers worked the knots around his wrists. Clearly, the woman was certifiable. She referred to herself and her 'people' as if they were a different species. He pegged her with a deadpan stare and tried to keep his voice flat. Ray knew better than to betray his bewilderment and fear—he'd learned that much in prison. "I don't have any idea what that means. But, by all means, do go on."

She continued her path across the worn concrete floor as if he hadn't spoken. "You know, I chose you for a reason. You were just the type of man I was looking for. Young, foolish, angry at the world. I knew that you would raise my daughter with the sort of...loose moral fiber that you yourself had been raised with."

As his outrage began to overshadow his fear, Ray was spurred on by anger. Not just at her words, but at the truth of them. "Now wait just a goddamn minute—"

She talked right over him, as if lost in her own thoughts. "She's half of us, and half of them, you see. She's a blank slate, playing for neither side. You didn't teach her about silly things like charity and karma, and other general do-goodery. You taught her, instead, to lie, cheat, and steal. To get what she wanted by any means necessary. To survive at all costs. Those are just the type of qualities that will eventually sway her in my favor."

When she paused, Ray remained silent. Once she'd begun speaking of Raven again, his back went up. He needed to know what this woman wanted with his daughter, and he figured the best way to find out was to keep his damned mouth shut.

"I've kept up with her through the years, you know. Watching her, waiting for the right moment to approach her. Unfortunately, that decision is out of my hands now. The die has been cast, and we must make our move against our enemies."

She looked at him then, and he was sure his face must have had a whole lot of what-in-the-holy-fuck splattered across it, because she threw her head back and laughed.

"She's a smart girl, our Raven. And strong. Her power is so strong already, she began to sense me, so I had to fall back. That's when I lost track of her. Seems you may have taught her too well, Raymonde."

Ray lifted his chin and met her creepy swirling eyes with a glare of his own and repeated his earlier question through clenched teeth. “What do you want with me?”

“I hadn't counted on you getting early release. I thought after I placed that ‘anonymous’ call to the LVPD, you'd get put away for the maximum. And I was right. However, I didn't plan for an underfunded prison system or you keeping your nose clean. So, now you're out, good and ready to mend fences with Raven and throw a wrench in my most carefully laid plans. We can't have that, now can we?

“You'll be our guest here for the next little while, Raymonde. I'm not going to kill you, though, not yet anyway. I'll be trying to ingratiate myself to Raven, and I'd imagine that killing her father—such as he is—would put a rather bad taste in her mouth. But I can't have you sabotaging me, either. So you'll stay. Although the comfort of your stay will be commensurate with your cooperation. How about it, Raymonde? Will you play ball?”

He said nothing for a moment, just eyed her warily. “Depends on what you want.”

“First, you'll tell me where Raven is at this very moment.”

“Don't know,” he said, and silently thanked every deity that he knew of that it was the truth. He had turned himself around in prison, but he didn't want his daughter's life balancing on the strength of his character against adversity.

“Really, Raymonde, if you're going to lie, at least make it an interesting one.”

The goombahs stepped out of the shadows like wraiths, flanking her and doing their best to look ominous.

“Not a lie. Raven wrote me off completely while I was in prison. Stopped talking to me altogether. I have my sources that tell me that she's alive and well, if she's happy. But that's the extent of it."

She thought it over then gave him a quick nod as if she believed him, and he relaxed slightly. "You'll just have to tell me who these sources of yours are, then we'll have an understanding."

Ray's blood ran cold, and his breath froze in his throat. Not only would he be endangering his daughter, but his three best friends, as well. Not an option. He closed his eyes briefly before meeting her gaze again. "I won't."

She clucked her tongue and looked at him sadly. "Oh Raymonde, I had quite hoped you would cooperate, and we would all get on fine together until our business was done." She nodded to one man then the other, turned on her sharp heel and walked off. "Pity, that," she said over her shoulder before disappearing.

As her two 'associates' advanced on him, Ray looked from one menacing face to the other and knew that he was in for a world of pain. And for a moment, he couldn't help but feel he deserved it.

The dark haired one pulled up a rolling tray—like the kind he'd seen in the dentist's office—with all manner of tools, from pliers to scalpels, knives to hooks. The blonde carted an IV pole over, where several fluid bags hung. When he noticed Ray's eyes on the instruments, he sneered. It was clear that the guy got off on the fear. "Can't have you kicking it before we're done with you."

Ah, so they planned to torture him to the brink of what his body could handle, then nurse him back to health only to start all over again. He was so fucked.

CHAPTER TWENTY ONE

By Monday, the storm had cleared. Oz had reopened the dig site, and the team was back at work. The interns had excavated the rest of Daisy's skull, along with several smashed pieces of scapula.

Drew had the pieces laid out on his makeshift lab table, and he was examining one of the shoulder blade shards under the high-power microscope. If he'd thought the striations on the skull were odd, the markings he found on the smooth, flat fragments of the scapula were inconceivable.

There was unusual scoring in the enamel of the bone, deep grooves like you would see carved into a school desk. The edges of the grooves, and deep inside, had a peculiar blackened coloration. It was almost as if someone went at her with a branding iron or an etching tool.

The tool would have had to burn through the skin and the underlying muscle and fascia, just to get through to the bone, much less carve it up like that. It would have been unimaginably painful, and Drew hoped the woman was already dead when the wound was inflicted. It would have been a small mercy.

One thing was for sure, he'd never seen anything like it before. The piece was too small to determine what had made the grooves, or how far they extended. "Fascinating," Drew mumbled to himself, pushing his glasses up on his nose. They had stayed up so late talking the night before, he just couldn't bring himself to put his contacts back in after only a couple hours of sleep.

His fingers itched with the need to get his hands on the rest of the skeleton, the broken pieces having created more questions than answering them. Increasing his magnification, he made another pass at the tiny fragment, absorbing himself in theorizing about what had scored the bone.

He was so caught up in his examination, he didn't hear someone enter the tent.

"Hey Professor!" Drew jumped a foot when Hammer tapped on his shoulder.

"Damn it, Hammer! You have got to stop doing that."

"Sorry, Dr. Deveraux. But you've gotta see this. We found something."

In the young intern's hands was a small, flat earthenware box. It was caked in mud from the recent rains, and dirt flaked off from it as he moved. The top was divided into a grid, and each square had part of an intricate design carved into it. But the design didn't make sense to Drew. It looked almost as if the pieces were mixed up, in the wrong order. Wait…

"Holy shit," he whispered. "I know what this is."

Hammer looked up at him expectantly and his wide eyes gleamed with the light of discovery. It was an expression that mirrored Drew's own. "Well?"

"Put it down on that table," Drew ordered while pulling out a pair of latex examination gloves. Hammer set down the box and backed away, as if he half expected a barrage of evil spirits to burst out from within. Drew was fairly sure that, unlike the mythical Pandora, whoever made this box was entirely human. Crafty, but human.

"It's a puzzle box. A somewhat primitive design, but I'm positive it is one."

Drew tentatively touched one of the blocks with his fingertips and was able to wiggle it slightly. "Ah, see, I think that in order to engage the locking mechanism, you have to arrange the pieces in the correct order. However, only the one who made it knows for sure what the order is. The rest of us can only guess."

"Wow," Hammer breathed. "Are you going to open it?"

"Maybe, if I can figure out the key. We'll have to be careful though. I've heard rumors of puzzle boxes being booby trapped to protect the contents." Drew carefully picked the box up and examined the sides. It was fairly heavy for its size—about eight inches square and three or four inches deep—and was a dark terra cotta color.

A series of glyphs were carved into the sides. While they resembled runes, they were unlike anything he'd seen before. There was one thing he knew for sure: this box was most definitely not a Native American artifact.

Drew gingerly tilted the box to check for any mark or signature of the maker. There was something, and when he brought it closer to his face to get a better look, he froze.

Carved on the underside of the box was the same symbol that was embossed on the leather cover of the grimoire.

"...figure out how to open it. I can't wait to tell the others..."

As Hammer rambled on about his discovery, Drew tuned him out. He studied the signa in shocked silence. There was no denying that's what it was, even though he brushed the dirt off the engraving, futilely hoping it would suddenly be something else.

Feeling a bit more akin to Pandora than he had at first, Drew had a strong hunch that nothing good could possibly come from this box.

"...doesn't look Native American. Wonder what's inside..."

Hammer's voice finally broke through Drew's perplexed stupor, and he instantly went on alert when he grasped the implications of what the kid was talking about.

"Hammer," he interrupted in a soft voice, eerily calm. Not being any kind of fool, Hammer shut up. Drew pegged him with a hard gaze and hoped he communicated the seriousness of the situation.

"Do you trust me, Hammer?"

"Of course, Dr. D. You're my favorite professor. And we're...kind of, friends, right?"

Drew hated to use the poor kid's admiration of him to get what he wanted, but he had no choice. Raven's life may depend on it—not to mention Isla, Brynna, Marduk, and all of the other Bruixi out there. "Sure we are, Hammer. I trust you, too, which is why I need you to do something for me."

"Anything, Professor," he said eagerly.

"I need you to forget you saw this box."

The kid's face fell, but, to his credit, he said nothing, merely waited for Drew to explain.

"I've seen some of these symbols before. I don't know exactly what they mean, but I can tell you, beyond a shadow of a doubt, that they were not carved by Catawba Indians."

"Okay, I get that. But why—"

Drew held up a hand to cut off the volley of questions that would surely be headed his way. "I don't know if this box is related to the remains we've found, or if it's from a different source altogether. But if the powers that be get wind of this, of the fact that we are no longer excavating a possible Native American burial ground, no one can predict what will happen. They may just pull funding and shut us down, or—depending on where exactly this box comes from—they might bring in a different team altogether. Do you want that?"

"God, no, Professor. I need this dig for my thesis!"

"Exactly. So we're going to keep this between us, yes?"

"Yes. But what about the box?"

"Until I can figure out how to open it, I'm going to put it in my safe back at the inn. I need you to promise me you'll tell no one."

"I promise, Dr. Deveraux," he said solemnly.

Drew smiled and patted the kid on the back. "Great find. I think you've earned the right to call me Drew. Listen, if you find anything even remotely similar to this box, you bring it straight to me."

"Got it, Prof—er, Drew. I'm going to get back out there. Let me know if you get that thing open," Hammer called over his shoulder as he left to join the team.

"Yeah, sure kid," he mumbled to himself. "When hell freezes over."

Drew carefully wrapped the box in a towel, slid it into his messenger bag and headed out of the tent. He called out to Oz that he was taking lunch and took a path through the woods to reach his car, without having to deal with the mob of protestors.

He'd have to get through the rest of the workday before he would have a chance to figure out the puzzle. God only knew what was hidden inside that box.

CHAPTER TWENTY TWO

Ray hit the floor hard. He spat out a mouthful of blood, watched it splatter on the concrete, and glared at his captors with the one eye that wasn't swollen shut. Feeling around with his tongue, he checked one of his back molars on the side where the goon had clobbered him. Yep, loose. Bastard.

He levered his body up with his hands and struggled into a sitting position. The clicking of high heels on the hard floor announced Azibel's return. She stopped in front of him and cocked her head to one side, ebony hair cascading over her shoulders. She looked entirely too innocent for the evil Ray knew was hidden inside.

Clucking her tongue and shaking her head at him, she crouched so they were eye level to one another. "Oh, Poppet, I told you to do this the easy way, didn't I?"

Ray swiped the back of his hand across his mouth, smeared the blood on his lips. He glanced at the red stain and laughed bitterly. "That was the easy way?"

"Of course, pet. You have information I need. And since you weren't willing to give it up with a little… encouragement, I shall have to take it from you."

That was all the warning he got before she seized his head in an iron grip. Claw-like nails dug into his skin and drew blood. Again, he felt the searing pain lance through his brain, scraping the inside of his skull.

It was all the more unbearable because of the direct contact with her. His entire being was paralyzed, his eyes frozen open. Tears streamed down his cheeks from his inability to blink. He tried desperately to fight, to even think about fighting, but it was impossible.

He felt a sharp tug deep in the back of his mind, as if she were extracting a piece of him. An image of Raven's face, swimming in his field of vision, was the last thing he saw before his world went dark.

ജ്ജ

All day on Saturday, Drew stared at the box. He had tried so many different combinations of the pieces to solve the puzzle, he'd lost count. He'd even come up with a formula to calculate all of the possible sequences.

Still nothing. As a rule, he wasn't a vain man, but he prided himself on his intellect. It annoyed him that he couldn't come up with an answer with deductive reasoning. Raven had been working on a system at Elcourt Manor, pulling eighteen-hour days, and he'd barely seen her. Drew didn't care to admit how much of his irritability was due to her absence.

At the sound of his door opening, Drew barely spared a glance as his friends trooped into his room and made themselves at home. He didn't need to look to see the worried frown on Isla's face or the disapproving set to Jeremiah's jaw.

They were, no doubt, coming to rescue him from his 'obsession'. Nothin' doin', he thought. He had to get inside that box—there was something very important there, he could feel it in his goddamn bones.

Jeremiah sat on the couch and hauled his ever-present guitar onto his lap while Isla sat on the arm of the couch beside him. Marduk flopped lengthwise on the love seat and turned on the television, chuckling when he found a rerun of *The Big Bang Theory* on a local channel.

The three of them tried so hard to ignore him, it proved to be quite distracting. Jere picked a twangy tune on the instrument until Marduk shushed him by throwing a pillow at his head.

With a sigh, Drew pushed back away from the desk and faced them but didn't stand. Didn't put away the box. "Get yourself a new git-fiddle there, brother?" he asked, gesturing towards the shiny six-string acoustic.

Jeremiah gave him a lopsided grin as he played a riff. "Sure did. Wedding gift from Callum and Jack. Not quite the same, but she travels a sight better than the Tele'." He stroked the neck lovingly, and Isla rolled her eyes.

She winked at Drew and smiled. "I'd be jealous, but he plays me just as well," she said, surprising a bark of laughter out of Drew and gagging noises from Marduk.

"How are Jack and Cal, anyway?" he asked.

Isla's smile softened as she thought of her friends. "They're doin' great. Cal's taken over running Expeditions full-time, and Jack's been helping him guide some tours. Jack even took on an associate veterinarian to free him up for a little well-deserved time off. I think he kind of figured, after performing surgery on a shapeshifting wolf-boy, what else was there to see?"

"Who are you calling a boy?" Marduk asked indignantly.

"Oh, stuff it, Fido," Jere retorted, returning the pillow with a well aimed toss. Before the two men could start bickering like old biddies again, the door burst open to admit the overwhelming presence that was Raven.

She was dressed simply in frayed blue jeans and a dark green cropped sweatshirt that showed just a hint of midriff. The neckline was wide and had slipped down to reveal one smooth, golden brown shoulder.

Bigger than life, she pulled all of the energy from the room into herself, taking Drew's attention and his obsession with the box with it. With a shy wave to Drew's friends, she walked over to him and slid onto his lap.

Unable to help himself, Drew buried his face in her neck, breathed deeply of her spicy scent. He pressed a kiss to her warm skin and felt her shudder slightly. Giving her one last nuzzle, he pulled away and looked up at her.

"Hi," she murmured with a tentative smile.

"Hey," he said, and answered her smile with a grin of his own. "Done with work for the day?"

When she nodded, her silken hair slipped over her shoulder to brush against his arm. "We're still working on the installation. Once that's finished, I'll do a series of system tests to make sure they're getting what they paid for."

"You mean break in."

Her smile turned rueful, but she met his gaze with a steady one of her own. "It's what I do."

"Darlin', no one knows that better than me," he said with a wink.

But she didn't see it. Her attention was focused on the puzzle box sitting atop the little writing desk. Tucking her hair behind her ear, she chewed on her lower lip and gave him a wary look. "Where did you get that?"

The change in her demeanor confused him, but he saw no reason not to tell her. "At the dig. Hammer dug it up and brought it to me. Not sure what to make of it, but it sure as hell isn't Native American. Why?"

"My father had one just like it," she said, as if that was explanation enough. She leaned over the box, moved a few of the pieces around and pressed down on one in the corner. Just like that, the lid sprung open.

Three heads swung around in the living room and gaped at her, while Drew just stared at the box. Drew nudged Raven off his lap and stood for a moment, dumbstruck. "*Seriously*?" he hissed, then lit the air on fire with a string of curses.

Jamming a hand into his hair, he spun on his heel and stomped off into the bedroom. Raven stared after him in bewilderment.

Damn, she'd only been in the room for five minutes and she had already managed to screw things up. Throwing her hands up in a gesture of surrender, she looked helplessly at Jeremiah. "What just happened?"

Jere gave her a sympathetic smile and shook his head. "That boy's my best friend, and I love 'im, but he can be the biggest drama queen at times."

Raven snorted, but cast a worried glance toward the bedroom. What could she possibly have said to piss him off. She was raised as a grifter, for fuck's sake. She could talk her way in or out of any situation, but she couldn't understand why she always felt off-balance around Drew.

When she felt a hand come down on her shoulder, she jumped and spun around to find Jeremiah behind her. How long had she been standing there, puzzling over the enigmatic Dr. Deveraux?

"It's not you," Jeremiah said softly. "He's worked straight through the better part of forty-eight hours trying to get into that box, eating little and sleeping less. We came in here to distract him, to give him a break, but it didn't work. Until you came in, and completely absorbed his attention."

"Until I opened the box."

He gave her a quick nod and sighed. "You couldn't have known, and he'll thank you later for opening it. He's just running on empty right now. I'd better go check on him."

Raven bit down on her own fear, gathered her resolve and looked Jeremiah in the eye. "No, I'll go. I upset him, so I'll fix it." She saw a look of grudging respect cross the man's face before he nodded and sat back down.

Her footfalls were soft as she crept down the hall and around the corner into the dark bedroom. The heavy drapes were shut, so she could barely make out the silhouette of Drew lying on his side in the middle of the bed.

She started to speak, then stopped herself because she really didn't know what to say. Instead, she did the only thing she could think of that might help. She crawled up on the bed behind him and molded herself to his back.

When her arm snaked around his waist, his body went rigid with tension. But she didn't move away, she just held on and let him be. After what seemed like an eternity, he relaxed against her and his shoulders moved with the force of a deep, shuddering breath.

She felt him stir, so she moved back and gave him room to turn over and face her. Her breath caught in her chest when she finally got a good look at him, her eyes having adjusted to the darkness.

His normally smooth face was covered in scruff, a shade darker blonde than his hair. His clear blue eyes were dull and shadowed from lack of sleep, and the hollows of his cheeks seemed deeper.

With a heavy sigh, he wrapped her up in his arms and pressed a kiss to her forehead. "I'm sorry," he said gruffly. "I'm an ass."

The apology tugged on something deep inside her, a part of her she'd thought was dead, or never fully developed in the first place. It felt a lot like a nurturing instinct.

She lowered her head to brush her lips across his softly, before pulling back to look at him again. "You're not an ass. You're tired and overworked."

He grunted noncommittally. The breath that fanned her neck had slowed and deepened, and she knew he was halfway to REM already. "Whatever's in that box will keep for a few hours."

She threaded her fingers through his curls before sitting up. "Get some sleep. We'll get everyone back together tonight and figure out what we've got, okay?"

He nodded drowsily, but opened for her when she kissed him one last time. When she was satisfied that he slept, she padded quietly out of the room where the others were waiting.

Chapter Twenty Three

Raven burst out of the back door of the tavern, headed for her bike, and pulled on the leather riding jacket she'd grabbed as an afterthought. She had to move, to ride. Needed to air out the uncomfortable tightness in her chest.

It wasn't running away, she told herself, not really. Just getting some air, spreading her wings, so to speak. When she reached the Ducati, she quickly slid on her helmet. Pushing the bike into a roll, she swung on and kick started it in one fluid motion.

As she sped off, she pressed the power switch to the iPhone control panel on the side of her helmet, letting Radiohead circa 1995 surround her. The speakers and the iPhone dock itself were embedded within the helmet. It was a prototype Trys had worked up for her—it sometimes came in handy to have an engineer for a business partner.

Raven longed for the comfort and safety of obscurity, like the dusty highway through the Mojave Desert. As it was, she'd have to settle for a winding mountain road. While she soared down the Blue Ridge Parkway, her head began to clear and her thundering pulse slowed. This was her sweet spot. This was where she lived, where she worked. On her bike, out on the open road.

Even as she sank into the familiar peace of the road stretching out before her, Raven couldn't help but wonder why part of her wanted to pull a u-turn and head back to the inn. Back to Drew.

She ignored the impulse but was unable to move on. She settled for pulling off the road next to the familiar brown signs that announced one of the many state-maintained landmarks and trailheads.

Raven was familiar with this particular trail, having hiked it before. She felt comfortable there because it was off the beaten path enough that she usually didn't run into tourists. The trail led up to the watchtower on Wagon Ridge, then wound its way down to Mountain Laurel Falls. She had always been surprised that more people didn't find the trail, as a scene from a popular movie had been filmed at the falls. However, it was a rather difficult trek, so that kept many exploring tourists away.

Rolling the Ducati into the cover of some trees, Raven set off for the peak. She wasn't an expert hiker by any means, but she kept herself fit and capable, so she reached her destination with little trouble.

The watchtower was a tall, wooden structure that had definitely seen better days. It had originally been constructed so the rangers could spot forest fires in the vast valleys and on the mountainsides. These days, the task had been relegated to fire department chopper crews and, when necessary, the US Forest Service's Smokejumpers. No one seemed inclined to tear down the old fire towers, but they were largely unused and unkempt.

She used a hand to shade her eyes from the sun as she gazed up at the watchtower. It was as good a place as any to spend some time thinking, and collect herself. Grabbing hold of one of the ladder rungs, she hoisted herself up and began to climb.

Once at the top, she looked out over the valley below and shook her head when she realized that somewhere down in that valley was the dig site. Drew's work. Her subconscious didn't seem to want to let her escape the man.

She paced the small, square platform while the aging boards creaked under her boots. There was a thick picket railing surrounding the platform. Without a thought for her safety, Raven hopped up and swung her legs over until they were dangling out into space.

As Raven looked out over the Blue Ridge Mountains, she began to feel a little less constricted, a little less claustrophobic. She knew the exact moment when Brynna climbed onto the platform behind her. How the other woman had managed to scale the crumbling ladder without making a sound spoke volumes of her "feline" half. It was irrelevant though. Raven knew. She always knew when the space around her was disturbed.

Brynna stepped up behind her and said nothing, just joined her at the railing. She just silently watched the breeze sift through the trees. Finally she broke the silence, turning to look at Raven. "You're gonna bail, aren't you?"

Raven looked over at her and suddenly just wanted to let it out, to tell the truth just this once, and let someone else help shoulder the burden.

"I'm not a part of this. Not really. Believe me, I was *not* born to save the world. I'm just dust in the wind here. Grift 'n drift. That's what Ray always said—"

Brynna cut her off with a sharp reply. "Will you take off your goddamned highway halo and stop acting like a spoiled brat for five minutes? You don't hold the monopoly on a fucked-up childhood. At least you *had* Ray, despite his faults. At least you had *one* parent who loved you."

Raven slung her head back as if she'd been slapped, temporarily stunned into silence. Brynna seized the opportunity to continue.

"Let me tell you a little story about Isla. By the time Isla's *signa* appeared, the man she'd believed to be her father had already left them, driven away by her drunk of a mother. Her grandmother had been thrown out of the house, and Isla's mother told her that she was dead.

"So on Halloween night of '91, Isla was living alone with her mother, Eileen, when the mark appeared. Although she pretended to fear it was the mark of the devil, Eileen knew exactly what it was. Her own mother'd had one, and the symbol inside of it was that of a demon—the one who'd seduced and impregnated her.

"Eileen knew that once that mark appeared, he would come for Isla, and perhaps her, too. So that night, Eileen drugged Isla and tried to carve the *signa* out of her skin with a kitchen knife."

Brynna paused, allowing that information to sink in. Any trace of anger had fled from Raven's pale face. Her eyes widened and she clapped a hand over her mouth. "What happened?" she asked, the sound muffled by her hand.

"Isla awoke in the middle of it. The drugs Eileen had given her must not have been strong enough. She fought Eileen off and ran, but Eileen caught up to her."

Despite the grim subject, Brynna had to suppress a smile at the riveted look on Raven's face.

"*And?*" Raven asked insistently.

"Eileen slit her throat."

Raven sucked in a sharp breath and shook her head. "Obviously not very effectively, thank Fate."

Brynna nodded and continued. "She was drunk, as usual, so the cut didn't go as deep as she thought. Isla was able to crawl outside, where the police found her."

"It's amazing that Isla turned out as good as she did."

"Yeah, it really is." Brynna put her hand on Raven's shoulder and waited for eye contact. "Raven, the point I'm trying to make is this. I know you were raised to rely on nothing and no one, and, believe me, I get how hard it is for you to suddenly have to depend on others—and have others depend on you. Okay? I really do get it. But Isla wasn't raised at all. And she still stepped up to the battle, because she realized that it's what she was meant to do. Do you see what I'm getting at?"

"You're telling me to get over my personal baggage and start thinking about others for a change? Damn, I never thought of myself as selfish until now."

"Not selfish, just...unenlightened. In the immortal words of Spock, 'the needs of the many outweigh the needs of the few'."

"Or the one," Raven finished with a wink, causing Brynna to snort. "I had no idea that mythical creatures could be Trekkies."

Sobering, Brynna turned serious, green eyes to Raven's. "So what's it going to be? None of us can force you to be a part of this. But I have a feeling you'll get dragged into it anyway, so you're better off being prepared, with others at your back."

Raven mulled it over for a moment. She really didn't have anything else to lose, except maybe a little bit of her pride, and a lot of her youthful delusions. "I can't promise to be in it for the long haul. Not yet. But I can promise to be in it for now."

Brynna smiled and nodded. "I think we can live with that. Where to now, *domina*? Raven must have given her a funny look, because Brynna proceeded to explain to her that *domina* was what a *feradux* called her *Vigile*.

"I wanted to hike down to the base of the falls before heading back." She heaved a dramatic sigh before continuing. "Then I guess we can go back and tell the others that I'm in, and see what's in this box of Drew's." Raven narrowed her eyes at Brynna's speculative look.

"That's another thing we should discuss—"

Raven raised a hand to stop the inevitable. "No. We're not going to discuss him now. Just let it be for a little while, okay? Please."

Reluctantly, Brynna gave in and followed Raven down the ladder.

ꙮ

The sun was low in the western sky when they finally made it to the foot of Mountain Laurel Falls. It was a magnificent sight, one Raven never tired of seeing. A gentle flow rained down over one-hundred feet of sheer rock face, gathering in a crystal clear pool at the bottom.

Boulders created a natural wall around the pool, and a low overhang shielded half of it from the beating sun. At the far edge of the pond, the landscape plunged down another two hundred feet to the valley below.

Raven turned and watched Brynna settle herself on one of the dry rocks, stretching languidly in the sun. *Freaking cats,* she thought. Always chasing the sunspot, no matter how big they were.

It was quite an unseasonably warm day, so Raven hop-scotched from one rock to another, in the mist of the falls. When she finally got across to the far side, under the overhang, she pulled off her boots, rolled up her pants, and dipped her toes into the cold water. She eased back on the warm flat rock, folded her arms underneath her head and stared up at the sky.

She lay there relaxing for so long she almost fell asleep. She would have, had she not felt the brush of something on the bottom of her foot. Too lazy to get up and look, she pondered over what it could be.

The falls would keep fish out of the pool, and it wasn't near slimy enough to be a frog. Tadpole, maybe. Or just some roughage floating by. She dismissed it, chuckling when she heard a tiny snore coming from Brynna's direction.

Then she felt it again, a silky caress wrapping around her ankle. Her brows drew together in confusion. *What in the hell?* She sat up, reached down and batted at the substance with a hand. The stuff clung to her fingers in wet clumps. It felt like...hair.

Startled, Raven jerked her feet out of the water and raised up on her hands and knees, bending to peer into the pool. It looked exactly as it felt, a great mass of dark hair that floated just below the surface. She groaned at the thought of what it might be attached to.

Distracted by mulling over the ramifications of finding a dead body in a mountain pond, she never saw it coming.

A hand shot up and grabbed her wrist, where she had been reaching to touch the hair. The skin was pale—deathly pale—but the grip was strong and sure. Even as Raven tried to snatch her arm back, it held fast.

Trembling with fear, she tried to pry the fingers off her wrist, the punishing grip sure to leave bruises. Slowly, a face emerged through the cloud of wild, dark tresses. Raven's mouth dropped open as eyes blinked up at her.

They were black all over, with no whites showing. The woman's skin was white and her lips were tinged with blue. If she hadn't been looking straight at Raven, she'd be convinced it was, indeed, a corpse. The thing that startled her most was the *signa* that stood out darkly against her pale throat. It was the same as Raven's, only without the glyph in the center.

So this thing—woman, ghost, corpse, whatever—was *Vigilati*. That couldn't be good. And it couldn't be a coincidence. Raven wanted to call for Brynna. She needed...help, but her voice was frozen inside her throat. The woman in the water cocked her head as she stared up at Raven, and the iron grip eased ever so slightly.

The woman spoke to her. Not out loud because, well, she was underwater. But Raven heard her nonetheless. Her voice was deep for a woman, husky and with a guttural intonation that hinted at some Slavic heritage. Or Russian, maybe.

"Take care, dark one. She will be here soon," she said in accented English. Raven heard the words as a suggestion in her mind, as she felt the woman's presence there.

"Who...will be here? Who are you?"

The woman, who appeared to be in her mid-twenties, shook her head violently, causing the cloud of hair to slither around her.

"You may call me Malenka. Hear me. Even now, she comes. She will find you, before the curtain falls. Hear me."

Raven swallowed visibly, unable to believe what was happening. "Do you need help? I don't understand what you're trying to tell me. *Who* is coming?"

"*Veliko zlo,*" she whispered, then frowned as if realizing she no longer spoke English. "The great evil. *Azibel.*" The name hissed through Raven's mind like a curse.

"Raven?"

She nearly jumped out of her skin when Brynna's voice came from right behind her. She turned wide eyes toward her puzzled friend.

"Who were you talking to?"

Raven looked back down to the water and was startled to find it empty. When she examined her wrist, she saw subtle bruising beginning to form in the shape of fingerprints. "There was someone in the water..." she said lamely, trailing off because she wasn't sure how to explain it without sounding schizophrenic, at best.

But Brynna just nodded and held out a hand to pull her up. "We'd better get back to Cliffdweller's and tell the others what's up. We agreed we would work together, yes?"

Raven merely nodded and arched a brow at Brynna. "So you believe me? Just like that?"

"Raven, I can turn myself into a cougar. Somehow, hearing that you saw someone in the water isn't that big of a deal. Let's go."

Chapter Twenty Four

"Come on, Deveraux, just open the box!" Jeremiah whined for the fifth time.

Drew just shook his head and continued to flip through channels on the television. "Not until Raven gets here. She opened the box, she should be the one who gets to see what's in it. Besides, if I'm right, this will have more to do with her than any of us."

Jere grunted but said nothing else. Drew knew he was bored. They both were. This being their first trip to America, Isla and Marduk had gone into town to have a look around. Raven and Brynna were also AWOL, so he and Jere were stuck by themselves.

"You're getting pretty serious about her, yeah?"

Drew rolled his eyes at his friend's deceptively casual question. He so did *not* want to have this conversation—with Jeremiah or anyone else. Sighing, he ran a hand through his blonde hair, pushing the curls out of his eyes. "I don't know, maybe. She's not exactly relationship material. She made that clear from the start. I'm not either, for that matter."

Jeremiah turned his head sharply and looked Drew in the eye. "The hell you're not! Listen, I know you went through some shit growin' up—I'm sure there's some of it you haven't even told me. I know your mama did a number on you and that makes you think there's something wrong with you. But that's bullshit, and you know it."

"Jeremiah—"

"No, don't. I know you better than anyone. You may try to close yourself off from everyone, but you've got a bigger heart than you're willin' to let on. I just don't want to see you get hurt."

Drew blinked back the unmanly tears that threatened to fall at his best friend's admission. "Thanks, brother. But you don't have to worry about me. Raven's been honest from the start about her lifestyle. I'm not going to get too attached."

"That might not be your call," Jere answered, and Drew knew exactly where he was going with that statement.

Drew's French-Cajun drawl came and went with his moods, but he could just as easily make it disappear into his haughty, cultured "Professor Deveraux" mode. Turning it up full blast, he glared at his friend.

"Jeremiah," he said in a warning tone.

"Don't 'Jeremiah' me. We can't go into this situation blindly. Not this time. You have to consider the possibility of the *laqueum*." The *laqueum* was a term they had discovered in the grimoire that referred to the bond of a *Bruixi* and her mate. *Bruixi* witches' mates were chosen by the gods, and once they declared their love for each other, a symbiotic pair-bond formed in which if one of them perished, the other would as well.

"The *laqueum* is a non-issue, as Raven and I aren't in love. We're just having fun. Relax."

Jeremiah shrugged, clearly not convinced. Drew chose to ignore him and turned his attention back to the docu-drama on TV. He looked up and nodded at Marduk and Isla when they let themselves in, laden with bags.

Isla giggled when Drew raised a brow at her. "Gifts for folks back home," she said in explanation of her shopping spree. "Callum and Jack have never been to the States either, so I had to stock up on goodies for them."

Drew snorted, but gave his best friend's wife an endearing smile. "Did you guys leave anything in the stores?"

"Very little," Marduk said in his heavy Italian accent, his eyes already riveted to the screen. "Where are Raven and Hello Kitty?"

Drew shook his head and brained Marduk with a pillow, which was becoming a daily occurrence. "What is it with you people and the nicknames?"

"I don't know," Jeremiah answered with a laugh in his voice. "What do you think, dog breath? What's with us?" That one earned him a middle finger from Marduk and a cackle from Isla.

"To answer your original question, Raven and Brynna went for a hike. Raven texted me a couple of minutes ago and said they were on their way back. And they have news," Drew said.

Half an hour later, the six of them sat around the coffee table, staring at the puzzle box with the slightly cracked open lid.

"Well?" Raven asked impatiently.

"Tell us your news first," Jeremiah prompted and leaned forward to rest his elbows on his knees.

Raven sighed and looked over at Brynna. Irish just shrugged at her and sat back in the armchair. What the hell happened to all that 'there's no I in team' bullshit. "I hiked up to the watchtower today, and Brynna followed. We decided to head down to the pond at Mountain Laurel Falls before coming back. We laid out in the sun for a little while and then...I saw something."

Drew wrapped an arm around her and pulled her close. "Saw what?"

"There was something—someone, in the water." Raven took a shaky breath and allowed herself to lean into Drew, to accept support from someone. Just this once. She relaxed her tense shoulders and let the whole experience pour out. For the first time in her life, she'd decided to let others help.

"Do you think it was a ghost?" Isla asked quietly, concern showing clearly on her delicate features. Raven blinked at her, just stared for a little while. She couldn't believe that this woman, someone who didn't even know her, wasn't questioning her story. She just accepted it as truth and moved on to the why and the how of it.

Something in Raven's gut she hadn't known she'd been clenching loosened, soothed. She gave Isla a grateful smile before she answered the question. "At first, I thought she was dead. Like, a corpse. But then she grabbed me."

Raven held out her arm so the rest of the group could see the bruised hand print on her wrist. "I don't have much—any—experience with ghosts, but I've never heard of one doing that." She shivered slightly when Drew raised her wrist to his mouth and brushed his lips over the contusions. His eyes never wavered, holding her gaze.

"Actually, that's not entirely uncommon," Jeremiah interjected. "I don't know how much Drew has told you about what I do for a living. I do paranormal investigations, and, although most recently they've involved witches," he paused to kiss his wife's temple, "they are usually centered around hauntings."

"You think a ghost could really hurt a human being?" Drew's brows pulled low over his eyes.

Raven swore she thought she heard a rumble in his chest, almost like a growl.

"Not exactly. Poltergeists can use inanimate objects to hurt a person. Beyond that, I don't think ghosts can directly cause lasting damage to a human, but there have been many reports of things like scratches and bruises. Demons are another story, though." Jeremiah turned back to Raven. "Did you get any sense of danger from this woman? Did you feel as if she wanted to harm you?"

Thinking carefully, Raven gave a quick shake of her head. "No. No, I don't think so. In fact, it almost seemed like she was trying to tell me something. It was obviously important to her, but I didn't understand any of it."

"Tell us more about her. Maybe we can ask around, find anyone who knows someone who looks like her," Jeremiah said.

Raven pinched the bridge of her nose as she felt the beginnings of a headache coming on. It was going to be a long night. "She said her name was Malenka. She sounded eastern European. Czech, or maybe even Russian. And she had a *signa,* here." Raven touched the left side of her throat, just over her thrumming pulse.

"*Praeda*?" Marduk finally joined the conversation. Raven was learning that the man didn't waste words. He only spoke when he thought it was important, except for when he was snarking at Jeremiah.

"No, she was just *Vigilati*. But still, how many could there be in such a small town?"

"That's a good point," Jeremiah said. "Isla and I can go into town and ask around, discreetly of course, maybe check some records at the library." He aimed a pointed glance at Marduk then Brynna. "You two should do some reconnaissance in your animal forms. You may be able to get around to some places we can't."

"Raven?" Isla's soft spoken question had everyone pausing. "What else did Malenka say to you?"

Raven fiddled with a strand of her long sable hair. "She said someone was coming for me, would be here before the curtain falls."

"Who?" Again, Isla's question was calm, quiet, but poignant.

"Malenka called it *veliko zlo*. The great evil. And she mentioned a name. Azibel."

"Azibel." Isla tested it out on her tongue, her dark, highly arched brows knitting. "Sounds like a woman's name."

"So?" Now Raven was curious, as she thought Isla was acting strangely, although she didn't know the woman very well.

"So, we were told that the *Lochrim* were all male," Jeremiah supplied, obviously following his wife's train of thought. "I can't imagine that anyone else would be coming for you. But then again, we've got a hell of a learning curve for all of this."

Drew smacked a fist against the leather covered arm of the sofa. "Damn it! We really need to find Ray," he said and turned apologetic eyes to Raven. "He's the one person who may be able to fill in the blanks for us. Like how is Raven a *praeda* if he's her biological father, and who the fuck is Azibel? Any word from Matty yet?"

Jeremiah shrugged, his irritation showing. "Not yet. All I got was a text from an unknown number that said 'cobra deployed'. I can only assume that means he'll find his way to me."

Clearly unsatisfied, Drew raked a hand through his hair. His curls stuck up at odd directions and Raven assumed he'd probably been doing that all day. Seeking to distract him, and overwhelmed with curiosity herself, she turned his attention back to the reason they'd all gathered there.

"So..." she trailed a chaste finger up the outside of his thigh and smirked as he swallowed convulsively. "What's in the box?"

CHAPTER TWENTY FIVE

Drew knelt on the floor beside the coffee table and reached for the box with shaking hands. He wondered why he was so damned nervous about opening that little box. Pandora's damage had already been done, so what could possibly be in there that was so bad?

It dawned on him that whatever was inside the box was connected to his dig, and also to Raven and the Vigilati. That could not be good. He shook himself inwardly. Time to man up, Deveraux. He couldn't deal with it until he knew what he was up against.

He slowly raised the lid and peeked inside. He wasn't proud of the sigh of relief he breathed when he saw that it was just a book. No snakes, scorpions, or demons. Just a thin, crudely bound book, with—naturally—a signa burned into the leather cover.

He pulled it out and carefully opened it to the first page. He was surprised to find it was handwritten, journal style, and definitely not in English. The handwriting seemed feminine, but scrawling, and was very hard to make out.

The others lowered down to the floor around the coffee table and looked at him expectantly, while Raven peered over his shoulder at the book. "What language is that?"

"The writing is really hard to read, but it looks like French."

"Well, damn. How are we supposed to figure out what it says?"

Drew shared a smirk with Jeremiah. While Raven knew that he was a dead languages expert, she didn't know that he was three-quarters French-Cajun and one-quarter French. "I think we'll manage," he said with a smile.

The scrawled title page read: Le Livre des Ombres, L. Montreaux, 1885. Interesting. Up until that point, all of the other literature he had found on the Vigilati had been in Old Latin.

"Do you know what it says?" Raven looked at him so seriously when she asked that he had to suppress a laugh.

He cleared his throat and smiled at her. "It says The Book of Shadows. I'm guessing L. Montreaux is the name of whoever wrote this." Silently, he began to flip through the scribbled pages and couldn't help but think that the handwriting seemed familiar to him somehow.

The first few pages were faded, and the ink had run, making them undecipherable. Drew perked up when he flipped to a page with a vertical line of crudely drawn symbols, each one with an inscription out to the side.

He sucked in a breath. Could it be? If this was what he thought it was, it could prove to be their most valuable weapon in the fight against the Lochrim. He flinched when Raven poked him in the ribs, and he turned to glare at her.

She shrugged, obviously unphased by his temperament. "Don't leave us in the dark. What is this? You've got an idea, it's written all over your face."

Torn between feeling irritated over the interruption and touched that she could already read him so well, Drew gave up and chuckled. "You're right. I have an idea, but it's just a hunch."

"Out with it, brother," Jeremiah chimed in.

"Okay. There are several pages of these symbols. In fact, it looks like they take up half the book. In early Wiccan culture, a book of shadows was kept by a coven, and it was likely to contain religious doctrine and ritual instructions unique to the coven. In more modern Wicca, it is more like a journal, where each witch records their own personal spells, rituals, and magickal information."

Jere raised a brow at him, but Drew just shrugged. His friend may be the expert on all things paranormal, but Drew was in this now, and he never did anything halfway.

"What? I've done my research. I'm thinking that, what if this is the Bruixi version of the modern book of shadows? Maybe this woman, most likely a Vigile, compiled all of the information she had gathered in her lifetime, and recorded it."

"For what?" Jeremiah asked. "Posterity?"

"Maybe. Or maybe she knew that someday, people like us would need the information."

"That's a little far-fetched." Jeremiah was frowning but looked like he was mulling it over. "So what do you think the symbols mean?"

"We've learned that each auchrim tribe—for lack of a better term—carries its own symbol, worn by the Lochrim. I think these must be the seals of the Lochrim that L. Montreaux came in contact with or heard about in her lifetime. She catalogued them for some reason, maybe so others would be able to learn what they were up against."

Jeremiah was already shaking his head before Drew had finished talking. "If that were the case, why would she put it in a box no one could open, in a place no one could find?"

"But we found it. Raven opened it. Maybe it ended up exactly where she intended it to be."

"Huh...," Jeremiah said, scratching his chin. "Well, I suppose at this point, anything's possible."

"May I see it?" Isla reached out a small hand, and Drew passed her the book.

He watched her face carefully as she leafed through the pages. She studied the book for a few minutes before her eyes widened and a gasp escaped her.

"Find what you were looking for?" Drew asked. He thought he knew exactly what she was skimming the pages for. The symbol of Alastore. Of her father. He was dead, but Drew knew he would haunt Isla always.

"Here it is," she answered, placing the book on the table so that the others could see. She pointed to a small glyph of an eye that exactly matched the one inside the smallest circle of her signa. "What does it say, Drew?"

He squinted down at the wild loops and scrawls to the right of the seal. While French came as naturally to him as English, the handwriting was killing him.

Alastore de l'œil maléfique: Sud îles écossaises.

"There's not much here," he said with a frown. "It just says Alastore of the baleful eye: Southern Scottish Isles."

Isla nodded concisely, and Drew knew she hadn't expected to find out anything new about her father. She had gotten closure when she'd killed him.

"That confirms your theory, at least," she said.

Raven slid the book over so she could flip through it, and Drew watched her out of the corner of his eye. Finally she pointed to a seal that matched her own, the spider, and she didn't need Drew to translate the inscription for her. It only said one word: Azibel.

Chapter Twenty Six

When Raven arrived at the dig site, Drew was nowhere in sight. She assumed he was probably in the lab tent and didn't want to disturb his work. Bex had called her, saying he'd found some things that were off when he'd showed up for his shift.

She'd told him not to bother Drew or Dr. Larkin, that she'd come check it out, see if it was anything to worry about.

Standing next to Bex, she stared at the footprints at the perimeter of the site with her hands shoved into the pockets of her ratty jeans. A section of the snow fencing was down where the prints marred the mossy ground.

The fence hadn't been put up to keep out intruders, just to mark the private area, but the fact that it was down was certainly troubling. In fact, it was a damn sight annoying. No, Raven was pissed. When she installed security at a site, it became her responsibility. It was personal. And this wasn't going to happen on her watch.

Her long ponytail whipped around as she turned to face her associate. "What'd we get on the video feed?" She rubbed her forehead when she saw Bex already shaking his head.

"We got shit, boss. Actually, less than shit. The two cameras that would have captured this area both blacked out for five minutes, starting at 3:09 am exactly. When the feed comes back, the fence is already down."

"What?" Raven's jaw dropped. Impossible. "That can't be a coincidence. Someone had to have deliberately tampered with the equipment. What did the night man have to say?"

"I didn't see this until after he left, and I haven't been able to get him on his cell. My guess is, he's sleeping. Third shift, ya know?"

Raven spat out a string of curses and began to pace, careful to keep her own footfalls away from the intruder's prints. "I'm going to have to let Deveraux know. We have to find out if anything is missing or damaged."

Bex nodded toward the lab tent where Drew and Oz stood outside with their heads close together in deep conversation. "Want me to tell him?" he asked.

"That's okay, I'll do it." She stepped forward, intending to walk over and interrupt them, when she noticed a man striding purposefully toward them. He walked briskly, his long legs eating up the ground, but his whole body was taut with barely restrained fury.

She sensed equal parts malice and despair wafting off the man, and she glanced nervously around. No one else seemed to be reacting to it, so it had to be her mutant "Spidey senses" kicking in. She watched Drew's face as he finally noticed the stranger coming toward him. His eyes widened briefly in utter shock, but he quickly covered it, nodding at the man.

Even from a distance, she could tell that this man was volatile and extremely dangerous. She fought back the urge to go place herself between him and Drew. She didn't think any man would appreciate having the woman he was sleeping with trying to shield him in a fight.

Besides, Drew wasn't showing any fear. He was his usual calm and unflappable self as he greeted the newcomer with a bright grin. He reached out a hand and looked like he was going to pull the other man into a quick hug, but the guy flinched away from Drew and his smile faded.

They talked for a few moments, shared a cautious handshake, and the stranger stalked off in the direction he'd come, giving Raven a chance to study him a bit. He was a couple of inches shorter than Drew, but bulkier—he was covered in thick, rolling muscle from his powerful shoulders all the way down to thighs the size of tree trunks and beyond.

His dark hair was shaved close to his head, and he oozed military from every pore. She would have known he was a soldier even if she hadn't seen the black t-shirt stuffed into desert tactical BDU's, with black combat boots laced over them.

A chain disappeared inside the neck of his shirt, and she'd be willing to bet money that it held dog tags. He was handsome, with a square jaw, straight nose, and high cheekbones. But his perfection was marred by a vicious scar on his cheek, from the corner of his eye all the way down to his jawbone.

There was also the scowl he wore that would repel anyone from thinking him too handsome, she thought as they made eye contact and he curled his lip at her. Then her eyes widened as she caught sight of the tattoo that stood out on his corded neck and dipped down to where his shoulder was covered by his t-shirt.

The tattoo was of a king cobra, coiled and ready to strike. Cobra. Hell, she had just figured out who the pissed-off stranger was. It was Jeremiah's brother, Matthieu. Operation Cobra had begun.

ꙮ

Drew ran a hand over the back of his head as he watched Raven approach. Though she was dressed simply in jeans and a white tank, she was all business as she scanned the perimeter and made eye contact with the camera checkpoints.

She approached the lab tent slowly, narrowing her eyes as she frowned at Matthieu's retreating back. When she reached him, she turned to face the direction in which Matt had left, and stood shoulder to shoulder with Drew.

Raising a brow, she turned her head toward him. "That the brother?" She asked it so matter-of-factly that only the nervous licking of her lips betrayed her unease.

Drew nodded, but realized she was no longer looking at him. Rather, she was watching Matt drive away in an oversized black pick-up, and still frowning. "Yeah, that's him. He's not too happy with me right now, or Jeremiah, but he'll help us."

"What's his deal, anyway?"

He looked at her in surprise, but then he realized that probably anyone would notice the cloud of menace that surrounded Matthieu these days. He breathed a heavy sigh and turned anguished eyes to hers. "He's broken, Raven. There's a stain on that boy's soul. Whether it's from the war or something that happened after, we don't know. Jeremiah and Esme—that's their mom—just let him be and hope he'll come around one day."

He watched Raven twirl the end of her sleek ponytail as she thought it over. "Tell me again why you're so sure he can find Ray?"

"Well...like I said, he was part of a special ops team in Afghanistan. No one knows much about it, but I think it involved finding people—either POWs or enemy targets—and he has 'special skills'. Kind of like you. Anyway, he does some private PI work now, but I'm also pretty sure he's working as a hired gun."

"Mercenary," she said to herself. Drew nodded, though it wasn't a question.

"My theory, anyway. But it works to our advantage, because he'll find his mark, and he isn't necessarily going to be worried about going through the proper legal channels."

Raven rounded on him, eyes flashing. "He won't hurt Ray."

"He wouldn't unless we told him to. What happens to the mark is up to the client's discretion."

Raven looked relieved, leading Drew to believe that she cared more about what happened to her father than she was willing to let on.

"Matt is already almost certain that Ray is still in Vegas. His Harley and all of his things are still right where he left them. After accessing his financial records, he saw that there's been no activity in his account. How far could he get with no money and no possessions?"

"He's already found out that much? Well, what about the blood? If he was taken against his will, there wouldn't be a money trail, would there?"

Drew placed his hands on her shoulders and turned her to face him. "He's good, Raven. The best. Those are possibilities he's already considered, which is why he's heading to Vegas now to follow the physical trail. He'll need to question Trystan and Ryder, so make sure that they are willing to talk to him."

She nodded, taking out her iPhone presumably to send an email to Trystan. Drew had been so distracted by Matt's visit that he'd forgotten to ask about Raven's unscheduled appearance. "So why did you stop by? Not that I'm not glad to see you," he added with a quick grin.

She looked up at him, her mouth set in a grim line, and his smile faded. "Bex called. Someone breached the perimeter last night. Cut the feed on both cameras with a view of that area—both the visible and the hidden—at exactly the same time."

Anger surged through him. After all he had done to try and keep things safe, one of those granola-crunching conservationists had hit them where they lived. "What the—? Is that even possible?"

"It is for someone who knows a hell of a lot about electronics. I'll need you to go over the grid and each of the tents and catalog anything that's moved, missing, or damaged as soon as possible. I'm going to have Bex track down the night security guard while I check the rest of the site."

He nodded curtly and stomped off, tossing a look over his shoulder. "Let me know if you find anything."

CHAPTER TWENTY SEVEN

Now, this was personal. Drew tried to bite back the fury he felt burning in his gut whenever he thought of someone breaking into his lab, such as it was, and disturbing his research.

As it stood, if he ever caught up with the bastard, he was so going to go Cajun all over his ass. He pushed his way into the lab tent and began meticulously going over every artifact, every bone fragment, every piece of equipment, looking for any sign of foul play.

The very idea that someone had rifled through his workspace—touched his things, moved his tools—made his obsessive compulsive tendencies sit up and howl at the moon.

After a cursory glance, nothing was glaringly obvious. Kneeling down, he spun the combination on the medium-sized gun safe they had purchased to store the artifacts safely. The skull and fragments were exactly as he'd left them, along with the few broken pieces of earthenware they had uncovered.

He checked each one of his handwritten notebooks to make sure they were intact, and they were. Luckily, the majority of his notes were on his laptop, which he kept with him. None of the equipment was destroyed either. On the surface, everything looked perfectly fine, but something was off.

Drew couldn't put his finger on it, but there was a taint in the room, like a black mark on the atmosphere that lingered after the source had long gone. The lab looked as if nothing had been touched, yet everything had. Everything was just...Slightly. Off.

He doubted anyone else in the *world* would notice it but him. Sometimes he felt like the mad scientist Jeremiah teased him for being.

Narrowing his eyes, his scrutiny homed in on the larger microscope where he'd last examined the scapula fragment. Had he put that sample away? No, he was sure he hadn't. He'd been so distracted, first by Hammer scaring the ever-loving shit out of him, then there was the box.

The sample should have been right on the microscope stage where he'd left it. Should be, but it wasn't.

Drew wanted to put his fist through a wall, but, unfortunately, he had none handy. After counting to ten to calm his temper, he started for the door to go find Raven, where she appeared as if he'd conjured her.

Her eyes darted around the tent much the same way his had done. "Did you find anything?"

Drew clenched his teeth to keep from spouting a string of undignified cursing. He could barely think with the static buzzing in his ears. They. Touched. Everything.

"Hey, Drew?" He jumped when she placed a hand on his arm and looked up at him with concern. "You okay?"

Shaking his head, he took a deep breath and tried to focus on what she was saying. "Uh, yeah. Fine. The only thing that's missing is the bone fragment I'd left on the microscope when we found the puzzle box. It was the only thing light enough to carry that wasn't tied down or locked up. Don't think they found what they were looking for though."

Her brows pulled low over her eyes and she cocked her head at him. "What makes you say that?"

"Because everything's been touched. They were very precise with trying to put things back exactly where they were, but I can tell. Everything in here is just slightly off. All of that for a piece of bone that was left in plain sight? It doesn't fit."

"The box, maybe."

"Yes, or the skull. It was in the safe."

"Or...," she trailed off, chewing on her plump lower lip and tapping a finger to her chin. She snapped out of it when he raised a brow at her. "What if they were looking for something you haven't dug up yet? What if someone knows there's something down there, and it's only a matter of time before the team brings it up?"

Drew scrubbed a hand over his face and marveled at the woman before him. He hadn't even thought of that possibility. If that were the case, the implications for the dig site and what it housed were troubling at best.

She looked at him questioningly when he groaned. "Problem? Other than the obvious, of course."

"If your theory is right, and it may very well be, this excavation will get a whole lot more complicated, real fast."

Once outside, Raven took Drew around the perimeter of the dig, distracting him by checking the rest of the snow fencing for any signs of damage. She was worried about him.

When she'd come into the tent and found him standing there with his fists clenched, he'd looked deathly pale.

She knew that the disturbance in his lab was upsetting him more than he'd let on, but she'd never seen him this way. It cut through her, straight to the heart, to see her vibrant, funny, charming Drew look so drawn and tense.

Startled by the overwhelming desire to pull him into her arms and hold him until he gave her that dimpled smile again, she wondered when she'd started thinking of him as *hers*.

All she could do for him—the one thing she knew he would appreciate—was help him find out who did this, and prevent it from happening again.

When they arrived in front of the stretch of downed fence, Raven put a hand on Drew's shoulder to stop him. "Here's where they came in. See the prints? Just one set from what Bex and I can determine."

Drew met her gaze with sky blue eyes that had turned hard and cold with anger. "Do you think we should call the police?"

Raven shrugged one shoulder noncommittally. She didn't trust the police, never had. But she couldn't let the way she was raised interfere with her better judgment when it came to Drew and his work. "I don't know. Maybe. Something tells me you won't get anything but more red tape out of it. But it's your call."

She studied his profile as he looked up to the ledge on Barron's Bald they had hiked to a few weeks ago. When he said nothing else, she assumed he'd dismissed the idea of calling the authorities.

Good, she thought. She and her men would take care of this, without interrupting the excavation. She caught Drew's attention and pointed up at a security light post.

"That one is the visible camera that covers this area. See the birdhouse in the woods over there? That's the hidden camera. Someone managed to disable both cameras at the exact same second—only for as long as it took to slip past the field of vision. Had to have some serious tech skills for that one."

"Bex ever get ahold of the night man?"

"Yeah. He said he didn't notice the downed fence before Bex and Eric had relieved him. Never saw or heard anything out of the ordinary."

"Then what are we dealing with here? A goddamn ninja?"

Chuckling in spite of the situation, Raven gave him a gentle push to get him walking again. "Maybe. Who knows?"

"What's your plan, Raven? I know you have one. This has got to piss you off just as much as me."

She gave him a swift nod and dismissed the comment. It wouldn't help him any for her to start ranting and raving while he was in such a volatile mood.

"I think we need to bury a line around the whole perimeter. Trystan's just come up with a new mechanism that will trigger an alarm and alert either someone's cell phone—say, the guard on duty—or the local authorities, whichever you prefer," she said. She gave him a pointed look and hoped he would consider the hassle it would be to involve the police.

"Breaching the line would also trigger all of the security lights to come on at once. There's no way the guard would miss all that commotion."

"Sounds like I'm going to be working at the fucking Pentagon. But you're right. Whoever is doing this is obviously much more advanced than your average burglar."

Raven nodded, her eyes flicking over to the constant crowd of protestors. More and more, she wondered about them. It seemed so irrational to get this worked up over an archaeological excavation. But what did she know about what went on in the minds of hippie types?

"The perimeter warning system would be controlled by an electronic touch-screen keypad, and armed or disarmed with a six digit code. My strong advice would be for no one to have that code except for you, Dr. Larkin, and myself."

Drew's head snapped up and he looked at her sharply. "You think this is an inside job?"

"It's my job to consider *all* the possibilities. Doing it this way eliminates the possibility of a security breach from someone associated with the dig."

"What about the guards?"

Raven shook her head and looked over to where Eric stood, dressed to military precision, sharp eyes scanning the site. "Not even them. We'll have to coordinate the guard changes with when you or Dr. Larkin arrive in the morning and leave in the afternoon. We have to eliminate all possible wildcards. Do you understand?"

He nodded, and she knew he did, but it was killing him to think that one of his crew—his students—might be responsible for this. She watched him rub his tired eyes, and it distressed her to see the dark circles under them.

Grabbing his hand, she dragged him back toward the little tent city. "Come on. Let's go give Dr. Larkin an update, then you're cutting out early. You're stressed and exhausted."

"Raven, I can't just—"

"The hell you can't. They can survive without you for one afternoon. I'm not taking no." She watched in fascination at the variety of emotions that played over his features. Irritation, defiance, gratitude, and, eventually, acceptance.

She smiled when he put his hand in hers and allowed her to lead him away. Away from the uncertainty, and the possible danger. Somewhere he'd be safe.

CHAPTER TWENTY EIGHT

They had come back to the inn, and once they were back in his suite, Raven started working him. She slinked past him and poured them some wine in the kitchenette, tossing her hair and a smoldering look back over her shoulder at him.

She was every bit the temptress, the black widow she liked to pretend to be. She took a sip of her wine, licked the blood-red liquid off her lips and stared directly at his mouth. "You look thirsty, Dr. Deveraux. What are you going to do about it?"

Though her little show had gotten him hard as stone, it irritated him that she was still playing him, still being someone other than just Raven. Maybe she didn't know any different. If she wanted to play the slick con woman part with him, this time he was going to let her.

He spun her away from him and pushed her up against the door in the darkened room. Placing her palms on the door, he nudged her legs just a bit wider apart with the toe of his boot. Hard and fast? He could do that. The mood he was in, he could definitely give her what she was begging for.

"Stay."

She flicked a glance over her shoulder at his gruff command, but she didn't move. Drew slid his hands along the ridges of her ribcage, trailed them down her flat stomach until he reached the waistband of her jeans.

He unbuttoned them, but made no move to push them off her hips. Instead, he skimmed his hands underneath the denim, underneath the fabric of her simple cotton panties, and began to lazily stroke her.

He could feel her body shuddering, her muscles tensing as she leaned into his caress, searched for more than just the ghost of a touch he was giving her. *"Facile, ma jolie,"* he whispered against her ear.

Just as quickly as he'd started it, he put an end to the delicious torture for both of them by pulling his hands free. He traced the lines of the muscles in her strong back with his fingers. They were covered only by the thin material of her simple white wife-beater tank—so thin that he could clearly see the outline of her ravens.

He wanted skin and was running low on patience. He gripped the neckline of the tank and rent it straight down the middle. Flicking the clasp on her bra, he bared the expanse of inked caramel skin to his touch.

He put his mouth to the skin of her back, felt the slightly raised lines of the tattoo and decided he liked it. Her skin radiated heat like a furnace as he rained light kisses up the length of her spine.

When he reached the back of her neck, he stroked a hand down the silky rope of her ponytail. Slowly, he began to wrap it around his hand until he had a grip tight enough to pull her head back, to stretch her neck out and bare it for his assault.

She let out a satisfying hiss as he scraped teeth along the sensitive skin of that long, long neck. Peeling one of her hands off the door, she tried to reach back to touch him.

"I. Said. Stay."

She tensed at his commanding tone but, ever so slowly, pressed her palm back against the door. He knew that she was straddling the border between pissed and intrigued. She seemed willing to see how far he would take it, but if he went too far, she'd knock him on his ass faster than he could blink.

With a hand on the back of her head, he gently pushed her until her cheek rested flat against the door. Her eyes flashed as she narrowed a warning glance on him, but she stayed where she was. Good.

He took hold of the waistband of her jeans and pulled them down her long legs along with her underwear. The graceful movement of her hips captivated him as she stepped out of the garments. He slipped the elastic band out of her hair and let the satiny mass fall down her back.

As she stood there, mostly naked, it was easy to grab her wrist and spin her around to face him. The tattered remains of her top slipped off as he pulled her in for a bruising kiss. Backing her up against the door, he assaulted her lips, demanded that she open for him.

With one hand buried in her hair, he allowed the other one to roam over her soft skin. He poured all of his pent up angst, fear, and anger into that kiss. She took it all and gave her best right back. Her own hands siphoned through his curls, took hold and pulled gently, as was becoming her favorite thing to do.

He could give her everything—lay it all out, the good and the bad—and he didn't have to be afraid she would break. She was strong as steel and just as unwavering. It was one of the things he loved about her.

While that thought did nothing to slow the need racing through his body, it calmed him. Soothed like a balm until all of his frustration drained away with it. He needed to see her, to just look at her. He broke the kiss and stepped back, shaking his head when she tried to follow.

She stood before him, unashamed, wearing nothing but earrings and ink. Her hair was tousled and fell to her waist as a dusky curtain that framed her face. Her body was sleek and toned, with the lithe grace of a jungle cat.

Her eyes flashed in the moonlight—in fact, they almost seemed to emanate their own light—and her lips were lightly swollen from his onslaught. She stared at him with an intensity that threatened to burn him to ash.

To him, she looked like magic.

She cocked her head and studied him right back. She was proud and confident, beautiful and vulnerable, all rolled into one. When he looked at her, he felt a peace he hadn't felt in years, if ever.

Drew's pulse began to speed up, but for different reasons than before. He rubbed his hand across his chest, over his heart, as if he could slow the ache, ease the burn. But it was impossible. He could so easily fall for her. Hell, he was halfway there already.

Pushing thoughts of love aside, he stalked toward her again. His unbearable sense of urgency was eased until all that was left was the desire to worship every inch of her. He took her hand again, brought it to his lips and brushed kisses across her knuckles.

Her eyes widened and she sucked in a sharp breath. He knew she hadn't been expecting tenderness, especially after the way things had started, but he wasn't one to do what was expected. He could be contrary that way.

Pulling her by the hand, he led her into his bedroom.

ꙮ

Raven felt twitchy and off balance. She found it happened a lot around Drew. He was a man she couldn't predict, couldn't con, and she still hadn't quite worked out how she felt about that. One second, all cylinders were firing, and the next...he was looking at her like he wanted to eat her alive. Slowly. With chocolate.

Dazed and disconcerted, she followed him into the bedroom and lay down when he gestured toward the bed. She couldn't help watching as he quickly stripped down to the skin, catching up to her own state of undress.

Lord, but he was magnificent. All muscle and sinewy strength, there wasn't an ounce of fat on him. Really, she could barely see him in the dimly moonlit room. The angular planes of his face cast eerie shadows, but every inch of him was etched into her mind.

She could see his eyes; they glittered as he tracked her. This time when she reached for him, he allowed himself to be pulled down to her. Covering her with that massive, powerful body, he reared up and looked at her.

Under the scrutiny of the glimmering blue gaze, Raven felt stripped bare and raw. It wasn't because she was naked; she'd always been comfortable with her body. It was just Drew. The way he looked at her—it was like he was flaying her open, all the way down to her soul. He pulled at everything in her, asked her for everything, without even realizing it. She didn't know what scared her the most, him asking for it or her wanting to give it freely.

With one hand, he lazily stroked her side from ribcage to thigh, leaving a trail of goosebumps in his wake. His other hand caressed her face, almost reverently. When she tried to turn her head, to break the spell that was holding her hostage, he gently turned her face back to him.

The intensity threatened to burn her up from the inside, to melt all of her carefully placed walls. He worshipped her body so painfully slow, so sweetly, it was more than she could bear. She twisted beneath him, she lifted her hips, trying to bring her heat in contact with his body.

She felt, rather than heard, the light chuckle that rumbled up through his chest, sending pleasant vibrations through her. Her breath caught as he laid his forehead against hers and sighed deeply.

"Damn, woman, you'll be the death of me yet," he rasped, but made no move to speed things up. No matter how hard she tried to make it otherwise, he was determined not to let himself be another nameless, faceless hookup. It was like he wanted her to know that he was seeing her, and to make sure that she saw him. Felt him. And that scared her to death.

Did she have feelings for him? Sure. She was a lot of things, but a liar wasn't one of them—even to herself. But she wasn't relationship material, had never pretended otherwise. She had no room in her life for such attachments, she thought, even as she leaned into the warm comfort of his palm against her face.

She could enjoy this without needing it. Couldn't she? When she stared into those deep blue eyes of his, she saw lust, awe, but also a fierce determination that hardened them around the edges. Feeling panic rise again, she looked frantically around the room for something to break the tension, to lighten the mood.

Sweat beaded on her skin, her breathing sped up and her vision narrowed, darkened around the edges. Oh, *God*. She couldn't do this, she had to get away. Away from all of the feelings, the expectations. She didn't do expectations.

His eyes took on a knowing gleam, and his mouth quirked up into a half-smile. "Stop thinking about it so much. This is simple." He punctuated the word "this" by rocking himself against her.

"What?" She didn't squeak the word—much. Damn if the man didn't scramble her brains.

"I can hear the wheels grinding up here so loud," he tapped a finger against her temple, "I think steam's about to come out your ears." He kissed away her reply, and she could feel him smiling against her lips as he continued his leisurely exploration of her body.

Astonishingly, she felt the panic slowly recede. His presence, his touch calmed her, even when her own racing thoughts threatened to consume her, to strangle her.

Pulling back, he treated her to that heart-stopping smile. "Raven," he whispered and then placed another light kiss on her lips. "Let it go. Let me..."

As she watched his eyes searching her face for some kind of answer, she felt the air around them ripple. The rafters groaned and the curtains fluttered as if lifted by an unseen breeze. The atmosphere in the room thickened, vibrating, alive with its own thrumming pulse. It was the sound of her loosening her death grip on the last of her tenuous control.

Her power over the air and space surrounding them relinquished its hold, as well, but, to his credit, he didn't even blink. He just waited. Watched. She swallowed what was left of her fear and met his unwavering gaze with a direct stare of her own. After a brief pause to take in a shaky breath, she tilted her head in an almost imperceptible nod.

He needed no further invitation. Drew pulled her leg high on his hip and slid inside her in one fluid motion. Sensation crashed over her like waves on the beach and radiated from the place they were joined.

Her breath hitched and she clutched at his massive shoulders, trying to find purchase in the flood. All she could focus on was the exquisite torture of his heat filling her. He held his body still, but she could see the muscles in his arms and shoulders bunch and shake.

Biting down on her earlobe, he began a slow slide that threatened to make her lose her sanity. She closed her eyes and stars swam behind her lids. She coasted her fingers over his rippling muscles and allowed her hands to settle at his hips, encouraging his rhythm.

He braced an arm on either side of her head buried his face in the crook of her shoulder. When he sped up, she matched him, and dug her nails into his hips to hang on. His breath began to spill out in halting gasps that fluttered over her heated skin, and his rhythm faltered. The feeling of being the cause of the dignified Dr. Deveraux losing control of himself mixed with the mesmerizing sensations of hard heat sliding over soft pliant skin, took her over the edge.

She cried out his name on a keening wail, felt him bite down on the sensitive skin of her shoulder. His thrusts were punctuated with gasping incoherent words, until he finally lost himself in her.

In the aftermath, Drew dropped like a stone. Raven welcomed his warm weight pressing her into the mattress. Smiling to herself when she felt him nuzzle closer into her neck and sigh, she stared up at the ceiling and sifted fingers through his curls.

I should be freaking out, she thought as she listened to his breathing deepen and slow. *Why am I not freaking out?* It was a question she didn't have an answer to. Things may look differently in the morning, but right then, in that moment, Raven was okay. She didn't feel panic or fear, only peace as she followed Drew—*her* Drew—into sweet oblivion.

Chapter Twenty Nine

Everything hurt. Ray figured that meant he was still alive, but, then again, maybe he died and went to hell. A hell in which his brains were scraped out of his skull with a dull butter knife. Okay, that was a bit melodramatic, but, *shit,* that's what it felt like.

He tried to sleep, to surrender into unconsciousness, but an incessant dripping noise echoed in his ear. He cracked one heavy lid open and was treated to a blurry, sideways view of the stark concrete floor. Drip. Drip. Drip.

What the hell was that anyway? Ray tried to turn his head and look, but his neck started screaming fucking bloody murder, so he stilled. Drip. Drip. Drip. Oh, right. Ray realized that the dripping sound was the blood oozing from one of his many head wounds, dripping down his nose to plop wetly on the floor, only to congeal in a puddle in front of him.

Ray squeezed his good eye shut again and took a deep, shuddering breath. Enough with this already. It would be so easy just to give up. But every time he started thinking that way, Raven's face would pop into his mind again. Had to survive. Had to warn her.

Ray hadn't seen Azibel in what felt like a couple of days, and it had been around twelve hours since her goons had last worked him over. Where were they? Maybe they had finally decided to kill him, and were working out what to do with his body. That would just figure.

A door slamming drew his attention, but he kept his eyes closed, feigning sleep. No need to invite torture if he could avoid it. He tracked the sound of heavy footfalls from the back of the warehouse until they stopped a few inches from his face.

Ray held his breath, did his best to look well and truly dead. Eventually, he felt the toe of a heavy boot nudge his shoulder. Seconds later, a gravelly voice pierced the silence.

"You dead?"

Ray's pulse began to pound in his ears, and his hopes soared when he realized that the voice was unfamiliar—meaning it wasn't Azibel or her muscle. There was no choice but to take the chance, so he opened his eyes and blinked rapidly to clear them. All he could see was a pair of spit-shined tactical boots floating in his field of vision.

"Who's askin'?" he groaned. His voice sounded unfamiliar to his own ears, like his vocal chords had been massaged with sandpaper.

"A friend," came the brusque reply. "Can you stand?"

Ray felt the stranger's hand on his arm, helping him to push his aching body up off the concrete. He closed his eyes and breathed deep when the room pitched wildly.

"Take it easy," the man said. "Just breathe. Let me know when you're ready to try and get up."

As he sat cross-legged on the cold floor, Ray panted and waited for his world to stop spinning. When the nausea receded a bit, he opened his eyes and looked up at the stranger. If he hadn't been getting the life beaten out of him daily for the last week, he might have been scared of the fucker. Kitted out in fatigues, the dude had a gnarly scar down the side of his face, but even scarier were his cold, dead eyes.

Uncertain that it had been the right call to show his hand, Ray gave the man a skeptical look. You didn't survive prison without heavy doses of suspicion and self preservation. "Who are you? Who sent you?"

"A friend," he repeated.

A friend, Ray thought. He wasn't sure which question that was supposed to be the answer to, but it certainly didn't satisfy his curiosity. "What's your name?"

"No names," the man barked, spoken like a soldier who was used to his orders being obeyed. "Need to get you up."

Ray couldn't stifle his yelp as the man pulled on his dislocated shoulder to help him off the ground. Batting his hands away, Ray managed to get his feet underneath him and push himself up into a wobbly standing position.

"Look, friend, if you're helping me get out of here, we need to go, before Ugly and Uglier come back."

The man raised a dark brow. "If you mean the two no-necks outside, they're not coming back." His face was hard and expressionless as he spoke of the fate of the two men.

"What about her?"

"Her, who?"

"Azibel. She's the one pulling the strings."

"I've been casing this place for three days and I haven't seen any woman. Whoever she was, she's long gone by now."

Panic gripped Ray as fear surged into his chest. If she was no longer in the city, then she'd probably found the information she was looking for and was on her way to find his daughter. "Raven," he whispered, suddenly unable to take a breath. He shook his head when the man gave him a what-the-fuck look. "My daughter. She's after my daughter. I've got to find her, and I need your help."

Rolling his eyes, the stranger pushed his shoulder up under Ray's good arm and helped him walk. "Way ahead of you, old man."

Ray glared, and the man smirked.

"Who the hell are you calling old?" he grumbled to himself.

Chapter Thirty

Drew whistled as he punched in the code and turned off the perimeter alarm, allowing Bex and Eric to pass through and relieve the night guard. He knew he was grinning to himself like an idiot—had caught more than one odd look from Bex—but he couldn't help it.

That morning, he'd expected to wake up alone, as he seemed to always do after spending the night with Raven. Certain she'd have had another attack of conscience, reality, panic, or whatever it was that always caused her to pull away, he'd prepared himself for an empty bed.

So when he'd woken and found her curled into his side with her head pillowed on his chest, warm and naked in his bed, he was more than a little shocked. When he'd brushed a hand over that thick mane of hair, she raised her face and gave him a sleepy smile.

His heart had stuttered in his chest, giving him the urge to rub it like he had the night before. He researched bones and artifacts from long-dead civilizations, spoke countless different languages, and was currently translating a text from a centuries-old race of witches.

All of that, and he was being brought to his knees by the smile of one tiny woman. A powder keg inside a deceptively delicate shell. God, he was in *so* much trouble.

She had kissed him sweetly, rolled onto her back, and stretched like a cat, unconcerned with her nakedness. Needing to take a walk before he said something he shouldn't, he dragged his tired ass out of bed and got ready for work.

A Stiles & Nash team had worked through the night to get the new system up and running, concerned with the new threat to the safety of the scientists and their students. Drew was happy to give it over to their capable hands.

The perimeter line had been buried, the keypad calibrated, and he and Larkin had been given the code. It was time for all of them to get back to the business of bringing up those remains.

Drew sighed as he saw Oz Larkin striding toward him from the makeshift parking lot, red-faced and fuming. *Great.* Drumming up a smile with control he didn't know he had, Drew stepped forward to meet him. "Oz," he said, nodding.

"Where the hell is she?" he demanded.

At a loss, Drew raised both hands then dropped them to his sides. "I give up. Where's who?"

"Your new intern from U of E. She didn't show up for her shift yesterday afternoon. I thought you said she was dependable!"

Drew could barely suppress an eye-roll. Damn Brynna and her ridiculous cover story. He rubbed his temple and sighed audibly. "Relax Oz, she was a little under the weather yesterday. I told her to sleep it off. I was getting ready to call her to see how she was feeling."

That seemed to mollify Larkin for the time being, his face taking on a more human color. "She is a looker, that one. Be a shame to let her go." He elbowed Drew in the ribs and cackled.

This time, he did nothing to stop from rolling his eyes. Larkin was an old horndog, all bark and no bite. He was harmless, but if he went sniffing around Brynna, he might not come back with all his parts intact. "Believe me Oz, you'd be barking up the wrong scratching post with that one," he said and headed for the relative quiet of the lab tent.

"What? She into chicks or something?" Oz called after him with an exaggerated leer. That's okay!"

"Oh, for the love..." Drew mumbled as he let the tent curtain close behind him.

Looking around the lab, he closed his eyes and breathed a much needed sigh of relief. *Bless Hammer and his neuroses*. The kid had worked with Drew for a couple of years now, and knew his professor's habits and preferences, as well as he knew his own. He had done his best to put the lab back exactly the way Drew liked it—and did a fairly decent job of it.

Before he could get to work, Drew had to call Brynna and warn her about the consequences of getting on the boss's radar. Digging out his phone, he hit the number five speed dial button and waited for her to pick up.

Voicemail, naturally. He did what the cheerful recording asked and left a message after the beep. "Hey Brynna, it's Drew. Look, I get the need for a cover story, but it only works if you actually show up. Get in here for your shift today or I'll have to tell Oz that I fired you."

After he flipped the phone shut, Drew sighed and stuffed it in his back pocket. He was just getting ready to go out to the grid to check out the progress when Hammer entered the tent. The young man dipped his head respectfully, but he was practically bouncing on the balls of his feet.

"Hey, Professor!"

"Morning, Hammer. How're things coming out there?"

Hammer was buzzing with excitement and grinning from ear to ear. "I think we're ready to bring her up," he blurted. "Daisy, I mean. We made some pretty significant progress in the sediment yesterday afternoon. We should have the skeleton completely excavated in the next couple of hours!"

The kid's excitement was catching, and Drew couldn't help but grin back at him. They were finally going to get some answers, and maybe even get the protestors off their back. *Or it could just get worse*, the little voice in his head taunted.

Well, regardless of what would or wouldn't make the conservationists happy, they had to find out what they were dealing with. "Sounds good. Let the rest of the team handle that for the moment. I need you here in the lab."

"Sure, Prof—er, Drew," he said when Drew raised a brow at him. Hammer grabbed one of the lab coats hanging on the rack and shrugged into it. "What're we working on?"

"We need to harvest a couple of bone samples to send back to the ASU research lab for radiocarbon dating. I have my suspicions, but we need it confirmed."

Hammer pegged him with a direct gaze. "You don't think this is a Native American Burial site, do you?"

Drew gave a quick shake of his head, unwilling to give away too much of his theory yet. "No, I don't. Not an ancient one, by any means. But I don't want to be shut down before we can figure out just what the hell it is."

He slid his laptop across the metal lab table to Hammer. "Each sample needs to be photographed and added to the log. If anything is moved, it needs to be signed-out then back in when it comes back."

Hammer nodded and blinked owlishly behind his thick black frames, already typing furiously into the log.

"I'm going to unpack the portable x-ray machine. We need to get films on the skull for documentation. They can also be used for dental identification, if need be." Startled, Hammer glanced up with questions in his expression that Drew wasn't ready to answer. "Just in case," he said with a reassuring pat to the intern's shoulder.

He couldn't put his finger on it yet, but Drew had a bad feeling about what they were going to unearth in the Black Valley basin.

ꙮ

By midmorning, the team had freed the skeleton and all remaining pieces where intact. Pristine, in fact, which didn't bode well for their discovery. Hammer assisted Drew and laid out the bones on the metal examination table.

They began meticulously cataloguing, tagging, photographing, and arranging the bones into a complete skeleton. Drew was searching for the fourth metatarsal to complete the left foot when he was startled by a tap on his shoulder.

He whirled around and found himself face to face with a chagrined Brynna. "*Fuck!* B—uh, Ms. Murphy. You scared me."

"Sorry to interrupt your work...Professor, but I wanted to let you know that I came in early. Also, Dr. Larkin wanted me to tell you that they've found more remains."

He was so distracted by her sudden appearance that it took him a few seconds to register what she'd said. "What? More remains, so soon?"

Brynna nodded, feline eyes serious. Too serious. "They were buried directly under the first skeleton," she said grimly, and it was obvious that she understood the implications. Native Americans were respectful of their dead, as were most cultures. Unlike his home town of New Orleans, there was no call to stack the dead this high above sea level.

"Damn," he hissed, shoving a hand through his hair. "Do you think Larkin has figured it out yet?"

Fiery curls fluttered about as Brynna shook her head. "I don't think so, but it won't take him long. He's not an idiot—in this respect, anyway. The dirt is loosened from the first excavation, so we may be able to bring the second one up today, too."

Dazed, Drew simply nodded and turned back to Hammer, wondering if he'd caught on to what they were saying. Luckily, the kid was staring after Brynna like a starving dog looking at the last steak. Drew smirked and clapped him on the back, trying to cover his trepidation. "Not for you, kid. She'd eat you alive."

They worked in silence for two solid hours before getting to the cervical area of the skeleton. They had to catalog and piece together the sternum and clavicle, both scapulas and the cervical vertebrae up to where the skull would be attached.

Hammer was in the process of photographing the fractured shoulder blade—the one the stolen bone fragment was from. After he'd photographed the inside of it, he gently turned it over to document the other side, and promptly dropped it like it had burned him. "What in the holy hell?"

With a frown, Drew looked over from the makeshift x-ray lab he'd set up. "Easy with the merchandise, kid! What happened?"

"You gotta see this," Hammer answered. He stared at the bone like it had suddenly grown four legs and a tail.

Heaving a put upon sigh, Drew powered down the machine and crossed the tent to look over Hammer's shoulder. He was sure his heart stopped when he looked down at the flat, fractured piece of bone.

They had found the origin of the strange etchings in the bone. Surrounding the missing piece was what was left of a *Vigilati* signa, scored—no, branded into the bone. "Holy fuck," Drew whispered, unaware that he'd spoken aloud until Hammer looked up at him.

"It's just like the box, right? The symbol."

Drew couldn't catch his breath. This couldn't be happening. He'd come here for a dig, met Raven by coincidence, introduced her to Isla and Jeremiah because they were his friends.

But *this*. This made it impossible to think of any of it as a coincidence. Now, the site he was excavating was the home of a...what? A *Bruixi* cemetery? Or something much, much worse. A dump site for the *auchrim*, maybe.

Clutching his head as a vicious headache pounded through, Drew groaned. "Oh, God."

Hammer stood up and put a hand on his shoulder. "Professor. Drew, you need to sit down."

Drew allowed his intern to push him into a chair and force his head between his knees. He took deep, gasping breaths, and tried to get himself under control. What were the odds of this? About a zillion-to-one. He suddenly felt like they were all dangling from the strings of some invisible puppet master who was just waiting to cut one.

"Listen, Hammer," he croaked.

"Let me guess. Don't tell anyone?" When Drew shook his head, Hammer's dark brows pulled low over warm brown eyes. "What's going on? I know you have an idea of what these symbols mean. Tell me. Maybe I can help."

"I wish it were that simple, kid, but there are lives at stake here. I just need a little more time," Drew pleaded, placing a hand on Hammer's arm. "Please."

Hammer acted like he wanted to say more, but then he gave a quick nod. "Like I said, Professor. I trust you. I just hope you know what you're doing."

He tossed Drew one last sympathetic look, then left him alone with the bones.

ജ൫

Drew was dead on his feet by the time he reached the door of room 213. He was still reeling from the implications of what they'd found at the site, couldn't quite wrap his brain around it yet. The team had started excavating the second skeleton but were cut short by the sudden onset of a storm. Such was the way in the mountains; storms blew in out of nowhere and were sometimes gone just as fast. But occasionally they lingered, like tonight.

Almost too exhausted to summon the energy to open the door, Drew rested his forehead against the door and took a deep breath. Once inside, because he didn't want to further aggravate his growing migraine by turning on the lights, he dropped his keys on a table and put away his coat from muscle memory alone. He rapped his shin on one of the desk chairs for his trouble, and nearly fell over. With a curse, he gave up and flicked on the lamp.

The room became illuminated with the soft glow of a dim high-efficiency bulb that cast shadows at odd angles. Drew's entire body went taut as a bowstring as it recognized what his brain had not. That he was not alone.

The remaining desk chair had been pulled out into the middle of the room, in the empty space between the desk and the living room furniture. A man was slumped over in it with his chin resting on his chest, and he wasn't moving. At first glance, Drew thought he may have been tied up, but his arms hung loosely at his sides.

Not tied, but definitely unconscious. *What the f...*Matthieu, he thought. The unconscious man must be Ray. Had to be. Never one for finesse, Matty must have tracked Ray down and dumped him where he was meant to be. Drew would be surprised if Matthieu had even let the other man get a look at him.

Drew pulled up the other chair and straddled it to face Ray Sabatier. Taking advantage of the almost comatose state, Drew took the opportunity to study the man who was Raven's father.

He was tan, but not as dark-skinned as Raven. His hair was black and going silver at the temples, and long enough to flop over his face, shrouding much of it from view. He had several days' growth of salt-and-pepper beard dusting his stubborn-looking jaw. That's one thing he knew the man shared with Raven.

With a scowl, Drew looked closer and noticed the bruises, scratches, and cuts that marred the man's otherwise smooth skin. The one eye that wasn't obscured by hair was bruised black, and his nose had clearly been broken at some point.

Bile rose in Drew's throat even as his fists clenched in anger. Hell, he didn't know the man, but no one deserved this—especially not Raven's father. Who had done this? Why had they taken Ray and held him hostage? Clearly, it was more than just a simple mugging, and if it was a hit, well, it obviously didn't go down the way it was intended.

Drew sat up straighter as Ray began to groan and thrash his head from side to side. "Easy," he said. He tried to keep his voice calm and non-confrontational.

Ray's hands came up to rub his face and when he lifted them away, his hair had been pushed back and revealed a jagged cut across his other eye. Drew sucked in a breath and cursed softly.

Ray's brows pulled low over his eyes as he stared down at his wrists. It looked as though he was surprised to find them unbound. What had the man been through? When his dark brown eyes met Drew's, he blinked rapidly to clear his vision. He tried shaking his head, but that just roused another litany of groans.

"Bastard drugged me," he said, his voice muffled by his hands once again covering his face.

Drew suppressed the urge to laugh at that. Just like Matty, bastard and all. "That's entirely likely."

Ray narrowed his eyes and looked at him suspiciously, and, just like that, Drew saw Raven in him.

"Where am I? Who the hell are you?" Ray croaked. His voice sounding to Drew's ears like he had gargled with sulphuric acid.

"A friend."

Ray barked out a bitter laugh. "The last *friend* I made drugged me, dumped me here, so...I think I can do without that kind of friend."

Damn it, Matthieu, would it kill you to develop a few people skills? Drew knew there was no hope for the kid, so he focused on the man before him. Cocking his head to study Ray, he extended his hand. "Andrew Deveraux."

"Great, nice to meet ya. Now back to my other question. Where am I?"

"We'll get to all that, Mr. Sabatier. The man who...delivered you here is a friend of mine. When you disappeared, we called him to track you down. One of his many very special talents. We were worried about you, but we also have some questions for you."

Ray held completely still, but his eyes darted around the room, Drew assumed, to find the nearest exit. "Track me down...Wait, *we*? We, who?"

"Me, a few of my friends. Raven," he said gauging Ray's reaction. To his credit, the only thing that gave him away was a slight widening of his eyes.

He tried to rise from his chair but flopped back down with a wince. "What do you know about Raven."

Rubbing his eyes, Drew sent up an internal plea for patience. "Like I said, I'm a friend. When you didn't show up for your lunch with Nash, he called Raven because he was worried that something had happened to you. Clearly, he was right. Care to enlighten me?"

Drew watched as the other man's expression went flat, completely blank. Good poker face, he thought. "I'm not telling you anything. You could just be makin' all of this up. I want to see Raven."

Drew pretended to mull that over for a moment while he regarded Ray silently. He could see exactly where Raven got her suspicious nature and her street smarts from. "All right," he said with a concise nod, "I'll go find her. If you take off, you'll never see her, so I suggest you stay put."

Ray raised that stubborn jaw and looked him square in the eye. "I'm not going to leave my daughter again," he said, and Drew believed him.

Getting up from the chair, he started for the door but turned around again to face Ray. "I'll say to you exactly what your buddy Micah said to me. If you hurt her, I'm gonna crazy murder you, dig?"

Ray look stunned for a moment, then burst out a bark of gravelly laughter that ended in a fit of coughing. The smile disappeared from his face as quickly as it had come. "That's supposed to be my line," he grumbled.

Drew stared hard at him for a moment then looked down. "I think you gave up that right years ago," he said in a quiet voice.

Ray nodded, but when Drew saw the anguish in the other man's eyes, his remorse was instantaneous. It wasn't his business anyway.

"You're right about that. I fucked it up good," Ray said.

Drew sighed and approached Ray's chair again. "Hey, you're both alive and *free*." He aimed a pointed look at Ray. "So it's not too late. The choices you made may have been mistakes, but it's never too late to turn it around, Ray."

Ray swallowed and stared down at his hands. "Hope you're right," he whispered. "Shit. Micah. We're at Cliffton's place, aren't we?"

"That's the one," Drew answered with a smile. "I'm going to go find Raven and ask if she wants to see you."

Without waiting for an answer, Drew turned his back to the sad hopefulness he saw in the other man's expression, and left him in the same spot in which he'd found him.

Chapter Thirty One

Raven had never had a woman in her life. Not once. And now she had two. It was a strange animal, the friendship of females, one that would take some getting used to. Nevertheless, she was supposed to meet the women in question today at the Watauga County Public Library to do some research.

She was early, as was her habit, when she arrived at the charmingly rustic A-frame building that housed the library. Walking up the sidewalk, she stopped short when she saw Isla and Brynna engaged in a heated discussion in the parking lot.

She quickly ducked behind a stone column and looked on with curiosity. As she watched the women argue, she resisted the urge to jump to the defense of her *feradux*. It was truly a bizarre relationship. She knew that Brynna could take care of herself, that Isla would never hurt her, but she couldn't help feeling the pull to step in.

One of the perks to having the power to manipulate the atmosphere was that sound waves were just another form of space. She had the ability to use the surrounding obstacles to reflect the sounds back toward her—much like the sonar of a bat, or echolocation of a whale. Using her power, she was able to pick up bits and pieces of their argument.

"...really need to tell her about it." Isla's voice was heated and emphatic.

"...so much to deal with already, she needs time to adjust."

"...*laqueum* won't wait for her t'be ready. She needs to prepare herself."

"...don't want her to run..."

"...need to tell her..."

Okay, enough was enough. It was clear they were talking about her, and if there was one thing she couldn't abide, it was people trying to make decisions for her, no matter how well meaning.

Raven masked her presence until she was right behind the two women. "Need to tell me what?" she asked, and she felt momentary satisfaction when they jumped apart guiltily.

Isla glared at Brynna, and Brynna heaved a massive sigh and shrugged. "Fine. Raven, come sit with us."

Raven allowed herself to be led to a bench just outside the library. She sat down and Brynna joined her, while Isla sat on Brynna's other side. They both wore expressions that bespoke trepidation, and a little sympathy.

Annoyed, Raven narrowed her eyes at them. "What's the secret? I'm a big girl."

Isla leaned toward her and spoke softly even though they were alone at the moment. "In *Bruixi* culture, there is a phenomenon called the *laqueum.* The term refers to the bond between a *Bruixi* witch and her mate."

Raven rolled her eyes. "What's that have to do with me? I'm not *mating* with anyone."

"Supposedly," Brynna interjected, "the mates are sort of...predestined. Chosen by fate as the perfect match to produce optimal qualities in their offspring."

"*What?* Offspring?"

Isla slapped a hand over Brynna's mouth. "Sssh, beauty. You're not allowed to talk anymore." With a warning look at the redhead, Isla turned back to Raven, "A *bruixi* will instinctively be drawn to her ideal mate, but the *laqueum* won't take effect until the two have declared their feelings for one another. It's sort of nature's loophole, an out clause, if you will. If she never claims her mate, she's free to be alone, to carry on relationships with others."

Raven pinched the bridge of her nose. "Okay, so what does it matter, then?"

"Well, all I have are my hypotheses, since we've found no evidence to back them up. But I believe that a *Bruixi* would only be able to have children with her chosen mate. While that may not matter to some," she gave Raven a pointed look, "it's something to consider. Also, it's possible that one could live her entire life feeling like something was missing. I know I would have."

"But...?"

"But I don't have to. Jeremiah is my mate. He makes me so much stronger. *Bruixi* mates have latent power that strengthens our own."

"How do you know? That he's your mate, I mean. How can you be sure?"

"That's the easy part. Once the couple voices their feelings for each other, the *Bruixi signa* will appear on the mate's body."

Raven's mind was reeling. She could feel the panic stir inside her. She hated the idea that someone was behind the curtain, controlling their lives. Struggling to slow her breathing, she tried to get a grip. Sure, she had feelings for Drew, but it wasn't love. Was it? No, no, Raven knew better than to fall in love. And surely, Drew did, as well.

When Brynna noticed Raven's distress, she tossed an irritated look at Isla and patted Raven's hand. "Easy, dearling. It only matters if you let it. If you don't have feelings for the man, then you won't be mated. And if you do, well, then it shouldn't bother you to be mates. Right?"

"Right," Raven managed to squeak through her rapidly closing throat. She coughed and stood abruptly. "Enough of that business. Can we get on with the research, please?" She didn't wait for an answer, just simply turned on her heel and headed for the library, but she didn't miss the worried look that passed between her two friends.

ഗ്ഗ

Once inside the library, the three women split up. Raven found a computer to do an Internet search about Malenka, while Isla attacked the microfilm machine. Brynna had decided to scour the catalog and shelves for any *Bruixi* references.

Raven quickly became frustrated with the wide range of results of her Google search. She just didn't have enough information to narrow down the search. Hell, she didn't even know if she was spelling Malenka right. She had no last name, no address, and no way of knowing if the woman was alive or dead—or just a figment of Raven's fevered imagination.

Laying her head down on the desk, Raven groaned when Brynna patted her on the shoulder. "Any luck?"

"Not even a little," Brynna said. "There aren't many books on witchcraft to begin with, and all of the ones I've found have been centered on Wicca. How about you?"

"I got squat. I just don't know enough. All I have is a first name and an image of her face in my head."

"Too bad you're not looking for a criminal. You could just go through a database of mug shots," Brynna said, walking off to go check on Isla.

Her words, however, planted a seed of an idea in Raven's mind. "Irish, you're a freaking genius." She brought up a fresh browser window, typed in *Malenka, Blowing Rock, NC* into the search bar, and clicked on the "images" link.

As she scrolled through pages and pages of thumbnail images, Raven began to get discouraged as nothing looked familiar. When she was just about to give up and go find the girls, she noticed a thumbnail of a young woman at the bottom of the tenth page.

Clicking on the image to enlarge it, she sucked in a breath when she saw the woman's face clearly. That was her, all right. Long brown hair, brown eyes, *signa* clearly visible on her neck. When Raven clicked on the link, it took her to an article in the Mountain Times newspaper.

Raven had to put a hand over her mouth to prevent herself from shouting as she scanned the headline then the article itself.

THREE LOCAL WOMEN MISSING - SHERIFF HAS NO LEADS

Malenka Jovanovich, a twenty-six-year old Slovenian immigrant, was reported missing this morning by her roommate. Jovanovich is the third woman to disappear in the last two weeks. The other two women – locals Erin Kelley, 24, and Mariah Truesdale, 23, were both reported missing last week.

All three women have brown hair, brown eyes, and similar builds. We tried to contact the Watauga County Sheriff's Office to confirm there may be a connection between the three disappearances, but they declined to comment.

Our sources in the department tell us the police have no viable leads at this time. Though, other than age and appearance, the three women share another unifying characteristic – a similar tattoo. Could we be dealing with gang related violence? Or worse, a serial kidnapper or killer? The Mountain Times continues to investigate.

The article was dated almost two years ago, and there were no other follow-up articles. It looked like the trail just went cold. Struggling to keep her mouth shut, Raven gestured wildly at Brynna, who grabbed Isla by the arm and pulled her over to the computers.

"You guys have to read this," Raven whispered.

She watched her friends skim the article, saw the point where their eyes widened as they put two and two together.

"Omigod!" Brynna hissed. "If this article is to be believed, someone out here may have been kidnapping and killing the *Vigilati*."

"Only they don't know it. The police think these are just random girls who may have been involved in some kind of gang, or visited the same tattoo shop," Isla said.

Raven printed out a copy of the article. "We need to show this to the guys. I don't know how it's all connected, but I'm sure it is."

The three of them packed up quietly and made their way outside. Raven's phone rang, and she smiled to herself when she saw it was Drew. She turned her back on the smirks and eye rolls from her friends.

"Hey"

"Raven." He said her name like a prayer, and it never failed to give her chills. "Where are you?"

"We just finished up at the library. I think I may have found something big, but we want to get your opinion on it."

"Great. I've got a couple of big things to share with you, as well. Can you come back to the inn now?"

Raven frowned at his tone, not impatient, anxious, though. She'd never heard Drew sound quite so uncertain, and it caused her stomach to clench with nerves. "Sure, we're headed your way. Shouldn't take us but a few minutes."

"Good," he breathed a sigh of relief. "Raven?"

"Yeah?"

There was a long pause, as if he struggled to find the words he was looking for. In the end, he gave up. "Never mind. Just be careful, okay?"

"Okay, Drew. We'll see you soon."

CHAPTER THIRTY TWO

Drew was waiting on the sagging porch of the tavern when Raven pulled in on the Ducati. Parking under the shade of some trees, she couldn't help but smile at the little flip her stomach did as she walked toward him.

The feeling quickly fled when she caught sight of his expression, an incongruous mixture of despair and hope. It caused her throat to clench and her heart to speed up. Something was wrong. Immediately, her eyes began to dart around the parking lot, looking for a threat.

"Raven."

He held a hand out for her, so she stepped onto the porch and placed her own hand in it. Drew pulled her into his body, wrapped his arms around her and held on tight. He held on like the embrace was the only thing keeping his world from turning on its ear.

"Hi," she said, her voice muffled by the soft fabric of his shirt.

Chuckling lightly, he inched back to allow her some room to breathe, but didn't break the contact. Raven looked up into stormy blue eyes and she wondered what was causing her man so much worry.

"Did something happen at the dig?"

With a sigh, he stepped back and shoved a hand through his curls, still clasping her hand tightly in his other. "Yes, but it can wait until later. I've got something to tell you." The way he looked at her—like she would go insane or dissolve into hysterics once she heard his news—was causing her nerves to sizzle under her skin.

"Oh hell, just say it. You're freaking me out."

"Matthieu found your father."

It was the last thing she expected to hear. Her mind reeled as she was bombarded with dozens of different emotions. Relief, anger...fear. Was he alive? Was he hurt? Or worse, was he on another bender? Unsure of how to respond, she went with her tried and true standby—snark.

"That quick, huh? Which means he wasn't bothering to hide from anyone. Just didn't give a shit, most likely. So where'd he find him? Holed up in some dirty motel room with his best friends, Jack and Johnny—black-not-red-thank-you-very-much? I can't believe he just stood Ryder up like that...making him worry. The selfish bastard!"

Drew grabbed her shoulders in a soft grip and gave her a gentle shake to put an end to her rant. "Raven, stop! Breathe, love."

His voice cut through her frenzy, soothed as it always did. She leaned her forehead against his chest she gulped in a few deep breaths.

"I don't know where Matthieu found him. He's rather unorthodox in his methods. Apparently, he drugged Ray for the trip and dumped him in my room upstairs without so much as a howdy."

"And you think he's still up there?" She said with an eye roll and a snort. She wasn't proud of herself for acting like petulant child, but that's what talk of her father reduced her to sometimes.

Drew's direct gaze never flagged. "Yes, I do. You need to prepare yourself, Raven. He's been roughed up pretty good."

That statement was like a knife in the stomach. Gone was the latent teenage angst, the anger, the disappointment. All that mattered was that her father was here, and he was hurt.

"What? Where is he? I need to see him."

"Just be sure."

"I am."

ꙮ

The trip up to Drew's room went by in a haze, and, before she knew it, Raven was standing in front of the door. Raven drummed up what was left of her courage, opened it and stepped inside. The first thing she registered was that the television was on. That was a good sign, wasn't it?

However, a cursory sweep of the room left her disappointed when she saw no one. Just when she was about to storm off in an impressive fit of rage, she heard a soft snore coming from the couch. Looking over, she noticed a pair of socked feet propped up on the arm of the sofa. Was it possible that her father was, at present, sleeping on the couch in Drew Deveraux's hotel room?

Drew closed the door loudly behind her, and she heard a startled cough come from the man on the couch. An unkempt mop of dark hair could barely be seen over the back of the furniture.

Raven allowed Drew to take her hand and lead her around the end of the couch to face their visitor. She experienced the revelation in a series of flashes. Black hair, graying at the temples. Warm, chocolate brown eyes. Weathered skin with a perpetual tan.

The visions turned dark. Bruises. Black eyes. Broken nose. Scratches and cuts marring that beloved face. Fierce protectiveness welled up inside her, the depth of which she'd never even fathomed. She wanted to find who had done this to her father. Her blood.

She heard a keening wail fill the room. It seemed so far away, even when she realized it was coming from her own throat. Before she could think, she launched herself at him. "Daddy!" she cried, wrapping her arms around him and sobbing into his neck.

She couldn't remember the last time she'd called him Daddy, if she ever had. But it didn't matter to her just then. He was her father, he was hurt. But he was safe and with her now.

He stroked her hair and whispered in her ear. She couldn't make out what he was saying, but the words didn't matter either. The meaning was universal. Her breath hitched when he squeezed her tighter, and she let herself sink into the feeling of being safe in her father's arms.

All the while, she felt Drew's presence, supporting but not invading. He knew just what she needed. She reminded herself to thank him later. He was a good man, her Drew.

When she laid her head down over his beating heart, she felt an answering sob wrack her father's solid chest. "Ah, I've missed you, little bird."

"Where have you been? What happened to you?"

Ray started to speak, but she cut him off. "Was this some kind of drug deal gone wrong? A busted up con?"

She couldn't keep the accusation out of her voice, even as she clung to her father's shirt like it was a lifeline.

Ray shook his head vehemently and turned tired, but clear, brown eyes up to her face. "I haven't had a drink or a fix since they hauled me off three years ago. Hell, I don't even smoke. And even I'm not good enough to set up a scam less than an hour after being released from the Pen."

"Then what happened?"

Before Ray could answer, Drew stepped forward, out of the shadows of the room. "Raven, let's wait until the others get here, okay? I don't want Ray to have to tell his story twice."

The older man's brows drew together in confusion. "What others?"

Drew sighed and sat down on the other side of Ray, stretched out his long legs and crossed his ankles on the coffee table. "Friends of ours that were involved in tracking you down. We're dealing with something that may be connected to you, so they have some questions, too." Ray gave him a skeptical look but he pressed on. "Please, just trust us."

Ray gave him a curt nod. "It's not like I have anywhere to be. My girl's here."

When Raven realized she was still clinging to her father, she slumped against the arm of the sofa. "Isla and Brynna should be here shortly. They left the library right after I did. I found something, Drew. Something bad."

Scrubbing both hands over his face, Drew looked over at her from the other end of the couch. "Yeah, me, too. Still, let's wait for the others. I'll text Jere to find the girls and the kid and get up here."

Chapter Thirty Three

Fifteen minutes later, there was a light knock on the door. "It's open," Drew yelled, too damn drained to get up. Jeremiah entered first, hand in hand with Isla. Marduk followed, and Brynna shut the door behind them.

Jeremiah ignored the somber mood in the room, walked through the living room and flopped down in a recliner, pulling his wife down with him.

"Where's the fire, brother?"

Drew cleared his throat to get his best friend's attention. Jeremiah looked at him, then at Raven, then at Ray. After he looked back and forth between Raven and Ray a few times, Drew knew the exact moment he put two and two together.

"Damn, my brother works fast."

Brynna sat on the floor at Raven's feet, while Marduk did the same with Isla. "Brother? What?" the redhead said.

"It didn't take him long at all to find him," Jeremiah answered.

Ray glared at Jeremiah, brows drawing low over his eyes. "That charming asshat was your brother?"

Jeremiah snorted, completely unoffended. "That's the one. A fitting description."

Ever the peacemaker, Isla, smiled sweetly at the newcomer. "Welcome, Mr. Sabatier. We're so glad Matthieu was able to find you, relatively unharmed."

Drew watched as Ray lost the struggle and smiled back at her. "Thank you, ma'am. However rough he was, that man saved my life, and I'm grateful to him."

"Oh, go on with your ma'am. I'm Isla, an' this brute is my husband, Jeremiah. Down there is Marduk, and over by Raven is Brynna. And, of course, you met Drew."

Ray nodded politely at them. "It's nice to meet you all."

Raven stood and began to pace restlessly. "Now that we've all met, can we get to the explanations? Please?"

Taking pity on her, Drew turned to Ray. "As you can probably tell, I was as surprised as you by your sudden appearance here. Matthieu didn't give us any details, so you'll have to fill in the blanks. What happened to you, Ray?

"I had just gotten released. From prison," he clarified for the rest of the group. "Ryder had sent a car for me because he had a meeting downtown. The plan was to go to my place first then meet Ry at a neighborhood diner for lunch."

Raven sat down on the coffee table and faced him. "Ry said you never showed."

"The diner was close, so I walked. Cut down an alley, got ambushed. They worked me over, knocked me out, and I woke up in some kind of abandoned warehouse. I was unconscious a lot of the time, but I was beaten and tortured every couple of days. I'm fairly sure they would have killed me," he turned to look at Jeremiah, "if your brother hadn't...disposed of them first."

Drew sensed that he was holding back, and prompted him further. "Why would someone do that to you?"

"Why does any psycho do what psychos do? I've lived a rough life, most of it on the wrong side of the law. I'm sure I've made a lot of enemies along the way."

His eyes cut to the left then fixed on Raven in front of him. Now Drew was sure he wasn't telling them everything, but he left it alone for the time being.

"Maybe I'll get Matthieu to look into it when he comes back into town." He was bluffing, of course. Jeremiah knew it, but Ray didn't. He saw the nervous look in the other man's eyes before his expression shuttered. "But first, we need to ask you some questions. They're not going to make any sense right away, but just bear with us."

"Hey, I've got nothing to hide," Ray said, his eyes flicking to the left again. "They kind of take care of that in prison."

Drew looked over at Jeremiah and Isla, and, knowing they were probably the leading experts on the *Praedos,* hoped one of them would chime in. No such luck. It seemed like he had been elected the unofficial leader of this inquisition by secret ballot. He guessed he could take the hit, for Raven's sake.

"Alrighty then. I'm not going to bullshit you, Ray. Is Raven really your daughter?"

Drew watched the man freeze with his glass of water halfway to his lips. Slowly, he set it down again with a shaking hand. His face clouded angrily as he rounded on Drew.

"What kind of fucking question is that? Of *course,* she's my daughter." He gave Raven a pained look. "Are you trying to prove I'm not your father?"

Drew remained calm as he figured the man had a right to his outrage. "I'm sorry if this offends you, I really am. But it's extremely important that we know for sure. Like, life or death important."

Ray gave Raven a helpless look, but she merely shrugged and hung her head. Drew's hands itched to reach for her—she looked so small and lost—but he knew she wouldn't be receptive to it just yet.

"Are you positive, Ray?"

"Hell, I'm as positive as any man can be! We've had three different paternity tests done, at different times, in different labs, and each came back with the same result—that I'm Raven's biological father. The first one was done by CPS when they were trying to locate Raven's next of kin.

"I had my own done when I petitioned to have my name put on her birth certificate. The last one was done when she was eighteen, when I made her my beneficiary and gave her my power of attorney. My lawyer suggested that one, just so that no one could possibly take away what was rightfully hers."

"Is there any chance they could have been forged?" Jeremiah asked with a sympathetic half-smile.

"I suppose there's a minute chance. But three tests, three labs, several years apart, same results? I wouldn't bet those odds."

Propping his chin on his hand, Drew tried to scroll through everything they knew about the *Praedos* in his head. It just didn't add up. None of it did.

Ray's insistent voice cut into his thoughts. "Wanna tell me what this is all about? Why are you asking me this?"

Raven winced as Drew looked over at her helplessly. She knew he was at a loss, didn't know where to begin, how to explain. But, then again, how should she? He'd known about all of this a hell of a lot longer than she had.

But Ray was *her* father. Her. Father. The words repeated over and over in her head until all she could hear was a high-pitched whine. White noise. Mental feedback. She covered her ears and exploded to her feet again.

"Because I'm different, Ray! Because I'm...other."

Good old unflappable Ray, he didn't even blink. She hadn't realized until that moment how much he and Drew had in common.

"You're going to have to give me a little more than that to go on, honey."

"All my life, I've always had a little extra...power," she said, waving her hand in the air as she searched for the right word. "I can move things. Make things happen. I can see in the dark using my other senses. I can hear things that I shouldn't be able to. I can *feel* people disturbing the environment around me. It's why no one can sneak up on me," she said with a nervous smile.

Ray eyed her warily and wet his lips before speaking. "Raven, I'm not exactly sure what you're talking about."

"Neither was I, Dad. Neither was I. You remember this?" She pulled down the neck of her t-shirt to reveal her *signa*. She continued when he nodded. "I know you think I hit some rebellious phase, that I ran out and got a tattoo. In reality, it was so far from that. It just showed up one day. When I turned eight, I woke up and there it was."

"Okay..." Ray's eyes tracked her movement as she paced back and forth.

"After I hooked up with the boys and started the business, I decided it was time to get some answers. I began researching this symbol, and my research led me to Drew, and through him, I met these guys.

"For the first time in my life, I learned I wasn't alone. That I'm part of some...club, clan, race—whateverthefuck—of witches. Powerful beings. Thing is, though? The only way to gain entrance to this secret fucking society is to be fathered by a demon."

His eyes wild, Ray choked on his water. "Sorry?"

"Take Isla, here," she said and pointed to the slender woman perched in her husband's lap. "She's got one of *these* too." Raven flashed her *signa* again, for emphasis. Hearing the psychotic story coming out of her own mouth, she was starting to feel a little hysterical. She silently thanked Isla for turning around to show Ray her own brand.

"You see, Isla found out that her father wasn't really her father at all. Her real father was an evil fucking demon named Alastore. Don't worry, though. She killed him. That's what we're here for, you see. To kill these demons. Apparently, they can only be killed by a blood relative. Go fig, huh?"

Crazy laughter started to bubble up, and Raven could practically feel the straight jacket binding her already. Making eye contact with Drew, she allowed his warm, sky blue gaze to soothe her. He knew she wasn't crazy. He knew, even if her father didn't.

Ray looked at her with a mixture of fear and sympathy. Yeah, pity the poor crazy girl. She pulled aside her t-shirt again and pointed to the spider glyph in the center of her *signa*. "See this? This is supposedly the symbol of the father. Isla has one too," Raven said, and, bless her, Isla turned around again to show him.

"Her father had *that* symbol, right here," she said, and furiously tapped her own forehead for emphasis. "That's how she knew. That it was for real. So if you're my father—and I never doubted that—why do I have one? Why do I have *this*? Why am I this way?"

Ray leaned forward to stare at the symbol, until she began to squirm under his scrutiny. Slowly, he sat back, face white as the driven snow. "Crap on a cracker, I just thought she was psychotic. Goddamn motherfucking black widow."

Raven gaped at him, while Drew sat up at attention.

"What?" he asked. When Ray realized that everyone in the room was staring at him, frozen, he began to babble.

"Black widow...that's what I called her, the crazy bitch. She looked like Lisette, she *was* Lisette. But then she wasn't. Then she was Ms. McCoy. Then she was someone else. And she had th-the thing," he stuttered, tapping his forehead, "the spider. Then the crazy eyes. Crazy eyes and the fangs."

Raven was too stunned to speak, to move. Drew leaned over and touched Ray's arm, but the man flinched away from him.

"Try to hold it together, Ray. You're freaking out."

Ray just shook his head and kept talking. "Don't remember much. The goons just kept beating on me, see. She kept asking about Raven. Where was she? How could she find her?" He turned pleading eyes toward Raven. "I didn't tell her. I wouldn't. Couldn't anyway. She said she was following you, that you gave her the slip, so she needed to find you." He looked at Drew, smiling overly bright. "My girl was always sharp. One step ahead."

"Dad, try to focus," Raven said when she recovered her breath.

As if suddenly remembering she was there, Ray whipped his head around and she could see the fear in his eyes. "You have to do it again, little bird. Give her the slip. Stay gone. She's nuts. She would do this thing to my brain...like she was trying to suck the life out of me right through my eyeballs—or blow it out the back o' my head."

Jeremiah sucked in a breath, and Raven wondered if he was remembering his own fight with the demons.

Brynna's lilting voice cut through Ray's manic monologue. "With all due respect...Dude, you're no' makin' any sense."

Ray finally slumped back in his seat, having worn himself out. Raven moved to sit beside him again, handed him his water and studied him carefully. She hated to admit it, but Ray had always been so strong and confident, and it scared her a little to see him losing it.

"I think he's making perfect sense." The softly accented, rich voice had come from the floor at Isla's feet. Marduk raised a brow at Brynna and gave a haughty little sniff. "If you really listened."

Jeremiah reached down and ruffled the young man's hair. "All right *Rougaroux*, you so smart? Why don't you enlighten the slow folks."

Raven narrowed her eyes at Jeremiah. "*Rougaroux*?"

"Legendary Cajun werewolf. No big, just an inside joke," he said, waving his hand in the air for Marduk to continue.

"It would seem that, among the seven of us, we are in possession of the most comprehensive database of knowledge about the *Vigilati* and the *Praedos*. Would you all agree?"

Most of the group nodded, and Ray just shrugged.

"We have no way of knowing if any other resources out there even exist. And half of what we have isn't even translated yet." He sent a pointed look across to Drew, who promptly flipped him off.

"I think that Raven is a *Praeda,* like we thought, but one that is unique among others. Before I continue, may I ask," he turned to Raven and Ray, "who is Lisette?"

Ray cleared his throat and once again sounded like he had gargled with something corrosive. "Lisette is, was, Raven's mother. At least I thought so. They had so many similarities, the timing was right. She was Creole, and, God knows, Raven didn't get her skin tone from my white ass."

"That's what I suspected. And Ms. McCoy?" Marduk asked.

"She was the social worker that tracked me down and brought Raven to me. I thought it was kind of weird at the time, that she would just leave a child with some guy—even with a paternity test. They found me because I was in the system, for fuck's sake."

Marduk nodded pensively, as if it all made sense to him. Raven could feel Drew's irritation before he spoke. "Oh God, Fido, would you get to the point already?"

Marduk snarled at him before regaining his composure to continue, and Raven wondered how he could seem like a five-year-old and a one-hundred-year-old at the same time.

"I think Raven is different from the rest of the *Praedos* because her mother is the *Lochrim.* Not her father. The *Lochrim* must have been posing as—or inhabiting the body of—the human woman that Ray thought was Raven's mother. I surmise that she had Ray kidnapped to get him to disclose Raven's whereabouts so that she can come for her. A female *Lochrim* is a phenomenon we haven't heard of up until now, but there is so much we *don't* know. It's simple deduction, really."

He looked around the room triumphantly while the others considered his idea. Turning to Ray, Drew kept his voice low and calm. "Did this woman give you a name, Ray?"

"Azibel," he whispered and flinched, as if calling her name would summon her.

The name lanced through Raven's mind like a flaming arrow. She could hear it echoing around in her head as she rose from the couch and stumbled to the window. "No."

"Raven."

"No! I just need a minute."

She heard Drew rise and take a step toward her, but he stopped. "Guys, why don't y'all take Ray down to the tavern. Get the man a soda, let him catch up with Micah, then give him the *Cliffsnotes* version of the last two years. Raven and I will be down in a bit, and we'll talk."

Isla hopped up, and Jeremiah followed, giving Drew a sympathetic pat. He held a hand out to Ray and helped the man up. "Come on, Ray, we've got *so* much to tell you."

Chapter Thirty Four

Drew hated feeling powerless. As he stood in the middle of the room, watching Raven stare out the window, hugging herself, he silently cursed the feeling of helplessness. He wanted to go to her, to wrap her in the protection of his arms and fend off all her demons—real or otherwise—but he was afraid of being turned away.

Fear was also another emotion he despised. It contrasted sharply with his calm, in control nature, so he quickly bit it back. He was a big boy, he could handle it if she slapped him back.

He crossed the room and reached for her but dropped his hands when he saw her tense. He expected her to move away, to ask him to leave, so he stepped back and tried to ignore the pain in his chest.

Instead, she spun around and faced him, eyes fierce and piercing. There was a pregnant pause in which they stared at each other, trying to find the answers to unspoken questions.

Suddenly, she fisted both hands in his shirt and dragged him to her, crushing her mouth to his in a feverish kiss.

Momentarily stunned, he allowed her to devour his mouth in her sensual attack, and shuddered when her teeth found his lower lip. Again, he reached for her, but she backed away as quickly as she'd grabbed him, breathing hard.

"Please," she said, and raised a hand to hold him back. "If I lean on you now, I'm not sure if I'll be able get back up. Please understand."

And he did. He realized how hard it was, for someone who'd always had to fend for herself, to let someone take care of her. He thought the kiss was her way of letting him know that she wasn't rejecting him—she just needed to stand on her own.

The fist that gripped his heart loosened, and his posture relaxed. He looked into those troubled amber-gold eyes and tried to convey his silent message. That he wasn't going anywhere. "Whatever you need, *cher*."

She blew out a relieved breath and treated him to a brilliant smile. "Dr. Deveraux, you are something else."

He snorted and smiled. "Somethin'." He held out his hand and she didn't hesitate to take it, which brightened his smile just a little. "Let's go check on your dad."

When they made it down to the tavern, their friends had stuffed Ray into the corner booth and were flanking him on all sides, guarding him like a pack of sheepdogs protecting an injured lamb. Drew smiled at the sight. They were good people, all of them.

The man himself looked completely shell-shocked. His arms were folded on the table and he rested his forehead on them. His Coke was sitting off to the side, forgotten.

Jeremiah waved when he saw them, and Drew steered Raven through the light Wednesday night crowd. There was a trivia game starting soon, popular with the college kids, so he knew their group would most likely be ignored in their little hidey-hole.

Raven slid into the booth beside Isla, while Drew pulled a chair up to the end of the table. He glanced over sympathetically at the top of Ray's dark head. "How you doin' there, Ray?" he asked.

"I think I'm having an aneurysm," came the muffled reply.

Drew chuckled, because he knew exactly how Ray felt. He'd been in the same position last year when Jeremiah and Isla had explained it all to him.

When Ray finally raised his head, his face was haggard and pale, which made the bruises and cuts stand out in shocking contrast. But, hell, he wasn't running away screaming either. Drew supposed it was a start.

"The whole thing actually makes some kind of ridiculous sense when I think back on everything that's happened up till now," Ray said, shoving impatiently at the hair in his eyes. "It it's still kind of hard, you know? To believe in that kind of stuff. And after spending so many days with that...thing...I don't want it to be true."

"Raven," Isla said in that soothing way of hers, "when I told my friends and, eventually, Drew, it was helpful to them when I showed them. It seems weird, at first, sort of like a circus act, but I think it really went a long way in helping them to process it. But, of course, we wouldn't want you to do anything you're not comfortable with."

Drew watched Raven's profile as she thought it over, saw her fear and uncertainty. He reached under the table and grabbed her hand and was happy when she gave an answering squeeze.

"I've never really tried to do something for display. I wouldn't know what to do."

Isla smiled reassuringly at Raven. "Just something simple and discreet, but irrefutable."

Raven thought about it for a moment, then her eyes lit up. She pulled her legs up and spun in her seat so she was facing the back of the booth, and Ray. This effectively put her back to the main tavern door.

She looked intently at Ray. "Watch the door," she said to whoever was listening, "and tell me when the next person comes in."

Drew turned his head obediently with the rest of them and waited for the next patron to enter the tavern. "Okay," he said when a young man entered.

Raven closed her eyes and reached out into the space around them, sending a wave of energy through the particles in the air. The energy caressed the stranger, slid over every inch of him and whirled around him. It created such a clear picture in her mind of what it was touching, she could practically see him as well as with her eyes.

All the while, the man felt nothing. When Raven opened her eyes, she was no longer looking at Ray and her friends. She was seeing nothing but the man in the doorway who was beginning to walk toward the bar.

"White male, early twenties, shaggy hair," she began softly, "about five-foot-ten with an athletic build. Jeans, UNCA t-shirt, douchy Japanese Kanji tattoo on his left bicep." She shook her head and blinked, allowing her vision to return to normal.

When she looked at Ray again, he was staring at her with wide eyes. Not from fear, she thought. Something akin to awe. Her stomach unclenched, and she smiled at him. "That comes in really handy in my line of work."

Ray seemed to surprise himself with his own laugh. "I'll bet," he said in a gruff voice. "I don't really get it, though. Are you psychic?"

"No, not exactly. I just have the ability to manipulate my environment to supplement my regular senses, to see what my eyes can't, to move things I can't. That's the best way I know how to explain it."

"Move things?" Ray asked.

Raven winked at him and turned her face toward the drapes on the window near their booth. She sent out a gentle ripple in the air and made them flutter as if lifted by a light breeze, although no windows or doors were open.

"Huh. Well. That's that then," he said, smiling at her.

Raven felt Drew give her hand another squeeze. "Now that Ray's somewhat caught up, why don't you tell us what you found at the library."

Raven reached into her pocket and pulled out the folded printout of the article she'd found. "I found her." She spread the creased paper out on the table and slid it over to Jeremiah. "Her name is Malenka Jovanovich and she went missing two years ago. She's presumed dead along with two other women. The only connection between the three is a similar tattoo."

She let her statement hang in the air as the others absorbed the shocking news. "I don't know how she was able to show herself to me, but I feel sure it was a warning," she said once the article had been passed around. "I think someone's been targeting the *Vigilati*. I don't know if it's the *auchrim* somehow orchestrating the disappearances, or if someone else knows about us. Either way, it's not good."

Looking over at Drew, she noticed he looked pale and drawn, and he was unusually quiet. She covered his hand with hers and waited for him to look up at her. Those beautiful blue eyes were clearly troubled, but he gave her a weak smile, raised her hand, and kissed her fingers.

She felt Ray's eyes on them, but she ignored him. He'd have to accept that his daughter had grown up while he was in prison, and he would have to accept her relationships.

"What's wrong, Drew?"

He closed his eyes and sighed against her hand when she said his name. "Found something at the dig. Was hoping I was wrong about it, but this article makes it hard to deny."

Dread coiled in her belly, but she asked anyway, determined to have all of their cards on the table. "What did you find?"

"The team brought up the remains we've been excavating. I had already been examining a fragment of the scapula that had some strange grooves on it, and that was the piece that was stolen when the lab was broken into.

"While Hammer and I were assembling the skeleton, I checked out the bone from which the fragment came. Even without the missing piece, I could tell that the etching formed a *signa*."

He paused when Isla let out a shocked hiss. "It seems as though when the *signa* forms on the skin, it forms on the bone, as well, and, I would guess, on the muscle and fascia in between."

"Maybe that's why it hurts so damn much," Jeremiah said, absently rubbing his own shoulder.

"You said scapula," Raven interrupted. "That's the shoulder, right?"

"Yes. The shoulder blade. Why?"

"After the article...I was worried that it might be Malenka. But it isn't. Her *signa* was on her neck."

Drew scrubbed both hands over his scruffy face. Raven's relief would be short lived when she realized what he actually thought they'd found, and he didn't relish telling her.

As if she could read his mind, Raven looked at him sharply and searched his face. "That's not all you found."

Shaking his head grimly, Drew's big shoulders heaved with a deep sigh. "No, I'm afraid not. As we were examining Daisy—the skeleton, that's what we call her—the team discovered another skeleton...right underneath the first one."

He had a sick feeling in the pit of his stomach as he watched his friends' contemplative expressions turned to shock, and for those who already made the connection, horror.

Ray looked across the table and made eye contact with Drew. "Is that normal for burial sites?"

Holding his gaze, Drew slowly shook his head again. "No. It isn't. Especially not in the high ground. In areas of lower elevation—New Orleans and Savannah, to name a couple—it's common to stack the bodies in tombs. Burial grounds, ancient or otherwise, are most always arranged with supreme respect for the dead. Stacking bodies in a shallow grave, well, that's more reminiscent of— "

"A dump site," Raven finished for him with a somber look. "So three women we believe to be *Vigilati* have gone missing in the last two years, and your team has found at least two bodies, unceremoniously buried—one of whom you've confirmed to be *Vigilati* as well."

With a groan, Drew lowered his head and rested it on the table. "That's about the sum of things."

"That can't be a coincidence. How long before Oz and the others realize what's going on and turn it over to the police?" Raven asked.

"I've been stalling. Hammer is the only other person who knows, and he's promised to stay quiet. But I can't keep it a secret for much longer. It will jeopardize both of our careers."

Drew remembered the puzzle box, grabbed his messenger bag from the floor and pulled it out. "Ray, I wanted you to take a look at this. My intern pulled it up from the dig, and Raven mentioned that you had one like it when she was growing up. Do you know anything about it?"

Drew had left the book of shadows in his lock box back in the room. One thing at a time, he told himself as he slid the box across the table to Ray. He watched Ray turn it over in his hands several times, tracing the symbols with a finger. Finally, he set it back down and looked at Jeremiah, his eyes filled with indefinable shadows.

"Yes, I do have one very similar to this. Some of the symbols are different, but, other than that, it's the same."

"How did you end up with it?"

Ray sat back against the cushion of the booth and lifted his head back to stare up at the ceiling. "When my father died," he said, failing to keep the snarl out of his voice, "I ended up with a box full of my mother's things. She passed away when I was two," he clarified. "The puzzle box was there with the rest of the stuff. I think it may have belonged to my grandmother, who died before I was born."

"Was there anything inside it?" Drew asked.

Ray shrugged and rolled his head back and forth against the booth. "Just some old family photos. Nothing else."

"What we're dealing with, even the smallest detail may matter. Is there any way you can have it sent to you here?"

"If you think it could be important, I suppose I could have Tristan or Ryder grab it from my place and Fedex it."

"I'll call the boys tomorrow and set it up," Raven said.

"Thanks, love," Drew said, rubbing his eyes. He felt the edges of another headache flickering over his sinuses. He'd been getting a lot of those lately.

While they were talking, trivia had ended and the tavern began to fill up with the late night college crowd. The music was turned up, and the sounds of excited voices and raucous laughter echoed around the large open room.

Ever the 'type A' guy, Jeremiah leaned over the table. "Okay, so we've got some homework to do, kiddos. Drew, obviously you should stay at the dig and keep your cards as close to the vest as you can, for as long as you can.

"Isla, why don't you go with Raven and Brynna and scout out a five-mile radius around the dig site. Maybe you'll be able to find the *locus* if you combine your efforts. Also, you may want to head back up to the falls to see if Malenka will show herself again. Marduk, you go furry and tackle a ten-mile radius around Black Valley. I'll head to the library and work on lookin' through the grimoire and the book of shadows, to see if there's anything we've missed."

"Aye, aye, Cap'n," Brynna said with a mock salute.

Grateful to have someone else take charge for the moment, Drew clapped his friend on the back. "Sounds like a plan to me."

"What should I do?" Ray asked

Jeremiah opened his mouth to answer, but Raven cut him off. "You, sir, are going to let Micah take you to the hospital tomorrow to get all of your injuries checked. Don't even *think* about telling me no," she said when he looked like he might argue. "You already scared ten years off my life once, I'm not going to go through it again."

Ray turned helpless eyes toward Drew, but he just shrugged in return. "I believe the only acceptable answer here is 'yes ma'am'."

He heaved a huge sigh that would have been comical if it weren't for the wince that came along with it, and gave in. "All right, have it your way."

"Well, I think we've all had about enough to deal with tonight," Drew said as he looked over at the quickly growing mass of drinkers and dancers.

"Ladies and gentlemen, canines and felines, what say we have a little fun for once?" Standing, he reached out a hand to Raven. "*Madame...*"

She rolled her eyes at him, but she was laughing when she placed her hand in his.

As Raven allowed herself to be pulled out to the dance floor, the last few chords of the latest Luke Bryan hit were blasting out from the speakers. Cliffdweller's wasn't a western bar by any stretch of the imagination, but the crowd definitely seemed to be on a country bent that night.

She smiled when the first few bars of Garth Brooks' *Friends in Low Places* floated over them, and Drew whirled her into a spin. He led her around the floor in a hip grinding mock two-step in time with the twang, inciting wild hoots of laughter from her.

When she looked to her left, she saw that Jeremiah was giving Isla a similar performance. Chuckling, she noticed Brynna trying to dodge the fervent attentions of their young friend with the Kanji tattoo.

Ray hung out at the bar to catch up with Micah, while Marduk was in the back, blending in with a group of college kids watching the football game. She turned her attention back to Drew as he maneuvered her around the floor.

He was all smiles and dimples, a light sheen of perspiration making his hair curl more around his ears and forehead. She got so distracted looking at the sheer perfection of him that she tripped over her own feet.

She would have fallen flat on her face if Drew hadn't been there to catch her against the solid wall of his chest. She felt the warmth radiating off of him in waves, and her heart did a little tripping of its own.

When was the last time she'd been able to spend time with someone, a man, that she genuinely enjoyed being around, that she genuinely liked? She couldn't remember. Maybe never. The way she'd grown up, there were never friends that hung around for long. Now, here she was with a whole gaggle of them. And her dad. And Drew.

The music changed again—a slow, hauntingly sweet ballad by Tim McGraw—and Drew tightened his arms around her, swaying gently. Good lord, had she ever even danced with a man? She sure as hell hadn't been on a date, not in the true sense of the word.

Drew encouraged her to lay her head on his shoulder and snuggle closer as they danced. And she let him. She snuggled right up like a cat to the milkman, practically climbing him. He stroked a big hand down the curtain of her hair, and she trembled. He made a small sound of approval deep in his throat and bent to kiss her gently.

She kept waiting for him to disappear, like people always did, but he was still here. Real, and big as life. Raven drifted dangerously close to contentment, the sensations that washed over her were overwhelming and not entirely comfortable. But for once, just for this night, she gave up and gave in. She'd worry about tomorrow...tomorrow.

CHAPTER THIRTY FIVE

Drew rolled up the sleeves of his work shirt as he stepped out of the lab tent. It was time for a break. He'd spent another morning cataloging and assembling, examining and sample extracting, and he needed to give his eyes a rest.

He spotted Raven over by the alarm control panel as she performed some last minute system checks, and smiled to himself. She had really let her guard down the night before, laughing and cutting up like he'd never seen her do. She was always so serious, though he knew it came from having to grow up so fast.

It had warmed his heart to see her have a little fun. He was just about to go talk her into having lunch with him when he noticed a large Suburban pull into the makeshift parking lot. Cars coming and going wasn't unusual—what drew his attention was the fact that the noisy mob of picketers tapered off to a low rumble, and most of them turned to watch the car.

He snorted when he saw the driver hop down from the running board—a tiny woman no more than five-two who teetered on towering heels. Her eyes swept the compound as if looking for someone to speak to, and he groaned inwardly when her gaze rested on him.

Damn it, almost made it out. He smiled politely and walked toward her like a man going to the gallows. Her frank stare followed his every move, and he got the feeling she was sizing him up and finding him lacking.

As he approached, he noted that she was probably in her early forties but took care of herself. Her skin was pale; her hair was a warm brown and curled down to her waist. She stared at him through a thick curtain of inky lashes with stormy gray eyes. When she spoke, he noticed she had a slight overbite that some men might find sexy.

Him? He just wanted her to say her piece and let him go the hell to lunch. "Ma'am," he said and nodded. "Can I help you with something?"

She extended a petite hand and he shook it with trepidation, fearing she might break. "Yes, thank you. Elisabetta Marconi, president of the Watauga County Historical Society."

Despite her obviously Italian name, she had the slight twang that was typical in the area. "What can I do for you, Ms. Marconi?" He asked politely, grinding his teeth to keep from hurrying her along.

"I was hoping to speak with whoever is in charge of the excavation. I'd like to get more information on the plans for the site and the findings, so I'll be better equipped to deal with all of the...publicity," she said, and angled her head toward the now quiet group to her right.

Drew rubbed a hand over the back of his neck and looked around helplessly for Oz. Of course, he was nowhere on hand. "You'd need to speak with Dr. Larkin. He's heading up the dig. I can go find him for you, if you like."

"That would be wonderful, Mr...?"

"Dr. Deveraux. Please, call me Drew. I'll just go check the tents and see if I can locate Dr. Larkin."

Drew jumped when a big hand once again clapped him on the back. *Good lord, the man is a motherfucking ninja.* "No need to go huntin' me up, Dev. I'm right here," Oz's voice boomed.

While he was speaking to Drew, his eyes were all over Ms. Marconi. He practically threw himself in front of Drew to shake the woman's hand. Good, he could have her. All Drew wanted was a goddamn sandwich and a few moments alone with Raven. But it wasn't to be.

After Ms. Marconi batted those killer lashes at Oz and told him what she wanted, he folded like a cheap suit and offered to take her to lunch so they could talk more privately. "Dev, hold down the fort here till I get back. You don't mind, do ya?" He continued on without allowing Drew to answer. "Good. Couple of hours, tops." Before giving Drew a chance to even draw breath to answer, he offered Ms. Marconi his arm and escorted her to his Lexus SUV.

Drew felt the urge to check for tire tracks down his back, but instead he turned around to go find Raven. He shook his head and set off in the direction where he'd last seen her. Maybe he could convince her to keep him company in the mess tent while he tried to choke down lunch in between assisting interns and directing the team.

He found her already in the mess tent, waiting for him. Her eyes were just a little too wide, her face a little too pale. He wondered what had happened to change her mood from that of the night before.

Drew sat down in the metal folding chair beside her and pushed a shrink-wrapped mystery meat sandwich her way—the only full lunch option from the food truck that came by daily. "Raven? *Cher*, did something happen? You look upset."

She stared down at her hands for a moment before shaking her head and looking up at him. "Um, it's nothing. Who was that woman?"

With a sigh, he propped his chin up with his hand. "Some fancy-pants from the Historical Society, wanting information about the dig. Something about publicity. To tell you the truth, I couldn't get away fast enough. Oz is handling it. Why?"

She had gained some color back and was looking at him thoughtfully. "Not sure. I felt...something, when I saw her. Like déjà vu. I feel like I know her from somewhere, but I couldn't tell you where. You think Dr. Larkin can get her to back off?"

"Honestly, Oz is more likely to get in her pants, if anything. But that might have the same effect. Believe it or not, he can be charming when he wants to be."

Raven coughed to unsuccessfully cover a snort. "I'd have to see that one to believe it."

"Fair enough," he said with a grin. He was happy to be back to the easy companionship they had begun to share.

When Raven finished her sandwich, she leaned over and gave him a peck on the cheek. "I've got to meet the girls at the falls. I'll see you tonight."

She made to stand up, but he tugged her down into his lap instead. Covering her mouth with his, he plunged his fingers into her thick hair, massaging the back of her head as he kissed her. He shuddered when he felt her melt against him.

He wasn't sure that would ever get old, the knowledge that he could break some of that fastidious control and scramble her brains as much as she did his.

With a soft sigh, she pulled away from him slowly, stroking a hand down his cheek. She gave him a quick smile and bit her lip as if she might say something. But in the end, she gave him another hard kiss on the mouth and was gone.

ഇഗ

Oh, hell. That was the only thing Raven could wrap her mind around as she sped up the Parkway on her bike. The litany rolled around in her brain like a record stuck on repeat. *Oh hell, oh hell, oh hell.*

She could feel the cold sweat trickling inside her helmet and down the back of her neck, and her skin was clammy with panic. She had not expected this, wasn't prepared for it. *Well, fuck me to pieces*, she thought.

She loved him. Like, absolutely, head-over-heels, shot-to-the-gut love. In. Love. She was aware that, to some people, this would be a warm-fuzzy type of feeling. For her, it was pure, unadulterated terror. Not for herself—she'd long since given up having unrealistic expectations of other people—but for Drew.

Loving her would be hell on anyone, she knew. Raven was prickly, cynical, suspicious, and independent to a fault. Loving her would only lead to heartache. And that was even before the *laqueum* became a possibility.

Mate? More like curse. She was unwilling to strap Drew down to someone like herself—his fate depending on her *not* self destructing. She wouldn't do it. Loved him too much to do it. Raven was many things, but she wasn't a coward. She could admit her feelings, at least to herself.

But she would keep her mouth shut for the safety of all involved. For Drew's especially. If words were never spoken, then they would never be bonded, and Drew could live a long, happy life. The thought of him living that life without her was like a knife to her heart, but Raven tamped down the feeling.

She clenched her teeth against the vibrations of the engine and strengthened her resolve. She could do this for him. She'd probably never done an unselfish thing in her entire twenty-six years of existence. But now she would.

She felt better now that she had a plan, a way to keep her feelings safely locked away. She nodded to herself as she pulled off to the side of the road at the trailhead where she'd spotted Isla's rental car.

As she removed her helmet and secured it to the motorcycle, she imagined how she must look to her friends. Wild-eyed and harried, clammy skin and messy hair. Pulling her hair back in an elastic band, she took a deep breath and tried to get a grip on herself.

Raven smiled and waved as she approached the two women standing next to the car. They would be hiking directly to the foot of the falls instead of down from the watchtower, so it would be a much shorter trek.

They marched in silence, each lost in their own thoughts, enjoying the beautiful early fall weather. The only sounds were that of boots crunching over bracken, toes stubbing on roots. When they reached a cleared area with a circle of rustic benches, put there so hikers could rest, Raven pulled up short and stopped.

She raised her face to the breeze, closed her eyes and reached out her senses to the surrounding area. Nothing seemed off, but she felt...something. The back of her neck tingled, and the hairs on her arms raised. The Watcher, she thought.

After the rest area, the trail would plunge down another thirty feet to the base of the falls. Once there, they would be out in the open and cornered by the falls and the valley below. She wasn't sure why, but she had the disturbing thought that today would be the day The Watcher would make his move.

Unwilling to let her friends get caught in the crossfire but knowing they wouldn't back down easily, Raven thought quickly as she turned to face them. They both looked at her with questions in their eyes, and she fought a moment's guilt over not telling them the entire truth.

"I'm worried that Malenka won't show herself if I'm with other people. Before, she only talked to me while Brynna was asleep, and disappeared when she came over to me. Maybe you two could give me a few minutes—stay here, or explore the outlying trails?"

Isla thought about it for a moment before speaking. "That may be best. We wouldn't want to scare her off. I'll look around up here an' Brynna can follow me in cat form." Brynna nodded when Isla raised a brow at her.

"We'll give you half an hour before we come back. Text Isla if you make contact and don't want us to come down yet, or if you want us to come down sooner. Good luck," Brynna said before shifting.

Raven gave them a grateful smile as she waved them off. She squared her shoulders and faced the descending trail. It wasn't a hard route, just steep, so it only took her a few minutes to make it to the bottom of the falls.

Raven skirted around the deep pool and edged past the trickling spray to make it to the flat rock where she'd been sitting when Malenka appeared. Sitting down, she pulled her knees up and rested her chin on them, settling in to wait.

Five minutes passed and nothing happened. Then ten. She felt herself getting frustrated and was about to get up and pace when a rustling from the trail caught her attention. Sensing a disturbance in the energy field around the pond, she went on instant alert.

Raven climbed to her feet and backed up until she was flush against the rock wall behind her—an easier spot to defend—and scanned the clearing. Several minutes went by in silence and when she was just about to convince herself that she'd imagined it all, a figure emerged from the cover of the trees.

For some reason, Raven had found herself imagining The Watcher to be some burly goon, much like the ones that grabbed Ray. She should have known better. But she certainly hadn't expected this impossibly tiny woman.

Dressed simply in a sweater and jeans with hiking boots, she shouldn't have been anything remarkable. But she was so heart-stoppingly beautiful, it hurt Raven's eyes to look at her. Dark, curly hair brushed her elbows as she crept carefully through the spray from the falls.

At first, Raven thought it was the woman from the Historical Society—she had a similar build and height—but she realized this woman had different features, different hair color. The person before her had dark brown hair, similar to Raven's own, and eyes so dark they were almost black. Still, she seemed so familiar; there was just a hint of recognition somewhere in the back of her mind.

Raven's skin shivered like a racehorse at the gate, ready to bolt. The air around them changed when the woman had shown herself. There was a charge, and it was threatening to singe her.

Her fingers clawed into the rock behind her, and she wet her lips nervously, having to clear her throat before she spoke. "Do I know you?"

The woman clucked her tongue disapprovingly. "I should hope so, Poppet," she said in a heavy British accent. "I'm your mother."

Raven's pulse ratcheted up a notch even as her blood ran cold. She'd been anticipating this confrontation for nearly a year, but with the new information they had from Ray about Azibel, she was thrown off guard.

Doing her best to mask her struggle, she curled her mouth into a sneer and forced herself to step away from the safety of the rock. "So you say."

"Don't test me, child. You've no idea what you're dealing with."

"Try me. *Azibel.*"

The small woman raised a brow and narrowed her eyes at Raven. "I gather you've spoken to Raymonde. That *is* unfortunate. I'll have to have a little chat with my associates when I return." She said "chat" the way normal folks would say "pulling teeth".

"Good luck. They're dead."

Azibel shrugged a delicate shoulder and pouted. "Pity, that. Good help is so hard to find these days. Ah, well," she waved a dismissive hand in the air, "*c'est la vie*, as they say."

Raven was rapidly losing patience—a virtue she had blessed little of to begin with—so she decided to cut to the chase. "What do you want from me?"

Azibel stepped forward, then reached out and trailed a blood-red fingertip down a strand of Raven's hair.

"So pretty."

Raven's skin crawled with the need to back away, but she stood her ground, raised her face to meet her *mother's* gaze.

Big mistake. Big. *Huge*. A thin but surprisingly strong hand snapped out and grabbed her by the wrist. Raven was helpless but to look on in horror as Azibel's face began to change. Eyes that were once black turned completely clear, with shadows swirling hypnotically inside them, as if they were trying to reach out to her.

An image of a spider emerged on her forehead, and her canines lengthened into lethal-looking fangs. Explains the overbite, Raven thought. And it was the last thought of her own before Azibel firmly rooted herself into Raven's mind.

"What I want...," she purred, "is to take my rightful place in this world, with my daughter beside me. Imagine, Raven, joining together with me to lower, no, to *destroy* the barrier that keeps my people confined to the hell in which they are imprisoned."

Raven tried to shake her head, to scream, but she couldn't seem to get her brain to send the signals to her body. She felt her mouth go slack, and her breathing ease as she stared into those mesmerizing eyes.

"You can't tell me you haven't always felt...different. Like something was missing. Like you weren't meant for this menial existence. Can you?" Obviously fully aware of Raven's inability to answer, she plowed on. "Of course, you can't. You would be a *goddess* among my people. They would revere and fear you—serve your every desire. Imagine it."

And, with a nausea roiling in her belly, Raven did. She allowed herself a moment to feel what it would be like to have a mother, to really *know* who she was and where she came from, and be exalted for it.

Smiling a knowing smile as if she knew Raven's thoughts, Azibel cupped her cheek with her free hand. Her skin was icy cold and shocked Raven a bit out of her stupor. "Say the word, pet. Everything I have is yours if you join with me. In fact, you don't even have to speak. Just nod, my precious."

While she fought the battle to stay conscious and regain control of her own mind, Raven had the absurd image of Tolkien's Gollum salivating over a piece of jewelry like it could answer all the questions in the universe.

The utter ridiculousness of it, of Azibel for what she was asking, and of Raven for even allowing herself to consider it, snapped her right out of it. Without hesitating further, she summoned her power over space to swirl the air around Azibel, creating an invisible noose around her neck.

Azibel's eyes widened in disbelief as she released Raven to claw at her own neck, and she scored bloody gashes into her delicate skin. She coughed and gasped for breath, then stumbled back. Somehow, she summoned enough power to send out a blast of energy to dislodge Raven's hold.

"You *bitch!* I would have given you everything, but now? Now you'll bleed like the rest of those insipid humans when I burn this world down around your ears!"

Before Raven even had time to process those threats, she felt herself being lifted bodily off the ground and hoisted into the pool behind her, though Azibel never moved an inch.

The first thing she registered was the mind-numbing cold of the water. In an Appalachian mountain pool in the fall, one could freeze to death in minutes. God, the cold. Like nothing she'd ever felt, it seeped into her skin and made her bones ache.

Survival instinct kicked in and she tried to struggle to the surface, but she was pushed back down and held by invisible hands. Then she was held by very real hands. More hands than she could count.

The hands came up from the dark depths of the pool. They groped and pulled, and grappled with her as if trying to climb their way to freedom. Opening her eyes, she could see them. Bodies in the water. With their gaping mouths and vacant, black eyes, they loomed in the murky pool. They reached for her, whether to pull her down or pull themselves up, she didn't know.

Finally, her body registered the lack of air, the need to breathe. And everything whittled down to that one simple, life-giving function. Allowing her body to go still, she stopped her struggles and tried to conserve what little oxygen she had left.

As she calmed, an insidious voice floated through her mind. "You see what happens to those who defy me, Raven? I don't just kill them, I torture them for eternity. I'll destroy you for spurning me," the voice said with an eerie calm, "you, and everything—everyone—you love."

Spots began floating in her vision, and Raven knew the end was close. She sent out a desperate message and hoped to the gods that Isla or Brynna would somehow sense her distress.

The need to breathe became the center of her universe. Once again, she tried to claw her way to the surface, but it was useless. Invisible bands of steel encircled her, weighing her down, squeezing the life out of her. Her body began to convulse, and she involuntarily let go the breath she'd been holding.

Her vision dimmed, and her head pounded, her fight or flight response screaming in her ear. With the very last reserve of her strength, she pushed out against the water, against the very oxygen in its makeup.

Water exploded around her, and, just as suddenly, all the hands that held her down released. At the same time, two pairs of blessedly real hands latched onto her arms and pulled upward. She shot out of the water, flailing and gasping, and landed on two warm bodies.

Small but strong arms cradled her as she coughed and retched, until all the dreaded water had leeched out of her lungs. More hands smacked her back to help her expel what was left. She rolled onto her back on the cool stone, stared up at the sky and breathed in great heaves of air. Damn, she loved air. It was way underrated.

A shadow blocked out the sun as Isla leaned over her. "Raven? Sweeting, can you hear me?"

Raven tried to speak, but all that came out was a strangled croak, so she gave up and simply nodded.

Another shadow joined the first, except this one had a flaming red halo backlit by the sun. "What th' bloody divil was that?" she squeaked, her brogue so thickened, she was almost unintelligible.

"Did you see her?" Raven managed to rasp the question out before dissolving in another fit of coughing.

"See who?"

"Azibel," she ground out before promptly passing out.

Chapter Thirty Six

While Raven slept, Drew paced. His friends' eyes tracked his movements with looks of concern and pity, and they were grating on his nerves. Isla and Brynna had recounted their version of what happened at the falls when they brought Raven to his room.

They hadn't bothered to take her to her own room. Brought her straight to his room, to his bed. Smart girls. They told him that when they had sensed some disturbing energy waves, they returned to the falls to check on Raven. Apparently they found her damn near drowned, struggling to pull her head above water in the waterfall pool.

The girls had pulled her out and she quickly passed out. After they revived her enough to walk with help, Isla had driven her back in the rental car while Brynna drove the motorcycle.

And here they were, Raven shivering in his bed and Drew wearing a hole in the carpet with his pacing and glowering. He had never felt such blinding terror as when he'd seen her that way, his vibrant Raven, ghost white and frail, collapsed on his bed.

Drew was glad Ray was currently tucked away in his own room at the inn, sleeping off some painkillers he was given for his injuries. It would be awful for the man to have to see his daughter this way, true, but selfishly, Drew needed to be alone with Raven for now. To assure himself that she was alive and would stay that way.

Speaking of alone...he thought as he listened with half an ear to the concerned whispers behind him… A strong hand landed on his shoulder, no doubt Jeremiah, but he shook it off violently.

He clenched his fists at his sides, and struggled to keep his temper under control. Raven had nearly died today, yet everyone was looking at him like he might self-destruct at any moment. Enough was enough.

"Everyone out. Please," he added to take away some of the sting. "I appreciate your concern," he grated through clenched teeth, "but I need some time with Raven. Just...stay close. Look out for Ray."

As they filed out of the room quietly, Jeremiah blocked the path of his pacing. "Call if you need anything, hear? We'll be just downstairs."

Drew could only nod sharply at his friend, who then turned and left. He let out a relieved sigh, stopped his pacing and sank down into the desk chair, lowering his head into his hands. It wasn't that he didn't appreciate his friends, they were just draining his energy with all of their well-meaning concern. Energy he needed to focus on Raven—and just how the hell he was going to keep her safe.

Standing to rub shaking hands over his face, Drew attempted to pull himself together. He moved silently down the hall to the bedroom where he stood in the shadows and looked at her. The dying light outside flickered over her pale face and cast ghostly shadows around the room.

He stayed and watched her chest rise and fall. It was a way to reassure himself that she was, indeed, alive. She had dark, bruising shadows under her eyes that stood out against her ashen skin, and her full lips were pinched as if from pain—or perhaps from reliving the memory of what had happened to her.

Drew longed to lay with her, but he was hesitant to wake her from healing sleep. He needed to see those eyes, clear and sharp. Needed to hear her voice. To know what had happened to her that afternoon.

Quietly, he padded across the room on bare feet and eased down onto the bed beside her. The dipping of the mattress seemed to jostle her enough that she turned her head and blinked up at him. The sight of those whiskey eyes staring up at him as they focused, and those lips curling into a weak smile was like a punch to the gut.

He released a breath he was unaware he'd been holding, leaned down, and pressed a kiss to her lips. Cold. They were still so cold. He shivered and closed his eyes. "Raven," he breathed. "Thank God."

When Raven opened her eyes to find Drew beside her, the first thing that struck her was the fear in his eyes. She savored the soft kiss he gave her and reached out and circled both arms around his neck. Feeling deep tremors wracking his big body, she squeezed tighter and smiled when he buried his face in the hollow of her shoulder.

Pulling up the edge of the covers, she encouraged him to slide underneath them to snuggle up. When he pulled her to him and flung a leg over her hips as if he would keep her pinned there forever if he could, her heart stuttered. *Focus, Raven. Don't forget*, she warned herself.

"Hey there, sexy," she said. She knew she sounded less than alluring since her voice was still coming out scratchy from swallowing half the New River. Instead of answering, he just stared at her with a serious gaze that made her squirm in her skin. What was he thinking?

He sighed and stroked a hand over her cheek. "What happened up there, Raven? The girls said you mentioned Azibel before you passed out."

Just thinking back to her experience at the falls made her shiver with a cold she never thought she'd be completely rid of. "I asked the girls to give me a few minutes to see if Malenka would appear if I were alone—but I wasn't entirely honest. I sensed The Watcher following us, and I wanted to make sure they weren't harmed."

"Raven—"

"Ssh. Just, let me..." She saw a muscle tick in his jaw, but he nodded for her to keep going. "I waited for a good while and nothing happened. I was beginning to think Malenka was a no show, but I sensed something on the outskirts of the clearing. Shortly after, a woman I didn't recognize approached me."

"Azibel," he said with menace.

When Raven saw the murderous look on his face, she was certainly glad he was on her side. She wouldn't want to face him in a back alley when he'd worked up a mad.

She nodded at his answer. "The Watcher. Ray was right, it was her all along."

"How can you be sure?"

"Each person has a different energy signature. New-agers call it an aura, but it's just the energy that's given off by each being's body and consciousness. No two are alike. They're just like fingerprints."

"What did she say to you?"

"She got in my head, Drew. She tried to make me want things. Tried to get me to join with her and turn against the 'insipid humans', as she called them. She'd latched on to my mind, and she almost had me wanting it. Almost."

"But you snapped out of it and bitch slapped her." He said it with such unflagging confidence, as if he knew, without a doubt, that she could never turn evil. Raven was glad he didn't know how close she'd come.

"In a sense, yes. I used my power to force her back, but she's infinitely more powerful than I am. She dumped me in the pool and held me down, waiting for me to drown. In the water, all of these bodies were floating around me, grabbing at me, pulling me down. I think they may be all of the people she's killed, or drained, or whatever the auchrim do."

She shuddered to think about being trapped in that ice cold abyss, surrounded by darkness. "I knew I was nearly a goner. I tried to signal to Isla and Brynna—telepathically—though I have no idea if I even have that power. Then I used the last reserve of my energy to break her hold. When I did, Isla and Brynna were there to pull me out. You know the rest."

"Did she say anything else to you?"

"No. At least, not that I know of. The last few minutes, I was solely focused on the act of not dying." She couldn't quite meet his eyes as she lied about Azibel's threats.

It seemed as though he was satisfied with her answer, because he pulled her into his arms and wrapped himself around her. Blessed warmth bled into her body, and she curled into it, soaking up as much as she could.

"Do you need anything?" he asked as he sifted his fingers through her hair.

"I would kill for a cup of coffee."

CHAPTER THIRTY SEVEN

When Drew awoke the next morning, once again, the bed was empty. He looked around the room but saw no sign that Raven had ever been there. His heart lurched, slamming against his ribs. She wouldn't leave...would she? Her father was here. Her friends. *Me,* he thought.

He breathed a sigh of relief when he heard a noise in the living room. He got out of bed, pulled on a pair of jeans, and went out to investigate. He found her sitting at his desk in her Saints jersey, pouring over the translations from the grimoire.

He leaned against the door frame and took the opportunity to study her. Her face was scrubbed clean, and her long sable hair was still wet from her shower. He couldn't believe he'd slept through it. Her color was back, and the shadows that had seemed so prominent the night before had all but disappeared.

She raised her eyes to meet his, unsurprised. Of course she would have known he was there. No one snuck up on Raven. Not even Azibel.

"Good morning," she said, too cheerfully.

He frowned at her—something was most definitely off. "Morning. How are you feeling?"

"Good. Much better. I thought I'd never get warm."

Drew ground his teeth to keep from reminding her how close she'd come to death. He'd known she was resilient, so it shouldn't surprise him that she bounced back easily. He decided not to press the issue. Yet.

"Good. I've got to go over to the site for a little while, see how things are going. I need to make sure Hammer's holding it together and hasn't told anyone about our little discovery. Will you be all right?"

She gave him a smile, but it didn't quite reach her eyes. "Of course. I'm going to do some more research with the girls," she held up a hand before he could say anything, "and I promise I won't go anywhere alone. Okay?"

He gave her a smile, again marveling at how well she was able to read him. "Okay. Call me if you need anything." He leaned over and brushed his lips over hers, but when he would have deepened the kiss, she pulled away from him. His brow furrowed as he tried to silently communicate the fact that she could tell him anything. Nothing would make him turn away from her.

Raven let out a shaky breath after the door closed behind him. He loved her just as surely as she loved him. She could see it in his eyes—and she saw that he'd wanted to tell her, last night and just now.

What scared her to death was the thought that she wasn't sure she had the willpower to resist him if he did. She'd kept her distance when he came out of the bedroom because she hadn't wanted him to say anything.

Drew had a determined nature about him, and he wouldn't give up on her easily. She had to make him believe that she didn't love him, had to give him a reason not to love her. She had to squeeze her eyes shut tight against the tears that threatened to fall as Azibel's last words to her floated through her mind.

I'll destroy you for spurning me. You, and everything – everyone – you love.

Loving her would be a dangerous prospect for anyone. Not only would Drew have to deal with her messed up lifestyle, her daddy issues, and the laqueum, he'd also have to deal with her homicidal demon of a mother trying to kill him. Like hell.

It didn't matter how much it hurt her. It couldn't. She had to find a way to get Drew to give up on her and get to safety. She could handle dying in a battle against Azibel. But it would absolutely destroy her if she got Drew killed instead.

Her mind made up, she just had to come up with a plan that would do the trick. Her phone beeped to signal an incoming text from Drew. Made it 2 the site. Pls be careful today. As she read the short message, an idea began to form.

Drew was anxious to see Raven when he returned to his room that evening. He'd struggled to concentrate at work when his thoughts kept drifting back to her. How he'd almost lost her.

He stopped short when he opened the door. Raven had one of her feet propped up on a chair, buckling up a heavy motorcycle boot. She was dressed head to toe in black, from her boots to her riding leathers and the turtleneck that poked out of the jacket.

Her hair was once again braided at the temples and pulled back into a thick ponytail. She was clearly decked out for a night of work. His heart flip-flopped at the thought of her sneaking around some compound in the middle of the night, alone, with no back up.

Drew tossed his keys on the desk and arched a brow at her. "Going out?"

Squaring her shoulders, she palmed her own keys in one hand and grabbed her helmet with the other. "Yep. Got to finish up this job. I've missed too many days as it is."

Drew was unsure how to approach the fact that yesterday, she'd almost died, and that, maybe, it wasn't the best idea to go out alone. But she was fiercely independent, and he didn't want to insult her.

"I could come with you," he said, testing the waters.

She gave him a patronizing smile, and he had a sinking feeling that this was not going to go down the way he'd hoped. "That's sweet, but you'd only slow me down."

Ouch, he thought. *Don't let her get to you. She's being deliberately argumentative.* "Raven, I'm just worried about you, okay?" He walked forward and took her hand. When he looked into her eyes, he thought he saw a flash of longing, and of fear, before she steeled her expression.

She wanted to run? He could chase. He laid a hand over her cheek and kissed her slowly. He took his time as he teased his way inside to explore her mouth. When he felt her relax, he pushed his advantage, sliding a hand up to the back of her neck and angling his head to deepen the kiss. When he finally pulled away, she was breathing hard, and her eyes held a dazed expression.

"I couldn't stand it if you got hurt again, Raven. I love you. I know that's going to scare you, and that's okay. I'm a patient man."

She sucked in a breath, and her eyes glistened before they widened in panic. She stepped away from him, and he felt the loss of contact like a small death. She turned away for a moment, but when she faced him again, her expression was hard.

"What did you expect was going to happen here, Drew? Did you think I was just going to fall into your arms, cry all over you, and tell you I can't live without you?"

Drew blinked. He'd expected resistance, not a full scale assault. *Tread carefully, Deveraux.* "Uh, I'm not expecting anything. I just wanted to tell you how I feel, so you would understand why I was worried about you going out alone."

She sneered at him, and laughed. Laughed. "Sweetie, I've been going out alone since I was ten. That isn't about to change because you've decided to stake some kind of claim. You don't love me. You love the idea of me."

He was completely at a loss. Where was this coming from? Her tirade was taking on an almost desperate quality. Like she needed him to believe her. "Raven—"

"I'm not a settler, Drew. I'm a drifter. Do you think you can just take me home to New Orleans and turn me into a good little wife? You want to domesticate me!"

She was beginning to piss him off, putting words in his mouth and telling him what he was going to want. "Just a goddamn minute. I don't want to turn you into anything other than what you are. Remember what I said to you? I said the real Raven is enough. I meant it then, and I mean it now. I don't care if you travel all over the fucking world! As long as when you come home, you come home to me."

For a moment, she just gaped at him. Then her face crumbled. She choked out a strangled sob and rushed past him. When he tried to grab hold of her arm, she shook him off. "No! Please! I can't do this, Drew," she stuttered, and another sob escaped. "I can't be with you. I'm leaving. It's long past time for me to go. Don't follow me," she whispered, and then she was gone.

As he stood alone in the middle of the room, rubbing his chest, Drew looked down at himself and was surprised to find his body whole—instead of broken and bleeding, ripped wide open, like it felt.

His heartbeat hammered in his ears along with her words. Alone. It was a state of mind he'd grown up in, lived in, and now he was back there. Old faithful. Somehow it didn't feel like he would survive it this time.

He needed to get out of the room, to get out of the space that was closing in on him and threatened to squeeze the life out of him. He grabbed his keys and whipped the door open before letting it slam behind him. As he passed, he rammed a shoulder into Jeremiah who was blocking his path.

"Hey, Drew. Where's Raven," he asked cautiously.

Drew turned slowly and gave his best friend the full benefit of his haggard expression. "Gone," he croaked.

Jeremiah ran a hand over his stubbled chin, a habit that used to always make Drew smile. He doubted he'd ever smile again. "Uh, okay. Want to talk about it?"

"Fuck, no," he answered, glaring at Jeremiah. "I'm going out to the site. I need to occupy myself."

Jeremiah held up two hands in surrender and nodded. "Okay, brother. But at least let me drive you. You're in no condition. I'll drop you off and come get you when you're ready."

Drew started to refuse but then remembered his own requests of Raven. He didn't want to be a hypocrite so he jerked a short nod. "Let's go."

CHAPTER THIRTY EIGHT

Drew felt numb, listening to the rumble of the Camaro's V8 as Jeremiah pulled it into the parking area at the dig site. Silently, he climbed out of the passenger side and gave his friend a haphazard wave. Jeremiah just stared at him, naked concern in his eyes. After a few moments, he nodded. "Call me when you're ready."

"'Kay," Drew said and turned without waiting for an answer. Once he heard the engine growl as Jeremiah pulled out, he was able to relax a bit. He knew he should be angry, furious even, over the things Raven had said to him. But he just couldn't feel anything but empty. He hadn't felt that empty since his mother had dumped him in boarding school so she could run off with that douche-bag.

He knew Raven was scared of her feelings for him, he could see it in her eyes. Drew's theory was that she somehow felt she was lacking, like she was not good enough because of the way she grew up, the way she lived.

Hell, with all of his issues and shortcomings, she was too good for him. But now everything was FUBAR, and he had no idea what to do. So he'd work himself into a stupor. It was as good a plan as any—better, in fact, considering he could be drinking himself into a stupor instead. When his mouth began to water over the thought of a stiff glass of whiskey, he shook his head and made his way to the perimeter gate.

He punched in the key code on the control panel so he could enter without setting off the alarms. He felt a brief moment of guilt over breaking his promise to Raven that even he wouldn't go to the site alone at night. After what had just happened, he figured he had a pass.

Besides, he wasn't going to be alone. The night guard would be around there somewhere. Drew set of in the direction of the lab tent and set down his bag, so he could go find Alex to let him know he was there.

Before he made it, he noticed a flash of movement under one of the security lights near the lower point of the grid. Thinking it was Alex, Drew changed direction to give the man a heads up.

As he neared the light post, he noticed it wasn't one person who stood in the shadows, but two. He recognized the larger form as Oz. He had his head tilted down to hear something the other person was saying.

As he got closer, Drew realized it was that Marconi woman from before. At least he thought it was. She looked different somehow. Sharper, and darker. Hearing his approach, she turned her head toward him and smiled. Her teeth glinted unnaturally under the glow from the halogen light, and he caught sight of something that couldn't be real. A fang. Huh?

Before that even sank in, Oz followed her gaze until he noticed Drew, as well. Oz looked...strange. His expression was empty, blank, and his eyes glowed like clear orbs in the night with shadows flickering inside them like a school of fish. Come to think of it, Elisabetta's eyes were the same

"The fuck?" Drew choked out as he stepped back, feeling like he'd suddenly walked onto the set of a bad remake of Invasion of the Body Snatchers. He heard a noise behind him and turned quickly, foolishly hoping to find Alex to call for help.

He found Alex, all right. He caught a flash of a dark beard and the same freaky stare before a shadow came flying at his face and pain exploded into the side of his head. He spun a one-eighty, staggered on his feet, trying to keep his tenuous hold on consciousness and get himself out of this.

Warm liquid slid down his face and into one eye. The burn of it made him blink rapidly as he turned to face Alex again. Fuck, what was he holding? A two-by-four? The thought barely registered before the man swung at him again, caught him in the chest with unnatural force and sent him flying. Drew hit the ground half on his side and his face bit the dirt. That was going to leave a mark, he thought as his vision fuzzed out.

While he fought his brain's need to check out from the pain in his body, Drew listened for the threat. He could hear footsteps crunching in the gravel as someone—probably Alex—walked toward him. The feet stopped beside him, and he actually heard the man tsking him.

"You should always stay down, Deveraux. Didn't your daddy teach you that?"

That little revelation went a long way in focusing Drew's few brain cells left unscrambled. What the fuck did this guy know about what happened when his father had beaten the shit out of him all those years ago?

"Ah, well. Too late now," he said in a tone that was entirely too chipper. The guy reared back and landed a steel toe right into Drew's ribcage. Snap. Shit. He coughed and gasped as the pain threatened to make him vomit and then pass out in it. Drew tried to do the 'horror movie crawl'—the one where the hapless victim pulls his body along the ground with nothing but his arms and drags his legs uselessly behind.

He knew he couldn't get away. So did Alex. The bastard was playing with him, circling like a shark. Drew turned his red-hazed vision toward where Oz stood with the woman, still watching him blankly. "Oz," he tried. "Do something."

'Elvira' smiled at Drew again and raked what looked suspiciously like a claw down Oz's cheek, drawing blood. The man didn't so much as twitch a muscle. When he realized that Oz wasn't going to help him, that no one was, he tried to get to his feet. A wave of dizziness and pain the likes of which he'd never experienced washed over him, and he sank to his knees.

Taking advantage of his semi-elevated position, Alex felled him with a haymaker to the jaw. His prey down once again, the man went to town with the shitkickers to the ribs. Drew felt himself slipping away. His mind checked out to that place it had always gone when his daddy got a drunk on and started wailing on him.

It was almost like an out-of-body experience, like he was floating above himself while he watched some guy make ground chuck out of his torso. And the final stage of his fuck you daddy defenses, he blanked out entirely. Goodnight, kids, thanks for playing. Seacrest, out.

ഌൾ

Normally, Raven would have been speeding down the parkway, on her way the hell out of Dodge. But instead, she took the curves at a sedate pace and fought with every ounce of her willpower not to turn around.

Tears rolled hotly down her cheeks inside her helmet when she recalled Drew's stricken look as she'd railed against him. She'd tried to piss him off, to make him resent her and think she didn't want him. But he'd seen right through her bullshit and called her bluff. When he'd told her, once again, that she was enough, she almost gave in and poured out all her feelings.

All it took was one second of imagining it was him drowning in that pool to shut her right the hell up. Raven was determined that it wouldn't be Drew who was caught in the crossfire the next time Azibel wanted to hurt her. Still, everything in her was straining to go back to him. It was as if she could feel his heart beating inside her, his breath flowing through her lungs.

Not the first time, she wondered if maybe Isla had been mistaken about the laqueum. Maybe it didn't have to be spoken by both people. Maybe Drew saying it out loud was enough. What if it didn't have to be spoken at all? What did they really know for sure? Maybe some feelings were stronger than words.

If that were the case, then he was doomed anyway. *No! I won't let him be hurt. I'll get as far away from here as possible, and she'll follow me.* But where would she go, Raven wondered. Where was home now that Drew was her heart?

All of a sudden, a white hot flash of pain lanced through her skull while her heart clenched inside her chest. Drew. Unable to control her reflexes, her arms seized on the handlebars, and the motorcycle skidded onto its side. She spun, still gripping onto the bike, until it finally came to a stop at the side of the road where it barely missed a large tree.

If she hadn't been wearing her leathers, she'd have been hamburger meat. As it was, she would have one hell of a case of road rash, and the Ducati was going to need a new paint job. "Fuck!" she screamed inside of her helmet.

Even though the crash was over, her heart was still jack-hammering at an alarming pace, her adrenaline ramped up to a fever pitch. She remembered what had caused her to swerve in the first place. Something had happened to Drew. She was sure of it.

Damn her arrogance! She thought that if she was merely out of the picture, Drew would be left alone. Which left him open, a waiting target, without her there to help him. "Stupid, stupid!" she growled.

She needed to keep it together. Had to get back to Drew. She steeled herself, hauled her aching body up off the shoulder and righted the motorcycle. She straddled it once more, gave it some gas and tried to kick start it. Nothing.

Oh, God, please start, please start. She repeated the chant over and over in her head as she tried it again, whooping when the engine roared to life. Carefully, she pulled back out onto the parkway and headed back towards town.

Hitting the bluetooth call button on her helmet, she gave the command to call Jeremiah. It rang once, twice. "Hello?"

She could barely hear him over the growling of the Monster, so she turned up the volume.

"Jeremiah? It's Raven."

"Oh, hey, Raven—"

"Where's Drew?" she asked, cutting off the questions that would surely come.

"Uh, he's at work—"

"Great, thanks. Bye." She hung up on whatever Jeremiah was going to say. She didn't want to alarm anyone, especially when this little hunch could just be her finally tipping the crazy scale a little too far. It was probably nothing, but she had to check.

Revving the engine, she shot off toward the site and prayed the blue lights wouldn't get in her way.

CHAPTER THIRTY NINE

Raven was already swinging off the motorcycle as she skidded into the parking area. She cut the engine and dumped the bike—figuring she already needed body work after her little bender on the Parkway—and took off at a run.

Fingers flew as she typed in the code to temporarily disable the perimeter alarm. Once inside, she scanned the site and frantically tried to locate Drew. She didn't know why she was feeling such a sense of urgency, such a certainty that he had been hurt.

It just was. It was like an invisible string connected the two of them, and someone was tugging on Drew's end.

She started toward the lab tent but thought better of it. There were no lights on inside bleeding out from under the canvas walls. Where was he? As she moved down toward the grid, her eyes scanned the creepy chessboard full of bones laid out before her, shadowed strangely under the security lights.

The cameras. She could go check the feeds to see if Drew was anywhere around. She changed her mind and backtracked to the lab tent, after all. Inside, she flicked on the lights and looked around. All of the equipment was meticulously cleaned, covered and put away, and whatever was on the examination table had been covered with a tarp and secured by clamps.

It was clear that no one had been in there working. Making her way to the back of the tent to the security feed computer, she wiggled the mouse and woke up the screen. The display was divided into eight sections, one for each camera.

Scanning them quickly, she saw no sign of Drew. She was about to give up and continue her search, but she decided to have one more thorough look at each camera. Visible #1, view of the southwest quadrant; nothing. Hidden #1, directly south facing...nothing. The same for northeast, southeast, east, and north.

Staring hard at hidden #4—the one that faced northeast, and the lowest corner of the grid—she narrowed her eyes. There was a strange shadow below the security light, one that didn't look like it should be cast by the dim halogen.

She stared at it until her eyes crossed, then stared at it some more. And then it moved. Just ever so slightly, a shallow rise and fall. *Shit!* "Drew!" she said aloud.

Raven knocked over the chair, tore out of the tent and took off down the small hill faster than she'd ever run in her life. Her eyes zeroed in on the shadowy lump she'd seen on the feed, and she pounded the dirt until she got to it—stopping so hard she skidded the last few feet and slumped down beside him.

He was lying on his side with his back to her, his breathing shallow, chest hitching on the inhale. She could see that his blonde curls were dark and matted to his head with a thick, sticky substance. Blood.

"Drew," she whispered, but all she got in answer was an agonized groan.

"Shit, what do I do? Drew!" She'd shouted it that time.

More groaning, then, "Raven?" Gingerly, he turned his bloody face around to look at her. When she saw those clear blue eyes peeking out from all of that blood, she choked back a sob. Carefully, she grasped his shoulder and helped him turn over onto his back.

His clothing was dirty and torn, especially across his ribcage and chest, and he couldn't seem to take in a deep breath.

"Ribs?" she asked.

"Broken," he croaked. "At least three."

Her cheeks felt hot and wet, and Raven knew she had tears streaming down her face, but she didn't care. Unable to help herself, she leaned over to kiss him, lighter than hummingbird wings. He sighed and leaned into her, tried to smile, but it looked more like a grimace. "Knew you couldn't stay away."

A sob turned into a snort, and she nearly choked on it. "God, Drew. What the hell happened?"

"Oz...Fuckin' Alex Webber," he slurred, not making any sense. "Batshit crazy... And then the woman, but she wasn't real. Was that before he hit me? Can't remember. Must have been after...Hallucination."

"Drew, honey you're not making any sense."

"Brained me somethin' good, Raven. Two b'four ah think." He'd slipped back into his Cajun, and that, plus the slurring, made it nearly impossible to understand him. But at least he was talking.

"You think you can walk if I help you?" There was no way he was getting on the motorcycle, but they'd have to make it to the gravel parking lot so someone could pick them up.

"Can try."

"All right, up you go." She pushed him upright so that he was sitting up, but he moaned and grabbed his head.

"God*damn,* that hurts."

"Sorry, love," she said, but she had to get him up while he had his momentum. She tucked a shoulder under his arm and pushed into him to give him something to hold onto as he pulled himself up.

Staggering, he leaned heavily on her. She was strong, solid muscle, but at only five-foot-four, she struggled to hold up his six-two frame. They stood that way for a few minutes while he dealt with the vertigo and was finally able to stand up a little straighter.

Painstakingly slowly, they made their way up the hill toward the car lot. By the time they reached it, Drew was breathing heavily and covered in sweat, but he was walking better own his own.

He leaned on a light post while Raven went to her bike and fetched her cell phone, so they could call Jeremiah for a ride. As she was walking back toward Drew, a car down the road backfired loudly. She watched him flinch and twist his body around, as if he thought he would have to deflect another blow.

His entire body went rigid, and his face drained of color so fast, she thought he'd pass out. Instead, he tried to take a deep breath, but all he could get was a gasping, sputtering wheeze. He exploded into a fit of coughing, and she watched in horror as blood dripped from his mouth and coated his hand.

Widened eyes locked onto hers, and, as if in slow motion, he dropped to his knees. *No!* The thought screamed in her head again, but she made no sound as she lunged for him. She slid behind him so she could catch him before he fell backwards onto the gravel.

Sitting down on the ground with her back braced against the light post, she pulled him against her with his back to her front. She slipped her arms underneath his, wrapped them around and placed both hands on his chest.

"Breathe, love," she commanded with a calm she surely didn't feel. His chest wasn't so much rising and falling as it was convulsing. She could hear the telltale whistle in his ineffective breaths. When he'd turned so sharply, one of his broken ribs must have punctured his lung, which was likely filling up with blood.

Whether he suffocated or bled to death, Raven knew that they only had minutes. She had to get him help. Cell phone in hand, she dialed 911 and gave them directions to the site. She didn't hang up, because she wanted them to be able to triangulate her position, but she laid the phone down and concentrated on Drew.

"R-Raven. Some-Something's wrong. Can't..."

"Ssh. Don't talk. Just breathe."

"Can't." This time he said it more forcefully, inciting another fit of bloody coughs.

"I know, baby. Help's on the way, you just have to stay with me."

"But...," his voice was barely a whisper, "...you left."

Raven squeezed her eyes shut against tears as a fist clamped around her heart. She'd never make that mistake again.

"I know, baby," she repeated. "Won't be leaving again."

"Promise?" he asked, and he sounded so much like a little boy, she ached for him.

"Promise. Now I want you to concentrate on breathing."

"Can't."

"Yes, you can. You will." She placed a hand over his heart, comforted by its steady beating. She took a deep breath, allowing him to feel her chest rise and fall. "Feel me? Just do what I do. Breathe with me. In. Out. In. Good. Keep going."

Tears escaped again. They slid down her cheeks and dropped into his hair. It was like she was breathing for him, literally coaching him to stay alive. To not leave her. Where the *hell* was that ambulance?

He was still breathing shallow, but he was getting weaker. She could feel the fight begin to leave him, could feel his muscles relaxing. No. She was *not* going to lose him. She was just about to call Jeremiah and risk him driving 120 miles an hour down the parkway to get Drew to the hospital when she heard the whine of the siren.

The sound grew louder, and she could see the lights as the vehicle careened into the parking area. Raven eased her way out from under Drew and stepped aside to let the paramedic team do their work. With quick and efficient movements, they secured a neck brace on Drew and strapped him to a backboard to lift him onto the gurney.

"What happened?" one of the men in blue jumpsuits asked her.

"I wasn't there when it happened. I found him beaten up pretty badly, wounds to the head and chest, several ribs broken, at least he thought. He was doing all right until he moved the wrong way and started coughing up blood and wheezing. I think one of the ribs may have punctured his lung. Please, he can't breathe, and he's getting weaker. You have to help him—" she had to clap a hand over her mouth to stem the flow of hysterical babble.

Besides, the man had already gotten what he needed, returned to the ambulance, and was assisting his partner in loading the gurney. The man she'd spoken to climbed into the driver's seat, and the other one—a rather small, mousy looking man—started to step up into the back.

"Wait! I'm going with you."

"Ma'am—"

"*Fuck* the ma'am, I'm going with you. I can ride in the back like a good little girl, or I can drive this bus. Which is it?" The little man blanched under her fierce glare, then jerked his head toward the back.

Once inside the ambulance, the man—Tim, as a patch on his suit indicated—quickly put an oxygen mask over Drew's face, started an I.V. drip and began hooking him up to a vitals monitor. Raven sat on the other side of the gurney, whispering to Drew.

His eyes rolled wildly as he looked around the ambulance, as if not sure of where he was. When he started to claw at the mask, Raven grabbed his hand and kissed it. "Easy, baby. Let him help you."

Breathing was becoming more of a struggle, nothing but a painful gasping sound. "Can't you do something to help him breathe?"

"He most likely has a punctured lung from one of the broken ribs. The oxygen should help some, ma'am. We'll be at the hospital in just a few minutes," Tim said in his Appalachian twang.

Suddenly, Drew's body began bucking violently and the monitors began beeping. A strangled, gurgling sound began to emanate from his throat, muffled by the mask, and a haze of red appeared on the clear plastic.

"He's fucking drowning!" Raven screamed. *"Do something!"*

"There's not much I can do. I could intubate, but there's already fluid in his lungs, so it won't help much," he said with irritating calmness. "We'll have a trauma team waiting at the hospital."

As Drew continued to convulse, Raven climbed on top of the gurney and straddled his hips. She placed her hands on his shoulders, held him still and leaned over, catching his eyes.

"Drew. I know you can hear me. Hang on a little bit longer. Just breathe, baby."

His beautiful sky blue eyes were round with fear, and a single tear slipped out of the corner of one of them. That alone was enough to break Raven's control. Hell, she was already breaking every rule she could think of by sitting on him. What was one more?

Abruptly, she turned to Tim and practically snarled at him. "Are you an EMT or a paramedic?"

He leaned back and gave her a horrified look. "Y-you can't...What?"

"EMT. Paramedic. *Which?*" She shouted.

"Para. Why?"

"You can do a chest tube. I want you to do it."

"We-we're in the field. Not really supposed to—"

"I don't give a *fuck* what you're *supposed* to do. He's dying! Now do it or I'm gonna snap you in half!" She growled that last bit, and when she caught sight of her reflection in the window glass, she saw that her amber eyes were glowing fiercely—she looked like she could live up to her threat. With relish.

Oh well, she would probably be arrested or shipped off to the nut farm for threatening the paramedic anyway, so who the hell cared? The small man cringed away from her, but with shaking hands, he began to prepare the supplies for the chest tube.

While he set up, she leaned over Drew again, looked deep into those terrified eyes, wishing she could make it better. He tried to draw another breath and absolutely nothing got through. His eyes widened from sheer panic.

"Drew, look at me." He obeyed, even as he began to shake from lack of oxygen. "Don't you *dare* leave me. I'm nothing without you. Do you hear me? Stay with me," his eyes rolled back in his head as she whispered, "I love you."

She held him still with her arms and legs as Tim found the spot to make the cut with his scalpel. Slicing a small hole, he inserted the tube, and his eyes widened as blood gushed through it from Drew's chest cavity and into the drainage bag.

When Raven felt Drew gasp a huge breath, she closed her eyes and sent up a silent thank you to whoever was listening. Her entire body felt weak as the adrenaline drained away, and she slid off the gurney to sit by his side once more.

She spent the rest of the trip to the hospital stroking his face and watching his chest rise. He didn't open his eyes again, but he was breathing. He was alive, and that was all that mattered.

Chapter Forty

When they skidded to a halt in the ambulance bay of Blowing Rock Hospital, Raven backed off and allowed the paramedics to unload Drew. She ran alongside the gurney as a team of doctors and nurses rushed it inside.

They quickly reached a set of swinging doors that were labeled *AUTHORIZED PERSONNEL ONLY*. Fuck that, Raven thought, and lunged forward to push her way through. A male nurse put a hand on her shoulder to prevent her from entering.

"I'm sorry, ma'am, you can't be back here. You'll have to wait over there in the waiting room."

Raven just stood there, seething, covered in Drew's blood, and stared at the doors swinging shut. Frustrated, she walked back to the waiting room and tried to sit, but her skin felt tight, her muscles twitchy. She began to pace, shaking her head as she recalled the events of the night.

Her hands unconsciously curled into fists and her nails dug into her palms hard enough to draw blood. How could she have been so stupid? She had some crazy demon genetics going on inside her, so it wasn't a huge stretch of the imagination that Azibel could sense her connections with people or, hell, read her mind, even.

And she'd still left Drew wide open, with a bullseye on his back. Raven couldn't catch her breath, and her vision began to swim. He had to be okay.

No longer able to take the waiting, and sure she was freaking out the other patrons with her muttering and pacing, she went to the front desk. The nurse on duty had a halo of hair an improbable shade of blonde and a bored, world-weary expression. She eyed Raven over the rim of her thick glasses.

"Name?"

"Dr. Drew Deveraux. He was brought in after an assault. Can you tell me what's going on with him."

Raven gritted her teeth as the woman unhurriedly tapped on her keyboard with her two index fingers. "All I can tell you is that he's in surgery."

"Surgery," Raven repeated, unable to grasp the severity of the situation. "What are they doing to him? Is he going to be all right?"

Mary Sue, as her nametag proclaimed, gave her a hard stare. "You family?"

"No, but—"

"I'm sorry, but I can only give medical information to the patient's next of kin."

"Please, can't you just—"

"No, I'm sorry."

Raven released a stream of expletives that caused Mary Sue to pale underneath a thick layer of Maybelline. Time to call in the cavalry, she thought. Such an odd thing, how comfortable she'd become with asking others for help. Drew and his friends were changing her. Healing her.

She pulled out her phone and hit redial on Jeremiah's number. "Raven?" he answered without so much as a hello.

"Blowing Rock Hospital. Now," she said and hung up. She was in no mood to explain over the phone. Going back to the waiting area, she resumed her pacing despite the dirty looks she was getting from others.

The drive from Cliffdweller's to the hospital should have taken ten minutes. Raven guessed that Jeremiah made the trip in about four. He burst through the door with Isla in tow, followed by Ray and Brynna, with Marduk bringing up the rear.

The lot of them made a beeline for Raven, surrounded her with hugs and a barrage of questions. She couldn't find the breath to answer any of them. Instead, she heaved a dry sob and sank down into the nearest chair.

Immediately, strong arms surrounded her, and the familiar sent of vanilla and Old Spice washed over her. Ray. Her dad. She needed him, and he was there. How was that for progress? He was silent, just held her and rubbed her back while the others gently questioned her.

Raven managed to give them a brief rundown of everything that happened, leaving out the part about their fight—although she expected Jeremiah already knew.

"I don't know what to do. They won't tell me anything. Said they can only talk to family."

Jeremiah flashed her a smile, one that Raven was sure must have charmed the pants off many a young lady over the years. "Let me see what I can do."

Jeremiah sauntered up to the desk with a little extra swing in his hips. He grinned broadly at the nurse with his overlong canines and his twinkling hazel eyes, then leaned in to read her nametag. Laying the Cajun on thick, he winked at her.

"Hello there, Mary Sue. Ah've got a little problem Ah was hopin' you could help me with. My best good friend was brought in here 'while ago after an accident. Could you be a doll and look 'im up for me?"

Mary Sue looked like she was doing everything she could not to fan herself and swoon. Raven heard Isla suppress an unladylike snort.

"Sure, sweetie," Mary Sue said. "What's the name?"

"Andrew Deveraux."

More hen-pecking on the keyboard. Mary Sue frowned and flicked an annoyed glance over in Raven's direction. "I'm sorry, sir. He's in surgery. I'm afraid that's all I can tell you unless you're family."

"Listen, ma'am. I—*we* are the only family that man has that will claim him. You won't find anyone else to contact. He's only got one living relative and she wants nothing to do with him."

Mary Sue pursed her lips, which were a garish shade of tomato red, as she considered him. Finally she sighed, and Raven knew they'd won.

"I'll go see if I can find someone to come out and talk to you."

Jeremiah sent her another thousand watt smile, causing her to pat her unfortunate hair and bat her eyelashes. "Thank you, *cher*."

As he swaggered back over to the chairs, Isla and Brynna struggled to cover their sniggering. "Shame on you for flirtin' wi' that poor girl," Isla said with an indulgent smile that was only for her husband.

"What?" Brynna asked. "He'll be the star of her wet dreams for weeks!"

Marduk, who had just taken a sip of coffee, sputtered and choked while the rest of them cackled.

Raven just leaned her head on Ray's shoulder and watched them. She was glad they were there. It felt good not to have to shoulder everything alone for once.

Raven caught sight of a slim figure in a blue jumpsuit over by the vending machines, excused herself and walked over to him. Tim, the paramedic, eyed her warily, as if, at any moment, he expected her to grow a second head. Not that she could blame him.

"Hey," she said quietly.

"Hey."

"Look, I just wanted to say thanks for what you did. And I'm sorry that shit got critical back there. I just..." she trailed off, unsure as to how to explain to a stranger what she barely understood herself. That Drew had somehow wormed his way into her heart and into the center of her universe.

"Don't worry about it," he said, shrugging his thin shoulders. "I've had worse. I hope he'll be okay."

"Me, too. Thanks again. And if they give you any shit about doing something you weren't supposed to, just tell them I threatened you. I don't want you to get in any trouble."

"It'll be okay. Thanks, though. See you," he said, then grabbed his soda and headed back to his rig.

The double doors swung open, and a short, bald man in green surgical scrubs walked into the waiting area. "Deveraux?"

Six people surrounded the poor man, looking at him expectantly. "How is he, Doc?" Jeremiah asked.

"Mr. Deveraux suffered—"

"*Doctor*," Raven hissed, "Dr. Deveraux." She didn't know why it was so important to her that this man made the distinction, but it was.

"Er, sorry. Dr. Deveraux suffered a pneumothorax, a collapsed lung, caused by a broken rib. Four ribs were broken, both kidneys were bruised. He also received a head wound—no bleeding was indicated upon CT scan, but we won't know the extent of the head injury until he wakes up. At the very least, he has a concussion. He also suffered severe bruising and multiple lacerations during his assault."

"But will he be okay?" Raven asked quietly.

"We've repaired the punctured lung and broken ribs in surgery. His ribs will have to be taped for a while but should heal fine. The only thing we have to watch for is any swelling or bleeding in the brain."

"Can we see him?"

The doctor eyed them carefully, and Raven realized they were about to get another 'only family' speech. Jeremiah cut him off at the pass. He gestured for the doctor to step over into the corner with him, where they had a quiet conversation. Raven assumed he was saying something along the lines of what he'd told Mary Sue.

When they returned to the group, the doctor nodded at them. "I'll go find a nurse to show you back."

ജ

Drew felt like he was wrapped in a sleeping bag, with an elephant sitting on his chest. He couldn't see, but he could hear and he could breathe—however shallow. Since he was pretty sure he hadn't been run over by a herd of panicked wildebeests in the last twenty-four hours, his pain must be from the attack.

He only remembered bits and pieces of it: the two-by-four, the crazy eyes, the splintering pain. Raven. Thoughts of the beating made his brain want to recede back behind the hazy curtain of unconsciousness, so he let it.

He awoke some time later to the sound of muffled voices in the room, and a searing white light shining in his eyes. No matter how tight he tried to squeeze his lids, he just couldn't escape the light. He flailed angrily and tried to swat the light away. Feeling heavy arms pin him down, he struggled harder, until he felt a cool, smooth touch on his hand, then his face. Raven.

Drew's heart sped up, and he tried to push toward the surface inside his fuzzy mind. She was there. She'd stayed. All of the murmurs receded, and he latched onto one voice. "...come back to us, baby."

Finally, he heaved his eyelids open but immediately squinted at the brightness of the room. The nurse who'd been giving him a lobotomy with a penlight must have gone. His eyes bounced frantically between one blurry face and the next, until he zeroed in on the one he was looking for. She was right beside the bed, holding his hand.

He could make out her bronze skin and dark slashing brows, could see the worry lines around her sensual mouth. She'd stayed. He gave her a weak smile, and everyone else in the room might as well have been invisible.

"Hey there, sexy," he said, repeating her words from the previous night.

A shaky laugh escaped her, and she caressed his face with uncharacteristic tenderness. Her face quickly became serious again. "How are you feeling?"

"Better than I look, I'm sure." His vision began to clear, and he was able to see the faces of all of his friends, even Ray. They looked grim. "That bad, huh?" he asked Jeremiah.

The other man didn't smile. "We nearly lost you, brother. If it weren't for Raven, we would have."

Drew narrowed his eyes at his friend. "What do you mean?"

"She went all vigilante justice on the paramedic, threatened to end the little dude if he didn't put in a chest tube on the fly. I kind of got the feeling they're not supposed to do that."

He turned his head to gape at Raven, who merely shrugged. "Desperate times and all that."

Drew frowned as a flood of memories from the attack rushed to the forefront of his mind, along with an overflow of unanswered questions. Why had the night guard wanted to hurt him? Who was the woman, and why the *fuck* hadn't Oz helped him?

Raven lowered her eyes and spoke in a quiet voice. "Shouldn't have gone there alone, Drew."

"I wasn't alone. Alex was on duty, and Oz was there with that...woman. But something was off."

"Like what?" Jeremiah asked.

"Well, the two-by-four Alex Webber swung at my head, for one. And then there was...," Drew trailed off with a careful shake of his head. He couldn't even find the words to describe the craziness of what he'd seen.

The slender young man who stood in the corner came over to the other side of Drew's bed. Marduk stared at him with those unfathomable arctic eyes until he began to squirm. "And then?"

"Something just wasn't right about them. All of them, but especially that woman. Ms. Marconi."

"The eyes...," Marduk said quietly.

"How did you know?"

"It's what the *Lochrim* do," Jeremiah said. They don't have enough energy to become corporeal to physically hurt a human, so they'll possess people to do their bidding. Usually the weak-minded or weak-willed."

"That explains a lot," Drew murmured. "Alex Webber was the one who did the beating, while Oz just watched. *Fuck!* We have to find out what they remember..."

He trailed off when the surgeon entered the hospital room, giving them a detached smile. "How are you feeling this morning, Dr. Deveraux?" he asked. He walked over and reached inside the neck of Drew's johnny to place a cold stethoscope on his chest. "Deep breath."

"Like I've been sliced open and sewn back together. Oh, wait...," Drew grinned, amused at his own cheekiness.

Raven snorted and swatted his arm. "Ding, ding, ding! Tell the man what he's won, Doc."

Dr. Myers chuckled as he made notations on the clipboard he had brought in with him. "Well, we stitched up the hole in your lung, and it should function normally after a couple of days of shortness of breath. Two of your ribs were completely detached, which we repaired with wire. The others were merely cracked, so you'll have to keep your torso bound for the next couple of weeks."

"Don't lie, Doc. You put *adamantium* in there, didn't you?" From the corner of the room, Marduk barked out a laugh, but Doc Myers just looked confused. Drew rolled his eyes at Marduk, then winked at the doctor. "Never mind," he said, "please, continue."

"Ah, yes, well, we also put a few staples in that nasty gash on the side of your head...Oh, and I had the nurse put a salve on that tattoo of yours. It was looking pretty ripe."

Drew gave Raven a confused look, and she mouthed *tattoo?* He gave a quick shake of his head and a shrug to tell her that he had no idea what the doctor was talking about.

Dr. Myers quickly checked the rest of Drew's vitals then asked if they had any questions.

"What am I looking at for recovery?"

"We'll need to keep you here for a week in order to keep an eye on the healing process. If all goes well, you can go home after that, but you'll need to take it easy for another two weeks. No working."

Cursing under his breath, Drew raised his eyes skyward. They didn't have that kind of time. The end of the world wasn't going to wait on his fucking ribs to heal. Hell, that was probably what Azibel had been counting on, if not outright killing him.

Drew sighed and looked into the doctor's kind brown eyes. "Thanks, Doc, I owe ya one."

The man just shook his head and smiled as he backed out of the room. "Just take care of yourself. Don't mess up my handiwork."

"Will do," Drew said, though he'd already turned away from the doctor to lock eyes with Raven. "Tattoo..." he breathed. Seriously?

The sounds of chairs scraping the floor and clothes rustling filled the room, along with a litany of hastily mumbled excuses, as their friends rather indiscreetly made themselves scarce. Drew ignored them, having eyes only for Raven as she pulled her chair closer.

"You don't think...," he trailed off, not really sure what to say or how she was going to react to this. Would she leave again? "I thought it had to be spoken. For the *laqueum*, I mean. But you never...Fuck." She was looking at him with an intense, unreadable expression in those whiskey eyes with their flecks of gold.

"Um, I sort of did."

His mouth fell open of its own accord, and he could do nothing but stare at her. She began to fidget, uncomfortable with the scrutiny—or the intimacy—of the situation.

"I thought I was losing you. And it was completely my fault."

Drew closed his eyes as his emotions overwhelmed him. This woman. This strong, capable, stubborn, bull-headed, drop-dead-fucking-gorgeous creature, may actually love him back. It was almost too much to comprehend.

When his eyes opened again, he locked on her face, and, immediately, a memory teased the edges of his mind. Raven's eyes, wide and terrified as she straddled him on the gurney and willed him to breathe. Raven, snarling at the paramedic, her eyes glittering with an unnatural light. Her breathless whispers as he began to lose consciousness, drowning in his own blood.

Don't you dare leave me. I'm nothing without you. Do you hear me? Stay with me. I love you.

His breath hitched as he hooked a finger in the neck of his johnny and pulled it down to reveal the skin over his left pec. They both gasped when they saw it. Scored deep into the flesh and, they now knew, the tissue and bone beneath it, was Raven's *signa*.

The area around the dark black lines was an angry red, as if they had been tattooed over freshly burned skin. Angling his head to get a closer look, Drew gingerly touched the inflamed skin and immediately winced. "Ow."

He looked back at Raven and noticed that her eyes were still riveted to the spot on his chest. What was she thinking? Planning her next bolt? Didn't matter. She was his now, and he was most definitely hers. He would wait for her to come to terms with it. As long as it took.

Drew reached out and entwined his fingers with hers, and she looked up at him. "You okay with this?" he asked, as if they really had a choice.

She seemed to consider it for a moment before blowing out a shaky breath. "Yeah. Yeah, I think I am."

That smile, when she really let it come out to play, had the power to strip him bare. He returned the smile and tugged on her hand. "Then get up here."

For once, she did what he asked and climbed up onto the narrow bed as he scooted over to make room for her. She turned on her side to gently lay her head on his shoulder and placed her hand over his heart, as if the steady beating reassured her.

Drew breathed deep of her spicy scent, and relished the feel of her compact body tight against him. He felt like, with her by his side, he could face any goddamned thing that came at him.

She sighed deeply as her eyelids fluttered to look up at him. "I was really scared, Drew."

He knew how hard that was for her to admit—let alone feel—and he respected her for saying it.

"I know, love. But you were there for me, as I'll always be for you. We make a hell of a team."

She smiled, rather pleased with herself. "I guess we do."

"I need you to answer a couple of questions for me."

Raven frowned, her dark brows lowered, but she nodded. "Okay. Like what?"

Drew looked down at her and suddenly felt every bit of the strain of his ordeal. "Why did you leave?" He wasn't sure he wanted to know the answer, but he knew he needed to, if they were going to make a go of it.

She closed her eyes, and her forehead wrinkled as if the memory hurt to think about. She exhaled slowly and looked at him nervously, gauging his mood. "I thought you would be safer."

He started to speak, wanted to argue, but she stopped him with a look. "Let me finish. At first, it was the *laqueum* I was afraid of. I didn't think it was fair for you to be irrevocably tied to someone like me. I'm a mess, Drew. My social skills are crude, at best, and my relationship skills are nonexistent.

"Plus, the way I live is...dangerous. Even more so now. It felt like tying our fates together was like issuing you a death sentence." She broke off, visibly upset but struggling to pull herself together. He covered her hand with his, where it rested on his chest.

"And then there was Azibel's attack. When she was drowning me, she got into my head. Told me that she would destroy everyone I loved. And fuck if I didn't believe every word. I thought if I could make you hate me, make you leave me, she would leave you alone. Focus on me. But you wouldn't. I could see on your face that you wouldn't give up.

"So I had to take off. I figured I'd get as far away from you as I could, and she would follow. Guess I was wrong. I almost lost you anyway," she said with a full body shudder.

"Oh, Raven," he whispered. Drew couldn't believe that this had all been about trying to protect him. He should probably be angry. Furious, even. But all he could feel was overwhelming, mind-blowing elation. This woman loved him. She loved him so much that she'd been willing to rip out her own heart to keep him safe. How 'bout that?

He pulled her closer and placed a kiss on the top of her head. It was all he could reach without ripping his sutures. He figured Doc Myers would be kind of pissed about that. "Raven, I get what you were trying to do. I'm actually honored in a twisted sort of way. But we're stronger together. You understand?"

He waited while she nodded. "Remember that. Not just you and I, either. The seven of us are stronger together. Safety in numbers. Got it?" he asked and nudged her with his shoulder.

"Got it," she said with an indulgent smile.

"Good. So no more leaving?"

"No more leaving."

"That leads me to my other question. How did you know I was in trouble?"

"I just...felt something. Like it was happening to me. A blinding pain in my head. Nausea. Vertigo. I wonder if the *laqueum* hadn't already taken effect, even then. I may not have said anything out loud, but I had admitted to myself that I loved you. Maybe my actions spoke enough."

"Maybe," he murmured distractedly. He picked up her hand, intending to bring it to his lips when he spotted the scrapes and cuts across her knuckles. "What happened to you?"

She seemed unwilling to look him in the eye, focusing instead on the pattern of his hospital gown. "Uh. I had to lay my bike down."

His expression turned thunderous as his eyes snapped down to her face. "What does that mean? Like, you crashed?"

Her eyes flicked to his and looked away with embarrassment. "A little..."

"Raven!"

"It's nothing. I was riding down the parkway when your attack happened. I jerked a little, spun out. Look, I'm fine. You're going to be fine. Everything's fine."

She began to make slow circles with her hand over his heart, and he felt the tension start to ebb from him. She was right. They were all fine—for now. Her hand stilled and she was quiet for so long, he thought she'd gone to sleep.

Drew looked down and noticed her eyelids fluttering, but her eyes were unseeing—as if she was concentrating hard on something he couldn't see. A warmth began to radiate from her hand, infusing him with a nourishing glow. As the feeling spread throughout his body, he felt his knotted muscles turn to mush and his eyelids droop.

God, he was tired, and the drugging heat that buzzed inside him was so comforting. He closed his eyes and told himself he would just rest for a moment. Just a little while.

CHAPTER FORTY ONE

Hours later, Drew awoke and found Raven still curled against him with one leg thrown across his hips. He barely suppressed a groan as she shifted in her sleep, her knee once again massaging his near painful 'below the belt' situation. Some parts of his body didn't seem to register that the rest of him had been beaten in the worst way. They were so on board for a little hospital bed action.

Thankfully, Raven chose that moment to open her eyes. She sat up on the bed and tipped her head back, and sleepily raked fingers through her tousled hair. Drew tried his damnedest not to drool on himself as he eyed the smooth column of her neck.

That time, he failed miserably at holding in a moan, and she heard. Turning to smile at him, she gave him a wink. "Down boy. You heard the doc. You've got to take it easy."

"You could be gentle. Very, very gentle," he said with an exaggerated leer. She chuckled and leaned in to give him her mouth. He held the back of her head firm as he explored, teasing her lips until she opened for him.

After long reluctant moments, she pulled away. "I'm going to go over to the dig, see what's what. Need to find Oz and see what he knows. Alex Webber ghosted on us. Jeremiah went looking for the asshat after your surgery the other night. Long fucking gone," she groused.

"Raven, I'm not going to ask you not to go because, well, I like my nuts right where they are. But I need you to be careful. Please."

Her face softened and she took pity on him. "I am. I will. I'm going to take the fur patrol with me. Between the cat and the wolf, my ass will be covered."

Drew breathed a sigh of relief when he realized she had no intention of going off half-cocked after Azibel. She was being smart. Strong and capable, he thought again. That was his girl.

"Good," he said. "You'll come back here after? Let me know what you find?"

"Of course," she answered. She gave him a smack on the lips and hopped down off the bed. "Get some rest, Deveraux. I'm so going to have plans for you in a couple of days." With a waggle of her eyebrows and a deviant smile, she flipped her hair over her shoulder and sauntered out.

Drew closed his eyes and was just settling in to do as he promised and have a rest when he heard the door creak open and close with a soft click. He tracked the light footfalls across the room until they came to a stop on the far side of his bed.

Cracking his heavy eyelids open, Drew found Ray standing over him. He wore a leather satchel across his chest and a scowl on his face. Drew had the feeling he was about to get "the talk" with the old man. While he didn't have a problem with Ray—hell, he kind of liked the guy—the *fuck* if he was going to take shit from the guy who had raised her with one foot in prison and the other in the grave.

Drew sneered right back at the older man as he spoke in a gruff voice. "If you're about to sit there and ask me what my *intentions* are, I'm going to give you an enema with this I.V. pole, hear?"

Ray blinked a couple of times, then threw his head back and howled. Like, the dude was busting a gut, Drew thought, and winced as Ray slapped a hand down on his leg hard enough to hurt. Drew was trying really hard to minimize the damage to his ego, but, damn. He wasn't a UFC champion by any means, but he wasn't scrawny either.

When the laughter finally subsided, Ray wiped his eyes and grinned at Drew. "I like you, kid. And as long as you're good to Raven and don't try to change her, we're cool. Thing is, though, that girl was the only thing that kept me going in prison. But I will not *hesitate* to send myself back there with a murder charge, wrapped up in a pretty little bow, you hurt one hair on her head. Dig?"

Drew rested his chin on his hand and stared Ray down. He couldn't fault the guy for trying to keep Raven safe now that she was back in his life. But Drew felt like he had just as much call to protect her from Ray, if not more.

He nodded at Ray, his expression deadly serious. "Same goes."

"Agreed," the older man answered with no hesitation. "You ready for your get well present now?"

"Okaaay," Drew stretched the word while raising a brow.

Ray tossed the worn leather satchel onto Drew's blanket covered lap. Drew looked at the bag then back at Ray like he'd suddenly grown a pair of horns. "Um, you shouldn't have?"

"Don't be a tool," Ray said blandly. "Open it."

Drew reached in and pulled out something hard and cool. It was the other puzzle box, nearly identical to the one Hammer had dug up. He held it up gently, turning it to examine the symbols and markings. Just like the book they'd found in the first box, on the bottom was etched: *L. Montreaux.*

Drew eyed Ray, his brows knitting. "You have no idea who this L. Montreaux is?

"Not a clue. Here, let me see it."

Drew handed the box over and allowed Ray to engage the lock mechanism. Ray gingerly opened the top and handed it back.

Drew pulled out a yellowed stack of black and white photographs and placed them carefully on his lap while he set the box aside. The first photograph was a young, dark haired girl with an older woman who was obviously her mother. The girl was frail looking, but her eyes were bright and fierce.

"My mother," Ray said, almost whispering. "I imagine that was my grandmother." He tapped the face of the older woman.

Pulling out the next photo, he saw an older version of the girl, with her riotous dark curls and that same piercing gaze. Only this image showed a dark, sullen boy clutching at her skirts.

The woman's smile was serene, though off in the corner, a shadow loomed. A man leaned up against the side of a modest looking house, the neck of a whiskey bottle clutched between his thumb and index finger, and he was scowling at the pair of them.

Drew studied the man, then the boy. It was the older man's eyes that gave him pause, and he grew very still. He'd seen those eyes before, and, indeed, they haunted his dreams and his waking thoughts. They were the eyes of the woman he loved. His...mate.

His eyebrows rose toward his hairline as he made the connection. "Your father?"

Ray nodded grimly, his upper lip curling as if even the memory of the man stuck in his craw. Drew could totally relate. "Yeah. Meanest sumbitch I ever met. Cagey bastard. I'll never understand how he convinced her to marry him. She was so pure. She was all that was good in my world. Maybe that was why he hated her so much."

"What happened to her?" Drew asked quietly, fearing he knew the answer.

"She died. Under suspicious circumstances. Case was never solved. But then, Andrés Sabatier was always good at covering his tracks—and keeping the bruises on the inside."

Drew cursed softly and thought about his own mother. Even while part of him hated her for abandoning him in favor of her own happiness, he was glad she'd been spared that particular fate. For all her flaws, he'd never wished her death.

"And you?" Drew asked.

"He remarried not long after, to a bitch of the first order, nearly as evil as he was. He beat the shit out of me at least once a day until I finally got big enough to take him down. The day that happened, I left and never went back."

"Fuckin' hell." Eloquent, as ever, Drew thought. But what else could be said? He felt a sort of camaraderie with Ray—a solidarity of the beaten, so to speak—and he had more in common with the man than he'd ever thought. Maybe they could come to an accord after all. Maybe even become friends of a sort.

"I think I was around five the first time Stanton Deveraux laid one on me," Drew said quietly. As always, he refused to call the man his father anywhere except inside his own head. "First, it was his belt, then the hickory switch...then his fists. Hell, he hit me upside the head with the yellow pages once. Believe me, I feel you."

Ray met Drew's eyes and winced, and they were acutely aware of one another's pain. Ray inclined his head solemnly, and, yep, they definitely had an understanding. Drew cleared his throat and turned his attention back to the stack of old photos.

Moving on to the next one, he realized that it wasn't a photograph at all, but a tintype. Reverently, he ran a finger down the side of the etched metal plate He'd never seen one in real life, much less held one, so he was fascinated by it.

The image was of a woman dressed in Victorian garb, but rather than have her dark hair piled on top of her head, as was the fashion of the time, it fell to her waist in thick, heavy curls. She smiled out at the image maker, as if she had a secret of great importance.

But what struck him most about her was, again, her eyes. They stared straight ahead, unseeing, covered by an opaque white film. And on her left cheek was some kind of large birthmark. Drew squinted at the grayed out image. No, not a birthmark. A *signa.*

Well, that was to be expected, he supposed. Their research had told them that the *Vigilati* was a matrilineal bloodline. But he wasn't sure how that worked out when the maternal lineage was *Lochrim*. As far as they knew, Raven was the only exception to the rule. Did that mean that the *Vigilati* blood came from *Ray's* maternal lineage?

At this point, all they had was speculation, but Drew couldn't help the niggling doubt that clawed at him, warning him that there was more to these photographs than just a family tree.

"Who is this?" he asked.

"Not entirely sure. My mother died when I was young, and she hardly ever spoke of her family. I think maybe it hurt too much, given the situation she'd put herself in. But, based on the time period, I would assume she's my great-grandmother. I used to dream about her though, especially back when Raven first came to live with me. I was terrified of raising a child, so it was as if she came to comfort me somehow."

Drew studied the man and tried to figure out if Ray dreaming of a long-lost relative had any bearing on their current predicament. Running his fingers over the cool metal once again, Drew felt more etching on the lower edge. "I think there's an inscription on the back."

Ray frowned down at the picture, and it was clear that he'd never noticed one before. Drew turned the metal plate over and brought it close to his face so he could read the tiny lettering.

"L. Montreaux," he breathed. "Looks like we have our connection. Both of the boxes must have belonged to your great-grandmother. Assuming that L. Montreaux was also from New Orleans, how did the second box get buried with a stack of *Vigilati* bodies in the North Carolina mountains?"

"That would be the fifteen million dollar question, wouldn't it?"

"We've got to get the crew in on this, run a differential. Would you mind rounding them up? I'm going to see if I can sweet talk Doc Myers into an early release."

"Sure thing, son," Ray said, casting him a worried glance. "You take it easy, though, all right?"

Drew nodded and closed his lids against the sting in his eyes caused by the man's well-meaning concern. Unwittingly, it made him ache for something he'd never had, never would have. The love and concern, the companionship, of a father.

Ray closed the hospital door quietly and leaned back against it. He shut his eyes against the quagmire of pain the little trip down memory lane had triggered. It was easy for Ray to imagine where the kid was at in his headspace. He'd seen that cold, bleak look many times before, staring back out at him from the mirror.

Deveraux carried a dark spot on his soul that could only come from that kind of heartless abuse at a very young age. Ray knew that first hand. He hoped like hell there was still enough of him left to love Raven like she needed, for both their sakes.

Hell, maybe he'd try to help the boy himself. Be there for Drew like he had been for Trystan and Ryder—like nobody had been for him. But as it was, they had bigger things to worry about. Namely Azibel and her unholy war.

Ray believed, as he'd been told, that Raven was the only one who could truly kill Azibel. He knew she'd have to be the one to deliver the K.O. for sure, but, by God, he would get in his potshot first. The bitch deserved it after all she'd done to him and his girl.

Rays lips curled into an evil sneer as he imagined his hands around her milky white throat. Oh yes, he would have his go 'round with the Black Widow, for sure. He just had to figure out how to make it happen.

CHAPTER FORTY TWO

Chaos reigned in the Black Valley when Raven arrived with her crew. The group of protestors had grown larger—and louder—since she'd last been there. They pushed each other and jockeyed for position as they crowded as close to the perimeter as possible.

As she swung the Ducati into the parking area, Raven wondered how much of the protesting could be blamed on Azibel's presence. She'd proven that she had the ability to actually possess the participants, but all the eat-shit-and-die vibes she was sending out also had the power to bring out the worst in people. Raven had experienced that first hand.

Brynna hopped off the back of the bike, and Raven cut the engine to join her. Moments later, Marduk emerged from the surrounding woods, having traveled 'by paw'. Raven narrowed her eyes and scowled at the crowd of protestors. Across the perimeter line, a hard-eyed Eric stood with his thick arms crossed over an even thicker chest.

She'd had to split up the guards, with Eric on days and Bex on nights, after they lost Alex Webber. Tristan was sending another one of her guys over, but he wouldn't be there for another couple of days, and they couldn't afford to trust any more outsiders.

Striding toward the perimeter gate, she was flanked by Brynna on her right and Marduk on her left. She keyed in the alarm code, let them all in and closed the gate behind her. Raven smiled to herself when she imagined what a picture the three of them made.

She was dressed in her leather riding pants and boots and her usual white tank. Her hair was braided in a heavy rope down her back, á la *Lara Croft*, and she had her thick leather motocross jacket slung over one shoulder.

Brynna was dressed similarly in head to toe leathers since she'd been riding with Raven. While Marduk came across as a harmless kid in day to day life, when he dressed to intimidate, he came out in full effect. He towered over her, decked in black BDU's and an ankle-length black duster. Raven had been told that Marduk used to lose his clothing during a shift, but he was still young for a *feradux* and had learned how to re-manifest his duds—lucky for all of them.

Raven suppressed a snort when she got a sudden mental picture of the three of them wearing black wraparounds and doing a slow motion walk. While it would be an amusing diversion to make the interns shit themselves, there was important work to be done.

When they entered the compound, they came upon a group of interns milling about and talking worriedly. Oh, for the love...Raven thought. Like a chicken with its head cut off. Snagging the arm of the one person she recognized, she pulled

Hammer out of the cluster and the three of them instantly surrounded him.

"What the hell is going on?" she asked him.

The young man's eyes bounced warily from Brynna to Marduk before they focused on Raven. "Ms. Sabatier, thank God. We can't find Dr. Larkin or Dr. Deveraux. No one knows what happened to them, and no one seems to know what to do about it."

Raven pinched the bridge of her nose and prayed for patience. "Dr. Deveraux is in the hospital. He had a bit of an accident, but he's going to be just fine. As for Oz Larkin, put the word out that if any of you see him, you call me immediately. Understand?"

The poor kid gave her a dazed nod, overwhelmed by the information. "When will Dr. Deveraux be back?"

"Probably in just a couple of days," she hedged, not sure how much Drew would want them to know. "As for you guys, what would you normally be doing?"

"Uh, well...working on excavating the second skeleton, I guess. And I would normally be in the lab, testing samples with Dr—er, Drew."

She wrapped an arm loosely around the kid's thin shoulders and leaned in as if she were sharing a secret. "Well, then. Hammer?"

"Yes ma'am?"

"Do that!"

He jumped at the shrill sound of her voice, and she immediately felt bad. It wasn't his fault that Alex Webber...She shuddered to even think about what had happened—or could have happened—to Drew.

"You're in charge until Drew gets back. Now's your chance to step it up and prove yourself. Think you can do it?"

"Yes, ma'am."

"Good." She paused for a moment while Hammer stared down at the toes of his boots. "Hammer?"

"Ma'am?"

"Now!"

"Oh, er, sorry," he babbled as he shuffled off to fill the other students and interns in on the situation.

The three of them searched the entire compound and the outlying area and found no signs of Larkin or Webber. Raven scanned the lush landscape as they descended to the lower point of the valley, below the dig site.

Rubbing her arms, she noticed the fine hairs there standing on end. There was a charge to the air in the valley, and it was unsettling. Raven dug the toe of her boot into the dirt and squinted back at her two friends.

"Think this is it."

Brynna merely raised a delicate auburn brow at her and waited for an explanation.

"The *locus*. I don't think it's something we have to search for. It's right here. Maybe even the whole valley. I can feel it. I'm almost positive the final round is going to go down here."

Brynna stepped up beside her, raised her face to the wind and sniffed the air. "You may be right," she said. She looked over at Marduk for confirmation and he nodded.

Raven started to speak further, but the back of her neck began to prickle. She turned around and caught sight of Ray up on the hill at the perimeter. He silently raised a hand in greeting as the three of them made their way back up to him.

"Hey, Dad," Raven said, though the word still came out a little rusty.

"Hey, Bird."

She smiled at the familiar nickname, and gave him a quick hug. What's up?"

"Drew wanted me to round y'all up, so we could meet with everyone back at the hospital. We have some stuff we want to run by you."

Raven breathed a sigh of relief. For a moment, she thought Ray had come to tell her that Drew had taken a turn for the worse. She swallowed her anxiety and mustered up a smile for her father.

"Sure. Just got to finish up here, and we'll be over in ten."

Ray nodded, studying her face as if looking for some kind of sign. Of what, Raven had no idea. Eventually, he gave her a smile and a wave and headed back to Drew's Camaro. Marduk tagged along after him for a ride.

A cloud slid across the sun and cast dancing shadows on the ground around them. Raven shaded her eyes and looked up toward the peak of Barron's Bald. "Storm's coming," she said quietly.

ꙮ

When Raven, Brynna, and Marduk entered Drew's hospital room, they were the last ones to arrive. Ray sat in a chair on the far side of Drew's bed, wearing a grave expression, while Jeremiah and Isla sat to his right and looked vaguely confused.

Marduk crossed the room to Isla and sank down at her feet, while Brynna pulled up the remaining chair. Raven figured there was no need for pretense, so she climbed into the bed beside Drew and laid her head on his shoulder. She felt, rather than heard, his small sigh, and her lips curled into a private smile.

Jeremiah snaked an arm around his wife's shoulders and gave his friend a pointed look. "Now that everyone is here, as you requested, can you *please* tell us what you've found?"

Drew smirked at his friend and pretended to be distracted by an invisible spot on his hospital gown. "Patience never was your thing, was it, Rousseau?"

Jere just stared back and raised a brow. "Bite me, Deveraux."

To save them all from an equally mature retort, Raven looked up at Drew and brushed a kiss over his jaw. "Just tell us. Please?" She tried to make her eyes look wide and innocent, and batted her eyelashes at him.

He knew she was working him, and yet, she still felt him relax against her just a little more. It sent a shocking jolt of power and lust through her body that this big man would melt for her. God, she couldn't wait for him to heal up and get sprung from this joint.

"Of course," he said with his eyes on her, and he didn't seem to notice anyone else in the room. "Ray got a hold of the other puzzle box. We think it may have been made by the same person. It was full of old photographs of his mother's family, including a tintype that has an engraving: *L. Montreaux*."

Raven's mind reeled at the implications. "So, you think the person who made those boxes and wrote that book could be related to me?"

Drew nodded. "At this point, I think it's likely. Ray, go ahead and show them the pictures."

Raven got the stack first, flipped through them slowly and handed each one to Jeremiah after she was finished. She paused when she got to the tintype. She took note of the woman's period dress and her smirking expression.

In the woman's long waves of dark hair, high cheekbones, and slashing brows, Raven saw parts of herself. Her eyes were startling, covered in a milky film—seeing nothing and yet, somehow, everything.

She had a large *signa* imprinted on one of her cheeks, and, God, if that didn't make Raven feel better about her own. It could always get worse, she reminded herself. She flipped the tintype over and noted the inscription. She didn't find any new information so she passed it on and moved to the next picture.

Jeremiah reached for the tintype while lifting his Coke bottle to his lips. Raven watched as he took a deep swallow before glancing down at the image in his hand. Those hazel eyes went wide with shock, and the man spit out his mouthful as if someone had punched him in the gut. Six pairs of eyes snapped to his face as he wiped his mouth with the back of his hand and stared at the tintype.

"What the *hell,* Jeremiah?" Drew gave his friend an irritated frown.

"Leora," Jere whispered, fingering the etched metal.

"What?" Raven asked. She thought she'd heard him say a name, heard him speak it like it belonged to someone he knew. Only that was impossible. Wasn't it?

"Seriously?" Drew asked.

"Leora," he said, stronger this time, and Raven noticed that his eyes flicked over to Isla before returning to the tintype. "*Ne t'effraie pas,*" he said quietly, stroking the etched face with his thumb.

Drew looked helplessly across the bed at Isla. "What is *wrong* with him?" he asked at the same time Ray spoke.

"What did you say?"

"I said...*ne t'effraie pas*. It means—"

"I know what it means," Ray interrupted. "Why did you say it?"

"It's what she said to me the night she saved my life. Leora. That's her name."

"She always said the same to me when I dreamed of her," Ray said, mostly to himself.

Raven watched as Drew sat up straighter in his bed and looked back and forth between Jeremiah and Isla. "Do you really think it's the same person?"

It was almost as if the three of them were speaking in code, and, gee, Raven had left her Enigma machine in her other purse. It irritated her enough to interrupt them, to call a halt to the cryptic dialog. "Can someone, please, fill me in?"

Drew pulled her closer and rubbed his hand up and down her shoulder. "Of course. But brace yourself, because this will be about as believable as all the rest of the bombs we've been dropping on you."

"Fair enough," she acknowledged with a nod, indicating for him to continue.

"Last year, when we were translating the grimoire, Isla came across a handwritten passage that she read aloud to the rest of us. It turned out to be a summoning spell for a *Bruixi* goddess. The spell caused her to inhabit Isla's body, and we were able to communicate with her."

"Jeremiah recognized her as the *Vigile* who saved him from an *auchrim* attack when he was a boy. The experience was what set him on the path of researching the *Bruixi,* and what eventually led him to me," Isla said with a smile.

"She told us that her name was Leora, and that we could summon her if we ever needed help. We wouldn't have found the *locus* without her," Jeremiah finished.

Raven pinched the bridge of her nose as she tried to sort through the new information. If she'd thought she was a freak before, well, damn. "So, if the woman in the tintype is your Leora, then not only is my mother a demon, but my paternal great-great-grandmother is a goddess?"

"'Bout sums it up," Jeremiah answered sympathetically.

"Maybe she can help us figure out how to get rid of Azibel," Raven said, thinking out loud.

"Only one way to find out," Isla answered, and her dimples appeared with her mischievous smile.

Jeremiah whipped his head around toward his wife, his eyes sparking. "Absolutely not! You're not going to put yourself at risk like that."

Isla's smile was patient, her jade eyes soft with compassion. "Love, I know you worry, but she didn't hurt me last time. It just took us all by surprise. I don't think Leora would let anything happen to me. We need to do this. It's like we're being led—like she wants us to know she's there."

Jeremiah sighed and ran a hand through his mop of sandy brown hair. "I guess you're right," he said. "I want to wait until Deveraux gets out of the hospital, though. We need all hands on deck."

Raven liked the sound of that. She could feel Drew vibrating with the need to be up and about, to delve into the mystery. But she wanted to make sure he took the time to heal properly.

"I think that's a great idea. On that note, why don't we let him get some rest so he'll get out that much sooner."

With a chorus of agreement, their friends packed up the photos and the puzzle box, and filed out of the room.

Drew yawned so wide his jaw popped, and Raven regarded the dark circles under his eyes and the lines of pain etched around his full lips.

"How were things at the site?" he asked.

Raven sighed deeply, wishing she could shield him from further stress, but he had a right to know. "Pretty chaotic. There's still no sign of Alex Webber or Dr. Larkin, so no one's running the dig. When I got there, the interns and grad students were just wandering around, at a loss as to what to do. I told them to do exactly what they would normally be doing, and I put Hammer in charge of directing everyone."

With a snort, Drew smiled weakly at her. "I'm sure he nearly shit himself. He's scared to death of you already."

Raven grinned at that, a little too happily. "I know. Listen, Drew, about the dig site...," she trailed off when she realized his eyelids were drooping low and his breathing was deepening.

"Hmm?"

"Nothing, love. We'll talk tomorrow." He nodded but didn't open his eyes.

She lay there for several more minutes, making sure he was sleeping deeply before she began her work. When you got right down to it, human beings were nothing but energy and matter—both of which she could manipulate.

Since Drew had been admitted to the hospital, every time he went to sleep, Raven had been giving his body a little 'push' toward healing. It was like a shot of Red Bull to his cells, infusing them with extra energy to complete the natural healing process.

She'd never tried to use her *own* energy to force someone's healing, and she certainly wasn't going to use Drew as her test subject. But the blast of energy she'd been giving him should, in theory, cut down some of his recovery time.

Besides, she thought impishly, it was fun to watch. Not only did the energy shot ramp up his body's healing properties but also all of its other processes. If he were awake, he'd be stronger, faster, more clear-minded...more sexually charged.

Raven smiled to herself as she placed a hand over his heart, leaned back, and watched the show. As her energy swamped into him, his breathing sped up and his heart began to pump more efficiently. His broad chest heaved with the exertion of an extended lung capacity, and more blood infused into all of his extremities. All. Extremities.

Drew groaned in his sleep as the first wave hit him, his body bowing up off the bed. His head was thrown back, and the tendons in his neck strained as his mouth opened in silent ecstasy. His breaths turned to pants as his hips undulated against the bed. Raven could see the telltale tenting of the hospital blanket as his arousal grew.

Even covered in the tacky johnny, his body was a sight to behold. Solid ropes of muscle and sinew stood out in taut relief as his back rose off the bed. While it was quite an entertaining side effect of the energy boost, the hospital was definitely not the place to play. She gently receded her power and hoped that it had done the job.

Afterwards, there was complete calm. He slept peacefully, not stirring in the slightest. Raven walked to the cabinet and grabbed a fresh warm blanket. She shook it out over him, wrapped him up in it and climbed up on the bed beside him.

She found that her own hand was trembling as she brushed sweaty blonde curls off his forehead. Honestly, she didn't know how many more times she could watch that without doing something about it—but she drew the line at molesting an injured man in his sleep. Even she had *some* scruples. Raven just needed to get her man home and into bed.

ℵ

"This is highly irregular," Dr. Myers said, scratching his chin while he studied Drew's x-rays and scans. He'd come in that morning to do an exam, and he brought the follow-up films with him. "I don't really have an explanation for it."

Drew gave the confounded doctor a patient smile and waited for the man to explain himself. He had a feeling he knew what was coming. Drew couldn't be sure, but he thought Raven might be doing something to him, something to help him heal faster.

"Your scans show remarkable healing progress—that which you'd normally see after a few weeks, rather than a few days. I don't believe I've ever seen someone recover this fast from these types of injuries."

Drew gave the doctor a dimply grin and shrugged. "Guess I'm just special, Doc." The doctor gave him a look that said he'd heard that line before, but Drew ignored it. "So what do you say? Can I blow this Popsicle stand?"

Dr. Myers considered it for a moment, frowning as he stared at the x-rays again. "Normally, I would advise against it, but I really can't argue with the pictures. I'll sign your release today, but you need to take it easy. You're not out of the woods yet."

"Sure thing, Doc," he said as he offered his hand to the doctor for a shake. "I appreciate all you did for me."

"My pleasure. I want to see you back here in a week for another follow-up," the doctor said with a smile. "Take care of yourself."

Drew watched as the small man made his way out of the room, and he turned to Raven. She was as beautiful as ever, but she looked tired. He imagined she hadn't been sleeping nearly as well as he had.

He couldn't help smiling at her because soon he would have her all to himself again. Combing his fingers through her long sable hair, he kissed her neck and whispered into her ear. "Take me home, baby."

Chapter Forty Three

Drew couldn't have been happier when he arrived back at room 213, just barely leaning on Raven for support. When they swung the door open, he was stunned by what he saw. The lights were turned down, and there were dozens of white column candles burning around the room. He would have thought it was a romantic surprise from Raven, except for the fact that all of their friends were there, sitting around the coffee table.

"Um, guys? This is romantic and all but, well, I'm already seeing someone," he said with a cheeky grin.

No one cracked a smile. Well, he'd thought it was funny. He tried not to be annoyed that he wouldn't get to be alone with Raven just yet. "What's with the ambience?"

Isla smiled and gestured for him to come and sit down. "We're going to try and summon Leora again. We thought doing it sort of like a séance might make it easier for her to appear to us," she said with a shrug. "Somethin' to try anyway."

Drew sat down on the couch, but when he reached to pull Raven down with him, Isla shook her head. "I think the four of us should sit together," she said, gesturing towards Marduk and Brynna. "The more power we have in a centralized location, the better."

He didn't like it. He didn't like not being able to protect her, to shield her if need be. However, the humbling thought occurred to him that she was more powerful. So he nodded at her as she sunk down on the floor beside Isla.

They had the grimoire spread open to the correct page, the paper browned with age and wear. Drew watched as Isla held out her hands, and the four of them linked fingers. "You guys ready?"

Raven licked her lips nervously and nodded. "Let's do it."

Quietly, Isla began to read the handwritten notation that contained the summoning spell. "*...Vetera novis per loqui et respondere monent.*" Isla squeezed her eyes shut tight and held her breath, obviously waiting for the goddess to inhabit her body. Only nothing happened.

The room was dead silent, except for the murmur of the crackling fire. The candles cast flickering shadows across her face, but Isla remained unchanged. Isla swallowed visibly and repeated the words. "*Vetera novis per loqui et respondere monent.*"

Silence.

Isla's brows pulled together and a line formed on her forehead. "She said she'd always come. I guess she would if she were able."

She looked crestfallen enough to make Drew want to reach out and hug her. He was at a loss as to why the spell didn't work this time. He rose to extinguish the candles but was distracted by a noise that seemed to come from the terrace. "What the hell?" he said.

He pushed back the curtain a bit and peeked outside, but saw nothing out of the ordinary. Just to be sure, he pulled the sliding glass door open to see what had made the noise.

He found himself face to face with a tiny woman with milky white eyes. A bizarre looking *signa* writhed on her cheek, and her face was barely visible through the curtain of pitch black hair. She wore some kind of white, flowing robe that dragged the ground, and her feet were bare.

"Um...," Drew said, as she glided past him into the suite. He followed behind dumbly as she floated to the center of the room, her feet barely touching the ground. In a casual move, she took a seat at the end of the couch and smoothed out the folds of her robe.

Not seeing any other option, Drew returned to his own seat, sat there and stared at her. "Um...," he repeated.

Leora turned and gave him a serene look and an instant sensation of calm washed over him. Safe. They were all safe for the time being, in the presence of the goddess.

"You called, my dear," she said to Isla in her musical French accent. Isla opened her mouth to speak, then closed it again.

Always calm in a crisis, Raven stepped in. "We've found some things we believe may be yours." She carefully laid out the two puzzle boxes and the book of shadows on the table.

Leora looked straight at Raven, without so much as a glance at the items in question. "Yes."

"So you *are* L. Montreaux?"

"That is a name I have been known to use when on this earthly plane, yes. Leah Montreaux."

Isla finally found her voice and was able to ask her own question. "How were you able to appear corporeally, instead of...inhabiting me?"

Leora seemed to consider the question for a moment before shrugging a finely boned shoulder. "We have four extremely powerful, magickal beings in this room, two of whom are mine own blood. Your combined strength allowed me to manifest." Suddenly, she swiveled her head around and turned her unseeing gaze on Jeremiah. "Good to see you again, dear one. I trust you are taking care of our girl?"

"Always," he answered sincerely.

Then she looked at Ray. "Ah, Raymonde, son of mine. So we finally meet in the land of the waking."

"Son?" Raven asked, raising a brow.

Leora smiled that inscrutable smile of hers as she faced Raven once more. "Once or twice removed, of course. You have some questions to ask of me." It wasn't a question, but a call to order. "Proceed."

Narrowing her eyes, Raven studied Leora. She thought about what she needed to hear most from this woman. She wanted to find out the connection between Leora, Ray, and herself, once and for all. There were so many things about this battle that they still didn't understand, and it would be nice to feel just a little bit less like pawns on a chessboard.

"We were led to believe that the *Vigilati* traits were passed down in the maternal lineage of a *Bruixi* bloodline. Was that wrong?"

Leora tilted her head, causing her ropes of black hair to slide across her knees. "Not wrong, no."

Like pulling teeth already, Raven thought to herself. "Then how do I exist? I've learned that I am a *Praeda*—that

Azibel is my mother, and I know that Ray's my father. So what *am* I?"

"What you are, is a genetic anomaly." Leora held up a tiny white hand to keep Raven from interrupting. "Let me explain. The odds are stacked against our race in this fight, as the *auchrim* have the ability to multiply at will. In order to balance the scale a little bit more, I was granted a *bréve*—a leg up in the game, if you will.

"Every hundred years, I am allowed to take human form long enough to mate and bear a child. It helps keep the bloodline pure, and insure that there are still warriors remaining. In your case, Raven, my granddaughter gave birth to a son and died before she could produce anymore offspring. But because Ray was my direct descendent, the *Vigilati* gene passed through him and on to you, despite your unfortunate mother."

"If you're allowed to pad the deck this way, why aren't there more of us?" Raven asked, sure that Leora wasn't giving them the whole story.

"The *Lochrim* are very cunning and ruthless. Little is written about our race, and oral tradition has died out with the majority of the prominent families. It is hard for the *Vigilati* to survive in a war they aren't even aware of. Unfortunately, only three of my bloodline remain. All the rest have been snuffed out by the *auchrim*," she said.

Isla slammed a hand down on the coffee table, and Marduk reached over to place a gentle hand on her back. "But you're a *goddess*! Can't you see it coming? Surely you have some manner of foresight. Would you not help your own family?"

Leora's face contorted into a grimace as she looked down at her hands. "Regrettably, my sight does not extend to my own descendants. And even if it did, I'm forbidden to intervene. If I did so, I could lose the *bréve* entirely."

"Can you tell us how to defeat Azibel?" Raven asked, not really expecting an answer. She believed that if Leora could tell them that, she would have done so already.

"Each *Praeda* must face her own demons. The way will always be distinct but contain a common thread."

"That makes no sense," Raven complained, and Leora merely nodded in solemn agreement.

"But I can tell you this—you'll not do it alone." Her stare pierced right through Raven's defenses, because that's exactly what she'd planned to do. Face Azibel alone, woman to woman, witch to demon.

"I have a question," Jeremiah spoke up. "Why *are* the odds so stacked against us? The *Vigilati* and their mates...Why are the *auchrim* allowed to multiply like goddamn bunnies while the *Vigilati* are just strugglin' to hold off extinction?"

"That is a good question, dear one. One that I do not have a good answer for, I'm afraid. In fact, no one on earth knows this. I can only surmise that long ago, the *Vigilati* must have done something to anger The Source—enough to sway the scales permanently."

"How do we find this source?" Drew asked. "Maybe there's something we can do to change things."

Leora's head whipped around in a cloud of ebony ropes, her milky eyes blazing. "There is *no* questioning The Source! To endeavor to even set eyes upon it would mean certain death. We all must accept our lot, and accept that there are some forces in this world we cannot change."

Drew clamped his mouth shut and said nothing more, but he glared right back at Leora. The sight of her man about to go ten rounds with a supernatural goddess had a smile quirking at Raven's lips. "You said there were three remaining lines descended from you. Besides the Sabatiers of Las Vegas, by way of Mid-City New Orleans," Raven said with a smirk, "who else is there?"

Leora's face slackened, and her eyes took on a faraway quality, as if she were seeing something else. Something the rest of them couldn't see. "There are three. One is dark as the shadow of the moon, like a blackbird. The other is like two halves of the whole, equal parts fair and dark. The Mackay."

Raven narrowed her eyes when Isla gasped and Jeremiah tensed. "I'm guessing you're the Mackay, then," she said, and Isla nodded.

Growing impatient with the guessing games, Raven turned back to Leora. "And the third?"

"The third is bright as the noonday sun, but she hides in shadows."

"How very vague," Raven quipped.

Leora's pale eyes refocused and honed in on Raven, and the scrutiny made her want to squirm. "This battle is *nothing*. A war is coming, the likes of which this world has never seen. In order to survive, you must find the Serpent's Fate. Fate is at the crux of it."

Raven was beginning to have serious doubts about Leora's sanity—but could a goddess even be insane? Probably not. She sensed that they wouldn't get much more coherent information from the goddess, so she asked one last question.

"How do we find the *locus*?"

Smiling, Leora arched a brow at her. "I think you already know." Suddenly her head swiveled around like something out of the *Exorcist*, and she once again pinned Drew with her fathomless gaze. "Storm's blowin' in, Dr. Deveraux," she said in a perfect Cajun drawl. Then, with a pop and a sulfuric flash, she was gone.

"The *fuck—*" Drew said, but was interrupted by his phone ringing. He answered it, but immediately had to hold it away from his ear as the person on the other line was shouting over a cacophony of noise.

Raven heard clearly what was said next.

"...storm's blowin' in, Dr. Deveraux..."

She sucked in a breath as Drew tried to calm his assistant. "Hammer, slow down. What's happening?"

Drew listened for a moment before his eyes widened. "Okay, stay calm. Start packing up the equipment so we can clear out until the weather turns. I'm on my way. "

Oh, hell if he was going to undo all of her hard work by going out to the dig and getting himself hurt, Raven thought. "Don't even think about—"

"A storm's coming in hard, and the valley's starting to flood. Being at the bottom of the valley, the site's at risk for a landslide and Hammer's getting worried. I need to go there to oversee breaking down the lab. You can come with me, or you can stay here, but I'm going."

She noted the determined glint in his eyes and the stubborn set of his jaw. What right did she have to try and tell him what to do, anyway? But at least she could be there to watch his damn fool back. Clamping her mouth shut, she nodded, rising silently to follow him.

ꕥ

The Camaro's eight cylinders and power steering were tested as Drew navigated the switchbacks on the Parkway at a speed that was probably less than safe in the driving rain. He couldn't shake the bad feeling he had after the encounter with Leora, so he wanted to get to the site to set his mind at ease.

He saw Raven's white-knuckled grip on the arm rest and knew his driving scared her, but she said nothing. Drew appreciated her silent understanding, even when she was in fear for her life. He just wanted to reassure himself that everything was okay in the valley.

When Drew pulled into the parking area, he got out and raced for the gate. He'd left the engine idling, but he knew Raven would take care of it.

He was pummeled by rain—and was that hail?—as he dashed through security and surveyed the pandemonium. The valley was so flooded, muddy water was already sloshing around his ankles.

The rain was so heavy that he could barely see that the mess tent had already been swept away, and that the wind was testing the strength of the lab tent's flimsy staked lines. Drew thought he saw movement over by the lab, so he headed that way.

He was relieved to see Hammer LeRoux outside the tent, barking orders at the other interns as they carried plastic covered equipment outside. Good man, Drew thought. Drew walked up and laid a hand on Hammer's shoulder. The young man whipped around, his concern clear on his face, but his expression eased when he saw Drew.

Drew found himself engulfed in the embrace of the stocky grad student, and, amazingly, he squeezed the kid right back. "Glad to see you in one piece," Hammer yelled over the thunderous storm. "We've gotten a good bit of the equipment out, but we're running out of vehicles. The water's rising too fast—one more good soaking, and, I swear, we'll get a slide. The remains—"

"Don't worry about the remains," Drew shouted. Hell, they weren't more than a couple of years old anyway. Not worth risking lives for. "We need to get whatever equipment we can and get you kids to higher ground. That's all we *need* to do, you hear me?" He waited until Hammer nodded, making sure he understood. The running out of vehicles would definitely be a problem. Wondering where Raven was, Drew eyed his Camaro and swore under his breath. They couldn't fit much in that. They had lucked out with the fact that the parking area was on the high ground, so they weren't risking the vehicles getting stuck. However, they'd be able to move the equipment faster if they could get the cars right up to the tent. What they needed was a fucking truck.

He could barely see through the haze of rain and wind, but Drew tracked some movement near the gate. He made out Raven as she opened the gate and waved someone through.

Drew whooped out loud as he saw a huge Suburban with the Cliffdweller's logo emblazoned on the side plow through the mud. The truck paused briefly while Raven hopped up on the running board, locked her hand onto the luggage rack, and surfed the truck down to where he stood.

Leaping off before it even came to a complete stop, she swaggered toward him, seemingly oblivious to the deluge. Her face was alight with the challenge. She'd rolled up her sleeves and was ready to get her hands dirty—literally. "Hope you don't mind," she said with a laugh in her voice, "I brought some company to the party."

Drew's jaw dropped as person after person hopped out of the truck. Jeremiah and Isla, the *feradux*, Ray, and even Micah, had all come to help them. Jeremiah clasped Drew's nape with his big hand. "Where d'you need us, bossman?"

"Uh, the lab. We've got to get all of the equipment we can out of there before the whole site gets washed down the Black Valley drain." The group turned as a unit and ducked into the ravaged tent. Raven made to follow, but Drew grabbed her wrist.

When she turned and gave him a questioning look, he yanked her to him and locked his mouth onto hers. He devoured her, trying to pour all his love for her into that one kiss, all his gratefulness for everything she'd done for him. Tangling his fingers into her mass of wet hair, he savored the scent and the taste of her. Reluctantly, he pulled back and stared into eyes that were darkened to a deep amber in the stormy atmosphere.

"Please, be careful. And stay close. This area is famous for its flash floods. The whole site could be swept away at any moment."

"Same goes," she replied, lifting her chin.

Clapping his hands together, Drew eyed the tent as their friends were already filing out with their arms full of million dollar lab equipment. "'Kay, let's do it."

With the Suburban parked right outside the tent, the loading went quickly. They had the whole lab broken down and packed up, along with the security equipment, in under twenty minutes.

Drew stepped up to Micah and offered his hand for a shake. "Thanks man, you're a lifesaver."

"Anytime, kid. You got somewhere to put all this stuff?"

"Uh, not really. I'll probably have to rent a storage unit until I can ship it back to the Universities."

Micah dismissed that idea with a wave of his hand. "I've got an empty storage closet back at the Inn that you can use for however long you need it. I'll lead the way, and the kids can follow me back. I'll put them all up for the night, too. Don't need anyone out driving in this."

Drew was speechless. He had no idea why this man, who barely knew him, would go to all this trouble. Micah just shrugged and winked at him. "'S'what friends do, ya dig?"

He just nodded back dumbly before turning and giving the kids instructions. "Listen, y'all did everything exactly right. Now I want you to get the hell out of here before you get hurt. Baldie over there is Micah. Y'all are going to follow him back to his inn and wait out the storm. I'm going to do one last sweep of the area to see if we missed anything. Then I'll be along. No arguments!" he said sternly when they started to protest.

Drew turned to Raven and pointed at her. He still had to shout over the deafening squall. "You...Stay. Here."

Drew turned away, but not before he thought he saw Raven roll her eyes. Fuck it, he thought. He was soaked to the skin, battered by the driving rain, and he was pretty sure he'd ripped a couple of his stitches out. On top of that, he was bone tired from nearly an hour of schlepping through the mud.

There wasn't much to check. It looked like the mess tent had been swept away and the lounge tent was pretty much collapsed. They'd lose the cameras, but there wasn't much he could do about it now. At least they were bought and paid for. The lab equipment, on the other hand, was on loan.

Descending the gently sloping hill, he surveyed the area where the grid had been. It was gone now, or buried under the quagmire of mud and probably a foot of water. Sighing, he ran a hand through his hair, now slicked from the rain. He figured they'd never get answers now—never identify the poor souls who were buried in this wicked boneyard.

He heard a noise behind him, almost imperceptible through the rain, and he swung around, ready to chew out Raven for following him. His voice caught in his throat, and his body went into high alert survival mode when he saw who was in front of him.

Raven had followed him, all right. And so had Hammer, against his wishes. The two of them stood about thirty feet away, huddled together, watching in horror as he faced his attacker. His would-be murderer.

Alex Webber approached him cautiously, his hands outstretched as if to show that he was unarmed. His expression was full of warring emotions, confusion, remorse...fear. There was no malice in his eyes—a warm brown instead of translucent shadows—as the man tried to speak. "Hell, Dr. Deveraux, I'm so—"

He never got to finish his thought. Even as the man looked as though he wanted to apologize, he raised a hand to Drew and Drew's brain shorted out. Reacting purely on instinct, he grabbed the guy's shoulders for leverage, and head-butted him in the nose. Hard.

Blood sprayed, and Webber dropped like a stone. When Drew realized the guy wasn't getting up, wasn't going to fight him like a man if he couldn't hide behind his two-by-four, he threw his head back and bellowed an unholy roar.

He felt as though he was outside of himself, as if the darkest part of him had taken over, Drew knelt down and straddled Webber, wrapping cold hands around his throat and squeezing.

Raven's heart pounded with dread and she had a death grip on Hammer's arm as they watched. Drew seemed to transform into some otherworldly beast. The veins in his neck and arms bulged as he screamed and squeezed, squeezed and screamed.

"Hammer, we have to do something!" she whispered, but the boy was rooted to the spot with open-mouthed shock. "Hammer!" she shouted this time and shook him a little to snap him out of it.

Finally, he turned to look at her, and she could feel him trembling under her grip. She reached into her jacket pocket and pulled out a pair of steel handcuffs she always kept on her, in case things got hairy on a job. She quickly pushed them into Hammer's palm.

His eyes bugged out of his head when he saw what she'd given him. "No time to queen out on me now, Hammer. I'm going to get Drew off of him, and, as soon as I do, I need you to restrain Webber long enough to cuff him. Do you understand?" she asked, looking directly into his wide, fearful eyes.

"You stay on him, no matter what you hear."

Hammer's head dipped in a weak nod. "But how are you—"

She turned her back on the rest of his question and took off at a full sprint, using the slope of the hill to gain momentum. As she neared the pair of them, Raven saw that Webber seemed to be unconscious—and turning blue.

Her legs burned as she kicked it into high gear. When she reached them, she didn't slow down even a little. She launched herself into the air and collided with Drew in a full body tackle. The force of the hit was enough to knock the wind out of her, but it did the job. They both went flying, landed hard in the mud and rolled a few feet away.

Raven landed on top, so she quickly sat up and straddled Drew's hips. He was like a live wire underneath her, bucking and screaming, his arms flailing enough that she had to duck a few blows. His eyes were wild and unfocused, but they were his own. That was something, at least.

Drew threw his head back, let out another yell, and tried to dislodge the dead weight that was Raven. In order to avoid the swinging arms, Raven scooted up and pressed her knees into his biceps. She sent a surge of energy into his body to pin him more effectively.

"Drew!" she shouted over his own screams. This was Azibel's doing, Raven was sure of it. Her evil presence leeched into everyone in the Valley, bringing out the darkest part of every soul. Drew's rage over being beaten and his thirst for vengeance festered like an infected wound—one that Azibel kept lanced and bleeding, goddamn her black heart.

No matter what she tried, Raven couldn't get a response from him. He just continued to writhe and squirm...and scream. Out of options, she reeled back and cracked her fist across his jaw. She smiled without humor as she was reminded of the night they'd met.

He'd stopped screaming as soon as she made contact, and she watched with relief as those baby blue eyes blinked twice and seemed to focus on her face. He frowned at her and his full lips pouted in a way that would have looked ridiculous on any other man.

"Why're you always hittin' me?" His voice was grittier than pit gravel from all the screaming, but she couldn't help the genuine smile that tugged at her lips. So he'd made the connection, as well, she thought.

Raven eased off of him and helped him sit up, as they were quickly becoming engulfed by the floodwaters. "What the fuck happened?" he asked, looking at her helplessly.

"You don't remember?"

"Last thing I remember was Webber reaching for me. I sort of lost it—vision went red, then I completely blanked." A horrified look suddenly crossed his face. " I didn't—"

"No, you didn't," Raven stopped him. Still, he had to understand how critical it had gotten. "But you would have. You were strangling the mess out of him, so I had to tackle you while Hammer handled Webber."

"Hammer?" he asked, and Raven turned to check on the kid, hoping he'd fared as well.

"Yeah, boss?" came the reply, barely heard over the rain.

"Why the hell did you come back? I told you to get to high ground."

The kid ducked his head and suddenly became fascinated by the mud flowing over his shoes. "I was worried about y'all."

As pissed as he was, Drew was also absurdly touched. "You good with Webber?"

"I got this," Hammer said.

Drew breathed a sigh of relief and slumped beneath Raven. His big shoulders shuddered as he tried to get a grip on what had just happened.

Raven gripped his face in her hands and tilted it until he met her eyes. "You are *not* a killer. Azibel was preying on your instinct to protect yourself. She's corrupting us all with her malignant evil, exploiting our weaknesses. We just have to circle the wagons, be more careful and guard our emotions, especially the darker ones.

He nodded and leaned his forehead against hers before he allowed her to roll off of him. After he stood, he reached out a hand and hauled her to her feet, once again making her feel weightless. "Let's go collect Hammer and get the hell out of here before we find ourselves down river."

When they approached the kid, he was standing with one leg propping up an unconscious and cuffed Alex Webber, to keep him from drowning. "Good job, kid," Raven said, and watched with interest as his expression bounced between irritation at being called "kid" and pride at the compliment. From the smile he gave her, it looked like he decided on pride. Smart kid.

Drew hooked a hand under one of Alex's arms and motioned for Hammer to grab the other. Together, they half carried, half dragged him back toward the camp. Raven brought up the rear, walking backwards so she could watch the storm ravaging the dig site.

As she watched, a deafening roar filled the air, and the water that lapped at her ankles began to ripple. She lifted her eyes to the top of Whistler Mountain, she saw the slippery mass of land plummeting down the mountainside.

"Uh, guys?" they were too far away to hear her.

It was like a train wreck. She was unable to look away as the massive mudslide struck the valley with brutal force. It churned the floodwaters and washed away everything in its path.

The slide was missing them and, instead, was crashing into the area where the grid had been. Raven gasped, then clapped a hand over her mouth as she almost choked on the rainwater.

In a surreal River Styx, the bones floated up from the churned earth and bobbed in the muddy water. They rolled with the current, spinning and dipping as the wind batted them around. God, there were *dozens* of them.

"Drew!" she screeched, and his head whipped around that time. He left Hammer supporting Webber out of the water and loped back to her. She didn't turn when he came up beside her—she was too riveted by the gruesome scene.

"Raven, what's—"

"Ssh, look."

He did, and she felt him tense. He sucked in a breath when he saw what had caught her attention. "Holy mother..."

"Yeah."

"I guess there's no mistaking what this was anymore," he said.

Raven shook her head. "What do we do?" she asked when she finally looked over at him, absurdly focusing on the way his long lashes clumped together in the rain.

"We tell the police. I think we need to drop off our little friend back there so we can give them a heads up about the site. Once the Valley dries up, they may be able to collect the bones, match some dental records. Hopefully, they can identify the remains and give the families some closure."

Raven nodded, and she suddenly felt every ounce of the soaking wet clothing she was wearing, as if they weighed a ton. When another surge of earth tumbled down the mountain, Drew urged her to turn and follow him. Raven tried to get the image of the river of bones out of her mind, but it was one she had a feeling would be etched there forever.

CHAPTER FORTY FOUR

It was close to three in the morning when they made it back to Cliffdweller's. The police had given them a good tongue lashing at the condition in which Alex Webber had been surrendered. Drew had explained the initial attack and that he'd felt threatened, so they eased up.

They eased up until they gave him another dressing down about not filing a police report on the first incident. He couldn't blame them, not really, but he hadn't wanted to involve the authorities in the messy fight with Azibel. In the end, Webber would probably walk because of it, and Drew was okay with that—long as they kept him out of their hair until Samhain. Samhain, the in-between-time during which spirits and demons can cross through the *locus*, would be when Azibel would make her move.

The police had also agreed to check out the dig site once the floodwaters receded, to see what they could find of the remains. Drew supposed that was the best they were going to get. He couldn't really think about it anymore that night. He was just too damned exhausted.

Raven unlocked the staff entrance at back of the inn, and they trudged wearily up the stairs to the second floor. Micah had texted that he'd gotten the team all settled in, and now the halls were quiet. Not an unsettling quiet, just an empty one.

Drew grunted his thanks when Raven pulled his room key out of his pocket and opened the door for him. He just couldn't seem to convince his brain to send any signals to his poor, battered body. He and Raven were both caked in a hardening shell of mud and completely soaked through. The October cold snap had finally begun, and both of them were turning a bit blue. Again, too tired to care.

Raven led him back into the bedroom and went about the business of removing his muddy armor. Her hands were steady and nimble as she undressed him and he sighed when he was finally wearing nothing but his boxers. He wondered how she could manage to be so coordinated when he felt like a walking corpse.

He pulled Raven against him, unconcerned with her muddy clothes and hair, buried his face in her neck and breathed deep. She was so strong. It was as if nothing ever threw her. At least not storms or mudslides, demons or men with two-by-fours. No, the things that scared Raven were things like trust and commitment. Love.

But he was working on her, as surely as she was working on him, teaching him how to accept another's care. And he, sure as hell, was beginning to like it.

Raven gave him a squeeze then backed away. She wrinkled her nose as she looked down at herself. "Go on in and take a shower. I'll start the fire and take one after."

Drew shook his head. His mother had taught him precious little, but basic manners had been among her repertoire. "No, ladies first. I insist."

She shrugged and began removing her own clothing, leaving a muddy trail to the bathroom. Once he heard the water start, Drew found an extra blanket from the linen closet to wrap around himself, and he went into the living room and turned on the gas fire.

When Raven came out wearing only her Saints jersey, he was ready to forget the shower altogether. He reached for her, but she side-stepped and made a face. "Get your dirty ass in the shower!"

Drew surrendered, picked up his discarded clothes and strolled to the bathroom. On his way in, he wiggled his 'dirty ass' at her and threw a goofy grin over his shoulder.

Drew started to bundle his dirty clothes into a towel so he could take them to get cleaned in the morning. He frowned when something dropped out of his jacket pocket and clattered onto the tile floor.

It was some kind of necklace, a string of gunmetal gray beads that resembled hematite. When he picked it up, he noticed that the stones were cool to the touch but instantly warmed in his hands. They felt alive against his skin, as if they were buzzing with energy.

Raven must have put the necklace in his pocket, he assumed. It certainly felt vital with a potency that reminded of her power. With a small smile, he clasped the necklace around his neck, although it barely fit, and turned on the shower.

The little room was blessedly warm and steamy after Raven's shower, and Drew couldn't suppress a groan of relief when he stepped under the spray.

He stood for a moment with his head bent under the steady stream of water and took a few deep breaths. It had been a hell of a night—and Samhain was still three days away. What would happen to them? Would they all survive?

Worrying began to cause a headache to pulsate in his temples, so he effectively shut down all thought processes that didn't involve getting clean and into bed as quickly as possible. He turned to grab the soap and hissed out a breath as water sluiced over his irritated surgical incision. It was red and encrusted with dried blood, but it looked like the stitches had held.

He gently cleaned the wound, and the water ran muddy as he washed the rest of his body. Quick to finish, he shut the water off before it ran cold. After he dried himself off, Drew wrapped the towel around his hips and went back to his bedroom.

The room was completely dark, but as soon as he stepped out, three of the leftover column candles on each bedside table spontaneously ignited. The warm glow illuminated the figure of Raven, stretched out in the middle of the bed. Naked. She was not within arm's reach of the candles.

He gave her a slow grin. "Heh, cool," he said, because it was. Really friggin' cool. Raven paid the candles no mind as she dragged her hungry gaze up and down his body. Slowly, she licked her lips and raised a brow at him.

"Lose the towel."

"Yes ma'am."

ꕥ

Raven drank in the sight of him like a woman dying of thirst. The skin that covered his steely body was bronzed and smooth. She wanted to taste every inch of him and then some.

When he loosened the towel and allowed it to slide to the floor, her eyes were immediately drawn lower. He may have been exhausted, but some parts of him were ready to play.

Biting her lip, she trailed her gaze over his abdomen, as the muscles there twitched in anticipation. His broad chest rose and fell just a little faster than normal, so she could tell he liked what he saw in return.

She frowned when she noticed he was wearing a necklace she'd never seen before. It was made of some metallic looking stone beads, similar to hematite, she thought, but darker. It nestled into the crook of his collarbone as it glinted in the candlelight.

"Where'd the necklace come from?"

He looked down at it and frowned as well. "Found it in my jacket pocket a minute ago. I thought maybe you'd put it there."

"Nope. I've never seen it." Interesting, Raven thought. She wondered if its sudden appearance had anything to do with Leora's visit. "Oh...Okay, I'll just get rid of it."

"No! I mean, what if Leora put it there? If she did, I'm sure she meant for you to have it. I think you should keep it on. Better safe than sorry."

Drew merely shrugged, then looked her up and down like she'd done to him. His muscles danced under his skin as he crossed the room, stalking her like prey. The sensation of being hunted mixed with her arousal and caused goosebumps to break out over her flesh.

It was when he was standing over her looking ready to pounce that she noticed the angry red incision curved underneath his left pectoral muscle. She gasped and bolted upright to get a closer look.

The wound was clean from his shower but red and puffy, as if it had been recently opened. God*damn* him. He should have told her he was hurting. They should have gone to the hospital. She tilted her head up to meet his eyes and glared daggers at him.

"Fucking hell, Drew! Why didn't you tell me you had aggravated your incision? We need to go back to the hospital..."

"I'm fine," he said, gently pushing her back until she was lying down again.

"But—"

He slid in on top of her and placed a finger over her lips. She raised her brows but said nothing. She was willing to see where he was going with it.

"I'm. Fine." He punctuated each word with quick kisses, then pulled back and grinned. "Besides, you're just going to fix me anyway."

Raven's cheeks heated as she felt the blush creeping across her skin. She looked away from his unwavering stare and became entranced by the lint on the comforter. How had he known?

"Thought you were being sneaky, didn't you?" He laughed when she jerked her shoulder in a moody shrug.

"A little," she answered.

He tipped her chin with his index finger. She had no choice but to stare in to the deep blue depths of his eyes. "Never underestimate our connection, Raven. Even in sleep...I feel you."

"I'm sorry if I...overstepped. I just wanted you to get better. I promise, I didn't *do* anything to you. I just stimulated your body's natural healing abilities."

His eyes took on that predatory gleam again, and Raven felt the heat coiling in her belly. Leaning forward until his lips were just a hair's breadth away from her own, he spoke softly. "I don't mind *anything* you want to do to me, love. But this time, you're going to do it while I'm awake."

Raven sucked in a breath, remembering the way his body had exploded under her care when he was in the hospital. To have complete control of him in such a way, while he was awake...Oh, *God*.

"Okay," she said breathlessly. "When the time is right."

"Okay."

Her eyes drifted closed as she felt his hands on her, her body being thoroughly explored like never before. He lay half on top of her with a heavy leg slung over her hips while his calloused palms ghosted over her skin.

Melting was too mild a word to describe what happened to her under his ministrations. Her muscles seemed to liquefy along the path of his hands, as they stroked over her shoulders and down to cup her breasts.

His mouth followed the wicked path of his hands. When he scraped his teeth lightly across the delicate skin of the underside of her breast, she arched off the bed. She was unable to control her reaction as much as he was unable to control the smug look he cast up at her.

Oh, he wanted to play, did he? Well, she had a few tricks, too. She used an invisible burst of energy to send a breeze through the room, extinguishing all of the candles but one. She adored the way the shadows flickered over his astonished face, and it always made her shiver to see the awe in that look.

She hooked a leg around his waist and rolled them until she was straddling his hips. She leaned forward slightly so that her mass of sable hair slid over her breasts and tickled his belly. It never failed to draw his immediate attention.

Her lips curved in a secret smile as his gaze dropped to her breasts, and he grabbed a lock of her hair and ran it through his fingers. "God, you're so beautiful," he said in a gravelly whisper, and her insides did that melty thing again.

He was the beautiful one. Lying against the pillow with his sexy blond hair curling as it dried, he looked like some kind of Roman god. His blue eyes were stormy with desire, completely riveted on her as she rose above him. Slowly, watching his face, she lifted her hips and lowered herself down on him.

The position reminded her of the first time they'd made love. The arrangement was so similar, and yet, so much had changed in a mere few weeks. She traced her fingers over her *signa* etched permanently over his heart.

He watched her face as she did it—probably searching for any sign that she was preparing to tuck tail and run now that she was well and truly stuck with him. Not a chance. Not this time, she thought.

"Regrets?" he said. His calm exterior belied by the worry that flickered in his eyes before he shuttered them.

"None," she answered without hesitation, then punctuated the sentiment with a swivel of her hips, taking him deeper.

His eyes rolled back before they slid shut, and he bucked up against her with a groan. She kept her hands on his hips and pressed their bodies against the bed. He was usually the one trying to slow down her frenzy, but tonight, the tables had turned. She was driving.

He released a sound that was suspiciously like a whine as she rode him, as she held him fast, not allowing him to speed up the pace. She wanted this moment, this little window of time, of perfect passion with the man she loved. Who loved her. And wasn't that something else, she thought.

"Raven..." he pleaded with her.

Raven refused to give in. Instead, she stopped moving altogether and leaned forward to capture his lips in an aggressive kiss. She invaded his mouth, pulling his tongue into hers and sucking, hard—which led to another round of struggle over the pace of things.

When she sat upright again, he raised his knees to support her back as she lifted herself in languid strokes. The torturously slow pace was having its own affect on her as she felt the sparks igniting in her belly, and lower.

Finally, when she knew Drew was about to lose it, and herself along with him, she snaked her left hand down and grabbed a hold of the stone necklace he wore. She used it as an anchor point—she was feeling as if she could fly apart at any moment—and placed her other hand over her *signa,* over his heart.

She gathered all of her strength and considerable power and pushed a surge of healing energy into him, concentrated from her hand. As he had in the hospital, he went wild beneath her. Muscles straining and veins bulging, he threw his head back and yelled.

Mesmerized by the sight of her tough, unyielding lover completely undone by her power, Raven raised herself up higher and gave him the room he so desperately needed to move.

Each movement was emphasized by a low moan, as the molecules in his body raged and strained to get at her. His white teeth flashed in the candlelight as he bared them, and his throat, to her. The temptation was too great to resist, so she leaned forward again and licked a trail up his neck and sucked up a mark on his pulse point.

The change in angle and another powerful thrust caused him to hit the perfect spot inside her, and she shattered. As she pushed back to meet his attack, her release washed over her, and her entire body shuddered.

Before she came down, Drew sat up and wrapped a heavy arm around her and used the other to lift her up. Biting down on her shoulder, he allowed his own release to swamp him as she sank back down onto him. Raven felt him deep inside her, and it was so much more than physical release. So much more. It was everything.

When they were finally able to move again, Drew turned and lay her down against the pillows. He laid his head on her stomach and looked up at her. It made her happy to see him looking so relaxed after the events of the day. God, she loved him. If anything ever happened to him...

She bit down hard on her lip to shut down those thoughts, and looked back at him. With a wicked grin, he licked a line up her sweat-slicked torso, between her breasts, to her chin. He ended the path with a sweet kiss on her lips.

By then, Raven could see the exhaustion creeping back into his handsome face. Without a word, she urged him to lower his head to her chest and rest, and he was asleep in seconds. Sleep didn't come so easily for Raven. She lay there for a few hours more, listening to Drew breathing—Drew, her love, her heart. She tried and failed to keep from thinking what would happen to all of them come Samhain.

CHAPTER FORTY FIVE

It was the day before Samhain and the seven of them had gathered in another one of what Raven was beginning to think of as their "round-table" meetings, although the coffee table in Drew's suite was a rectangle. Drew's phone had rung and he'd excused himself onto the terrace, where he paced and gestured in an intense conversation.

Raven frowned, pulled her attention back to the conversation, and focused on what Jeremiah was saying. "...and Leora said that she thought you know where the *locus* is," he said with a hard stare. "Have you been there?"

"Yes," she said, staring hard back. "We all have. It's Black Valley itself—more specifically the lowest point, just below where the dig site is...was."

"You sure?"

Raven nodded as she watched Drew in her periphery. "Positive. I felt it when I was down there the other day. I think it explains all of the things that have been happening there.

Drew's attack, the escalating behavior of the protestors, maybe even the mudslide. The locus—mostly Azibel's presence in it—brings out the worst in people." She left out the part about Drew almost killing Alex Webber. That was a need to know situation, and they didn't.

She breathed a sigh of relief when Drew ended his call and came back inside, but her stomach dropped when she caught the look on his face. "What happened?"

"Just got of the phone with a Detective Willis of the Watauga County Sheriff's office. Looks as if they've identified some of the remains from the dig site using dental records. Three of them to be exact—Mariah Truesdale, Erin Kelley, and Malenka Jovanovich."

Isla gasped and grabbed onto Raven's hand, and Raven squeezed back because, to be honest, she was just as freaked the fuck out. "The three missing girls," Isla whispered.

Drew nodded, and a muscle twitched in his jaw. "Yeah. Cause of death is as yet unknown."

"So we could have a serial kidnapper slash killer on our hands, or a crazy, homicidal demon who's killing off *Vigilati,*" Raven supplied.

"I'm leaning towards the latter," Jeremiah said.

Ray startled them all by surging to his feet and rounding on Drew and Raven. "What the hell are we going to *do* about this? We can't just go stomping into the Valley on Samhain in some fucked up 'Custer's last stand' and expect Azibel to just surrender. We need a plan!"

Touched and scared at the same time, Raven went to her father and slid an arm around his waist. "I get that you want to have some kind of strategy here. But how can we, when we're not even sure how to take her down? We know how Isla killed Alastore, but Leora said it will be different for every *Praeda.*"

"Still, we can be prepared. We can decide who's going to be positioned where, and what we're going to do if we get separated, and so on. I didn't survive three years in the joint by closing my eyes and hoping for the best, so it's hard to do that now!"

"Ray's right," Drew interjected, "we do need to strategize. We won't be able to control everything that happens, but we can try to anticipate how we'll react."

Raven nodded and squeezed her father a little tighter. She'd only just got him back, and she may lose him too. Not. Gonna. Happen. She locked eyes with Brynna, and she felt the connection that defied space and time, that of a *Vigilati* and her spirit guide.

"*Feradux*. You two move quicker and quieter than any of us. Think you can track down a topo map of the Valley?" she said, nodding her head toward Brynna and Marduk. Both of them hopped up, obviously relieved to be able to do something productive.

"We'll be back within the hour," Brynna called over her shoulder as the two of them left.

ജ്ജ

They reconvened down in the tavern, spreading the large map out on the table of the corner booth. Drew gave Micah a grateful smile when he brought them all drinks—and a soda for Ray, thank you very much—having learned all of their favorites by then.

Without a word, he went back across the room to tend the bar. Drew knew the big man could tell that something big was going down, and while he was watching out for them, he didn't press them for answers. Bless him; the man was the definition of discreet, Drew thought.

Drew looked down at the topographical map the *feradux* had obtained from God knew where. He pulled out a pencil and circled a position on the map. "This is the area that Cliffdweller's sits, more or less...agreed?"

They all nodded, so he circled a second point. "This is the waterfall where Azibel attacked Raven. And this is the dig headquarters, where I was attacked," he said, circling the third location.

Seeing his theory take form in front of him, Drew pointed out that the three points made a triangle. He used a piece of paper as a straight edge and drew a line from each point of the triangle to its corresponding opposite side. Then he circled the point at which all three lines intersected.

"This is the lowest point, where Raven thinks the locus is. I think it's safe to say that she's right. On the east side of the Valley, you have the hill that led up to HQ. We've got woods on the north and south sides, and the foot of Barron's Bald on the western border. That gives us several defensible positions, but the Valley itself...wide open."

Raven leaned forward and studied the map, and Drew's thoughts momentarily scrambled as he thought back to the other night. Shaking his head, he tried to concentrate when he realized she was speaking.

"This is good. I think I have a plan," she said.

"By all means, do share," Jeremiah said. "We've come up with jack so far."

"Azibel knows we're all here, right? So she's going to be expecting an entourage—she'll think we're going to come in musketeer style, all guns blazing."

"Musketeer style?" Isla asked, genuinely confused.

"You know, all for one, one for all. So we're going to do the exact opposite. When she gets there, she's going to see me and only me."

Drew's heart shot up into his throat when he imagined Raven facing down Azibel alone. *Like hell.* Everyone turned to look at him, and he realized that he'd growled that last bit out loud.

"...out of your frigging mind—"

"Absolutely not!" Drew spoke over Ray's protest and tried to ignore the stab of pain he felt that Raven didn't want him fighting by her side. "If you don't want me with you, fine, but you'll take the *feradux*. Non-fucking-negotiable."

Raven's eyes softened and she took his hand. "Easy, love. Let me finish." She waited for his curt nod before she continued. "It will appear as though I'm alone, to throw her off. But you'll all be hiding in strategically defensible positions."

"Go on," Jeremiah said.

"I'll approach from the main entrance of the compound—what's left of it—and make my way down into the valley proper. Isla, Jeremiah, and Marduk will cover me from the southern tree line. I want Isla close, because we seem to amplify each other's power." She looked to Isla for confirmation, and she smiled and nodded.

"Drew, you, Brynna, and Ray will flank the open valley and take up a position at the northern tree line. That will cover all of the approach points. If anyone approaches from the hill, I'll see them right away and sense them even before that. Barron's Bald is sheer rock, so no one's coming from that direction unless they're repelling or falling. What do you guys think?"

"I think it's a solid plan," Jeremiah said. Drew nodded his agreement, infinitely relieved that Raven was accepting the help of their friends—and his, as well.

Raven cocked her head at Isla as a line of concentration formed between her delicate brows. "What is it?" she asked.

"Alastore knew nothing of what the *Praedos* were capable of, so he came unprepared. He thought a man to woman fight would be cake for a demon like him. He was wrong. But I think Azibel has some idea of what you are—hell, maybe she knows for sure—and I don't doubt that she's infinitely smarter than him. She won't come alone."

"We must teach all of them to fight the *auchrim*," Marduk interjected, gesturing towards Ray, Raven, and Drew—the only ones who haven't been up against the soulless demons before. "I am sure she will bring hundreds of them. They are easy to dispatch, but they *will* be a distraction, so you must learn to cut them down quickly, yes?"

"We will," Drew said with conviction. "Just tell us what we need to do."

Marduk's lips twitched as he thought over what he wanted to say. "Have any of you ever seen *The Walking Dead*?"

"Like the one with the zombies?" Raven asked.

"Yes, exactly like that. The *auchrim* aren't zombies, exactly, as they can reason and think for themselves, but they are under the control of the *Lochrim*—using his, or her, energy to remain corporeal. They can be disposed in much the same manner as the television zombies."

Jeremiah rolled his eyes at the wolf and took pity on his friends. "What Rain Man is trying to say is that anything that would ordinarily kill a human being is enough to send an *auchrim* back inside the *locus*. There's no need for firearms, as blades, clubs—hell, a tire iron—will work just as well."

"But we can't kill them?" Ray asked, casting a worried glance to Drew. Obviously the guy wasn't any crazier about the idea of Raven risking her life than Drew was.

Brynna's eyes flashed feline and she bared a delicate fang when she spoke. "If only. The only way to kill the *auchrim* is to kill their source—the *Lochrim*...Azibel. Their fate is wrapped up in hers, as well as any live captures she may have."

"Live captures?" Drew didn't like the sound of that.

"The *Lochrim* feeds off the energy of living things. They collect it to become corporeal, and to use in their various shenanigans," Marduk answered. "Occasionally, they'll keep live captures inside the *locus* to have a continual source of energy—because if they collect enough of it, they may become strong enough to permanently break through the *locus* for good. Of course, I'm not aware of an instance in which one has ever been able to accomplish that."

"We released several live captures when I killed Alastore," Isla said, "along with a few trapped souls."

Drew felt Raven shudder beside him, so he pulled her close to his side and ran a hand up and down her arm. "Okay, so we have a plan, then."

"Not quite. I wasn't finished," Raven said, looking at him warily. Uh oh. Drew had a feeling that he wasn't going to like whatever was coming next. "Azibel is too smart to buy the idea that I've come alone. She'll anticipate an ambush...unless I give her a reason not to."

"Which is?"

"I'll tell her I've decided to join her."

"What?"

"No!"

"Are you insane?"

Raven closed her eyes to the protests thrown at her, and Drew just wanted to shake her to her senses, then lock her in a room until the demons had been exorcised. But he'd learned from Jeremiah that that would most assuredly not work.

In his quiet, cultured accent, Marduk had the most shocking reply. "It's fucking brilliant."

Drew rounded on the young man, glaring at him. "How can you *say* that?"

"Because it's true. You are blinded by your fear for your mate—I don't begrudge you that—but I am not. There's no other way she'll get anywhere near close enough to Azibel to defeat her without it. The Valley is just too exposed."

Drew slammed a hand down on the table, startling the entire group, and whirled his head around to look at Raven again. "I hate this. Fucking hate it." It took all the strength he had in his body to back down and concede the point. "But the goddamn-motherfucking wolf is right." He frowned and rubbed his eyes. "But what if she asks you to prove your loyalty to her? What then? How far are you willing to take this?"

"I've got a plan for that, too, but you all are going to have to trust me. If everyone knows about it, it won't be convincing." She turned pleading amber eyes up to Drew, and her gaze was strong and sure. He knew she was perfectly capable of fighting this battle, and they'd all be there in case something went wrong. "Please, Drew."

"Of course. I trust you, you know that. So next on the agenda, we need to weapon up."

"That could present a problem," Jeremiah said. "Where the hell are we going to buy enough weapons to support a small revolution, without raising any eyebrows."

Drew merely laughed and swatted his friend in the back of the head. "And I thought *I* was forgetting my Southern roots! We're in the heart of Appalachia, brother. We'll just go to the Army-Navy Surplus store," he answered with a shit-eating grin.

ꙮ

The next morning, their motley band descended upon the Military Surplus store with hurricane force. They swam in a sea of camo and camel, of boots and blades, and they had entirely too much fun doing it.

The idea had been to outfit their group with weapons, but Raven looked on like an indulgent mother as her friends rifled through fatigues and packs, trying things on and laughing at one another. Danger would come soon enough, so she let them have their fun, and chuckled when she caught Drew eyeing a bin full of ninja stars like a kid on Christmas.

Raven closed her eyes and wished she could be so lighthearted while facing their impending doom. But she had a plan to hatch. One that could save them, but could also very well destroy the tenuous bond they'd formed as a group.

Their lives were worth it, though. She smiled at them sadly before catching sight of Brynna drooling over a display of bowie knives. Trying to be as discreet as possible, Raven crossed the room and grabbed the *feradux* by her elbow, then pulled her toward the back of the room.

"*Ssh!*" she hissed when Brynna tried to speak. Once she was sure they hadn't been noticed, Raven ushered the other woman behind the curtain into the small fitting room. Immediately, Brynna jerked her arm away and eyed Raven suspiciously.

"Dude, I'm flattered and all...but I *so* don' swing that way."

Raven rolled her eyes then glared at Brynna. "Shut. Up. Keep your voice down. This is serious."

Her *feradux* senses snapping her to attention, Brynna lowered her head in a submissive gesture. "Anything you need, *domina.*"

"I said before that I was going to try to convince Azibel that I've turned. You and I both know that she's going to ask for proof. If it comes down to it, and I have to give it to her, the others can't know what's happening. Their reaction needs to be genuine. You following me?"

Knowing feline eyes stared back at her, and Raven knew that she was. Brynna gave a curt nod, and Raven could see the gleam of battle sparking in that stare. Good. Leaning in, she pressed her lips up against the redhead's ear and began to outline her plan.

In the end, they spent hundreds in the little store, and Raven could practically see the dollar signs flashing in the old owner's eyes. They'd all gotten various forms of camo gear and survival packs—because who knew what would happen—and a selection of weapons.

Raven herself chose a machete and a gnarly looking crescent blade. Drew got a machete, as well, along with a bowie knife and a handful of ninja stars. The others were armed much the same, with the exception of Brynna, who chose a matching pair of tantos in blood-red scabbards. Raven wasn't sure what Samurai swords had to do with the American military, but they looked pretty deadly, regardless.

There would be no sleeping on the eve of Samhain. No dancing, no lovemaking, no laughing. Raven lay on their bed facing Drew and tried to memorize every line of his face, because it was that image that would get her through the next few hours.

She would have to hurt him tonight, hurt all of them, to save their lives. Unable to tell him exactly what she was planning, Raven still wanted to make him understand that no matter what was said—no matter what happened—they were solid.

She must have been frowning, because she suddenly felt Drew's hand on her face, caressing the line between her brows. "What is it?" he asked.

What wasn't it? Raven thought with a sigh. That was more apt a question. "I just want to prepare you as best I can. If I'm going to fool Azibel, I'm going to have to act like I hate all of you. Like I'm ready to sacrifice your lives for my own. Like I hate you. God, Drew, the things I'll have to say...Are we strong enough to survive that?"

She appreciated the fact that he took time to think about her concerns, to give them their due. Then he dismissed them.

"I meant what I said to you the other night. Never underestimate our connection. I feel you like you're a part of me, and I think it's the same for you. How else would you have known that I was in trouble the night I was attacked? No matter what you have to say, or do, I'll feel your heart."

"But Drew—"

"No. It's enough Raven. We'll get through it. And we'll dance on Azibel's grave together when it's all over."

"Maybe so," she answered gravely. "Maybe so. But not before that Valley runs with blood. That of the innocent and the evil alike. Hope to gods we'll all be strong enough to survive that."

Chapter Forty Six

Raven figured if she was going to pretend like she'd come to take her rightful place as the daughter of the Queen of Evil, she may as well look the part. She dressed in her black leather riding pants and a high-collared leather jacket, topping the outfit off with knee-high bondage boots and black lambskin riding gloves.

Her hair was braided intricately along the sides of her head, woven through and tipped with black feathers. The rest of it was brushed back away from her face and tumbled down her back. A makeshift weapons belt was slung low on her hips, from which the machete hung on the left and the crescent blade on the right.

She'd blackened her eyes dramatically, giving them an eerie smoky effect, and her lips were painted a deep blood-red. She regarded herself critically in the mirror and smirked at the effect the getup had. She looked a lot fiercer than she felt.

Gathering up her keys and a pair of Ray-Bans—they would make it easier for her in the event that she needed to use her spatial senses for sight—she went to meet the others.

Once outside, Raven took note of the blood-red harvest moon that cast its wicked glow upon them. Her friends, her family, stood in a circle in the gravel parking lot, and they all looked up at her when she stepped through the door.

Her gaze immediately sought out Drew, who came to her side and pulled her against him. She chanced a quick look at Brynna, and the *feradux* gave her an almost imperceptible nod, signaling that she'd gotten the things they needed to carry out the plan.

Raven gave Drew a small smile. "Are we ready for this?" she asked to no one in particular.

"As we'll ever be," Drew answered for all of them. "You sure you want to do it like this?"

The evident worry in his eyes made Raven's heart lurch, because she knew there was much more to come. She wished she could spare him any pain, but that would be impossible. He'd make it through. He was strong. *They* were strong.

"Yeah, I am. I have to. Let's ride."

Raven led their little cavalcade on her Ducati, and Drew followed behind in the Camaro with Ray and Brynna. Jeremiah, Isla, and Marduk brought up the rear with their rental. They saw no one else on the road as they barreled down the Parkway.

When the caravan reached the turn-off that would snake its way down to the southern border of the valley, Raven raised a gloved fist as the signal for Jeremiah's group to split off and get into position.

Next, they came to the driveway of the dig site where Raven pulled over and waved Drew on. She couldn't miss his grim look as he nodded to her on his way past. She would wait in the relative safety of the driveway while Drew flanked the valley to the north to get his team in place.

After about ten minutes, Raven kick-started the bike and descended the long, curving driveway. When she caught sight of the compound, she was in awe of the destruction the mudslide had wrought. There was barely anything left.

She made quick work of the hill, and when she got to the deepest point of the valley, she placed a foot on the ground while idling the motorcycle. She reached out with her senses to examine the space and atmosphere of the sheltered meadow.

Sure enough, there was some kind of invisible circular border around the bottom of the valley. It was like a current of energy, swirling like an unseen wall cloud. Raven had no doubt it would shock the body to pass through it.

"Oh, well. No turning back now," she murmured. She righted the bike, gunned the engine and surged forward. When she breached the barrier, shockwaves sizzled across her skin—like getting shocked by an electric fence in various places all over her body. It was all she could do to keep from biting it.

Just inside the border, Raven killed the engine and parked the bike on its kick-stand. She removed her helmet, reached into her pocket and pulled out her Ray-Ban Warriors. The glasses helped block out her optical vision so she could focus on her spatial vision.

She was able to locate each of her friends so she knew they were all in position. She'd managed to snag some earpieces out of her Stiles & Nash goodie bag for them to use to communicate. She didn't wear one herself—couldn't risk Azibel seeing it—so her senses were all she had.

So Raven waited. And waited. It had to have been close to an hour that she stood there, propped up against the Ducati, using her senses to bounce energy waves around the valley. Finally, when she was starting to wonder if she'd gone into some kind of crazy Samhain time warp, she caught a bit of movement at the foot of Barron's Bald.

A nebulous cloud of black smoke wafted towards her, disappearing and reappearing across the field as it moved ever closer. When it was just a few feet in front of her, it began to gain form until it materialized as Azibel.

The woman looked deceptively innocuous, but Raven knew otherwise. Azibel wore a long black gown with her sable hair falling loosely in curls. She was as deadly as the night was long, and that was evident even from the delicate fangs that poked out from under her ruby red upper lip.

Azibel gave the illusion that she'd come alone, but Raven's spatial vision picked up on a group of bodies just a few feet behind her. *Auchrim* waiting to materialize, to be sure. Gliding forward, Azibel smirked and raised a brow at Raven's sunglasses.

Raven merely shrugged, determined to keep up an appearance of outward calm. "The better to see you with, Mother dear."

With an un-demon-like snort, Azibel surveyed the open field in which they stood. "Come to sacrifice yourself for your putrid little human friends, then?"

"No," Raven answered. She had to force herself to meet those unnerving shadowy eyes without blinking. "I've come to join you."

The *Lochrim*'s jaw dropped, and Raven considered it an advantage to have shocked her. "I've grown tired of their neediness, their paltry little problems. They're suffocating me. And I've decided that I'll be more powerful with you than without you."

"Too true. An intriguing idea. What about your dalliance with the handsome scientist? I tried to take care of it myself, but I fear I had incompetent help."

Raven rolled her eyes and examined her fingers, while her heart was breaking. "Oh that? That's over. I'm a traveler. He knew from the beginning that I didn't want to be tied down. He tried anyway, so I ditched him."

Wanting to steer the conversation away from her loved ones, Raven began to question Azibel. "So how do we do this thing—take over? I'm sure they'll try to stop us. After all, they did take out Alastore."

Her eyes flashed, and she bared her fangs when Raven mentioned his name. "*Alastore* was a fool! Weak and stupid. How he managed to let himself get ended by that insipid little human girl, I'll never know. No matter, they'll not be so lucky against us, my daughter."

It was in that moment that Raven realized that Azibel had no clue how Isla had been able to kill Alastore. She knew nothing about the order of the *Praedos* and what their purpose was. Interesting—score one for the humans. She didn't have anymore time to think on it, because Azibel spun around and pegged her with a chilling glare. "You say you're with me, daughter?"

"Yes," Raven answered with a steadiness she didn't feel.

"Prove it."

There it was. The moment she'd been waiting for, dreading, since they'd come up with their plan of attack. It was time for Raven to deploy her *feradux* def-con one failsafe. She just hoped the others could hold it together.

Pokerface, pokerface, pokerface. She kept chanting it over in her head, whether to her friends or to herself, she couldn't say.

If she didn't make this convincing, it could kill them all. But no pressure, she thought with a sneer.

With a haughty sniff, Raven raised her chin and glared at Azibel. "I'd expect no less. I'll give you your *proof,* don't you worry. *Feradux,* away to me," she said in a quiet voice.

Azibel glanced over to the northern tree line as they both heard a rustling. Raven's stomach flipped as the cougar emerged from the shadows. The cat flanked them in a wide counter-clockwise circle, and eventually approached at Raven's left side.

"That'll do," Raven whispered, and the cougar immediately changed back into the form of the woman. She'd worked out a code with Brynna the day before, adapted from sheepdog herding cues. She hoped it would keep Azibel from realizing that Brynna was aware of what was going on.

The *Lochrim* bared her fangs at the *feradux,* and cut her eyes to Raven. "You'd better be going somewhere with this, daughter. Make it fast, before I lose interest and slit both your throats."

Raven snaked an arm across the back of Brynna's shoulders, curled it around until it hooked across her throat. She had to make it good, so she squeezed firmly, eliciting a tiny cough from Brynna. "There," she whispered, "There." It was the code to let Brynna know she was doing everything right.

Raven swept her jacket back with her free hand and reached, not for the crescent dagger or the machete, both which hung at ready access. No, she reached behind her for the knife that was concealed at her back.

As if in slow motion, she brought the knife around in front of Brynna while taking deep breaths through her nose but keeping a steady gaze on Azibel. The demon's eyes glittered with malicious excitement.

Raven squeezed Brynna's throat tight, never taking her eyes off Azibel, and plunged the knife downward into Brynna's chest. A keening wail wrenched out of her as blood flowed like water. Raven released the other woman abruptly, and she sank to her knees, gasping.

Raven couldn't allow herself to look at Brynna, couldn't check and make sure everything had gone right. She only hoped their friends realized it was a hoax, and stayed hidden. She forced herself to ignore the fading sobs coming from the woman on the ground. Instead, Raven pokered up and curled her lip at her mother. "Happy now?"

"Ecstatic," she retorted, and Raven got the feeling that she truly meant it.

"Fuck!" Drew shouted over the screams in his ear piece. He spun around, reeling as he tried to erase the gruesome scene from his mind. "Fuck, fuck, *fuck*. It's not real, it can't be."

He felt an arm come around his shoulders to steady him. "I'm to blame for this," Ray said. "I raised her to survive at all costs, no matter who she had to take down. I just never thought..."

Abruptly, Drew turned again, fisting his hands in Ray's shirt and backing the older man into a tree. "It's a trick, Ray. She's a witch, for God's sake. *They* are witches. It's not real, no matter how convincing it looks. Trust me. Trust *her*."

He didn't look all that convinced, but before they could discuss it further, Ray focused on something over Drew's shoulder. "Got company," he said.

Drew let go of Ray, turned and saw a group of people standing behind him. They had the peculiar swirling eyes he now associated with Azibel and those under her control, but they didn't have pale skin and black hair like Isla said the *auchrim* would.

He actually thought he recognized a few of them, but he couldn't put his finger on where. He made the connection to the conservationist protestors at the same time he heard Jeremiah's panicked voice through his earpiece.

"Fuck...humans!"

CHAPTER FORTY SEVEN

Raven cast wary glances around the valley, but none of her friends broke their cover. She breathed an inward sigh of relief before glancing at Azibel who had cocked her head as if listening to something Raven couldn't hear.

"I'll just have my...associates come and take care of that," she said, nudging Brynna with a dainty foot.

Raven's heart began to race as she frantically searched her mind for an excuse not to let them take her. "Leave it," she said, "We've got more important things to deal with. And besides, we both know your minions are already here."

She leveled an accusatory stare at her mother, and got an astonished look in return. "You're more powerful than I had imagined, child. I'm glad I don't have to kill you after all."

"Oh, stop it, Mother, I'm getting all warm and fuzzy."

Raven tried to keep Azibel engaged while she waited for the opportunity to make her move. It would only come around once and most likely would be ineffectual, but it was the best shot she had.

At a signal from Azibel, the *auchrim* finally materialized. They were a gruesome lot with their almost translucent skin, empty, dead eyes, and razor sharp fangs. They'd almost pass for human if they wore sunglasses and shut their drooling mouths.

Azibel whispered something to the one in front, a gaunt-looking male who towered at least six-foot-four. He glared at Raven with open hostility as he walked up and grabbed Brynna around the ankles.

No! Raven couldn't let them take Brynna. What if they tried to dispose of her body? If they found out she wasn't really dead, they'd slaughter the both of them. She mustered all of her courage, drew her crescent blade and lunged at the man, plunging the dagger into his neck.

Azibel screeched as his body exploded in a cloud of sulfur and ash. "I said leave it!" Raven growled. "My *feradux*, my problem. We need to concentrate on opening the gateway before the sun rises."

Some of the wind had been let out of the *auchrim*'s sails, and they inched backward as Raven stepped forward. Azibel regarded her silently before flashing her fangs in a horrific facsimile of a smile. "Well done. Pity, he was one of my favorites. No matter, you are right. We must get on with our agenda."

ຮOca

Drew turned to fully face the group of humans with Ray at his back. There were four—no, five—of the bastards to their two. Not great odds. "Ray," he whispered, "got any rope in your pack?"

"Bet your ass."

Drew touched the com button of his earpiece and spoke quietly into it. "It's a ploy to slow us down. She knows we won't kill them. Neutralize them quickly, with minimum damage. This isn't their fault any more than it's ours. Use the rope from your packs, disable, restrain, regroup. Got it?"

"Ten-four," came the crackling reply from Jeremiah.

Drew tensed when one of the humans, a fresh-faced young man no more than twenty, started to walk toward him. "I'm going to distract them while you cut some lengths of rope to tie them with," he said without taking his eyes off the guy.

"Could do that, I suppose. Or we could just use this bag of zip-ties I brought. This ain't my first rodeo, kid," he said when he caught Drew's astonished look. Then his eyes widened, and Drew whirled around just in time to catch Opie's fist before it plowed into his head.

"Give me some of those," he shouted back to Ray who pushed a handful into his outstretched palm. Since it had worked so well on Alex Webber, Drew head-butted the kid right in the kisser, and he crumpled to the ground.

Quickly, Drew trussed him up with zip-ties and turned to see Ray fending off two attackers. He took a step to go help, but an arm circled his neck from behind and squeezed him into a choke hold. Seeing spots, Drew struggled to keep conscious as the man strangled him with inhuman strength.

Drew grabbed the guy's arm, pushed all of his weight forward, and flipped his attacker over his head, but not before he wrenched his neck painfully on the way down. Hitting solid ground flat on his back stunned the man long enough for Drew to roll him over and sit on his back while zip-tying his hands together.

Breathing hard, he hopped up to go help Ray, but the man had subdued his two attackers and was engaged in a brutal fight with the last one. *Damn, High Desert Prison ain't no joke,* Drew thought. He circled around and got behind the guy who had just clobbered Ray with a haymaker that sent him reeling.

Drew jerked the guy back hard and jabbed him in the kidney with the handle of his Bowie knife, which was enough to drop him. By that time, Ray had recovered enough to help him secure the big bastard.

Once the threat was neutralized, he and Ray leaned back on their hands to catch their breath. Touching his com again, Drew tried to raise Jeremiah and the others. "Come back, Jere. What's your status?"

It took him a few heart-wrenching seconds for him to reply, and Drew breathed a sigh of relief when he heard it. "Attackers are down. No fatalities. Only minor injuries on our side. You?"

"Same. Go ahead and give the signal. I'm sure Raven's freaking by now."

"But Drew, did you see—"

"Just give the fucking signal, Rousseau!"

"Ten-four."

ꙮ

Raven scanned the tree line while pretending to pay attention to Azibel, who was outlining her plan for death and destruction, and basic world domination. Where was the signal? They should have let her know they were ready long before now. What if there had been more *auchrim* in the woods?

Her heart gave a painful lurch when she realized she'd have to carry on with the plan, with or without her friends. She had to try. Her hand was already curling around her crescent knife when she heard it. A long, mournful howl of a wolf. And then another. The signal. Time to move.

Raven's lip curled into a sneer when she realized that Azibel had her back turned as she was talking quietly to her minions. Pulling the knife from its sheath, Raven winced as she drew the blade across the skin of her forearm, coating it with her blood.

She silently came up behind Azibel and grabbed hold of her neck with her free hand. She pushed a wave of energy into the demon's body that set her molecules buzzing, and rendering her temporarily unable to move. She hoped.

Raven brought the bloody knife around and laid it at Azibel's throat. She gave her mother just a moment to fully realize what was happening. Raven smiled when she saw her friends flanking the band of *auchrim,* forming a semicircle behind them. She dug the knife in just a little farther.

"I should have known you were too worthless to see reason," she croaked as she tried unsuccessfully to twist her head around and look at Raven.

"Yep, you should have known."

"But the *feradux*—"

"Is just fine," Brynna answered from behind them.

Oh, thank the gods, Raven thought. She was worried the trick knife had failed, that she'd killed her for real. Damn, the cat was a good actress. She felt Azibel's power begin to push back at her, and she knew it was time to end it.

Putting all of her strength into the strike, Raven sliced the blade deep, pulled it across the *Lochrim's* throat, and let her drop. There was bleeding, screeching, and gurgling...but no dying. Not yet, at least. Isla had said, when she stabbed her father with a knife covered in her blood, he'd imploded almost instantly, burned from the inside out.

Each Praeda *must face her own demons. The way will always be distinct, but contain a common thread.*

Leora's words haunted her, and she knew. This was not the way Azibel was going to die. Behind them, her friends engaged the *auchrim,* dispatched them with efficiency while they tried to multiply. It would all be for nothing if Azibel lived—she'd kill them all.

Raven gasped as Azibel began to struggle to her feet, glaring daggers at her. "You'll pay," she said, choking on her own blood and the gaping hole in her throat. She stomped her foot and sent a current through the earth that exploded underneath Raven's feet and sent her flying to land on her back a good fifteen feet away.

Before she had a chance to regroup, Azibel was on her. The demon queen straddled her waist, wrapped bloody hands around her throat and squeezed. Raven could feel Azibel sending the same kind of pulse through her own body, the one that paralyzed. Choking, gasping, she struggled against it, but got nowhere.

Blood dripped on her face as Azibel leaned over and whispered to her. "Mortal weapons? It's a coward's way. But I'll oblige you if it's what you prefer." She removed one hand from Raven's neck and pulled the machete off her weapons belt.

She gripped it with both hands now and raised it high, preparing to plunge it down into Raven's chest. Raven saw a streak of gold out of the corner of her eye, and suddenly the weight was lifted off of her. The cougar tackled Azibel hard and they both went down together. It broke the demon's concentration and Raven was able to get free and stand up.

A cold fist gripped her heart when she saw Azibel struggling beneath the cat. She was struggling against the weight of the cougar, not the attack of it. To her horror, the *feradux* had taken the machete in the chest, the blow that was meant for Raven. And she wasn't moving.

The ground beneath them began to rumble, and a dazzling light emanated from the wound in the cougar's chest. It blinded them all momentarily and when it disappeared, Brynna was gone.

Raven choked on the tears that spilled over unbidden as she walked toward Azibel. "I'll kill you," she said in a cold voice, "I'll rip out what's left of your goddamn throat myself."

She prepared to leap, but was caught by two *auchrim* who had snuck up on her. But they didn't attack, they merely held her, waiting for Azibel to get free and finish it herself. And she did, but as she rose, she was body blocked by Ray.

"*No!*" Raven screamed. "You can't fight her, Ray. This is between her and *me*."

"Fuck that," he spat and swung his own machete at the demon. Azibel easily dodged the blow and her arms shot out to latch on to his skull with her claw-tipped fingers. She forced him to look into her eyes, to become mesmerized by the shadows of the souls dancing there.

Ray's face went slack, and he stopped struggling. His body convulsed violently before going still. And she just dropped him to the ground.

Raven went wild, squirming, kicking, biting, trying to get free and help her father. She looked to her friends, but they were engaged in a battle that was quickly turning against them.

"Now where were we?" Azibel asked primly as she stalked Raven. She left a trail of blood in her wake. "You, yes, you were talking about ripping my throat out. Sounds like a plan."

She moved so fast, Raven couldn't track her until she was right in front of her. Azibel bared her fangs before lurching forward and locking them onto Raven's throat, while the *auchrim* still held her fast.

Pain exploded from her neck and radiated through her body as Raven felt those razor sharp fangs tearing at her flesh. What the *fuck?* The bitch was biting her! It was like they were suddenly on the set of some bad vampire movie. Raven felt the absurd need to look around for George Clooney.

Get a grip, girl. Clooney's not going to save you. As she tried to think through the pain while the fucking demon chewed on her, Raven reached down deep for what was left of her power. The surge blasted through her and the demon went flying, but Azibel took a chunk of Raven's flesh with her.

Raven prepared to go on the offensive, but something was off. Azibel was stumbling back, clawing at her own throat, gagging. She reached out for Raven with a scream that held both terror and loathing, but before she could reach her, her body exploded in a sulfuric cloud of ash. Only her bones were left behind.

The *auchrim* soon followed suit and disintegrated one by one. Raven clapped a hand over the blood gushing from her flesh wound, and she went to her father. She checked his vitals—he had a pulse, was breathing—and she tried to rouse him, but he seemed almost...catatonic.

Raven turned around searched desperately for Drew. When she saw him, covered in blood and dirt, but alive, a sob escaped her. He was by her side immediately, hugging her to him as he checked on Ray. Raven just couldn't stop the flow of tears at all she'd lost. She'd probably saved the entire human race, but lost a dear friend and, possibly, her father. It was just too much. She turned and buried her face in Drew's shoulder and let go.

The others approached as Raven wailed, poured out all of her grief onto him. They had to get Ray to the hospital, figure out what happened to Brynna. But just then, all she wanted was to be comforted by the man she loved.

When she'd finally cried herself out, Raven raised her head and wiped her face with grubby hands. "What happened back there?"

Isla knelt down beside her and put a hand on Raven's shoulder. "I have a theory. In some ways, it was the same as Alastore...your blood was poison to her. Alastore succumbed just by blood contact while Azibel, apparently, had to ingest it. Seems like she killed herself. Accidentally, of course."

Raven sniffed and looked up at Marduk, who was standing behind Isla. "What happened to Brynna? Where did she go?"

"Where all *feradux* go to be judged. Back to The Source—to the *Antisanctum*."

Five heads whipped around as they heard a noise behind them. Raven gasped as Leora approached, her white gown dragging on the bloody ground.

Drew helped Raven to her feet as they faced the goddess. "Well done, child."

"Is she really dead?" Drew couldn't help but ask it. He had to know if Raven was safe for good.

"Indeed. Another victory on our side. Because of this, I think we have been granted another *bréve*." Drew watched as Leora turned and stared at Jeremiah, then Isla. "Something stirs within you, child."

Isla jolted and looked down at herself, then back at Leora. "What?"

The goddess smiled and slowly began to disappear. "Hope."

Chapter Forty Eight

Raven awoke from a fog to an incessant beeping sound and a dull throbbing in her neck. Instinctively, she reached a hand up to check the area and found it covered in thick bandages. Her eyes flew open and darted around the room. Hospital, she thought.

She heard a sound to her left, looked over and saw a haggard looking Drew leaning over a chair. "Hey. You're awake."

Confusion swamped her, and her head began to swim. She remembered fighting Azibel, crying over Ray, and seeing Leora. Then, nothing. Total blackness. "What happened?" she asked, and winced when her voice creaked like a rusty gate.

"You passed out from blood loss," he answered, his brows knitting with concern. "Azibel nicked your carotid. You nearly bled out. Why didn't you tell me she'd gotten you so bad?"

The anguish was so evident on his face, it brought tears to her own eyes. "I'm sorry. I didn't realize. I thought it was just a flesh wound."

He pushed forward, laid his head on her thigh, and looked up at her. "Almost lost you." His voice was choked with unshed tears.

"You didn't. No more leaving, remember. I promised." She gave him a weak smile and sifted fingers through his soft curls.

"Yep, you promised.

They stayed that way for a long while, and Raven felt herself drifting in and out of consciousness. When her head finally cleared, she remembered to ask about Ray. Drew frowned, and she knew it wouldn't be good news.

"Physically, he's healthy. All his body functions are normal. He's just...gone. They want to discharge him. Been pressuring me to check him into some kind of long term care facility."

Raven felt panic surge up in her chest, and she gripped Drew's hand, hard. "No! He'll die in a place like that. Too much like prison. We have to think of something else. Please."

She had visions of padded cells and straightjackets that were probably fueled by late night movies, but she couldn't help it. Raven needed her father. She'd only just gotten him back. "I need to see him."

She moved to pull at the wires connected to her and tried to sit up in bed, but Drew stopped her. She felt herself pulled into his arms, and as he ran his hands up and down her back, she felt herself calming. "Easy," he said. "You've got to stay in bed a little while longer. Don't worry about Ray just yet. I think I have an idea. How would you feel about living in New Orleans?"

Raven narrowed her eyes at him. She couldn't quite believe he was talking bout living arrangements when her father's future was so uncertain. "You want me to move in with you?"

"Well, yes, of course. But I know of someone who can take care of Ray. She lives in New Orleans, too. So if you came home with me, you'd be close to him. You can work from anywhere, right?"

Raven nodded dumbly and watched with a full heart as the emotions played over his features. Fear, hope, panic, desperation. His expression screamed please say yes, don't run from me again. She let him squirm for just a moment more before turning to kiss him deeply—a slow, lingering kiss. The kind that made you forget your own name.

"New Orleans sounds like a good place for all of us." She gripped his shoulders like a lifeline, leaning on him. Raven had no doubt that he would take care of her—they would take care of each other. Because Ray was a part of her, she knew Drew would take care of him, too. Together, they could all heal.

ജ

Drew was smiling so brightly when he stepped out of the hospital room, his cheeks ached. He had to call, make some arrangements for Ray, and Raven had to get well. But once all was said and done, his woman, his beautiful, incredible Raven, was coming home with him.

He was still smiling when he picked up his phone to make the call. The answer came on the second ring, and he closed his eyes when he heard Esme Rousseau's sweet Cajun accent float over the line. That voice sounded like home.

"Hey, Mama E. How you doin'?

"Drew Deveraux, you rascal. You haven't called me in ages! Shame on you." The laugh in her voice took the sting from the words. Still, he felt a bit guilty for having neglected his surrogate mother.

"Yeah, I'm sorry about that. Work's been busy, but that's no excuse. I'm afraid I'm calling you now because I need to ask a favor of you."

"Anything."

"You haven't even heard what it is yet."

"Doesn't matter," Esme said cheerfully. "Anything for my boys."

Drew squeezed his eyes shut tight to stave off another spontaneous outburst of tears. He couldn't believe he'd ever wallowed in self-pity, ever thought himself alone in the world. "I love you."

"Love you, too, honey. Now, what did you need?"

"How would you feel about taking in another stray?"

"Friend of yours?"

"Family," Drew answered honestly. He hoped to make that official in the near future. "He's suffering from some kind of PTSD or shock from a trauma. They're kicking him out of the hospital, and we don't want to put him in, you know, some kind of institution."

"Well, of course you don't! That wouldn't be right. You send him to me, and I'll make sure he's taken care of."

Relief flooded in and Drew sagged against the wall. Ray had somewhere to go, and Raven...well, Raven was his.

"I love you," he said again, speaking both to the woman who'd raised him, and to the love of his life, who was standing in the doorway, smiling.

Raven came to him as he hung up the phone and, for once, she wore her heart on her sleeve. His heart stumbled when he looked into her eyes and saw gratitude, yes, but more importantly, trust and love—two things both of them thought they'd never find.